THE HIGH GROUND

THE HIGH GROUND

THE IMPERIALS SAGA

MELINDA SNODGRASS

TITAN BOOKS

The High Ground
Mass-market edition ISBN: 9781785654091
Ebook edition ISBN: 9781783295838

Published by Titan Books
A division of Titan Publishing Group Ltd
144 Southwark Street, London SE1 0UP

First mass-market edition: May 2017
2 4 6 8 10 9 7 5 3 1

A CIP catalogue record for this title is available from the British Library.

Printed in the USA.

This one is for George R.R. who loved this universe so much that he wouldn't let me give up on crafting the right story. And when we couldn't make it happen as a shared world project where we could play together he generously gave me the despicable—oh, excuse me, George—the charming, handsome and debonair Boho to abuse... er... use. Thanks, dear friend.

CAST OF CHARACTERS

THE IMPERIAL FAMILY

His Imperial Highness Fernán Marcus Severino Beltrán de Arango,
Emperor of the Solar League

Her Imperial Highness Mercedes Adalina Saturnina Inez de Arango, the Infanta

Her Imperial Highness Estella de Arango

Her Imperial Highness Julieta de Arango

Her Imperial Highness Izzara de Arango

Her Imperial Highness Tanis de Arango

Her Imperial Highness Beatrisa de Arango

Her Imperial Highness Delia de Arango

Her Imperial Highness Dulcinea de Arango

Her Imperial Highness Constanza de Arango, Emperor's consort

THE HIGH GROUND
OFFICERS

Vice Admiral Conde Sergei Arrington Vasquez y Markov

Captain Lord Manfred Zeng

Captain Baron Tarek El-Ghazzawy

Commander Lord Trent Crispin

Commander Jeffery Baldinini
Commander Father Tanuwidjaja
Commander Phillip McWhinnie
Commander Michael Westfield
Recruit Commander Nathaniel Deal
Recruit Commander Yas Begay

STUDENTS
Marqués Clark Bennington Kunst
Marqués Ernesto Chapman-Owiti
Vizconde Beauregard (Boho) Honorius Sinclair Cullen
Vizconde Mihalis del Campo
Vizconde Yves Riccardo Petek
Baron Jasper Talion
Lord Arturo Espadero del Campo
Lord Sanjay Favreau
Ensign Prefect Caballero Marcus Gelb
Caballero Davin Pulkkinen
Caballero Hugo Devris
Lady Cipriana Delacroix, daughter of the Duque de Nico-Hathaway
Lady Danica Everett, daughter of the Conde de Wahle
Lady Sumiko Tsukuda, daughter of Caballero Arashi Tsukuda
Thracius (Tracy) Ransom Belmanor
Mark Wilson
Donnel (Cara'ot batBEM)
Mela (Isanjo batBEM)
Tako (Hajin batBEM)

THE FORTUNE FIVE HUNDRED (FFH)

Rohan Danilo Marcus Aubrey, Conde de Vargas

Analise Aubrey, Condessa de Vargas

Duque Musa del Campo

Duque de Argento y Pepco

Marqués C. de Vaca

Lord Estevan de Vaca

Caballero Sasha Olsen

Caballero Malcomb Devris

Lady Pearl Devris

Lady Opal Devris

Lady Ruby Devris

Lady Topaz Devris

Lady Citrine Devris

Caballero Stefan Devris

Caballero Rafe Devris

Caballero Brandon Devris

Father Jose del Campo

THE COMMONERS

Alexander Belmanor

Bajit (Hajin)

Flanon (Hajin)

PROLOGUE
SECRETS AND SCHEMES

They listened to the screams of pain and terror and watched the humans die courtesy of the monitoring devices that had been slipped into the hull of the spaceship by the Isanjo builders as it was being constructed. Ma'utea gave a slow beat of Cara broad, fleshy wings and took a slow turn through the thick mist on the bridge, then returned to Cara post.

It was difficult to watch sentient creatures die but the task of the Cara'ot scout ship was just that—to witness and report. Never to intervene. Not that they could have; the enemy that was currently destroying the human ship was beyond the Cara'ot's ability to defeat.

Perhaps if the humans had not fired upon the spires they would have survived, but when the crystalline creatures had begun to nudge at the small vessel there had been the predictable human reaction. The guns had fired, torpedoes had shattered spires and death had been the response. Ma'utea sighed and returned Cara attention to the main screen.

It was split into several sections. The center

showed an exterior image of the ship under assault. Others revealed the humans inside that fragile metal shell, their bodies being rendered by the touch of the crystalline scales that had broken off from the main alien body, and were slicing through their ship.

Weapons fire lit the corridors of the Solar League's warship, and alien scales were shattered. But not enough and not quickly enough to save the human males fighting inside. Hours passed and the Cara'ot watched as the human frigate, the *Ave Rapaz*, was reduced and rebuilt into a tiny glittering latticework of crystal. The scales became ropes and towed what had once been a ship to the main snowflake-like body of the alien hive. Another ship was gone.

"Did they get off a message buoy?" Ma'utea asked Cara comm officer.

"Yes."

"Track and destroy."

"Is it not time for them to know what they face?" asked Cara first officer. The long proboscis waggled as Cara spoke.

"No, they fear the unknown that might lurk beneath the bed far more than the reality," Ma'utea replied.

"And fear breeds anger," piped up Silea from Cara comm station.

"And their anger is their greatest asset," Ma'utea added softly. Cara spun slowly in the dense atmosphere, and briefly wondered when that anger would be turned against the Cara'ot. Soon was Cara guess given the truculence of the species.

Ma'utea touched the control panel with Cara prehensile feet, and their ship lifted away from the head of the comet behind which they had been sheltering on the edges of this star's system. The engines sprang to life, and their ship overtook the human distress buoy. A quick blast from the port weapons and it was reduced to debris.

Ma'utea switched screens to show the rapidly receding system. Of the seven planets in this system, four had already been transformed. The strange crystal lattices that had replaced the planets glittered in the light of the system's sun, and like tumbling silicon snowflakes the alien colonies were already spinning toward the next planet. There the strange Star Ants would kiss, enfold and reform every bit of matter that formed the world and rebuild it into an inexplicable shape of unknown purpose.

Alien vanguards had noticed the flare of power from the Cara'ot ship and were speeding after them. If they did not wish to join the dying planets they needed to be gone. The Cara'ot ship slid into the heliosphere, and entered folded space just as the crystal vanguard arrived.

• • •

The naked human lay on the surgical table. Hair curled on his chest but thinned as it scaled the thrusting belly. It was as if the climb had exhausted the pale red strands. The harsh light of the operating room was not kind to the supine, pasty figure. Shadows pooled at the edges of the room and figures moved in the darkness with the soft *ting* of metal on metal as they prepared.

The man's twin stood next to the table dressed in a

high-collared coat and the tight pants that were all the rage, but not kind to a man of his age and girth.

He tugged at the collar that only accentuated his double chin. "Well, I'm off to home and the wife."

"They're not all that fond of one another," a female voice spoke from the pools of darkness at the edge of the room.

"Oh, I'll soon have the condessa billing and cooing," the man said as he walked out of the room.

1

TWO FATHERS

His Most Noble and Puissant Emperor of the Solar League stood on a large footstool while his tailor knelt at his feet, pinning the hem of his dress pants.

"A little more break over the instep, Your Imperial Highness?" the tailor asked. The Emperor turned slightly to survey his image in the gilt-edged mirror.

"That looks good."

The tailor marked the edge with a bit of chalk and moved to the other leg. "How are your children, *Majestad*?" the stoop-shouldered man mumbled around a mouthful of pins.

The Emperor noted and appreciated the tactful phrasing of the question. *Children* rather than *daughters*. He glanced down at the grey head bent over its task and decided to say what he was thinking.

"What a shame I can't tap you for the diplomatic corps. You are far more judicious and thoughtful than many of my so-called diplomats."

"You're too kind, Your Imperial Highness."

The Emperor turned back to the mirror and

studied the tired face of the man reflected there. Emperor, Highness, *Majestad*—so many words to connote his power, and all of them nothing but meaningless sound. He sighed. For the ruler of the humans' far-flung galactic empire had managed to sire only daughters, nine of them from five different wives in his fruitless attempts to obtain a male heir. Two years ago a clandestine medical test had made it clear that approaching a sixth young woman of impeccable birth and breeding would not alter the situation.

He had broken laws to obtain that information and hidden his transgression by the discreet removal of the creature who had run that test, but the reality remained. If he did not change the laws governing succession, his cousin or his cousin's children would succeed him, and that he would not accept. He was determined that his eldest, Mercedes, would take the throne upon his death.

Sadly it was proving to be a daunting task. Not because of political resistance. It had taken over a year, but he had rammed the amendment through parliament, changing the right of succession to include daughters. No, the problem was Mercedes. When presented with his legislative triumph the girl had refused to take the first, necessary step to ascend to the throne—entering the League's military academy The High Ground. She had done so in a show of the famous Arango temper, and had spent the last two days locked in her suite.

Emperor, Highness, Majestad, but at the end just a baffled father.

The Emperor pulled his thoughts away from

his damaged sperm and his recalcitrant child. "And your... son, isn't it? How is he?"

"He's fine, *Majestad*. Kind of you to ask." A sigh seemed to arise from the depths of the tailor's soul.

The vast levels of rank fell away and the Emperor realized that this father was also having problems with his offspring. Two perplexed fathers separated by rank, wealth and power but sharing an eternal human problem.

• • •

"Trouble?"

The tailor stared up into the jowled face. Fatigue gouged lines around the Emperor's mouth, and hung pouches beneath the brown eyes. The tailor knew he shouldn't speak, propriety dictated he not. The Emperor seemed to sense his dilemma, and he gently encouraged: "Go on, it's all right."

He couldn't hold it back. Discretion was thrown aside and the tailor blurted out, "He's won a full scholarship to The High Ground, but he refuses to go."

The Emperor stared, then burst out laughing. The tailor stiffened, hating himself for speaking. He had opened himself up to mockery. He forced down the flash of pride and resentment, and managed to assume a tone of humble gratitude as he said, "You are right to laugh at my foolish child, *Majestad*."

"No, no, you misunderstand. I am facing the *exact* same dilemma with my eldest."

The tailor's eyes flicked up to briefly meet the Emperor's, and he rose stiffly to his feet, feeling and hearing his knees crack.

"My Tracy has an opportunity to move up. Men have won titles in combat. I don't want him to have *my* life," he murmured, gazing down at his gnarled hands.

"And I moved heaven and earth to give her *mine*. I guarantee her the throne and she says I've ruined her life. What the devil is wrong with these kids?" the Emperor demanded. The tailor merely shrugged. "Why is your son refusing? The scholarships have always been a way to reward the deserving poor."

And that attitude, thought the tailor, *is* exactly *why he is refusing*. He stared up into the face of his sovereign and sought the diplomatic answer. Once again they stared at one another, but this time from distant vantage points. The tailor was saved from answering by a knock on the great double doors.

"Come," the Emperor called.

An aide dressed in the uniform of the *Orden de la Estrella* hurried in. He bowed and said, "Highness, we have lost another ship."

2

REFUSALS

Thracius Ransom Belmanor, known (despite his best efforts) as Tracy, stared at Principal Naranjo, seated behind his scarred and tap-pad laden desk, and tried to process what he was hearing.

"...So sorry, but it comes directly from the school board and I can't..." The older man spread his hands in a gesture of futility and helplessness.

The blood rising into Tracy's face made him feel like he had a fever, and rage quivered deep in his gut, an angry animal waiting to tear free and destroy the man across the desk. He yanked his focus away from Naranjo's face, studied the ugly faded paint on the walls of the office, the diploma and the few commendations, the picture of the principal taking part in a pep rally in the gym.

"I had written my speech," Tracy mumbled, then realized that sounded pathetic so he added with appropriate heat, "And Hugo is a meathead. How many grades had to be changed for him to suddenly be the top student? Which teachers were willing to do that?"

Naranjo folded his hands in front of him, the knuckles flaring white, and remained silent, but his jaw worked as if he were holding back unwise and unwary words. "Doesn't matter. Caballero Hugo Devris will be the valedictorian."

Tracy clutched at the strap of his tap-pad case that was slung over his shoulder. "Caballero? Hugo? When did that happen?"

Naranjo simply said, "His father was just knighted. *Hereditary* title, not a life grant."

Tracy understood now. The newly minted noble at this working-class high school clearly had to receive the top honor. It would be an insult to the FFH—the Fortune Five Hundred—if the son of a tailor took that title over an aristo, however recently his blood had been turned blue. The College of Peers had probably stepped in and applied pressure to the school board who had pressured the principal who had leaned on the teachers, and now Hugo—*oh excuse me,* Caballero *Hugo*—was the best student in this year's senior class.

It was clearly magic. Just as magical as the touch of a sword that had turned Hugo's crass, big-bellied and sweating father, the so-called Flitter King, into Caballero Malcomb Devris, Knight of the Solar League and worthy to join the Fortune Five Hundred. Word in the *Alibi*, the only really independent news outlet in Hissilek, was that Devris had been selling flitter cars to the FFH at well below market value.

"I'm applying to universities. I needed this for my scholarships," Tracy said.

"But you *have* a scholarship," Naranjo said pointedly.

"I'd be the only *intitulado* at The High Ground. It's nothing but aristos up there. And I hated RCFC. I never want to be a soldier."

"There's a big difference between the *Reserva Combata Formación Cuerpo* and The High Ground. That's *Orden de la Estrella*, not the *fusileros*. You'd be on a ship, not humping a gun dirt side or getting wet in the navy. And you'd graduate an officer. There have been commoners who have won high honors in battle."

"Yeah, how many more died and we never heard of them?"

Naranjo just shrugged. "You're smart, Tracy. Probably the best student to come through these doors since I've been principal. Don't let pride hamper your chances." They stared at each other for a few more moments then the principal pointedly picked up a tap-pad and studied the line of text scrolling past.

Tracy spun on his heel and walked out into the hallway of the school. The smell of spinach, macaroni and cheese, and male gym sweat still lingered in the air. Most of the students had already fled on this Friday afternoon so Tracy's footfalls seemed loud as they echoed from the concrete floor and bounced off the lines of lockers.

He stepped outside, and the late May heat from Ouranos's blue/white sun immediately had sweat popping on his forehead and his T-shirt sticking to his chest. He found it an effort to put one foot in front of the other, and it wasn't just the heat that had his footsteps dragging. On Fridays he and his dad always met for dinner in Pony Town where they enjoyed one of the spicy alien cuisines that could be safely ingested by humans. Normally he looked forward to this ritual, but how could he bear to tell his dad that he was no longer the valedictorian? Especially coming on the heels of his refusal to accept the scholarship to the military academy.

There was a subtle trembling that came up through the ground and into the soles of his shoes. Tracy looked up as a big passenger ship lifted off from the Cristóbal Colón Spaceport. The massive vessel glittered in the sunlight as it balanced on a tail of flame. He had only been on one of the great ships twice. He didn't remember the trip out, he had been barely four. The trip back however was etched in acid memory. He had been seven when they returned to Ouranos. His mother had died, their attempt to become carpet baggers on a newly discovered Hidden World had ended badly, and Tracy, his father and grandfather had returned deeply in debt and utterly defeated to the capital city of Hissilek.

The memory brought a sudden tightness to his chest, a new grief that had nothing to do with the news he had received this afternoon. Tracy was shaken and bewildered by the emotion and then he found the context. He had wanted to see the stars from the observation deck and his father had tried to sneak them up to the upper levels where the well-born, wealthy and well-connected traveled in luxury, but they had been stopped by a supercilious steward who ordered them back down to the dorm quarters. Tracy never had gotten to see the stars from space.

His father had. The shop "made" for some of the young gentlemen who attended the academy and occasionally crises would demand his father's presence on the great floating space station. There were moments when he wanted to beg to go in Alexander's place, but his father didn't want him missing school and the FFH families were particular about who served them. Maybe now, since his life and education were over he'd get to go and see the stars.

You would if you went to The High Ground.

He pushed away the traitorous thought. He had made his decision. He wouldn't give the *pendejos* the satisfaction. His errant, agitated thoughts had him walking without looking where he was going, and Tracy suddenly found a beefy hand against his chest and he was shoved unceremoniously against the wall of a building.

He looked up into the face of the bodyguard dressed in the livery of House C. de Vaca de Basaf, and realized he was in that no man's land of commerce that separated the estates and palaces of the Palacio Colina from Pony Town and Stick Town and Slunky Town, the alien neighborhoods farther inland and well away from the cooling breezes off the ocean.

He recognized the livery because his father had made him memorize the coats of arms of every noble house so if any member of the FFH were to grace the tailor shop they would be greeted by name and title. Truthfully the shop only catered to a handful of well-born clients; men of a more conservative bent who preferred Alexander Belmanor's understated tailoring. The whole thing had been a massive waste of time in Tracy's opinion and in fact he was faintly embarrassed by his father's pride at being one of the four tailors who "made" for the Emperor.

A flitter bounced lightly on its maglev cushion while a Hajin chauffeur held open the door of the vehicle. The alien's mane was thick and golden, falling in a forelock over the long face. The thick hair ran down the back of his head and disappeared beneath the collar of his elaborate livery. The alien looked hot and uncomfortable, as uncomfortable as Bajit, the Hajin who pressed clothes for the Belmanors in their stifling workroom. One of the chauffeur's large dark eyes, set on the side of its bony head, was cocked at Tracy, the other stared at the door of the bank on the other side of the street.

The Marqués was being bowed through the tall steel and glass doors by an obsequious bank manager. He headed down the steps accompanied by a second guard. His eyes skimmed across Tracy, bored and uncaring. The bodyguard at the flitter cuffed Tracy lightly on the cheek. Reminded of his duty, Tracy bowed as the nobleman walked past. C. de Vaca stepped into the backseat of the flitter. The guards took their seats in the flitter and the entire entourage flew away.

I wonder if he has a son going to The High Ground? Tracy thought. *Of course he does if he's got a son.* Every Fortune Five Hundred male had to attend the academy unless they'd been promised to the church. Just like every *intitulado* had to spend six months playing soldier in the *Reserva Combata Formación Cuerpo* during their last year in high school. *So we can be cannon fodder if there's another war,* Tracy thought.

With an angry shake of the head he forced away the thoughts. It wasn't that he was regretting his decision. It was just like being told not to think about pink elephants. He checked the time on his ScoopRing, realized he was going to be late and set off at a jog.

The glass, stone and steel buildings that housed the engines of the economy gave way to less towering construction, cheaper materials, and subtle inhuman differences in color choices and design. It was also decidedly shabby. Signs for strip clubs, massage parlors, nail and hair salons blossomed down side streets. Tracy knew that many of them were in fact brothels despite the laws that made sex between humans and aliens strictly illegal. The ban had been put in place out of fear of the mysterious Cara'ot and their uncanny ability to blend the DNA of wildly divergent species to create new and strange hybrids. But sex was a potent drive, as was the lure of the exotic, and now the authorities mostly turned a blind eye. Unless it was some prominent politician who had fallen out of favor with the Emperor. It was a convenient way to remove a problem without leaving Imperial fingerprints.

Tracy moved deeper into Pony Town and the crowds on the streets began to change as well as the architecture. There were still humans, but in addition there were Hajin clip-clopping past on delicate hooves, their long arms swinging at their sides, and their manes fluttering. Tiponi Flutes, like animated groves of bamboo, hooted and swayed as they played their incomprehensible math-based stick and tile game. The betting was frenzied and the Reals piled up.

Isanjo, fur-covered and wide-eyed, their prehensile tails waving like pennants, flowed through the crowds. Tracy spotted a tail dart quickly into a human's pocket and emerge with a wallet. The Isanjo vanished into the crowd, and the human walked on, unaware of the robbery.

There was a shadow in one of the narrow side streets that met no known shape or form. It vanished into a doorway, and Tracy realized he might have actually seen a Cara'ot. They were normally found only aboard their ships, and in the warehouses surrounding spaceports where they sold their goods.

His father was waiting on the corner by the bodega where they bought groceries. Slight and stoop-shouldered, his greying, dishwater-blond hair lay limp on his skull from the heat and humidity. The older man's eyes lit up when he spotted Tracy, and Alexander waved. He had almost abnormally long hands and the swollen knuckles from his work intensified the sense of freakishness.

Panting, Tracy came to a stop, and Alexander hugged him. "You're late."

"Sorry." Tracy almost added *Naranjo wanted to see me*, but bit it back just in time.

"Where do you want to eat?"

Tracy pointed at an open-air café bracketed by wooden trellises. Overhead thick ropes crisscrossed with the complexity of a spider's web. Isanjo ran along the ropes, trays balanced expertly in their six-fingered hands. Alexander sighed.

"Well help me pick something mild. My old gut just can't take that much spice any more."

They were guided to a table by a female Isanjo with deep red fur. Her enormous golden eyes flicked away from them and as soon as the menus were in their hands she scurried off toward a better-dressed couple who had just entered.

The father and son settled into woven rope chairs.

A waiter hurtled down from the ropes overhead, landed with a thud beside their table and deposited a bowl of dipping sauce and a basket of bread. The alien's neotenous dark eyes were wide pools in the broad, fur-covered face, but despite their size their expression was unreadable. The upturned corners of the creature's mouth cocked even higher, but was that really a smile, Tracy wondered? Or was the Isanjo just aping human behavior for the sake of the customers?

The waiter's order pad hung from a chain around his neck. He picked it up and tapped it to life. "What would you like to drink?" The shape of the muzzle gave the words an odd lisp and burr.

"Milk," Alexander said.

"Enchata," Tracy said. The sweet beverage distilled from the petals of flowers on the Isanjo homeworld went really well with their hot spicy food.

With a powerful thrust of his legs the alien launched himself back up into the tangle of ropes, gripping with his hands and feet and the prehensile tail. The pungent scent off the sauce set Tracy's eyes to watering and anticipation of the peppery taste had his mouth watering as well.

"Are you really sure about turning down The High Ground?" his father asked. His tone was hesitant, pleading. "You know we can't afford to pay for college…" His voice died away and he began shredding a hunk of bread into small crumbs. While the tailor shop turned a reasonable profit his father carried a substantial tax burden because he hadn't remarried after his wife's death, and further penalties were applied each year for his only siring one child. *At least we no longer have the debt from the disaster on Riker's World*, Tracy thought.

He hunched a dismissive shoulder. "If I'm good enough that the academy wants me then I can for sure get a scholarship at a university *and* I won't have to be a soldier. Besides, there's no merit involved. The fleet is filled with rich men's sons who are there solely because of their birth. It's a wonder we ever won a battle."

His father's eyes drifted toward the aliens surging and milling on the sidewalk and hawking their wares from portable stalls. "They," he said with a nod toward the aliens, "might not agree with you. We beat them all pretty decisively. Even the Cara'ot."

"That was hundreds of years ago!"

"Back when humans were real men?" his father teased gently.

Tracy gave him a reluctant smile. "Back when ordinary people could… well… get ahead. Before rich and titled assholes got everything handed to them." The conversation had circled back to the news that lay like a stone in his heart. The thing he couldn't bring himself to tell his father. He went on talking, nervous words with no meaning. "I mean, the whole thing is so stupid. Acting like all of us are going to get called up and be ready to fight. Do you even know where your gun is?" Tracy asked, referring to the rifle that every human household was required to keep close to hand.

"I believe it's in the hall closet with the umbrellas," Alexander said thoughtfully.

Tracy gave a sharp humorless laugh. "Yeah, we're totally ready to fight off the alien menace."

"Tracy, what's wrong?" his father asked. "You're angry, I can tell."

To buy himself some more time Tracy dipped a small square of bread into the sauce, chewed and swallowed, but his stomach, clenched into a tight hard ball, rebelled, and the food had him gagging. Alarmed, his father was out of his chair, and came to wrap a comforting arm around Tracy's thin shoulders. Alexander waved down a waiter.

"Water!"

The creature nodded and bounded away. Alexander laid a hand on Tracy's forehead. Tracy jerked away. "I'm fine, Dad. I'm not sick." *Not in the way you think.* With another worried glance his father returned to his chair.

"But something's wrong."

The gentle tone broke his control. Tracy's throat ached as a boulder lodged itself just above his Adam's apple so the words emerged as a harsh croak. "Don't bother closing the shop for graduation," he said. "I won't be making a speech."

● ● ●

Princess Mercedes Adalina Saturnina Inez de Arango had cried until her chest ached, her throat was raw and her eyes were burning. It had been something of a waste, for the person who needed to witness her grief had been stubbornly absent. Always before Papa had rushed to her side when she'd fallen in the gardens and scraped a knee, when her beloved dog had died, when her first mad crush on Duque Sanje's eldest son had ended in heartbreak. But this time when he had *ruined her life* he was ignoring her.

Her stepmother hadn't come either. Perhaps because Constanza felt awkward or because she resented the fact that Papa had done everything to give the throne to Mercedes rather than her own daughter, Carisa. Of course the girl was only six so Constanza could hardly expect such a thing. Carisa couldn't attend The High Ground. *No, that horror is reserved for the Emperor's eldest child*, Mercedes thought resentfully.

She pushed aside the floating curtains and rose from the elaborately carved canopied bed. She would not go. He could not make her. There was nothing wrong with Cousin Musa, and his son, Mihalis, would be a worthy heir. She didn't understand why her father was so opposed to that side of the family. Let Musa take the throne.

Her rooms looked out over a small garden. Wisteria with trunks the size of small trees overhung the marble walls with a riot of purple blossoms. At the center was an elaborate herb knot garden and a small pond with a fountain. Cushioned benches surrounded the pool, strategically placed so any breeze would carry a soft spray of cooling water onto those who sat on them.

Mercedes considered going outside, but then caught a glimpse of herself in the dressing-table mirror, and decided that none of the guards needed to see her with a blotchy face, bright red nose and tangled hair. She rushed into the bathroom with its large sunken tub, and quickly splashed cold water on her overheated face. It helped a little. Back into the bedroom where she ran a brush through her long dark brown hair.

What if they make me cut my hair?

But I'm not going, she reminded herself again. *He can't make me.*

He's the Emperor. Ruler of the Solar League.
And I'm his daughter and he loves me.
Really?

Hurt and anger and insecurity blended in a toxic stew, and almost before she realized she had done it the brush crashed against the mirror and a jagged crack appeared. Mercedes felt a spasm of guilt and sadness that she had ruined something pretty because of one petulant act.

Was she about to ruin the League too because of one petulant act?

She shouldn't have been surprised that an internal voice was counseling duty and protocol. She had been schooled to serve ever since she could be trusted to wield a fork and not misbehave in public. The crack in the mirror formed a scar across the image of her face. She turned her back on it. Most fleet officers sported scars, for dueling was accepted and indeed expected at The High Ground. Would she be expected to fight as well? She had never been trained to fence. Dance, play the piano, paint. The various imperial wives had taught her how to check the palace books to be certain that no majordomo or servant was stealing from the imperial purse. Her education was good, but there was going to be a lot of math associated with ship duty. Was she up to the task?

But I'm not going!

There was a soft tap on her door. Mercedes ignored it. Then a sweet soprano called through the heavy wood paneling. "It's Estella and Julieta. Please let us in, darling."

Mercedes ran to the door and threw the lock. Her

two full blood sisters slipped through, and Julieta quickly locked the door behind her. Estella was sixteen; Julieta fifteen, born a scant ten months after Estella. The trio was proof that her mother had tried, *Dios* had she tried to produce the required son, but in the end she had been put aside, and it had been Agatha's turn to try... and fail. Followed by Inez, Greta and finally Constanza. Five imperial wives and nine princesses between them.

Mercedes studied her sisters. They all had the same dark brown hair and brown eyes. Julieta had taken after their mother. She was tiny and vivacious with a mischievous smile. Estella was the avowed beauty of the first three imperial daughters. She had skin like old ivory and her eyes were the color of caramel. Mercedes, the eldest, was the least attractive; she had taken after her imperial father and had a rather jutting blade of a nose. Many of her attendants assumed she resented it, but she actually didn't. She loved her sisters and took great pride in their beauty, vivacity and accomplishments.

"We've brought chocolate and a vid," Julieta said.

Mercedes slipped her arms around her youngest sibling's shoulders. "That's sweet, but I don't think that's the cure for this."

"Papa hasn't come to see you?" Estella asked. Mercedes shook her head. For a long moment they just looked at each other. "I don't think he's going to back down, Mer," she said.

The muscles in Mercedes' jaw tightened. "And neither am I."

3

MEETING BY CHANCE

Three weeks passed. Tracy refused to attend his graduation. His dad made sad eyes, but Tracy pointed out it was just high school. *"Wait until I graduate with honors from SolTech, or New Oxford or Caladonia. That'll be worth attending."*

Tracy was in the back sewing a cuff on a jacket when he heard the bell chime. He and Bajit were both working shirtless in the sweltering workshop. They could only afford to run the air conditioning in the front of the shop and the fitting rooms. The workshop and the small apartment upstairs were torturous in the summer months. The Hajin's sweat had a sharp, almost medicinal smell. It mingled with the rank smell of Tracy's sweat in a really unpleasant way. He hoped the stink wasn't working its way into the bolts of cloth that lined the walls.

Tracy pulled on a shirt, the material clinging uncomfortably to his damp skin. Walking to the back door dislodged a bead of sweat that ran into his left eye, stinging as it landed. He opened the door to find a deliveryman holding a long white box and a tap-pad.

"Thracius Belmanor?"

"Yeah." The tap-pad was shoved out for his signature. "What is it?" he asked as he scrawled his name.

The man shrugged. "It's from the Admiralty."

Tracy shoved the box back at him. "I don't want it."

"Too bad, you signed for it." The man returned to his flitter.

The dumpster across the alley beckoned, but he was curious now. Tracy carried it back into the shop. His father came into the workshop, muttering to himself as he stared at his tap-pad.

"Outrageous. The cost of spider silk. *Everything's* gotten so expensive. And what the bank is charging for my loan— What's that?"

Tracy held out the box. Alexander carried it over to a table, sliced through the static tape and lifted away the lid. There was a cadet's uniform inside. Tracy watched his father's eyes slide to the bolts of the shop's stock of spider silk, their color a deep midnight blue. The uniform in the box was pale blue, constructed from cheap synthetic material, and the low-grade silver piping was beginning to flake, leaving metallic dandruff across the cloth. There was a letter lying on the uniform.

Tracy lifted it out, unfolded the paper, scanned it. After the usual salutations he read:

> *While it is normally required that all recruits at The High Ground possess a dress uniform as well as an undress uniform an exception has been made for our scholarship students. They may wear this undress blue at all times.*

He thrust the letter at his father and turned away. He tried to return to his work, but his hands were shaking too hard to set a stitch.

"I suppose the deserving poor are only *so* deserving." Tracy jammed the needle through the material. "And like this wouldn't have set me apart from all the others." He then hastened to add, "If I were going. Which I'm not."

"Though your tailoring relation in my set could never pass, though you occupy a station in the lower middle class," Alexander sang, altering the *H.M.S. Pinafore* lyrics somewhat. He had a pleasant baritone voice, and had bequeathed his singing ability to his son. It was as close as Tracy had ever heard his father come to criticism of the FFH and it both surprised and comforted him.

Alexander once again looked at the bolts of fabulously expensive spider silk that would become the uniforms for Space Command officers. His father sighed, shook out the cheap uniform and hung it on a rack.

"Should we send it back?" Tracy asked.

"Best we not draw attention to ourselves," his father answered.

Tracy checked the watch set in his sleeve. "Shall I go get us lunch?"

His father nodded. As Tracy left he saw his father walk over to Bajit, lay his hand on a bolt of spider silk, bend in close and say something.

• • •

That night Tracy ate alone for his father had gone to deliver new evening wear to Lord Palani. It was a horribly hot July night, and he found the leftover paella nauseating. Grabbing his tap-pad he went out in search of a breeze, and rode the loop rail down toward the one public beach near the capital city.

The beach was more rock than sand, and dangerous rip tides could sweep the unwary far out to sea, but it was the one place where "cottages" of the wealthy didn't commandeer the coastline. The scent of brine and rotting seaweed filled his nose as Tracy scrambled down a hillside toward the seawall. Coarse grass clung to his pants legs, and the sand shifted and squeaked beneath the soles of his sandals.

He settled onto the wall, feeling the rough surface of the rocks bite through the fabric of his trousers. There was a breeze off the ocean. Tracy threw back his head, allowing the sighing wind to cool his cheeks and carry to him the boom and hiss of the waves hitting the shore. After a few moments he opened his eyes. The nebula blazed across the sky, a riot of twisting colors with stars inset like diamonds in the fabric of a mad painter's dream. The smallest moon—Lynx—was already up. Soon the other two, Panacea and Thalia, would join her.

With a sigh Tracy pulled his gaze from the display overhead, and pulled out his tap-pad. He had two new messages and they were from SolTech and Caladonia. A hard knot settled into his gut, and Tracy's breath shortened. He clasped his hands together, both desperate and terrified to open the messages. With shaking hands he opened them both in quick succession, putting them up side by side on the screen.

For a moment his heart tried to fly to meet the glowing nebula. Both universities had accepted him!

Then he hit the next to last paragraph in each missive.

We are, however, unable to offer you a scholarship at this time as our records indicate that you have been offered a full scholarship to The High Ground, and we would prefer to offer our funds to a student who has not already qualified for aid at another institution of higher learning.

The final paragraphs detailed registration, the dates classes began, and links to housing requests. None of it mattered. There was no way his father could afford to send him to either premier institution. For a moment he allowed himself to hope that New Oxford would still offer him a scholarship, but he knew it was a vain hope. He had been offered a full ride to The High Ground, and the other colleges knew it. He should take the Fortune Five Hundred's largesse and be appropriately grateful.

His throat ached. Tracy stared stonily at the frothing waves and examined possible plans for his life. He wasn't very successful. All he could see was continuing to work with his father, ultimately inheriting the tailor shop, becoming as blind and stoop-shouldered as Alexander, and then dying.

• • •

A ghost in the palace, that's what I've become. Mercedes walked the halls.

That hadn't stopped her being saddled with a new title. A public announcement by the Office of Peerage declared she was now to be known as the Infanta, signifying she was the heir to the throne. Even thinking about it set her stomach roiling.

Despite her elevated title her attendants had been withdrawn and reassigned among her sisters and stepsisters. Servants still cleaned her rooms and brought her meals, but she was barred from all other public and social events. Her stepmother had carried her father's directive, and had seemed to enjoy delivering the news that Mercedes was no longer welcome at any state or family events.

So many women with nothing to do. We are like caged and bored animals so we tear at each other, Mercedes thought as she slipped out a door and into a side garden.

Her dress was sticking to her back in the heat of this July night. Through the windows she could hear the roar of conversation and *tink* of silverware on china as the state dinner rolled on. They were entertaining the governor of Kronos tonight. Mercedes should have been sitting at her father's right with Constanza on his left. Instead she sweltered in the garden.

Is it cooler on the coast? she wondered. Usually the palace's position on the highest of Hissilek's hills caught a breeze, but not this night. She was struck by a mad thought. She would check out a flitter and go down to the beach.

Usually such an outing required days of planning. Traffic had to be blocked, security details arranged, but she was the lost daughter. The one nobody cared about because she had defied the Emperor. She could probably dispense with even a single guard. Excitement and terror warred in her breast. The thrill and sense of an adventure won out over the fear. She hurried off toward the garages.

• • •

The hum of a flitter coasting in for a landing pulled Tracy's attention skyward. The vehicle was a shadow ringed by lights against the glow of the nebula. Tracy sat on the seawall and watched as it came in for a somewhat inexpert and wobbling landing on the sand down near the water. Whoever was piloting it also wasn't very familiar with the tides. All three moons were now up and soon that inviting beach would be underwater. The door irised open and a girl stepped out. Tracy waited, but she was unaccompanied. A thrill of excitement was followed almost instantly by the prick of worry.

Unchaperoned young woman on a beach with an unchaperoned young man, and judging from the make and model of the flitter and the dress she wore the girl was wealthy. She stood at the edge of the water, the sluggish breeze tugging loose tendrils of dark brown hair from the mane that hung down her back. She suddenly danced back as a chuckling, white-frothed wave lapped at her feet. Tracy wished she would turn around so he could see her face. He was sure she was pretty.

An internal debate began. Tracy knew he should leave, but if he didn't warn the girl soon she and her expensive ride would be waterlogged, and the flitter might not lift off if the jets got flooded. But approaching an upper class and unchaperoned woman could bring down trouble on his head.

Tracy also had little experience talking with girls. His entire world was male dominated aside from the alien females he met. After his mother's death his father had given up their female clients and took to catering only to gentlemen. He said he had no ability with the frills and furbelows that graced a lady's gown. There was no way his father was going to remarry so they would have had to hire a seamstress, which would have been expensive, and human women who worked were viewed with distrust by the FFH. In their world there was no reason for a wife or daughter to ever have to work, and they assumed the same held true for the working class as well.

Every school in the Solar League, both private and public, was gender segregated. The only opportunity Tracy had to speak to this mysterious and intriguing sex was at carefully chaperoned dances and picnics. And since Tracy didn't dance well and hated to look a fool, he usually leaned against a wall, glowered at the couples twirling past and tried to pretend he was being aloof and mysterious. In more honest moments he suspected that he only ended up looking surly, shy and awkward.

She turned. Her skin was café au lait, and the rather straight eyebrows accentuated the almond shape of her eyes. Her nose was too long and very patrician, and her jaw a bit too square. She didn't fit the current standards for beauty. Tracy thought she was gorgeous, and his chest was suddenly too tight to hold air. He jumped down off the seawall, forced himself to breathe, and headed down toward the strip of rapidly disappearing sand.

"Hoy," he called. She stared at him with alarm. "The tide's coming in. You need to move before the flitter gets swamped."

. . .

It was a boy with wind-tousled pale hair and equally pale skin, gaunt cheeks and an adolescent's gawky boniness. Not a threat. He was trying to help her. The fear remained, but it was no longer directed at him. It was focused on the rising waters. Mercedes hit the key bracelet and the flitter doors irised open. The water was coming up fast. The boy ran to her, swept her up in his arms and sat her in the cockpit just before the water reached her feet.

At first she was shocked, then offended. "How dare you!"

"Fine. I should have just let you get wet since you're an idiot!"

They glared at each other. The boy stood in rising water now up to his knees. Offense faded to gratitude. She wouldn't have wanted to try and explain a pair of ruined shoes.

She snapped at the boy, "Well, come on! Get in!" He gaped at her. "Or do *you* want to be an idiot and get even wetter?"

He gave a nod, and climbed into the flitter. She settled the headband on her forehead, and her fingers flew across the virtual screen that shimmered to life in front of her. The engine coughed rather than hummed, but they managed to lift off and bounced more than flew over the seawall to land on the coarse beach grasses. She opened both doors.

"Thank you," they both said at once. Then fell into an awkward silence. She waited for an introduction that didn't come, and Mercedes decided she had never met anyone as socially inept as this boy.

"You are?" she finally asked, exasperated with his silence and darting gaze that would never quite look at her.

"Tracy. Belmanor," he added hurriedly.

"Tracy?" she repeated. The pale skin went blotchy red as he flushed.

"It's really Thracius, but who wants to get saddled with that? I wanted people to call me Trace, but it never—" He broke off, pressing his lips tightly together. Clearly an unpleasant memory had surfaced. "Sorry, I'm sure you're not interested in any of this."

"Do you live near here?" she asked. He gave her an incredulous look, and that was when she was finally able to see his eyes. They were far and away his best feature: pale grey surrounded by a dark ring around the iris and set beneath arching brows.

"No, I live in Pony Town."

Now she felt embarrassed and awkward. She should have seen from his clothing and demeanor that he didn't live in any of the "cottages" that dotted the coast. He could have been a servant in one of the households but it was clear he was an *intitulado*—untitled.

"I wanted to get away from the heat," he explained.

That shared experience delighted her in a way she couldn't explain. "Me too."

"It's always cooler at the beach," he continued. It was inane, but this conversation with one of the lower classes and a male while unsupervised was proving to be very exhilarating. "Are you going to get in trouble?" he asked. "I mean, should you be here? Alone?"

"Nobody cares what I do any more."

"Why?"

"I've refused to do something my father wants," Mercedes said.

"Me too," Tracy said and he smiled. It transformed his face. He still wasn't handsome, but the large grey eyes were suddenly bright and expressive as well as beautiful. "He pretends like he's supporting my decision, but…" He fell silent for a moment. "After what I learned tonight he's going to start pushing me." Mercedes stayed quiet. Caution and discretion had been trained into her from the cradle. The boy went on. "I worked hard, and I'm really smart." He shot her a contrite glance. "Sorry, that sounded really conceited, didn't it?"

"Yes, but it's all right," Mercedes said.

"Anyway I thought I would have options. The League needs smart, hard-working people. I'm very good at math so I thought maybe I could become an auditor or work in purchasing or a big accounting firm."

They sounded like dreadful jobs to Mercedes. She schooled her features so none of that would show. "So, what's happened?"

"I've had a lot of doors slammed in my face, leaving me with just one option. I feel like a cow going down the chute at a slaughterhouse." Tracy seemed to realize he had been monopolizing the conversation. He cocked an eyebrow at her. "You?"

"I think I'm the opposite of you. Why are options such a wonderful thing? I know what I've been trained for. I thought I knew what my life would be. Now I've been told I can't have that life and I have to do this other thing."

"Sounds like you don't actually have choices either," Tracy said.

She stared at him, then said slowly, "I hadn't thought about it quite that way. I don't have to decide anything." The knot in her chest began to relax. "I just have to do what I'm told."

"And doing what you're told is a good thing?"

"Yes." She impulsively held out her hand. "Thank you."

He took it, his grip loose and awkward. "Uh... you're welcome?"

"I must go now."

"Okay." He climbed out of the flitter.

"Thank you for saving me."

He grinned up at her. "Oh, you wouldn't have drowned. Just gotten really wet and had to get the flitter towed out."

"Well, *adios*, Tracy."

"Goodbye." The doors began to close. "Hey, what's your name?"

"Mercedes."

She took off. His head was canted back watching her climb into the nebula-bright sky. He dwindled to a small figure and then was gone.

When she reached the palace the state dinner had ended. She caught the majordomo overseeing the cataloging of the silver as it was returned to its drawers.

"My father?"

"The Emperor is in his study."

She moved through the halls, busy even at this time of night. She found herself studying the faces of the passing servants. None of them would meet her gaze. Rather like Tracy at the beginning. Then he had really started talking to her. She wondered if she could do the same with all these people? Probably not. Setting was everything.

The door to the study was closed. Mercedes gave a gentle rap on the ebon wood panel.

"Yes? What?" came her father's voice.

"Daddy, it's me."

A moment later the door opened. He looked down at her and he seemed tired and rather sad.

"Daddy, I'm sorry. I'll do what you want. I'll go to The High Ground."

He folded her in his arms and the world righted itself. She was still scared, but facing those fears could wait for another day.

• • •

When Tracy got home his dad still hadn't returned. Tracy sent the university letters to the flimsy press and laid the physical copies on his father's desk among the litter of invoices and bills. He climbed slowly up the stairs to the personal quarters and tossed his sandals into the shower to wash away the sand and salt.

He then crawled into bed, folded his arms behind his head, stared at the ceiling fan beating slowly against the overheated air like a tired boxer flailing at an opponent. *Mercedes.* From her accent and the pricy flitter it was clear she was a member of the FFH. He wondered if he could find out which family.

An instant later he realized the idiocy of that thought. What was he going to do? Go visit her? He gave a snort. He'd be booted off the property. And it appeared she had slipped out. He shouldn't betray her by revealing her illicit nighttime flight. He had seemed to help her though he wasn't sure what he had done.

He remembered the feel of her breast pressed against his chest as he carried her to the flitter. The memory elicited an embarrassing physical reaction. He squeezed his eyes shut and thought about her face. There was something familiar... The thought slipped away, and he gave his head a shake.

By breakfast time tomorrow his father would know the worst. Know that there would be no university education. There was no doubt his father would start in on him to accept the commission to The High Ground. Tracy wished there was somebody to help him.

4

CONFRONTATIONS

The "young gentlemen" had begun arriving over the past week to be fitted for their uniforms for The High Ground, and his father had made sad eyes at Tracy, and once said hesitantly, "Are you sure?" Tracy's blazing look had his father stuttering into muteness. Since then there had been tense silence in the shop and the apartment.

One such noble scion stood on the raised platform idly sipping champagne—Beauregard Honorius Sinclair Cullen, Vizconde Dorado Arco, Knight of the Shells, Shareholder General of the Grand Cartel and heir apparent to the 19th Duque de Argento y Pepco. Tracy knelt at Cullen's feet, marking and pinning the cuffs of the pants. The spider silk had the consistency of flowing water against his skin. His father stood behind the young nobleman, smoothing the material across the broad shoulders and checking the fit of the coat at the tapering waistline.

"Good God, Arturo, military victories? Don't be so conventional," Cullen mocked, responding to a remark from his friend, Lord Arturo Espadero del Campo, one of the three sons of the Duque Agua de Negra. The man who had been the heir apparent to the Solar League until Mercedes Adalina Saturnina Inez de Arango, the Infanta, had agreed to attend The High Ground.

Tracy lowered his lashes to veil his eyes and hide the secret he had hugged close ever since the news services had announced that the Infanta would attend the military academy, the first required step of her ascent to the throne. There had been pictures of the girl in the modified uniform that had a long skirt instead of pants, and it was then that Tracy realized the identity of the girl on the beach.

The girl who had filled his thoughts, and had him waking sticky and panting from vividly erotic dreams. In some ways Tracy felt a fool. How could he have failed to recognize her? But she had been so out of context that it had never occurred to him, because context was everything in the carefully structured world of the Solar League.

I met the eldest child of the Emperor. We talked, and I said something. Something that helped her in some way. I wonder what it was?

If he had accepted the commission he might have found out. Tracy gave a quiet, derisive snort. As if he'd be allowed anywhere near her up on the space station—the *cosmódromo*—that housed the academy.

Cullen continued, "Military governor, that's what you want. You can make a fortune when you have a planet to squeeze. Especially if you land a Hidden World. The government doesn't care how much you bleed them."

Del Campo sprawled on the sofa twirling his glass by the stem and watching the bubbles rise. "I don't need money," he said. His voice was a soft drawl. Both the young men had that FFH upper class accent, but it was even more pronounced in del Campo. Maybe because he was a cousin of the Emperor, Tracy wondered. "I want the people's love," he concluded.

"Why? Are you planning on going into politics after you leave the fleet?" Cullen laughed as if the very idea were absurd. He drained his glass and thrust it out.

Bajit minced over and refilled the glass, bowed and backed away. Tracy caught his father's pained look. It would have reduced their status even further to have humans waiting on other humans so they had pulled the Hajin out of the workroom to act as waiter. Of course that meant Bajit wasn't sewing which meant they were falling behind on orders, which meant more late nights for all three of them. Tracy swallowed resentment and found it lay just as uncomfortably in the gut as in the mouth.

"I'm a third son. I need to find some way to make my mark. Especially since it seems that neither my father nor Mihalis will become emperor now."

Cullen shifted so he could look directly at his friend, his foot coming down hard on Tracy's fingers. Tracy gave a hiss of pain, and for the first time Cullen seemed to be aware of him. He actually looked down. Tracy stared up into startlingly green eyes. With his jet-black hair and impressive physique Cullen was an extraordinarily handsome man, and at six foot four he made Tracy feel short even though he was six feet tall. The Vizconde was still standing on Tracy's fingers.

"Watch what you're doing," he snapped and only then did he move his foot.

All of the slights and insults over the years and especially the past month coalesced into a hard burning ball and settled in Tracy's throat. He felt his jaw tighten. Then he caught his father's look— pleading and frantic.

Tracy returned his gaze to Cullen's. "I beg your pardon, sir." But he didn't bow his head or look down.

Cullen's eyes narrowed. "Dolt." He returned his attention to his companion. "This whole thing with Mercedes is just nonsense. I loathe the fact our class has to be part of an experiment. One doomed to fail, no doubt."

Tracy had read every article, following each breathless discussion about how one bathroom was being refitted for the ladies. How many attendants the royal princess would bring. It had turned out to be only three rather than her usual seven ladies-in-waiting. There had been speculation about how the three were selected, what the presence of women on the station would do to good order and morale.

As if reading Tracy's thoughts, del Campo spoke up. "I think she's bringing a few attendants so there might be an opportunity for shagging as opposed to drilling." The elegant dandy cocked his head. "Or perhaps drilling is the proper term."

Cullen gave a shout of laughter. "I claim Cipriana. That nose and jaw on Mercedes are far too off-putting." He paused, stroking his chin in deliberately theatrical and calculating manner. "Still, that ass is certainly appealing." He paused for another sip of champagne.

Tracy reached into the pin box. It was almost

involuntary, fueled by his rage at the nasty and suggestive remark. He jabbed the pin into Cullen's ankle. The man bellowed and jerked. Tracy lifted his head and stared challengingly up into the Vizconde's face. He then slowly removed the pin.

For a long moment there was only silence, then Alexander broke into hurried, stammering speech. "Ah, your lordship. I beg pardon. My boy has been at school. He's a bit out of practice—"

Cullen ignored the older man. He stared down at Tracy. The rage in Cullen's green eyes should have flayed the skin off him, but Tracy was oddly calm. Cullen embodied everything Tracy hated. He couldn't strike back against the FFH, and Mercedes would never know he had defended her honor, but that was okay if he stood up to Cullen.

"If I didn't already have a competent servant I would hire you so I could have the pleasure of beating you until you became less of an oaf. But perhaps that's unlikely. You seem slow."

Tracy gave Cullen a thin smile. "I won a place at The High Ground. You're going just because your daddy is a duque—"

He was suddenly rocked by a hard blow across the face. But not from Cullen. Tracy had been prepared for the blow, but not the source. It was his father who had struck him. Tracy reeled less from pain than shock. Bajit reacted in alarm and went galloping out of the fitting room, champagne slopping from the bottle. Alexander grabbed Tracy by the collar and dragged him, choking, to his feet.

"I should give him to you, my lord, so you could

teach him manners, but you probably wouldn't want him." His father gave him a shake as if displaying a piece of particularly unpleasant trash.

Never in his life had Tracy heard such a tone from his father. His bitter pleasure and anger melted into grief and anger. His cheek and jaw burned from the blow.

His dad glared at him. "Now apologize!" Alexander grated.

Obedience won out over pride and betrayal. Tracy bowed his head and muttered, "I beg your pardon, sir, for my clumsiness."

"Still too proud. Whine. Make me pity you," Cullen said.

His father shook him again. Fear and fury and grief combined to leave Tracy unable to draw in a full breath, much less speak. He endured another blow to his sore jaw, but no words emerged and he watched the dread bloom on his father's face. They were saved by the royal cousin. Del Campo languidly drained his glass and stood.

"Oh leave off, Boho. He's not worth the effort. And I want to get a ride in before Lady Maria's party."

Cullen tore off his jacket and threw it at Tracy who caught it instinctively. He turned to Alexander. "I should take my custom elsewhere, Belmanor, but I'll give you another chance. Make sure my uniform is perfect and I won't blacken your name to the entire FFH." He walked toward the small dressing room and paused with his hand on the curtain. "But don't expect payment. That will be your punishment for your son being an ill-mannered lout."

A few moments later and they were gone. The

faint echo of the bell over the door hung in the air. The anger was fading leaving only nausea. Tracy balled up the jacket and pressed it against his aching stomach.

"Dad," Tracy began, but Alexander stepped away and glared at him.

"I took out a loan to buy that material from Dunlap's. *Now* how do I pay for it? You're right not to go to The High Ground. You haven't got the skills—socially or emotionally—to make it. And after this performance today I doubt you have the brains for it either." He whirled and strode into the workroom.

Tracy stood, stunned for a few minutes, then plunged after him. Bajit was frantically pressing shirts on the big heat press, the steam coiling around his face. Tracy flung Cullen's jacket to the floor.

"You're wrong! I could do it."

Alexander whirled on him. "No! You couldn't! You are what you are and it's time you accepted that. This is your life." He threw open his arms indicating the workroom.

Tracy stared at the bolts of material, the sewing machines, the boxes of thread. Pictured a life spent among the scraps. He had thought his father was proud of him, loved him. Now he knew the truth. He was nothing when compared to his father's sycophantic adoration of the Fortune Five Hundred. A boulder had landed on his chest, crushing and painful. He wanted to wail like a child, or scream profanities. Tracy fought for control, threw back his head, and said in a low, cold voice, "Your little kingdom. Well, enjoy it because I'm going." He went to the rack and tore down the cheap uniform provided by the academy.

"If you walk out that door you are never coming back," Alexander called after him, his voice shaking.

"Fine! I hate you and I hope I never see you again!" Tracy said, spitting out the words. He plunged up the stairs to their apartment. He didn't have much to pack. Toiletries, underwear, his tap-pad and ScoopRing, his mother's rosary, the uniform, and shoes. A couple of changes of clothes. He had a feeling he'd be in uniform most of the time. He pulled out a travel sewing kit that had also been his mother's. It was well stocked with thread, needles, pins and a tape measure. Tracy bounced it in his hand. It was a reminder of a life he was leaving behind. He should leave it too. But he had a vague gauzy memory of his mother packing it away as she headed out for the final fitting of some grand lady's gown. He shoved it into his holdall.

He knew better than to take any posters, but he did take the crucifix down and added it to the holdall. He sealed the corners, slung it onto his shoulder and headed back down the stairs. He hesitated. What if his father was still in the workroom? It would be so awkward and anti-climactic. It might even shake his resolve. There was nothing for it. Gritting his teeth Tracy entered the stifling room. Alexander wasn't there. Just Bajit, now seated at a sewing machine. One of the alien's large and expressive eyes rolled toward Tracy.

"I am so sorry to see you go, young sir," Bajit lisped. "But may your path lead you to great reward."

"Thank you, Bajit, that's kind." Tracy moved to the door into the alley. He tapped his ScoopRing and deleted the key code for the shop. He was never coming back here again.

"And, sir," the alien called. Tracy looked back. "Your papa will be reconciled, of that I am sure. Know that he loves you."

"If you think that then you really don't understand humans."

• • •

Three expectant faces stared up at her. Mercedes stood at the front of the shuttle looking at the women who had been tasked with accompanying her to the academy. They had known each other since childhood, and they had been among the seven attendants who had been assigned to her once she reached sixteen and set up her own household. How or by what standards they had been selected to join her in military service she wasn't sure. She just hoped it wasn't based solely on political clout. There had been more than a few editorials questioning the Emperor's decision so if any of them failed it would just weaken him further. Mercedes realized she had been wool gathering and she returned her attention to her companions.

Lady Danica Everett, daughter of the Conde de Wahle; fine-boned with dark golden hair and brown eyes, filled with worry at the moment. She was small; her head barely came up to Mercedes' shoulder.

Lady Cipriana Delacroix, daughter of the Duque de Nico-Hathaway, a true beauty with ebony skin and black hair with a hint of red among the raven. She was tall and slim, and a martial light flashed in her dark eyes.

Lady Sumiko Tsukuda, daughter of Caballero Arashi Tsukuda. She was the lowest born of the trio.

Plump, a little unremarkable, but known to be bookish and far too ready to engage in a debate over any and every topic. They were debates Sumiko often won.

They were all clad in spider silk uniforms. The skirts were to the floor, which Mercedes knew to be absurd. At least they were split down the center like culottes so they could maintain decency in freefall. Instead of pumps or sandals they wore black knee boots. White shirts held with a gold clip at the throat and jackets identical to those worn by the men, but adjusted to accommodate a woman's breasts and hips. Mercedes had to admit that the severe lines of the jacket were very flattering. All of them wore their hair in a single tight braid down their backs.

"Remember, you are not there to wait on me. Just to act as chaperones. We'll be assigned servants—"

"*One* servant," Cipriana said, looking up and allowing the holo to slide back into her ScoopRing.

"It's not like we need more. We eat in the mess hall, we're not going to be changing clothes five times a day. Our title for the first year will be simply 'cadet'. Second year we'll become midshipmen. Senior year we'll be ensigns—"

"If we last that long. And why are you telling us all this?" Cipriana asked.

The insolence drove the blood into her cheeks, but Mercedes realized she had been babbling and let it go. "Point being we leave our privilege at the airlock."

"No one is going to forget who *you* are," Danica said.

"Maybe, but it won't be spoken of. We'll be going to class and drilling and eventually flying alongside the

men. And we cannot fail. Not any of us. Otherwise…"
She didn't finish. Otherwise her father's enemies
would tear him to pieces for the foolish experiment
of putting women in the military and by extension his
daughter on the throne.

"Pity your father couldn't just pass another law
and make you an officer and give you a ship."

There was something in Cipriana's delivery that
raised Mercedes' hackles. "He probably could have,
but it would be nice if I actually knew what I was
doing. So I'm going to study. We're all going to study."

"Three years," Danica said mournfully. "I hope we
won't miss out on everything."

"My understanding is that leave off the station
is limited the first three months. After that we'll be
allowed to attend more social events down the gravity-
well," Sumiko spoke up for the first time.

"Point is we must try to fit in," Mercedes said.
"Take part in the traditions of The High Ground."

"Does that include the dueling societies?" Cipriana
drawled.

Mercedes had to work hard not to obviously gulp.

●   ●   ●

It had only taken eleven years, but Tracy was finally
going to see the stars while aboard a spaceship. *Shuttle*,
he corrected himself, and this was just a jump into high
orbit. They weren't going to Fold space and cross light
years. It didn't matter. He couldn't tamp down his
excitement. He had taken an acceleration couch at the
front and against the curving side of the shuttle so he

had a view to the side and ahead. They were streaking through the thermosphere. It would be only a few seconds before they left all atmosphere behind and were in space.

He wasn't alone on this flight, but he wasn't traveling with any of the other cadets. Tracy shared the shuttle with the servants who had collected the luggage of the well-born cadets. At first he had tasted sour resentment, then he'd let it go. He had a feeling there were going to be many more slights and insults to be endured before the three years were over, but he would graduate an officer in the imperial star command, the *Orden de la Estrella*, and that status was many rungs above his previous station. It wasn't just hyperbole—a man could win a title in war.

The last veil of atmosphere whisked away and they were in the darkness. Only they weren't. The backdrop was what he had expected, but Tracy found himself squinting as the sun's rays flared off the hulls of passing shuttles, communication and weather satellites, a freighter, and a large passenger ship. Near orbit was an astoundingly busy place. They slid past a missile battery, its deadly cargo pointed belligerently outward ready to repel any invader.

The shuttle's maneuvering jets fired again, the pressure pushing him deeper into the acceleration couch. He was feeling cocky that he hadn't felt any nausea then he realized there had been enough thrust that he hadn't really experienced true weightlessness yet. The big capital ships were outfitted with gravity units, but the devices were expensive and weren't mounted on shuttles. Tracy didn't mind.

Weightlessness was part of space travel. It was what the pioneers Glenn and Armstrong had experienced five hundred years before at the dawn of the space age, and one hundred years before the discovery of the Fold technology and gravity units.

Orbital mechanics kicked in, sending the shuttle racing around Ouranos. With a flash of disappointment Tracy realized he was on the wrong side of the shuttle to see the planet. It was something he'd dreamed about. He tried to tell himself that there would be plenty of opportunity when he began fighter craft training, but it wouldn't be the same. It wouldn't have been the first time he went into space. The engines shut down, and Tracy's stomach gave a slow roll then settled.

There was a handhold conveniently placed on the curving wall above his head. Looking across the aisle he saw others dotted along the wall and ceiling. He couldn't resist; he unhooked the restraints and floated upward out of the couch. He caught the handhold and bounced there. Some of the servants glanced at him curiously, but most kept reading the holographic projections off their tap-pads.

Running the numbers in his head—the orbital speed, his weight—Tracy calculated how to kick off from the wall. His trajectory was fine, but he hadn't anticipated how little thrust it took to set a body in motion. His forehead connected painfully with the rim of the porthole, and he grabbed for the handhold, missed, and was ricocheted back across the shuttle. Tracy braced for his back to slam against the far wall, but one of the Isanjo servants reached up with his tail, wrapped it around Tracy's ankle and brought him to a bobbing stop.

Humiliation was a bad taste on the back of his tongue. He prepared to issue a rebuke to the alien, but the servant ducked his head respectfully, and said, "May I assist you, sir, in viewing the planet?"

The humble tone and the *sir* went a long way toward ameliorating Tracy's bruised feelings. He gave a curt nod. "Yes. Do so."

The Isanjo unclipped, and using feet, hands and tail he quickly moved them to a port that offered a view of Ouranos. Tracy forgot to be angry. Forgot to be haughty. The world rolled beneath him. Only one of the two great continents was visible, a mix of green and brown. The globe wore its ice caps like silver yarmulkes. A gossamer belt of clouds banded the belly of the globe.

"It's beautiful," he breathed.

"Yes, but you should see Cuandru. The trees stretch up to heaven and it glows like an emerald," the Isanjo lisped.

"I expect I will someday." Tracy paused then added impulsively, "Thank you."

There was a flicker of surprise in the alien's huge eyes, then he ducked his head and murmured, "My pleasure, sir." A braying klaxon rang out. "That is the signal for boost," the Isanjo explained. "It would be best if you returned to your couch. Do you need assistance?"

"May I try on my own? Then if I need help you can step in."

"Of course, sir. As you wish."

This time Tracy modulated the amount of thrust, and he easily floated to the other side of the shuttle and caught the handhold. Twisting around he caught the arm of the acceleration couch with his right hand, pulled himself down into the form-adjusting foam, and buckled the restraints. He was surprised at the soft ripple of applause from the servants.

"Well done, sir. It's unusual to see a human take so readily to zero gee. You appear to be a natural, sir," his new friend said.

Tracy felt a flush of pride heating his cheeks, then he wondered if he'd showed too much familiarity? Aliens would take advantage if a human wasn't careful. Instead of the pleased smile he instead gave a curt nod as the engines fired again, sending the shuttle hurtling out to the LeGrange point in orbit where the *cosmódromo* was located.

Forty-three minutes later the Apex *cosmódromo* began to grow in the front window. The space station was immense, but also squat and rather ungainly. Tracy had seen pictures and had been reading up on the *cosmódromo* since he'd decided to attend the academy, but the pictures couldn't capture the wallowing size of the thing. There was a fat central hub that extended above and below the central ring, which looked like a belt on a fat man. Four large spokes attached the bulbous ring to the hub, and eight massive cables stretched from the central ring to the top and bottom of the hub. Two stubby legs jutted out from the base of the hub in a V shape. Each cylinder ended in two round pill-like structures that looked to be about four stories high.

Extending from the top third of the hub were vast solar arrays comprised of interlinking hexagonal panels like glittering blue and gold wings. They gave the illusion that the *cosmódromo* was some kind of exotic spacefaring insect.

Tracy knew that one of those circular structures at the base of the hub held the academy. The other held the *cosmódromo*'s plant facilities—water recycling, oxygen production, waste disposal, and the fields that grew fresh food to help provide oxygen and also recycle the waste as fertilizer. The fresh food grown there also landed on the tables of the restaurants that served travelers, the students and the support staff of the *cosmódromo*.

The ring was basically an upscale spaceport for those making their way from distant worlds to the League capital or transferring onto ships to other worlds. In addition to restaurants and stores there were also hotels, casinos, and joy houses, which were technically illegal on a planet's surface, but completely legal on a *cosmódromo* or at a military *Estrella Avanzada* or "star port" as the aliens termed them.

They were again in the midst of traffic. Everything from wallowing, fat-bellied freighters to elegant racing pinnaces, luxury space liners and utilitarian shuttles. All were dwarfed by the *cosmódromo*. The ships converged on the Apex *cosmódromo* like silver bees returning from a day's labor, and vanished into the hive of docking bays. Their shuttle broke away from the pack and headed toward the docking bays that lined the circumference of the module housing The High Ground.

The klaxon sounded, three sharp bleats. Front thrusters fired and the shuttle slowly slipped into a bay and settled with a bump onto the steel floor.

He had made it. Now he just had to *really* make it.

5

GIFTS AND GUILT

They had been met on the shuttle by an *estrella hombre* who had introduced himself as Farley and told them he would guide them to the quadrangle for muster. He was an older man, in his forties with short-cropped grey hair and skin like cracked leather. He had taken the lead and Mercedes and her ladies trailed after him like desperate ducklings. The bay smelled of hot oil and graphite. The metal decking rang beneath their boot heels, the sound driving like a spike into Mercedes' temples and making her headache and nausea worse. She had not enjoyed zero gee. Only Sumiko had managed the flight without vomiting.

The sour taste still filled her mouth and burned at the back of her throat. Some wisps of hair had pulled loose from her braid and clung to her sweaty face. She desperately wanted to bathe and then sleep.

They were walking down a curving corridor. At one end were double doors, and Mercedes felt a breeze tickle her face that smelled of growing things and water. She caught the briefest whiff of gardenia and was seized by desperate homesickness. They were led away from those scents of home, through another set of sliding doors and into a flagstoned courtyard with a viewing platform at one end and jet columns all around the sides. It had the look of a parade ground, and it was filled with a seething mass of young men in uniform. Their voices were a rising and falling cadence of bass and tenor sounds with an occasional outbreak of nervous high-pitched laughter. No words could be distinguished and even in the large space the rank smell of male sweat, aftershave and hair pomade was carried to Mercedes. She gagged, turned away and started breathing through her mouth.

That was when she saw him. It was the boy from the beach. His back was against a column as if trying to merge into the stone. His fair hair stood out against the dark surface, and his uniform was a pale blue unlike the midnight blue of the others. He turned his head and looked at her, and Mercedes held her breath, but not by the twitch of an eyelash or the smallest quiver of a muscle did he indicate that he knew her. She felt herself relax and was a bit surprised at his delicacy. Her view of Tracy was cut off by an expanse of chest, the material pulled tight across the pectoral muscles.

"Highness," the man said, and kissed her hand. The green eyes were dancing with enjoyment as he glanced at her from beneath his lashes.

"Hello, Boho." Mercedes wasn't a small woman, but Beauregard Honorius Sinclair Cullen always made her feel so.

"Let me be the first to welcome you."

"I rather think that duty and honor belongs to the

64

commandant, not a mere cadet," she said dryly, and was pleased when his cheeks turned a dull red. Boho's conceit was legendary. As were his appetites. More than a few of Mercedes' set had had to withdraw to discreet country estates for a number of months after Boho had managed to cajole them into his bed.

Upperclassmen and older men who Mercedes assumed were professors began circulating through the group of new cadets. One of them stopped by her and Boho, and executed a perfect court bow.

"We understand you don't yet know proper military order, but if you would all stand at your best approximation of attention the commandant will be here soon. And, ladies, if I may escort you to the front." He indicated the raised platform at one end of the room.

There was a door in the center of the wall behind the dais. To either side were flags. On the right was the flag of the Solar League which was blue/green with tiny globes all around the edges, and a cross of gold in the center. On the left was the flag of the *Orden de la Estrella*. It showed the Milky Way galaxy with a spear thrusting through its center, and over the door was the seal of The High Ground, a spaceship lifting on a plume of fire. Its landing pad was an open book, and on either side were crossed rifles. The bare expanse of the platform was broken only by a single podium.

Mercedes inclined her head. "If you will excuse us, Boho." She didn't need to say that, but her father had driven home the idea that courtesy was the privilege of kings and cost them little.

As their guide led them through the milling crowd of males Mercedes looked for the boy from the beach.

He was being shoved, none too gently, into place at the very back of the crowd by a young cadet whose stripes indicated he was a second-year student. Tracy's head was thrown back, chin up, glaring at the upperclassman. Mercedes noticed another young man also dressed in the pale blue uniform who was scuttling into line while an upperclassman paced behind him. This boy's head was down, shoulders hunched in submission.

The shifting and coughing, the mumble of conversation and the scrape of booted feet on the flagstones slowly subsided. There were a few final coughs and then Vice Admiral Conde Sergei Arrington Vasquez y Markov emerged through the door in the wall at the back of the dais. He was an imposing figure, tall and very broad, though some of it was due to a thrusting belly. Light gleamed on his nearly hairless skull. From her position in the front Mercedes could easily see the scars that twisted across his left cheek and fat-blurred chin, white against his dark skin. He stepped up to the microphone.

"Welcome to The High Ground." He paused and swept them all with a ferocious blue-eyed gaze. "This institution has stood for three hundred and forty-one years. First on the surface of old Earth, then on Ouranos, and for the past seventy-three years aboard this orbital station. Ours is a proud tradition. We honor the past. We also train officers and heroes for the challenges of the future. We have always been willing to embrace change in an effort to defend the Solar League and the billions of humans who live under its protection. This year we welcome a new change. This year The High

Ground and the *Orden de la Estrella* welcomes the first class of women to these hallowed halls. Highness." He saluted Mercedes.

Her hand rose in the accustomed royal gesture of acknowledgment. Then she tried to turn it into a salute, misjudged and knocked her hat off. Danica leaped to pick it up and returned it to Mercedes' head. There was the briefest ripple of laughter. Mercedes choked back a blazing flare of anger.

"God save the Emperor."

"God save the Emperor," several hundred male voices roared out, and went on to conclude with the *Orden de la Estrella* motto, "May we touch the stars with glory." Markov saluted, whirled and left.

Another man took his place, as spare as the admiral had been broad. He had an elongated head and a pointed chin that made him seem like a living embodiment of an ancient painting called *The Scream*. "I am Captain Lord Manfred Zeng. I am in charge of operations at the academy. If you have issues come to my office. First a few rules. Reveille at five thirty a.m., breakfast followed by physical training. Classes begin promptly at nine hundred. Lunch at thirteen hundred. In the afternoon there will be more classes and drills. Dinner is at nineteen hundred. The evenings are yours. I suggest you use them to do homework. No one is permitted down the gravity-well until three months have passed. You are permitted in the civilian areas of the station on Saturdays. Services on Sunday are mandatory. No male cadets will be permitted within five hundred feet of the ladies' quarters. Their corridor has been blocked off with new pressure doors. You will display courtesy and behavior becoming an officer at all times toward the ladies."

Or what? Mercedes wondered. They had been set apart, caged like exotic animals in need of protection, but there was no mention of the penalty to any male who might try to break those rules. Or would the penalty be exacted against the woman? Mercedes had had a tutor (safely gay) who had talked about the Madonna/Whore dichotomy throughout human history. He had been replaced shortly after with an even safer governess who had been dull and very respectable and never said anything controversial.

Zeng was continuing, "Please leave through the planetside doors. Your personal servants will be there to escort you to your rooms where you will find your undress blues. Those will be worn during regular classes. You are permitted civilian attire only on Saturdays. Tonight there is a welcoming banquet at twenty hundred in the mess hall, dress uniform required as the Emperor will be attending. I suggest you all see to your toilettes. Dismissed!" He saluted, whirled and was gone through the same door that had swallowed the vice admiral.

Mercedes and her ladies found themselves in a bubble, separated from their classmates by ten or fifteen feet. At least for now the men were reacting as if the women were toxic.

"Well damn. It's going to be hard to find a husband now," Cipriana said. Danica once again seemed on the verge of tears.

"We're trained to impress them while dancing," Sumiko said. "Surely we can manage to make an impression during hours of class or hand-to-hand combat training."

Mercedes stayed silent. In addition to *don't fail* there had been another instruction her father had given her in the days before she left for the academy. *Find a consort. Pick the man who will share the throne with you. To protect yourself against the conservatives he will have to be a military leader. I can give you the throne. He will help you keep it.*

Her eyes slid across the hundreds of young men streaming toward the exits. *Which one of you will I marry?*

• • •

Tracy was at the back of the crowd heading out. *Courtesy and servility at all times.* His father's mantra. It seemed to have been deeply ingrained in him because when the older student had muscled him into line Tracy had only briefly considered shoving the man back. The rebellion had quickly died, and Tracy hated himself for falling back into the old pattern. He comforted himself with the thought that perhaps a fight on his first day wouldn't have been prudent. The other scholarship student was also at the back of the pack. He looked scared. Tracy wondered if his face mirrored that fear. He hoped not.

As he reached the double doors he heard his name. "Tracy!" He looked to his right and saw Hugo Devris. "Hey, it is you. This is such a flare. I was afraid I wouldn't know a soul up here."

Frozen with shock Tracy stared into the face of the boy who had taken his place as the class valedictorian.

"What are you doing here?" he blurted.

Hugo had tightly curled dark gold hair that set an odd contrast to his dark skin, and wide set, rather round eyes that gave him the look of a surprised lemur. He shrugged a gesture that seemed to encompass both regret and resignation. "We didn't realize when the old man got knighted it meant I had to come here. Every FFH son has to do at least a year here. It kind of sucks—" He broke off then added mournfully, "I had a *fútbol* scholarship to New Caladonia." Hugo had led the soccer team at their high school, and he had been a strong defense player. "Hope I get to play up here."

"I'm sure you will," Tracy heard himself answering automatically. Why was Hugo greeting him like a long-lost brother? They'd scarcely interacted at school. Tracy pushed ahead, eager to escape this unwelcome and forced comradeship.

Just outside the parade ground Hajin and Isanjo servants waited. Tracy noticed that the aliens waiting for the ladies were all female which was going to make the term "batman" a tad difficult to adapt, Tracy thought. A Hajin female whose greying mane and the deep lines around her muzzle indicated her advanced age approached Mercedes and dropped into a low curtsey, an awkward movement given the way a Hajin's legs were jointed. The alien servants quickly paired off with various freshmen cadets. An Isanjo approached Hugo and bowed.

"If I may guide you to your quarters, young lord."

"Hey, looks like I need to go. We'll catch up later, okay?"

Tracy nodded, not trusting his voice. All the cadets

and their servants flowed away down branching corridors, vanishing as quickly as rain on the desert uplands. Tracy found himself alone with no idea where he was supposed to go.

There was the sound of heavy breaths approaching from around a curve, and moments later the strangest creature Tracy had ever seen came racing along the wall of the corridor. It had three segmented legs and four appendages that appeared to be arms that ended in long hands with six fingers. Its head was too round and seemed to sit directly on its shoulders. It also had four eyes, two set in the center of the face and two others on the sides of its head. There was something about its feet that allowed it to cling to the Durabond material that formed the station. It tucked its legs, bounded off the wall and landed in front of Tracy with the air of a gymnast making a perfect dismount.

The face was basically humanoid, but the mouth was a small O, and the eyes in the center of the face were small, the beady stare of a spider adding to the overall impression of an insect. The voice that emerged was a rich baritone, completely at odds with the physical attributes.

"Cadet Belmanor, I am Donnel, your batBEM."

"What?"

"I am a Cara'ot," the creature said.

"I figured that out! No, I mean… BatBEM? Bug Eyed Monster? Seriously?"

"A little funny on the part of one of the early commanders of the academy," Donnel said.

"And is it? Funny?"

Donnel bowed. "That wouldn't be for me to say,

young sir. You humans seem to think so."

"Are you the only Cara'ot among the... batBEMs?"

"I am."

"But what are you doing here? I thought you people never lived off your ships except to trade."

"An unfortunate confluence of debt and a disagreement with my captain trader." Donnel turned and began walking down the corridor. Tracy assumed he was supposed to follow and did so. "I was designed for space work so seeking employment on the station seemed the optimal choice. I have been eager to move out of the freighter bays, and when the opportunity arose to serve you I took it. Mela told me of your graciousness. I thought we might be a good match."

"Mela?"

"An Isanjo batBEM assigned to Ensign Craddock. You were on the shuttle with him."

"Was he the one who helped me?"

"I could not say. He was struck by your courtesy."

"Yeah, well, sometimes it's not the best approach," Tracy muttered, thinking of his father's servile manner toward the FFH.

"If you say so, sir." Donnel stopped in front of a door, touched the panel and the door slid open.

The room was larger than his bedroom above the shop, and had that neat and well-designed feel of a ship's cabin. There was a desk and chair. Tracy's tap-pad had already been set out on the desk. On his left was a closet where his civilian clothes hung. To the right was a bathroom, where his toiletries were carefully arranged on a towel. There was a chest of drawers forming the pedestal of the narrow bed.

It was what was laid out on the bed that caught Tracy's breath in his throat. A uniform. A dress uniform sewn of spider silk. A uniform that was the deep midnight blue of the other cadets. The silver piping was of the finest quality.

Tracy stepped to the bed and lifted the garment. The material slid across his hands like a whisper. Now that he was close he could see how smaller pieces of silver braid had been expertly sewn together. How the coat and slacks had been done piecemeal from smaller remnants, but in the hands of a master tailor it didn't show. The only reason Tracy could see what had been done was because he had been trained by that master tailor.

He sank slowly down onto the bed, clutching the uniform to his suddenly aching chest. Donnel cleared his throat, turned away, and fussed with the tap-pad, straightening it though it didn't need it. Tracy flashed on a memory of his father placing a hand on a bolt of spider silk, leaning in close to Bajit. He now knew the conversation that ensued. A request that Bajit cut as close as possible and save every excess scrap of material.

Understanding finally dawned. His father had been planning and hoping for Tracy to attend. The blow that had broken Tracy's heart had been part of that plan, an act of terrible calculation and ultimate sacrifice. His father had risked losing the love of his only child in an effort to win a better life for that child. Tracy's pain must be nothing to what his father had felt.

"How did this... Did you see..." Tracy fumbled.

"An older gentleman stopped by and delivered the uniform. He was on his way to make a small repair to Cadet Lord Arturo Espadero del Campo's uniform."

"Did he... did he have any message?" Tracy forced the words past a constricted throat.

"No, he seemed a bit taken aback to have found me here. He merely said he was making a delivery for Cadet Belmanor."

I hope I never see you again! His hot, hateful words returned to tear at Tracy.

Tracy shot to his feet. "Do you think he's still on the station, Donnel?"

"I couldn't say, sir."

"Could you find out?"

"Don't you require assistance dressing, sir?"

A corner of his mouth quirked up in a wry smile. "I'm not one of your helpless aristos. I've been dressing myself for at least fifteen years," Tracy said. "Please, just look, okay?" he pleaded. "It's terribly important."

"Very well." The alien went scuttling out of the room. The door closed with a sigh.

"Thank you, Dad," Tracy said softly to the walls.

• • •

The cadets were entering by class—upperclassmen first, the plebes last. She might be the Infanta, but she would come behind all the others despite outranking them all.

She glanced around hoping to spot Tracy. At first she failed to see him. She had been looking for that pale blue uniform, but instead he was wearing a midnight blue dress uniform just like all the rest of them. It was beautifully tailored and seemed molded to his body. As she watched, Boho walked past Tracy and cuffed him hard on the back of the head, knocking off his hat, and then treading on it.

"So, which one of us did you rob to get your hands on that uniform, *intitulado*?" he asked while several of his comrades laughed.

Mercedes was baffled. She knew Boho was arrogant but she had never thought him a bully, and all of the FFH were trained to show courtesy to the lower classes. Something must have happened between the two men, but how they could possibly have crossed paths was a puzzle she couldn't solve.

Tracy bent to recover his hat but Boho kept his boot firmly planted on it. Glancing up from beneath his long lashes Tracy said, "Since you seem to wish for my hat, sir, I'll most humbly and happily make the trade." And lightning quick he straightened and swept Boho's hat off his head, and placed it on his own.

Mercedes gave a gasp of laughter and several other cadets of lower nobility, after glancing from Boho to her, followed her lead. Tracy glanced at her and the barest of smiles touched his lips. She realized she was smiling back, and quickly schooled her features. Blood rushed into Boho's face, but the grizzled old spacer was calling for them to enter now that the other classes had made their way into the hall. Boho had no choice but to pick up the crushed hat and try to punch it back into shape. Fortunately it was hats off as they entered so he was able to tuck the abused chapeau beneath his arm.

Mercedes snuck one final look at Tracy. High color flew in his cheeks and his grey eyes were alight with pleasure. He had his shoulders squared and he looked taller than he had even moments before. Then they were in the mess hall, a large utilitarian space softened only by the battle banners hanging from the high ceiling. On some the colors were faded, the metallic threads tarnished by time. Others were scorched. Still others displayed ragged edges where sections had been burned or torn away. A history of human conquest written in fabric.

There was a raised dais at one end of the room that held the high table. The rest of the tables ran perpendicular to the high table, and each of those was headed by an officer with the rank of commander or captain. Mercedes assumed the men were teachers. A military band was in one corner staffed by low-ranking spacers.

At the high table the commandant and his second were already in place. A chaplain sat at one end of the table, and at the other was Rohan Danilo Marcus Aubrey, Conde de Vargas, who served as the direct patron to The High Ground. His plump hands were folded over his paunch, and the light reflected off the scalp showing through his thinning red hair.

Alien servants were flowing through a set of double doors. Each time they slid open Mercedes had a glimpse of the kitchen beyond and the laboring cooks, none of them human. Among the fur and hooves and tails she spotted one human. An older man, stoop-shouldered with greying hair. He was trying to stay hidden at the side of the doors, but leaned out now and then to scan the crowd of students. She frowned at the incongruity, then saw his face light up with pride and pleasure. She followed his gaze. He was looking at the young man from the beach and now she could see the resemblance. If she had to guess she would bet they were father and son. The older man lingered for a brief moment longer, pressed the tips of his fingers to his heart and then his lips. The doors closed again. When they reopened the man was gone. Mercedes looked to Tracy, but he hadn't noticed. He had been focused on scanning the long tables for his place card. When he finally found it his table was well in the back and next to the doors leading into the kitchen, which made it ironic that he had missed seeing his parent.

As she expected, Mercedes and her attendants were at the middle table closest to the dais. Their companions were the sons of the highest born families with one notable exception: her cousin, Mihalis, eldest of the de Campo sons, was not present. She and her ladies were clumped at one end of the table, a small island of femininity in the midst of a sea of testosterone. Mercedes knew for a fact that Vice Admiral Markov was married, but even spouses weren't permitted at this welcoming banquet. Clearly the rituals and traditions of The High Ground were uniquely male. Would they be adjusted to accommodate the four nobly born women? *Only time will tell*, she thought.

The band struck up the League anthem and with a scrape of chairs and scuff of feet everyone stood. A *fusilero* slapped his rifle, and banged the butt of the gun on the floor announcing with a roar:

"All rise for His Imperial Highness Fernán Marcus Severino Beltrán de Arango!"

Her father entered and walked toward the high table. As he passed he glanced briefly over at her. For the briefest instant her father's eyes, cold and demanding, met hers.

She received the message loud and clear—*don't fail me.*

He looked away, and the image of a work-weary father miming his message of love to an unaware child flitted across her mind. She wished that gesture of love had been given to her. Instead she was left with only the crushing burden of expectation.

6

UNPLEASANT TRUTHS

Reveille had sounded, piped through speakers in the rooms and echoing down the halls. Tracy was already up, dressed in his workout clothes—sweat pants, T-shirt and running shoes—and heading down the corridor toward the mess hall when the recorded bells rang and the bugle blew. At home he'd risen with his father at five so there was time to work before school. His interior alarm had brought him awake at the normal time, and he saw no reason to linger in bed. Drills were scheduled for eight, and he wanted to be sure his breakfast had time to settle before some drill sergeant laid into him.

It meant he once again dressed without assistance from his batBEM, and he wasn't sorry. Last night when he'd returned to his room after the banquet he found Donnel waiting for him. As the Cara'ot helped him out of his jacket he said, "I took the liberty of laying out your gym clothes for tomorrow, and loading your text books on your tap-pad, sir."

"Uh... thank you."

Donnel motioned for him to sit on the bed as he pulled on gloves. Tracy jerked when the creature knelt and carefully removed his mirror-bright boots, giving them a brush with the sleeve on one of his arms. "I also added a map to your class schedule. Wouldn't do to be late on your first day."

"Thank you," Tracy muttered again. Donnel motioned for him to stand. Once again he found himself obeying, and jerked nervously when the alien unbuckled his belt and unzipped his trousers.

"I will be waiting in the shower area with your undress blues after drills."

"Really, you don't need to do that. Really you don't," Tracy objected as he stepped out of the puddled material. He could hear the desperation in his voice.

Donnel rocked back onto two of his three legs and gazed up at Tracy out of those strange eyes. "If I may be so bold, sir... it will place you at a disadvantage if you do not show the proper attitude toward the serving class. Again, your pardon, but you are already operating at a deficit as a scholarship student. If you wish to hold your own you must behave as if there is no difference between you and the FFH. One way to demonstrate that is to seem at ease with personal servants. I hope you will forgive my bluntness, sir."

"Yeah. Okay. I see your point. I'll see you after drills. And... uh... I can handle... the rest." He gripped the waistband of his shorts, determined to hold them in place.

"Very good, sir." Donnel brushed down the dress uniform and hung it carefully in the closet. "If that will be all I will see you in the morning."

But fortunately Tracy had dodged that by rising early. He was finding this level of attention rather creepy. He might have to ape his betters—his mouth twisted at that unconscious use of the word—when he was around them, but in the privacy of his quarters he'd look after himself.

• • •

It hadn't been a restful night. The bed was too narrow and Mercedes constantly woke to find that her foot was hanging off the edge and exposed to the cold air. She was also intensely aware of the other girls sleeping all around her. As the hours crawled past she discovered that Cipriana snored and Sumiko talked in her sleep. Mercedes hoped *she* didn't have any embarrassing sleeping habits.

Their quarters were clearly an awkward retro-fit. The walls between what had probably been individual rooms had been removed to leave a large ungraceful space with closets bulging like growths into the room and toilets and showers exposed. All four beds were set in a star pattern and only two of them were placed where the overhead reading lights could provide illumination. Between the beds and the desks the space felt cramped and unwieldy.

Mercedes wondered why the rooms had been twisted and deformed in this way, and then the answer hit her with blinding clarity—the administration was worried that if the women had private rooms they might find ways to slip boys into those rooms and into those beds and sex might occur. Instead the women were forced to live and sleep cheek by jowl to act as duennas for each other.

According to their class schedules physical training occupied the first two hours of the morning. As their maids—batBEMs—fussed and flitted about assisting them to undress after the banquet, Mercedes had inspected her gym attire. Once again it was a split skirt but not as long as the skirt for the dress uniform or her undress blues. The workout skirt ended mid-calf, a singularly unattractive length. There was a bulky tunic to be worn on top that hung to mid-thigh and would effectively hide her figure. Mercedes suspected the abundance of material was going to interfere with movement.

The four Hajin BatBEMs appeared a few minutes after reveille had sounded and started the water in the showers running. Mercedes slid out of the bunk and headed to a toilet. Pulling up her nightgown she sat down on the metal seat and felt her bladder tighten.

Cipriana apparently didn't suffer from embarrassment over having to urinate in front of other people. Her pee tinkled loudly into the metal bowl but even with that encouragement Mercedes couldn't relax and relieve herself. Her servant, Tako, sensed her discomfort and positioned herself in front of the opening. Mercedes sighed and finally let go.

A quick shower was followed by all of them standing in front of the mirrors and quickly applying makeup while their hair was brushed and braided by the servants. The chrono set into the sleeve of Mercedes' tunic showed that twelve minutes had elapsed.

Sucking in a deep, steadying breath Mercedes

faced her ladies. She wondered if her expression was as trepidatious as theirs.

"Well, all right. This is it then. *Touch the sky with glory*," she added though she felt silly intoning the motto.

She turned on her heel, the rubber of her gym shoe squeaking on the hard composite floor, and led them toward the door. Behind her someone giggled. She didn't look back to find out who.

• • •

Tracy entered the mess hall and found that of the first-year cadets only he and the ladies had arrived. Tracy was startled to see Mercedes. *The Infanta,* he mentally made the correction. He had no idea what a noble lady's life was like, but he doubted early mornings played any part in it. She was looking at him, and a sharp frown furrowed the pale chocolate skin between those sweeping brows. Apparently he'd allowed his surprise to show on his face.

He ducked his head and hustled to his table near the kitchen doors. He was relieved to see only a knife, fork and spoon instead of the array of flatware that had daunted him the night before. He had tried to surreptitiously watch his dinner companions, but he knew he and the other scholarship student, a young man from Nueva Terra named Mark Wilson, had made mistakes and that those mistakes had been noted by their better-born classmates. Even Hugo had known how to use the extra forks and spoons. The Devrises might not have had a title until recently, but they had the next best thing—money.

The FFH progeny with whom Tracy shared the table hadn't been all that happy. It wasn't just the presence of the commoners that had aroused their noble ire. There had also been a lot of bitching about the table itself. Its placement near the kitchen doors had been viewed as an insult, just like having to share the table with *intitulado*. The professor at the head of the table—who had introduced himself as Commander Trent Crispin—had cast the fulminating aristos an amused glance and said, "Look on the bright side. Our food is hot when it arrives."

That had drawn a laugh from Hugo. It had rung out too loud and too forced, and Hugo had wilted under the looks. Tracy almost felt sorry for the boy. Then he remembered that Hugo had taken what was rightfully his, to be the valedictorian, and Tracy quashed the feeling.

This morning Crispin was not present at the table. Since the dais was cleared of emperors, commandants and patrons the teachers had commandeered the high table and the task of supervising the first-year cadets had fallen to upperclassmen. Ensign Prefect Caballero Marcus Gelb had been the only other formal introduction that had been made last night. A ribbon on the left shoulder of the third-year student's uniform marked him as the prefect for their table. His only other notable feature had been an angry red cut across his receding chin. The man had noticed Tracy staring, frowned and Tracy had quickly looked away.

A Hajin servant appeared at Tracy's side, pulling him out of his reverie. "Traditional breakfast or oatmeal," the alien inquired softly. "Tea or coffee? Juice?"

Tracy considered the Sims he'd seen about life in the corps and books he'd read. He decided to opt for the less heavy alternative, at least until he knew what physical training was likely to entail.

"Oatmeal, café au lait, apple juice." The Hajin bowed and slipped back into the kitchen.

The food appeared quickly and Tracy began to eat. The food at the banquet had been first rate, and Tracy had assumed that would be the exception since they were hosting royalty, but breakfast was equally delicious, the oatmeal subtly flavored with cinnamon and cardamom and an alien spice he couldn't identify. *Well of course,* he thought, *the FFH isn't going to start slumming just because they're in the military. Servants to wait on us hand and foot and gourmet meals.*

A few moments later Wilson arrived. They had surreptitiously exchanged names and handshakes the night before. The better-born cadets at their table had not offered their names to the two scholarship students, and indeed seemed to pretend they weren't present. Wilson had looked enviously at Tracy's spider silk and tugged ineffectually at the poorly tailored coat of his pale blue charity uniform. Tracy had wanted to suggest that Wilson bring the coat to his room and let him fit it properly, but he quashed the impulse. He didn't want to be known as the tailor's son, the tradesman, the low-class lout. That life was behind him.

"Morning," Wilson muttered.

"Morning," Tracy grunted back.

At some point he and Wilson would have to talk, and decide just how much interaction they were going to have. Tracy felt it would be a mistake for them to spend too much time together. The next three years wasn't just an opportunity for an education. They needed to use it to make contacts and form alliances. Assuming any of their FFH classmates ever decided to acknowledge them, much less speak to them, Tracy thought as he watched Gelb, frown furrowing his brow, stalk to the table.

The prefect leaned toward them. "I will have good order at this table. So don't fucking embarrass me, *intitulados!*" he hissed in an undertone.

"Absolutely, sir, yes, sir," Wilson gabbled and there was not a hint of irony in his voice.

Tracy just stared at the older student. Gelb was no fool, Tracy had to give him that. The prefect's eyes narrowed as he correctly interpreted the challenge implicit in Tracy's silence and level gaze. Gelb opened his mouth but before he could utter a rebuke the rest of their table arrived.

"You weren't on my shuttle coming up," Tracy said in an undertone to Wilson. He was prepared to be offended if it turned out the other scholarship student had actually travelled with the well-born cadets.

"I came directly to the station from Nueva Terra," Wilson muttered back. "Seemed stupid to spend money on a ticket down to the planet." Tracy felt better and also felt small because of his suspicions.

The chair to Tracy's left was taken by a student he'd noticed the previous night because of the man's unusual coloring—grey hair and brows set against a youthful face, but cut with ropey scars across one cheek. Tracy tensed when Hugo took the chair directly across from him. "Morning."

"Morning," Tracy muttered back.

Hugo leaned across the table. Tracy retreated against the back of his chair. "Look. I want… I need to say something."

"What?"

Hugo's eyes widened at Tracy's harsh tone. "I want to apologize. It wasn't right… what they did. You were the best student in our class. It should have been you."

Both the grey-haired youth and Wilson were listening. Tracy writhed in embarrassment. "Yes. It should have been," he snapped.

"Look, I know it doesn't mean much… *now*, but I tried to get out of it." Hugo hung his head. "They just wouldn't let up. My dad and those guys from the palace. I'm not as smart as you. Nowhere near. I'll probably flunk out of here. But as long as I am here… well, I owe you. You can call on me if you need anything."

The humble apology and confession had Tracy's rage in tatters. He tried to gather it again, to find that hot, hurting ball that had lived in the pit of his stomach since May, but it refused to return. It had become a weary pity. Apparently nobody's life was going as they had planned. Tracy gave a sharp nod.

"Thanks. I appreciate… well, just thanks."

Deferential servants appeared and took orders. A hum of nervous conversation, the clink of silverware on china began to fill the cavernous room. Tracy was acutely aware of the voices of Mercedes and the ladies dancing like chimes and bells over the basso rumblings of the men.

Scar Face was eating his omelet and sausage with almost finicky care. The fork seemed small between his blunt fingers. Tracy forced aside his natural shyness, half turned and offered his hand.

"Thracius Belmanor," he said.

The grey-haired boy looked down at Tracy's outstretched hand, up to his face, back to the hand, then he lightly brushed Tracy's fingertips with his.

"Cadet Baron Jasper Talion."

"Pleased to meet you," Tracy said.

Talion didn't respond; he turned back to his plate, though he kept his eyes on Gelb, watching as the prefect chewed very carefully, trying to avoid moving his jaw and pulling at that livid wound.

"Sabers or the Black Feather?" Talion asked abruptly.

Tracy had read about The High Ground's dueling societies, and hoped he could avoid that bit of nonsense.

"Black Feather," was the curt reply from Gelb.

"I hear the Sabers are better."

"You won't get into the Sabers, Talion."

The muscles in the back of the powerful hand that held the coffee cup tightened, and Tracy momentarily expected to see the delicate china shatter beneath that grip. He was glad now that Talion hadn't actually taken his hand. "And why is that... exactly?" Talion's voice had dropped to a low purr and the hair on the back of Tracy's neck stood up.

Gelb sensed the menace and came to his feet. "Because we don't hold a high enough rank."

Talion lounged back in his chair. "I can see where that would be a problem for *you*. I'm a baron, and my father—"

"Yeah, yeah, I know. Your daddy is provincial

governor of that shit hole Nephilim, and if you think that will carry any weight with *those* guys..." He jerked his head toward the table directly in front of the dais where Mercedes and her ladies were seated. Cullen, Arturo del Campo and various other young men were making their way toward them. Gelb winced as the sharp move pulled at his scab then shrugged and concluded, "...then you're an idiot."

Tracy pushed back his chair and left the table. Mark scurried after him. "And what does that make us?" Wilson said in an undertone as they headed for the doors.

"Smarter," Tracy snapped.

• • •

Mercedes watched Tracy leave the mess hall. She admired how the material of his grey T-shirt hugged his back. He wasn't a muscled Adonis like Boho, but she liked his whipcord leanness. She was certain her gym clothes were far less flattering.

Approaching footsteps pulled her back to her surroundings. Vizconde Mihalis del Campo was approaching the table. It was the meeting she'd been dreading. It should have happened last night—Mihalis was the prefect for this table—but he had been absent at dinner. The professor had blandly mentioned a sudden illness, but Mercedes hadn't been fooled. She suspected her cousin had sipped from a cup of gall and that was the source of his indigestion.

The bite of soft-boiled egg she'd just eaten curdled in her stomach. If her father hadn't taken his radical step

Cousin Musa would have become emperor and Mihalis would be the heir apparent. Instead she was the Infanta, and Mihalis would end his life as a royal duque.

At Mihalis's side walked his younger brother Arturo. Arturo had his usual smug, faintly amused expression. Mihalis was also smiling, but it seemed tight, and obsidian would have been warmer than his eyes.

Find a consort. Pick the man who will share the throne with you. Once again her father's words roiled her thoughts.

Would it make sense to pick Mihalis? The del Campos were more golden skinned than their imperial relatives, and people accounted Mihalis handsome, though for Mercedes' taste his eyes were set too close to his nose. Another pair of eyes, grey and passionate, floated briefly before her. She pushed the memory aside and focused on the eldest del Campo. Looks weren't everything. In fact they shouldn't weigh with her at all, and Mihalis had a number of traits going for him. He was related by blood, already trained to rule—

The thought brought her up short. It was probably the best reason *not* to pick Mihalis. Being the consort would seem like crumbs to a man who had expected the throne. He would try to rule through her at best or undermine her authority at worst.

She glanced at her companions. Sumiko was focused on her plate, eating as if this were her last meal. Danica was staring down at her tightly folded hands, too shy to look at the group of men settling into chairs across from them. She hadn't touched her food as far as Mercedes could see. Cipriana stared boldly at the phalanx of males arrayed across from her with the air of a woman deciding between a set of Sidone scarves. *Or perhaps a housewife deciding which plump chicken looks more appetizing*, Mercedes thought and choked back a giggle.

She let her eyes drift to the others, this flock of the highest born males among the FFH. *Or perhaps they should be a pride like lions or a pack like wolves*, she thought. She realized her mind had gone there because she did feel like prey. Not only the professors would be watching her every move and reporting back to her father, all the students would be watching as well, and their reports would go to their families in the form of gossip and gossip was like pollution. It spread fast and wasn't easily combated. She pushed aside the uncomfortable thought.

Hunching his shoulders and sliding into a chair at the end of the table was Vizconde Yves Riccardo Petek. The tight T-shirt displayed his paunch, and his eyes with their epicanthic fold gave him a perpetually worried expression. He had a delicate mouth, and a pointed chin that was starting to lose its shape as fat blurred his features.

Boho and Mihalis jockeyed for the seat directly across from her and Boho won. He gave her a blazing smile as he took his chair. He was flanked by two of his toadies, Davin Pulkkinen, a simple caballero known more for his schoolboy "wit" than much else. The other was the Marqués Clark Bennington Kunst. Mercedes didn't know much about him beyond the fact he was a very good dancer. Neither of them were as handsome as Boho. It was a trait of beautiful women to pick less attractive friends to highlight their superior appearance. Mercedes was amused by the idea that men might do the same.

"So, you're happy to be here," Mihalis said.

"What?" Mercedes asked.

"You're smiling."

"Was I? I suppose I was. Silly thought. Nothing important…" She realized she was babbling and she shut her mouth so firmly that her teeth clicked.

Mihalis's smile broadened and the hard light in his eyes softened. "Come on, Mercedes, a joke is better when it's shared," he coaxed.

She noted the use of her given name, and irritation had her snapping before she considered, "Not when some of you are the butt of it."

Mihalis's smile was gone and all the young men exchanged glances. *Was it me? Did she mean me? Maybe it was you.* The wobbling deep in her stomach was distracting and irritating. Mercedes pushed aside her nerves and clung to the small advantage she'd seized.

"You weren't at dinner," she said bluntly.

"An unfortunately timed stomach bug," Mihalis replied with a courtier's smooth delivery.

"Throne-itis I hear is quite debilitating," Mercedes shot back. A frightened squeak emerged from both Danica and Petek. There were quick indrawn breaths from the other men and Arturo gave her a thoughtful and calculating look.

"You're very direct, Princess," Mihalis said.

"The title is Infanta now, and we're not playing court games, cousin. The fleet is essential to the League's security."

"Which is precisely why a little experiment in social engineering seems… foolish."

"Nonetheless I am here."

"But will you stay?"

"Depend on it."

Mercedes pushed back her chair with enough force that it set up a shriek as the metal legs scraped on the stone. Danica gave a gasp and leaped to her feet. Cipriana unfolded with the grace of a swan taking flight. Sumiko also stood, plump and solid at Mercedes' side.

"Well, see you all at training," Mercedes said.

Mercedes led them away. Her stomach was still wobbling.

7

SO IT IS TO BE WAR

It was an impressive room made even more impressive because it was on a space station. Overhead a clear dome arched against the stars and the blazing nebula. It seemed a fragile thing to separate them from the cold and vacuum of space.

Beneath it a running track circled a grass-filled soccer field. Directly across from the door through which they had entered was a shooting range, and at one end of the huge oval room were free weights and machines. At the other end mats were laid out. Tracy expected those were not for yoga classes, and in fact a barrel-chested man dressed in a star command blue martial arts gi stood waiting. He bounced on the balls of his bare feet, hands clasped behind his back. The light from the nebula poured down through the clear dome and glinted on the man's shaved head.

Arrayed all around the walls of the training center were suits of armor. The earliest honored Earth's history. Shining plate worn by the knights of the middle ages, exquisite lacquered bamboo armor from

China and Japan, ceramic and Kevlar combat armor from the late twentieth and twenty-first century. The suits worn by the astronauts who first tested the Fold technology that defeated the limits prescribed by light speed and opened the stars to humans. Those were puffy and white and looked as if the wearer were encased in marshmallows.

Tracy's eye skipped from suit to suit seeing not only the advance of technology but the militarization of the space program until it had morphed into the Solar League space command, the *Orden de la Estrella*. His gaze came to rest on the suit directly to the right of the doors. It was a familiar sight from hundreds of SimPlays, SimTourneys and recruitment Sims streamed to his ScoopRing. O-Trell battle armor. At some point he would wear one of those suits. He reached out to touch the glistening material only to have his hand slapped aside.

"That armor was worn by Vice Admiral of the Blue Margrave Øystein Nass at the battle of Xinoxex. Keep your dirty hands off it, *intitulado*."

Tracy had no idea of the midshipman's identity, but he bet he knew something the arrogant ass probably didn't. He turned on the other student, felt his lips twist into a sneer. "Nass was a scholarship student. Won his title at the battle of Xinoxex. Just another dirty *intitulado*. You can never tell where we're going to end up."

"I know where you're going to end up if you don't shut up. Now get on the track!" The older boy gave him a hard shove between the shoulder blades.

An officer, hands clasped behind his back, stood rocking gently on the balls of his feet at the edge of the track. He eyed them all. "Three miles, cadets! Go!"

There was a confused jumble as they all began to run. Tracy managed to use the scrum to casually trip the midshipman who had shoved him. The guy went sprawling, but in the crush he couldn't totally identify who had tripped him. Once on the track there began a contest for position. Tracy noted that Cullen immediately moved to the front of the pack. Jasper Talion, the baron from Tracy's breakfast table, matched him stride for stride—two big men fighting for primacy.

A light soprano voice asked incredulously, "We're all going to run *together*? With the boys?"

A single snapped word. "Yes." Tracy recognized Mercedes' rich alto voice even with just that one word.

Tracy picked a pace he thought he could maintain. It put him well back in the middle of the pack. From here he could watch the struggle playing out in front. Several other cadets tried to challenge Cullen and Talion for the lead, but they always wilted. The practical effect of all the dick waving was that the pace kept increasing.

Tracy realized he was lapping a fat boy who was staggering more than running. Sweat streamed down his face and darkened the neck, back and armpits of his T-shirt. His mouth was twisted in agony and his wheezing breaths could be heard above the slap of running feet and the panting of the other cadets. Tracy felt a momentary flash of pity for the suffering boy. Apparently the FFH wasn't kidding about requiring all its sons to attend The High Ground. Tracy's eyes went to Hugo a few feet in front of him and running easily.

As for Tracy, pain stitched its way up his side and

his lungs were burning. Material twined around his left shin and he almost lost his balance.

"God *damn* these skirts!" Mercedes gasped. She gave him a sideways glance and added in a puffing whisper, "Sorry."

"S'okay."

"You didn't say—" she began.

Tracy became aware of the contemplative gaze from a pair of brown eyes set in an ebony-skinned face. The cadet's black hair hung in ringlets to his collar, and he sported a gold ring in one ear. A large gold signet ring glittered on a slim hand.

Tracy clenched his fists at his side and forced his legs to pump harder, leaving Mercedes behind mid-word before any more of their classmates noticed their exchange.

At the end of the run the fat boy threw up, and two of Mercedes' ladies were looking decidedly unwell. The tiny one wasn't sweating, and her skin was unnaturally pale. The stocky one had blotchy red spots all over her face. Tracy didn't feel much better, but he had made it and hadn't humiliated himself.

Three more drill instructors joined their first torturer, and separated them into four groups. The women were kept together and led away toward the mats. Tracy found himself in the group heading toward the shooting range, while Cullen, Talion and Arturo del Campo were among the students heading toward the weights. Cullen draped an arm over Talion's shoulders. The other man lifted it off. Tracy was surprised to see Cullen laugh. Apparently he would accept disrespect from a fellow aristo no matter how marginal the title or how provincial the planet.

• • •

After the far-too-brief recovery period Mercedes and her ladies were herded over to the mats. Mercedes had hoped that the resentment toward the female invasion of this traditionally male domain would be limited to the officer class. Perhaps the enlisted spacers would be more sympathetic? That hope was quickly put to flight by the look the bald, fireplug-shaped man bestowed on them. Well, maybe it was unique to just *this* man.

"I am Recruit Commander Nathaniel Deal. You will refer to me as Chief. Now get those shoes *off*!"

Cipriana leaned in and whispered into Mercedes' ear as they unlaced their shoes. "Does everyone in the army feel it's incumbent upon them to shout?"

They shared smiles that quickly died when Cipriana was grabbed by the back of the neck and yanked erect. "First, Cadet, we are *not* the motherfucking footsore army. We are not air force limp dicks or even wet-footed navy boys. *We* are *Orden de la Estrella*. We might have been an out-growth of the navy, but our captains are smarter, our *Infierno* fighter jocks faster, and our *fusileros* tougher. We get the prettiest whores and the Planet Patrol fears us the most. And that's why I'm not a fucking drill sergeant. We don't have sergeants in O-Trell. Now what are *you*?" Cipriana gaped at him. Mercedes sensed her expression wasn't much different. "*What are you?*" he roared into her face.

"Lady—" Cipriana whimpered only to be cut off by a roar.

"Wrong!"

"Cadet," Mercedes blurted. "We're cadets."

"Still wrong! You are worms." Deal released Cipriana. "But I'm going to try to turn you into big damn heroes. Now get over here. The first thing I'm going to teach you is how to fall."

So she fell. A lot. Thrown to the mats with contemptuous ease by Chief Deal. Even with the mats the landing was hard, and Mercedes could feel the bruises beginning to blossom on her hips, shoulders and elbows. Sometimes she fell when she didn't mean to, tripped up by her absurd outfit. The entire experience was made all the worse by the ring of young men who surrounded the mats and watched their struggles. Oddly enough it was Cipriana who was sniveling. Mercedes thought it would have been Danica, but the tiny blonde just had the look of a person trapped in a nightmare; swept along and hoping she would wake up sooner rather than later. Sumiko was hobbling. The knight's daughter couldn't seem to grasp how to slap the mat and roll onto her shoulder so she kept hitting the floor like a sack of rocks.

Mercedes climbed to her feet and looked at Chief Deal. His fleshy lips were curled in disdain as he surveyed the women. "Okay, enough. Since you can't fall worth a damn I'm going to try and show you how to keep from getting knocked down. Do any of you know the right way to throw a punch?" They shook their heads. "Okay, make a fist. No, not like that." He stepped forward and peeled Mercedes' fingers open. "Never put your thumb inside your curled fingers. If you hit hard enough—not that that's likely, but if you do you'll end up breaking your thumb. So, like this." He demonstrated. To Mercedes' weary mind his hand looked more like a flesh-colored block than anything organic, much less human.

"Now line up and hit me," he ordered.

Mercedes found herself at the front of the line. She stared at his chest, the muscles cutting lines against his T-shirt. His neck was almost as wide as his head. This close she could see the pores on his nose, a few incipient blackheads. She had no idea where to aim. Deal tapped his chest.

"Just hit me."

She clenched her fist, careful to place her thumb over her fingers, and punched. It hurt her knuckles and Deal didn't even sway. He stood like a stone effigy. "Next!" he bawled and Mercedes moved aside.

One by one they hit him. None of their blows seemed to affect him in the least. "Useless," he muttered. "Take a break." He turned to the watching men. "Gentlemen."

Mercedes and her ladies retreated to the edge of the mat and sat down. Her hair was coming loose from her braid, tendrils sweat-plastered to her face and catching on her dry lips. Their servants rushed over carrying cups of water. Tako whispered to her.

"May I rebraid your hair, my lady?"

"Please."

The Hajin pulled a brush from the satchel she wore slung over her shoulder. Mercedes relaxed and enjoyed the scratch of the bristles against her scalp, and the languorous tug as the brush made its sweep through her heavy curls. She watched the men go through the falls. Most of them were far better at it than she and the other girls had been.

Deal moved to a pile of what she had taken to be giant

cushions. He lifted one and Mercedes saw the straps. Holding it like a shield he began to engage the male cadets, having them punch the cushion. Resentment began as a small coal deep in her chest. Deal had stood unprotected against the women. Dismissing them in a way that was utterly contemptuous and offensive. She wanted to react, but indecision held her immobile.

"He doesn't think we can hit like a boy," she whispered to Sumiko.

"And he'd be right," the other girl muttered back. "This is idiotic. We're not going to be punching people. We'll be aboard spaceships shooting missiles and... and things."

Mercedes fell silent. She sensed that this was the first battle in the war to make a place for herself at The High Ground, and that she was losing already. Trouble was she had no idea how to respond. A few minutes later and Deal motioned for the women to join them. He kept four of the male cadets with him.

"Let's try a little sparring." With sharp jabs of his forefinger the chief positioned them opposite their male counterpart.

They were being coerced into a situation where they could not win. She ought to speak up and object. But was a cadet allowed to point out that a drill instructor was being unfair? Weren't they supposed to be unfair?

Confused and afraid, Mercedes gingerly took her place across from Arturo as if they were taking their places in a line dance at a society ball. She glanced over at her companions. Their expressions ranged from outright terror to dumb confusion. The entire situation was bizarre. They all knew each other.

The FFH from Consular worlds came to the capital on a regular basis. The children socialized together while their fathers arranged business deals and their mothers arranged marriages.

"Okay, Caddies, spar."

No one moved. Sumiko's voice rang out. "This isn't fair. You haven't taught us anything. Certainly not how to spar."

Shame lay like a bad taste on the back of Mercedes' tongue. She was the daughter of Emperor Fernán Marcus Severino Beltrán de Arango. She should be the one defending her ladies, not a mere knight's daughter.

Deal shoved aside Sumiko's opponent, Boho's friend Clark Kunst, and thrust his face into hers. "War isn't fair, Princess," he said.

"Wrong girl," Cipriana said and pointed. "*She's* the princess."

Deal turned to Mercedes. "You have a comment… Your Highness?" If the man's tone wasn't enough, the delay in offering her title made the contempt plain.

Mercedes' stomach seemed filled with quaking jelly. She looked away from Deal's steel gaze. Her own eyes darted from face to face seeking help, support, comfort.

Arturo caught her glance, and she saw a flash of pity in his caramel brown eyes. He took a step back, and stared down his nose at Deal. "They're women. A gentleman does not strike a woman."

A complex and elaborate move that involved an arm and a sweep of the leg, and Arturo was on his back on the mats gaping up at the burly chief. Deal leaned over, and gripped Arturo by the throat.

"There are going to be women on the other side.

I lost a friend when he underestimated an Isanjo bitch. She was holding a cub, sweet little mother. She disemboweled him." He flicked the fingers of his free hand, and curved them. "They've got claws." Deal jerked a thumb over at the four women. "Don't think they don't have claws too."

Straightening, the chief raked the rest of the men with a cold glare. "Any of you pussies strong enough to overcome your programming? We know Peaches here," he glanced down at Arturo, "can't." There were awkward glances all around and not one of the men stepped forward.

Mercedes found herself remembering all the shocked headlines and disapproving editorials that had poured from the news outlets after her acceptance at The High Ground had been announced. There had been many arguments against the inclusion of women at the academy, ranging from how their presence would inflame and arouse the men and sexual license would abound, to the possibility that a man's natural inclination to protect the weaker sex would distract him from the serious business of killing enemies.

Judging by what was happening at this very moment, the latter concerns had been well founded. Word of this would leak. It would be all over the news services, trumpeted with their usual high decibel hysteria, that the Emperor's foolish action had weakened the military and that the League was now under imminent threat.

She stepped over to Arturo who was just climbing to his feet. "It's all right. You must do this," she said firmly. "Fight me."

For an instant his confusion was evident, then the calculation began. She sensed he was reaching the same conclusion as her. He stepped back, bowed and said, "I would not presume."

So it is to be war between our families, she thought.

• • •

The pulse rifle vibrated in Tracy's hands as it streaked death toward the distant targets. He knew his rate of fire was far slower than the other cadets. Theirs was an angry snarl while his was a slow buzz as he tried to line up his shots. He had done the same thing during RCFC training, and gotten roundly mocked and abused for it by the drill instructor. Memories of those painful classes had his shoulders tensing.

He was also distracted by what was going on over on the martial arts mats. The sound of the rifles made it impossible to hear what was being said, but he didn't need words to know that some kind of drama was playing out. Mercedes looked devastated. The men had all stepped back as if an invisible barrier now separated them from the women.

Recruit Commander Yas Begay's surprisingly delicate hand landed on Tracy's shoulder. "You're thinking too much, Cadet. What did I say right at the start?"

Tracy pulled his attention away from Mercedes and glanced up at the round-faced man. "The pulse rifle is a spray and pray kind of weapon."

"Exactly." Begay released Tracy's shoulder, and stroked his chin. "You're a thinker. You might be a sniper prospect. Takes coolness and a desire to analyze to be a sniper." The short, stocky man glanced over at the hand-to-hand training area. "So what's your analysis of what's going on over there?" he asked quietly.

Startled, Tracy glanced up at the chief, fearing some trick. The man's expression was blank. Tracy looked back to the mats in time to see del Campo stepping away from Mercedes and giving a deep and sweeping bow.

"They won't train with the women." He paused, considering all the ramifications. "That's not good."

"Depends on what you think is good, doesn't it?" Begay took the rifle from Tracy's hands. "We'll resume tomorrow and arm you with a Raptor. Young gentlemen often think shooting from cover is cowardly, not sporting, but people like us—we're not as *well bred*. You take my meaning?" Begay jerked his chin toward the mats. "Chief Deal will have you in his tender mercies next. I'd get over there now. Dismissed!"

Tracy walked quickly toward the martial arts area.

8

A LACK OF MANNERS

I wonder what instructions your father gave you and your brother before you arrived? Mercedes thought as she stared at Arturo. *Undermine me at every opportunity, I'll bet.*

Impasse. The other three men stepped away from her ladies. Danica slumped in relief. Sumiko and Cipriana relaxed and they all drew together. Mercedes wanted to cry and knew she couldn't. She swallowed several times trying to force aside the ache in her throat. Then a soft baritone voice said, "If the recruit commander will permit I'll spar with my fellow cadet."

She knew that voice. She had played it back during late nights so as not to forget her very first adventure. Tracy stood at her elbow, hands clasped behind his back, staring straight ahead. Not by so much as a glance did he acknowledge her.

"You're not in this group."

"No, sir. But Chief Begay saw your dilemma and thought I might be able to assist."

"And why is that?"

Those grey eyes flicked briefly to her face then turned back to Deal. "He thought my manners probably wouldn't be as nice as the young gentlemen's in your group."

"*Intitulado?*"

"Yes, sir."

"You'd hit a woman?"

"Yes, sir."

"All rightie then." Deal turned back to the nobles. "You gonna let this one show you up?"

There were more glances and shuffles then three of the men stepped forward to confront her ladies. Sumiko looked resigned, Danica gave her a desperate look and Cipriana shot her a poisonous one. Then she and Tracy were facing each other.

He was pale. She could sense that she was flushed. "I keep waiting for the music to start," she whispered.

"I don't dance," he muttered back. "Look, I'll make it real clear when I'm going to swing. Just get your forearm up and block me. Or grab my hand with yours and push it away."

"You know how to do this?"

"Studied a little martial arts. Been a while though—"

"Spar!" Deal shouted.

Tracy was true to his word. He would even glance down at which hand he was going to use, and then slowly raise his arm. Mercedes had plenty of time to react and also to sneak glances at her companions. Sumiko had her hands and arms up, trying to protect her face. Cipriana was dancing away from her attacker, keeping out of his reach.

Danica wasn't even trying. She just stood, hands

hanging at her sides, and cried. The boy facing her was dark-skinned and his dark red hair set an odd contrast to his pale brown eyes. Right now he was looking at the delicate blonde in frustration. Sanjay Favreau's father had large holdings in banks and investment companies whose home offices were clustered on Kronos. He had been discussed as a potential match for her sister Estella.

Wedding money to the crown was always a good plan, Mercedes thought and realized she sounded like her father. Her mind was wandering and she missed Tracy's windup. His fist connected with her cheekbone.

• • •

Tracy yanked his hand away. Horrified by the reddened mark on her cheek, aware of the softness of her skin against his knuckles. "Sorry, sorry," he muttered.

"It's okay. I got distracted," Mercedes whispered back.

Then they were both distracted when Deal bellowed, "This dumb *punta* boo hoos and you stand there with your dick in your hand? She's giving you a fucking gift! Take it. Or are you a liar as well as a pussy? You stepped up here. Now really step up!" The chief slapped Sanjay hard on the back of his head.

Tracy watched the pack mentality set in. A potential rival was getting his dick knocked in the dirt. It was too good an opportunity to pass up. The other males whipped out theirs, figuratively speaking, and the measuring began.

"Little performance anxiety there, Jay?"

"You offered, *hijo*."

"You going to cry too?"

Tracy watched as a frown furrowed the boy's brows. He shot a furious glance at his tormentors. Then the blonde girl made doe eyes at him. The young man's jaw tightened at the attempted manipulation.

"That's torn it," Tracy muttered.

"Oh, no," Mercedes breathed. "Sanjay's got a temp—"

She was interrupted when Sanjay growled, "I'll give you something to cry about."

His fist lashed out and took the girl full in the face. Her nose smashed against her cheeks, blood flew in all directions. The blonde screamed as the force of the blow drove her backwards onto the mat. The girl's hands were at her face, blood welling from between her fingers, both her eyes already blackening. Her sparring partner turned assailant lunged toward her, fist upraised, clearly ready to strike again.

Tracy moved to intercept, but not as quickly as Mercedes. She interposed herself between the sobbing girl and the furious boy. Tracy saw her hands close into fists, but she didn't swing. Instead her right foot flew up and took Sanjay in the crotch. He shrieked in pain, and bent forward to clutch his abused privates. Mercedes danced from one foot to the other and lashed out with her left foot, connecting with Sanjay's descending chin. Sanjay's head snapped back, and he collapsed moaning onto the mat.

Mercedes was hopping on one foot and clutching her toes. "Ow," she panted. Tracy tried to choke back laughter and was only marginally successful. "You try kicking a jawbone with your bare feet!" Mercedes flashed at him.

"Looks more like that jaw was made of glass," Tracy chuckled. A rueful smile told him he was forgiven. Then he was forgotten as Mercedes whirled and rushed to the whimpering girl. She dropped to her knees next to the blonde.

"It's all right, Dani. It's all right." She pinned Deal with an imperious look. "She needs to see a doctor. Now!"

Deal stepped forward. "The medicos are on the way." He held out a broad, blunt hand. "Well done you, Cadet Princess. I think I know the fighting style that will suit you. We'll make you a big damn hero yet."

Mercedes ignored the drill instructor and held out her hand to Tracy. He hustled forward and assisted her to her feet. For a moment they stood face to face, her hand in his. He knew he was beaming. She gave him a tiny nod. He gave one back, released her hand and stepped away.

• • •

The scent of sweat, farts, soap, hair pomade and aftershave mingled with the steam from the hot water pounding from showerheads. The locker room was crowded with students and their batBEMs. Donnel was waiting at a locker, a towel draped over one of his arms, a bar of soap and a bath sponge in one hand, shampoo in a second, shaving gear in a third. Only Tracy had a servant so rich in appendages. The other batBEMs carried their cadets' toiletries in small shower caddies.

Tracy stripped off his sweat-soaked gym clothes,

took the towel from Donnel's arm, wrapped it around his waist and joined the gaggle of men heading to the showers. Donnel trailed after him with his odd lurching walk. The tile floor beneath Tracy's bare feet was almost hot, and heat lamps set into the ceiling bathed his shoulders with warmth. There were no stalls, just a long row of showerheads throwing water onto the tiles and drains to carry it bubbling away. Mirrors were set on the back wall between the showerheads, made from some material that kept them clear of the clouds of steam that obscured the naked bodies of the men. Tracy handed Donnel the towel—he was getting too comfortable with this, he thought—took his toiletries and stepped under the water.

It was hotter than he was used to. At home they kept the water heater turned down low to save money. He began to scrub down. Suds foamed cloud-like on the sponge. Figures edged out of the steam, flanking him. Their faces were reflected in the mirror. Sanjay and one of the men who had stepped forward to face the girls. They didn't look friendly. Tracy stiffened, bath sponge in his hand.

Sanjay's jaw was swollen and bruised so his words were mumbled and muffled. Their meaning, however, was clear. "You need a lesson in manners, *intitulado*. You don't laugh at your betters—"

"And you need to learn when to *duck*," Tracy shot back, and he jammed the soap-filled sponge into Sanjay's face.

Sanjay yelled as the soap stung his eyes. Tracy spun to face the other man, but slipped on the suds and water-slick tiles, banging his hip hard against the wall.

He was directly under the shower, the water blinding him. A fist slammed into his belly. Air exploded out of him, and he doubled over in pain. A knee was rising toward his face. Then suddenly the knee was receding, and he was being hauled into the air.

The showerheads were beneath him now. Tracy craned to look over his shoulder. Donnel was scurrying across the ceiling on his three legs while all four arms cradled Tracy. The alien scuttled down the wall, and deposited Tracy under the last bank of showerheads at the far end of the room. Right in the midst of Cullen and his two brown-nosers.

Naked, gulping and breathless, Tracy decided it wasn't the moment for attitude. He ducked his head, muttered, "Excuse me," and headed out. The big aristocrat looked startled, then amused and finally thoughtful. His hand landed on Tracy's shoulder, holding him in place.

"What?" Tracy snapped. "You gonna teach me manners too?" *So much for discretion.*

"A word of advice, *intitulado*. You shouldn't take liberties with the ladies." The hand was lifted and Tracy started away. "Oh, and a warning. Stay away from the Infanta."

Donnel was waiting beyond the spray of water. He handed Tracy his towel. As he dried himself Tracy muttered, "I can fight my own battles."

"Maybe you'd like me to put you back?" There was a pointed pause and the alien added, "Sir."

"No. And okay, I get it." Tracy headed for the locker room, stopped and muttered, "Thanks."

"My pleasure, sir."

• • •

"This is ridiculous!" Mercedes raged at Captain Manfred Zeng's impassive face. She stood before his desk, fists braced on the marble surface, body quivering with nerves and indignation. The captain sat behind the desk in his oddly cluttered office, fingers tented in front of his lips, looking up at her intently.

"The whole thing is ridiculous, starting with these damn clothes!" She pulled open the tear in her skirt. The flash of skin got a reaction. The captain's eyes widened and he looked momentarily alarmed.

"Cadet Princess, please won't you sit down? I find conversations so much more productive when the parties are comfortable."

The mild tone left her deflated. She was also embarrassed about displaying her thigh. It wasn't the sort of behavior in which a well-bred young woman engaged. Mercedes had screwed up her courage to bring her complaints to the chief administrator by stoking her anger. Now she didn't know how to react. She looked around, and backed into one of the overstuffed armchairs that Zeng had indicated.

The office was a total contrast to Zeng himself. It held the usual and expected array of holos showing Zeng with various famous politicians, nobles and military leaders. What Mercedes hadn't expected was the clutter more in keeping with the salon of a fussy maiden aunt. Knick knacks adorned the desk and the side table that rested between two armchairs. In addition to the holos there were actual painted pictures on the walls, but not what one would expect from a military leader. No capital ships against a dramatic backdrop of stars, no brave *fusileros* storming a stronghold. No gauchos riding the steppes and plains of Nueva Terra following their herds, her father's personal favorites. Instead Zeng's taste veered to the fantastic—dreamy, misty landscapes or seascapes with sailing ships whose sails were made of flowers. Given Zeng's appearance Mercedes had expected an ascetic monk's cell.

"Now, what may I do for you?"

Mercedes' eyes narrowed. On the surface the words were innocuous, but she heard the faint echo of a man humoring a recalcitrant child. She remained silent as she marshaled her arguments. She decided to start by tossing it back to Zeng.

"First a question, Captain… after graduation we will be assigned to ships, correct?"

"Yes."

"And when a ship is in combat all personnel are wearing armor, correct?"

"Again yes."

Mercedes picked up the material of her skirt. "We start *Infierno* training at the end of the first quarter. You wear armor in an *Infierno* fighter too. Have I got that right?" This time Zeng just nodded. He was looking wary. Mercedes gave him a smile. "So, will our armor have a skirt? And how exactly will that work? Granted it would be a challenging technological problem and might lead to some real innovations, but is it really worth the effort? Wouldn't it be better to just give us regular armor?"

Zeng leaned back, hands gripping the arms of his chair. He no longer looked like he was humoring her.

A frown furrowed his brow. "What are you suggesting, Cadet Princess?"

"Let us wear slacks. Give us gym clothes that allow us to move so we can learn something. Otherwise we're just going to be burdens to our fellow officers."

"I'll have to take this to the commandant."

"Why? You said you were in charge of operations. Wouldn't attire fall under that?"

"Your presence here represents a profound change to this institution, Highness. We gave very careful thought to all the ramifications."

"May I speak frankly, sir?"

"You mean you haven't been?" His lips quirked in something that might be called a smile.

"No, you didn't think anything through. No one thought past the press releases and the holo ops and the first weeks of class because none of you think we're going to make it. Here's something you can pass on to the commandant. *I'm* going to make it."

He contemplated her for a long moment. "Is there anything else, Cadet Princess?"

"No, sir."

"Then you are dismissed."

9

A FRAGILE CONSTRUCT

With a few coughs the class settled into their seats in the raked auditorium. Commander Crispin sat on his desk in the well of the chamber, one gleaming boot swinging idly back and forth. Stands folded up out of the desktops to accommodate the students' tap-pads. Tracy unfolded his pocket keyboard. Half the screen on his pad held the opening chapter of a history book, and the other side awaited his notes.

Silence. It continued for several moments then Crispin lifted up his own tap-pad. "So, this is Imperial History 101, and according to the syllabus I'm going to teach you the historical precedents of the academy, why we fight, why we are the best fighting men…"

Crispin paused to incline his head toward the ebony-skinned girl and the stocky girl who were in the class. Tracy had been disappointed when neither Mercedes nor the blonde girl, Danica, arrived.

"And now women in the known galaxy." Crispin slid off the desk and began pacing. "First, I am Commander Lord Trent Crispin. Yes, I know you got all that from your course schedule, but it's polite to offer introductions. So let's do that. Starting here." He pointed at the front row left corner seat and the student occupying the chair. "Please stand and introduce yourself. And tell us something salient about yourself. Something that will go in the history books when they write about all your glorious exploits."

Tracy didn't miss the irony that edged Crispin's words. What surprised him was how few of his fellow classmates seemed to hear it. Only a few of the FFH were frowning. Most were looking unperturbed, seemingly accepting this as their due.

The introductions began. Tracy wasn't sorry to start to put names with faces since almost none of the FFH had offered him an introduction. And he now had names for the final two ladies. Cadet Lady Cipriana Delacroix, and Cadet Lady Sumiko Tsukuda. After that there were a lot of cadet conde, and cadet caballero, and cadet sir, and cadet lord, and cadet vizconde. Mercifully most of the students didn't decide to expound beyond their noble lineage. It was his turn. Tracy stood, tilted his chin up and said, "Cadet Thracius Belmanor." He sat back down. No need to say he was a scholarship student. His cheap, pale blue undress uniform announced it to the world.

Once this odd form of roll call was over Commander Crispin inclined his head and said, "I'm pleased to meet you all."

The doors sighed open. Tracy and a number of other students looked back to see who was the latecomer. It was the Infanta and the blonde girl. Both of Danica's eyes were swollen nearly shut, the surrounding skin purple and black, a contrast with the stark white bandage that covered her nose. Mercedes had her arm around the smaller girl's waist.

"Forgive our belated arrival, Captain Professor," Mercedes said. Her husky alto voice made music of the mundane words.

"I understand Cadet Lady Everett had a medical issue to be resolved. You, however, Cadet Princess, have no excuse. Meet me after class and I'll assign your punishment."

Mercedes looked scared and hurt. She opened her mouth as if to argue, then thought better of it and found a seat. Unfortunately it was on the opposite side of the room from Tracy, but as close to the other ladies as she could manage. Perhaps there was safety in numbers and he ought to be more amenable to Wilson?

Tracy turned his attention back to Crispin. The man stood, head bowed, shoulders tense. He gave a nod as if answering an unspoken question and looked up. His gaze was focused only on Mercedes.

"So, why do we have an aristocracy?" the professor asked. Glances were exchanged. *Is this a trick question?* No one responded. "Too hard? How about this one? When did we acquire a hereditary aristocracy?"

Tracy saw Cullen nudge the man to his left and whisper to him. The man who had introduced himself as Caballero Davin Pulkkinen hesitated then raised his hand and said, "Uh… we've always had them."

"Technically correct if a rather broad and overly general answer."

Oh, you got one of your buddies to test an answer for you, didn't you? Cullen was a clever bastard, Tracy decided.

"Anyone else care to try?" Crispin asked.

Tracy gritted his teeth. Men had won high honors and titles in the service. *But not if they sit cringing in the back row*, an inner voice prodded him. He tried to force his hand up, but his arm seemed boneless, limply refusing to obey his brain's command.

Del Campo raised his hand. Crispin acknowledged him with a raised eyebrow. "By the twenty-first century there were only a few noble families on Earth, and they didn't have any power. They were mostly... ornamental," Arturo drawled.

"Quite true." Crispin's pale eyes swept across the assembled class. "Do you find our current crop ornamental, Cadet?"

The imperial cousin smiled. "Oh, we are very ornamental, sir. Especially the ladies." He bowed toward the four girls. "But our fathers, now, they have a great deal of power. I'm assuming your task is to whip us into shape so we can exercise power as efficiently as our paters."

"Correct on both counts, but I return to my original question. Why did that happen?"

"Aliens. Aliens happened." It was the plump girl Sumiko who spoke up.

Once again Crispin's eyes swept the room and he tsked. "Put to shame by the fairer sex, gentlemen. Yes, Cadet Lady, we found we were not alone." He touched a panel on his desk and a holo screen sprang to life. Turning, Crispin wrote in the air, the words appearing on the floating holo.

"In 2127 scientists under the leadership of Tamil Al-Shabaz working at the Musk Institute built the first prototype Fold engine. By 2143 the exodus had begun. For twenty-three years we sought out and settled habitable planets, but then we stumbled across the Hajin. While they had inter-system space flight, their lack of a faster than light speed engine meant they offered little threat to our home world. Still the contact caused significant consternation back on Earth. Particularly among the more traditional religious sects."

Crispin glanced back over his shoulder and gave them a tight smile. "At base we really are just aggressive monkeys, and very fearful of *the other*. And we had found the Other." His voice gave a capital to the word. "It made us far more sanguine about the superficial differences between our races, creeds and colors. Whatever our outward differences might be we were at least human. At any rate the conquest of Belán was easy—"

"Yeah, we kicked the shit out of the BEMs," Davin Pulkkinen yelped.

Crispin went on. "But… *but* on the Hajin home world we found the embassies and trade goods of other alien races. Which strongly indicated that someone other than humans had access to faster than light—FTL."

"We know all this." Cullen's voice freighted with ennui cut through Crispin's lecture.

The professor turned slowly to face the class. "Cadet Vizconde Cullen. I believe your title appends to the words *dorado arco*. Am I correct?"

"Yes."

Crispin began walking up one of the two stepped aisles that cut through the desks. "Golden arch."

Cullen was frowning. "I know what it means."

"Do you know what it refers to?" Crispin stood at the end of the row, looking at Cullen. The cadet was looking less annoyed and more worried. "It refers to a chain of hamburger stands from old Earth. Vastly wealthy, international in its reach, but none the less a restaurant selling cheap food to the poor."

Crispin climbed a few more steps and stared down at the fat boy. "Cadet Petek, your father is the Duque de Telqual. The name derives from Telcom. A phone company."

There was a growing rumble of outrage. Several of the students had come to their feet. To Tracy's delight Crispin drove on undeterred by the shouts of fury.

"Cadet Lord Favreau. Your father's last name is Nestlé—that company sold chocolate as well as various other snack foods." The professor had switched on a lapel microphone so his voice powered over the offended din.

"I'll have you fired!" Cullen shouted and he had enough charisma and sheer physical presence to silence all the other ranting students. "My father will not tolerate—"

"SIT DOWN." Crispin's voice echoed off the walls. "All of you. I've been teaching history at The High Ground for seventeen years. I fought in the battle of Hells Point when we reintegrated the Hidden World of New Mecca. I will not be threatened by some spring of nobility. And I will be heard!"

The realization hit Tracy—this wasn't Crispin's normal lecture. *So why?* Tracy wondered. Once again Crispin was staring at Mercedes. Tracy looked from the man to the girl. She was flushed, uneasy at the close scrutiny. Tracy looked back to Crispin. His mouth was working. He looked almost as uncomfortable as the Infanta.

"What is it you're trying… wanting to say, sir?" Tracy called.

Crispin shot him a glance that was an odd mix of anger and relief. The professor walked up a few more steps until he stood abreast Mercedes.

"Cadet Princess, our society is a construct that grew out of insecurity, fear of the Other, and a need to establish beyond any doubt that we were better than the aliens we had subjugated. And we reinforced that superiority in ways both actual and symbolic by creating an aristocracy based on corporate wealth and power.

"It was logical to use these entities as the foundation for the League." The man's voice had taken on the cadence of a lecturer as he gained confidence. "They had helped finance our initial settlements, but make no mistake, the FFH is an anachronism. We managed to contort this outdated form of governance into something that can actually rule a hegemony spanning light years, *but* it is as fragile as a soap bubble. Rapid change can affect stability."

"And I'm that kind of change. That's what you're saying, isn't it, Commander Lord Crispin?" Mercedes' voice was calm and low, her nerves expressed only by the faint tremor on the final word.

"Yes, Your Highness. You and your ladies. And not just to this institution, but to our very way of life. What is happening is a cultural experiment and those rarely turn out well."

"There were economic studies in the late twentieth and early twenty-first centuries that indicated that integrating women fully into society resulted in a better outcome for those societies," Tracy called. His early timidity burned away in the face of the attack on Mercedes.

"That might have made sense when we were limited to the finite resources of a single planet," Crispin said, turning on Tracy. "But resource scarcity isn't our problem now. Our problem is population density or more precisely the lack thereof. We need more humans. Therefore our women are precious, their role in society sacred."

"What is it you want me to do? Quit? Become a royal broodmare? Well, I'm not going to quit. I'm going to make it."

To Tracy's ears it sounded like a cry of desperation rather than a statement of certainty.

Crispin's expression hardened and he turned again to face Mercedes. "Then let us see if you can." As he stalked back down the steps toward the desk he called, "We'll begin with the Climate Wars of 2077."

• • •

"You need to step on that encroaching little *cucaracha* and depress his pretension," Boho said over lunch.

"I don't think the faculty would appreciate my condescending to a professor," Mercedes said mildly as she dipped up a spoonful of asparagus soup.

"Not Crispin. The *intitulado*, the tailor's son."

"So, that's Tracy's background—" The words were out before she thought better of it.

"Tracy? How do you know his name?" Boho demanded with a frown.

"I… I must have heard it during… during roll call."

"Crispin didn't call the roll and you weren't there

123

when we all introduced ourselves," Cipriana pointed out. Mercedes shot her a venomous look. Cipriana gave a bland smile in return.

"And he gave his name as Thracius," Yves Petek added unhelpfully, mumbling around a large bite of croissant spread thickly with cheese.

Mercedes gave a sharp gesture with her spoon like an agitated conductor, and demanded, "Why are we discussing this boy? And I noticed none of *you* stepped up to defend me… us." Mercedes raked the males at the table with a cold glance. "Perhaps you agree with Commander Crispin?"

"Well, of course we do," Arturo said with the air of a parent talking to a particularly slow child. To Mercedes' eyes her cousin looked like a smug otter with his sleek brown hair and superior half-smile.

"Well, I don't," Boho said.

"And I detect a decided browning of your nose," Arturo said, his tone pure acid.

Mercedes tensed but Boho merely smiled. "I stand as friend to the Infanta, and will be ready to serve her as she sees fit." He inclined his head in respect. He glanced over at Arturo. "As should we all. We will all owe her our allegiance… in time."

"For now you owe my father your allegiance." Mercedes stood. "And it is *his* will that I am here so it behooves you to… to…"

"Back off and butt out," Sumiko said. She also stood. Cipriana and Danica rose but more slowly. The blonde girl looked particularly pathetic, her mouth half open as she struggled to breathe past the packing in her broken nose.

"And now we have class and I won't be late again," Mercedes said.

"So what's your punishment?" Yves asked.

Mercedes stiffened ready to take offense then realized the question was prompted more out of fear than a desire to gloat. She decided the fat boy had reason to be worried. He was likely to come in for more than his share of demerits and punishments.

"I have to clean the bathroom in our quarters for the next week."

"By which she means us," Sumiko said in response to Boho's and Arturo's outraged expressions. "*We* know our required roles."

You too? Mercedes thought as she watched the plump girl walk off in her stolid flat-footed way.

10

CABALS

Tracy was working through a particularly tricky orbital mechanics problem. It wasn't like high school where you were clearly in geometry or calculus class. He realized early on that he was going to have to be flexible and jump from discipline to discipline to reach the solution.

The buzzer on his door sounded. The nasal blare broke his train of thought and he lost the thread of the problem. Irritated, Tracy threw down his stylus and considered ignoring whoever was disturbing him at—he glanced at the time code in the corner of his tap-pad—9:17 at night. The buzzer sounded again. Hitching the belt of his bathrobe tighter Tracy strode to the door. He tapped the door camera and was stunned and alarmed when Mercedes' strained face appeared in the screen.

He touched the admit icon and the door slid open. Tracy was relieved to see she was accompanied by the plump girl. The next thing he noticed was the stack of folded undress uniforms held by the Infanta.

"May we come in? Good, thank you," Mercedes said in a harried whisper as she darted past.

Tracy was acutely aware that he wore only his jockey shorts beneath his tatty old bathrobe. As Sumiko stomped past she gave him an amused look as if she'd read his thoughts. "Shut the door," Sumiko ordered.

Tracy did before he thought better of it, then the reality and the dangers inherent in the reality came crashing home. "Princess... Highness... You can't be in here—"

"I need your help." Her voice throbbed with despair like the toll of a bell in a minor key.

"What do you need?" The words just emerged. Tracy comforted himself with the thought that it was his duty to serve his ruler.

"Boho said you were a tailor's son. Do you know how to sew because—"

Resentment lodged in his chest hot and heavy. "Of course he did." Tracy jerked his head at the slacks Mercedes held. "Did he send these to me for pressing?"

Mercedes gaped at his harsh tone. "What? No. Why do you two hate each other so? Oh, never mind. I don't care. Look I went to Captain Zeng to complain about our *absurd* clothing, and when we returned to our quarters after dinner *these* were sitting on our bunks with a message that we were expected to be dressed appropriately by the first class tomorrow but they don't fit—"

"They especially don't fit *me*," Sumiko interrupted, and she gave her rather ample rear end a pat.

"I was hoping you knew how to... that you could maybe help us make them fit," Mercedes said. She held out the stack of trousers like a priestess making an offering.

Tracy lifted up a pair of slacks, flipped them inside out and inspected the seams. As he had suspected, there wasn't enough material that could be let out to accommodate a woman's hips. He said as much. Mercedes let out a doleful sniff and drooped toward the door.

"Sorry to have disturbed you."

"Wait." She turned back. "Do your ladies know how to sew?"

"Of course," Sumiko said. "Well, embroidery."

"That'll do," Tracy said. "Go back to your rooms and bring me your undress skirts."

"Why? We're not going to be allowed to wear them any longer," Mercedes said.

Tracy waved the inside-out trousers at her. "As my dad would say—we can teach or we can do. Your choice, Princess."

For an instant she gaped at him, then she gave a decisive nod. "Right. Got it. Okay." She headed for the door. Tracy lifted the remaining slacks out of her arms as she passed. A wild idea was coming into focus.

The door sighed shut behind the women. Tracy dumped the trousers on his bunk, knelt and opened the drawer that held his sewing kit. Draping the tape measure around his neck he pulled out the box of pins.

Moving to the desk he pressed the call button. A few moments later Donnel arrived.

"Yes, sir."

"The Infanta came here tonight—"

"That could be problematic, sir."

"So they'll know?" Tracy asked.

"The administration will find out—they check the cameras."

Tracy sank down into his desk chair. "Oh crap, 'cause she really needs to come back. All the ladies need to."

"We might be able to alleviate that problem," Donnel said smoothly.

"We? Who's we?"

"Those of us who serve."

"The batBEMs."

"Yes."

"Do you guys have a network or something?"

"Something like that." The alien's tone was imperturbable.

"I don't know if that's reassuring or alarming," Tracy muttered.

"Let's just say we stay in contact so we can better serve."

"Do you take sides? I mean do you support your cadet against the others? Try to undermine the other guy?"

Donnel didn't answer that question. Instead he said, "I'll get on the cameras. Is there anything else you need?"

"Yeah, I need thread." Tracy held up the undress blues. "In this color. Several large sheets of paper, chalk, and probably a few more needles and pins."

"Would a sewing machine help, sir?"

"You could get that? Never mind, I don't want to know. Yeah, that would help. Oh, and scissors. Good ones."

"I'm on it, sir."

• • •

The room really wasn't designed for five. Cipriana, Danica and Sumiko perched side by side on the bunk. Their hair, unbraided, fluffed around them like the feathers of nesting birds on a cold day. Skirts and trousers and jackets were stacked on the closed lid of the toilet. Mercedes stood in front of Tracy.

She was shocked when he said, "I'm willing to help you, but I want something in return."

There was that inward cringe. She had felt it on the beach when he'd run toward her. She knew the lower classes liked to take advantage. Granted he had only been warning her about the rising tide, but perhaps he had thought to bide his time and now he would make his move. Boho's words about "encroaching cockroaches" came to the forefront of her mind.

"What?" Mercedes asked in her most forbidding tone.

He looked hurt then annoyed and said, "Give me these undress uniforms and your new dress uniforms too."

"Why? Why should I?"

Tracy moved to the closet and pulled out his cheap synthetic undress blues. He tossed the coat with its fraying silver braid onto the floor between them. "Because I'm tired of looking like the poor relation. I know you're all going to treat us that way, but we should get to at least start out even. I want a decent undress uniform for me and for the other scholarship student, and this way he can have a dress uniform too."

She sagged with relief. "Oh, is that all? Well, that

seems quite fair and reasonable."

"Okay. Then we better get to it. I need to get your measurements." Tracy dropped to one knee and placed the end of the tape measure at the top of Mercedes, thigh against her crotch.

No one apart from an elderly female doctor from one of the repatriated Hidden Worlds had ever touched her there, and certainly no man had ever done so. A sudden heat washed through her belly. Sometimes late at night Mercedes had begun to tentatively explore her privates causing just this reaction, but she'd immediately felt guilty, had confessed to Father Francisco and been assigned twenty Hail Marys.

Tracy's hand felt hot even through the material of her gym clothes. She squeaked; Tracy gasped and threw himself backwards, falling hard on his rear end. Cipriana choked on a giggle. Danica gave a shocked moan.

"Uh… maybe you better do the measuring," Tracy said, flapping the tape desperately at Sumiko.

"That would probably be a good idea," the knight's daughter said in her blunt, matter-of-fact way.

"I'll just write down the numbers," Tracy gabbled as he snatched up his tap-pad. His embarrassment was rather sweet, Mercedes thought, and she swallowed a giggle.

One by one they measured each other—inseam, hip, waist, length of torso. Partway through the door slid open, and terror shut down the breath in Mercedes' chest. It turned out to be Tracy's very odd-looking batBEM. He had a small portable sewing machine under one arm, spools of thread in another, scissors and chalk in another, and a roll of white paper under his fourth arm.

"Mela has a cousin in maintenance. The cameras have been seen to, and the lady cadets' batBEMs have created the illusion they are all safely asleep in their beds."

"Your Highness, please get on the bed. I need the floor," Tracy said.

Mercedes climbed onto the bunk with her ladies. It took some shifting around to get them settled. They formed two rows—Danica and Sumiko in front, Mercedes and Cipriana behind them, their backs against the wall. *Like a little box full of girls,* Mercedes thought.

They watched as Tracy laid out the paper, and using the measurements he drew a pattern for each of them. While he was working the Cara'ot set up the sewing machine on the desk.

"Donnel, give me one of those skirts." A small frown of concentration wrinkled the skin between Tracy's pale brows. Mercedes noticed that he chewed his lower lip with his teeth when he was really concentrating.

Next he ripped out the seams on the undress culottes and laid out the material. As he gathered up the first pattern Cipriana said approvingly, "Oh well done, you. That's why you wanted the skirts. There will be plenty of material to make trousers."

Tracy flashed her that blazing smile. "Exactly, my lady."

Danica leaned back against Mercedes and whispered, "He's rather cute."

Yes. Yes, he is was what Mercedes wanted to say, but in this new environment where undercurrents flowed in all directions and none of them good she realized she needed to be cautious.

"Really? Do you think so? I find him rather

ordinary," she whispered instead, and she infused boredom into the words.

The alien watched, then pulled down the remaining skirts and began tearing out the seams. Tracy cut out the pattern, gathered up the material and moved to the sewing machine. Mercedes watched fascinated as the alien used his four arms to cut out two patterns simultaneously. She wondered if the Cara'ot's brain was partitioned like a cloud drive on a computer.

A few minutes later and Tracy stood up from the desk. He held a pair of slacks in his hands. "Okay, Your Highness, please try these. We need to sew on the waistband and set the hems, but that's something you and your ladies can do by hand while I put together more trousers."

Mercedes wiggled out from between Sumiko and Danica, took the slacks and headed into the tiny bathroom. The door closed behind her. She stripped out of her gym culottes, and tried on the pants. They fit and were only a little long. She emerged, and Tracy nodded in satisfaction.

"Not bad, if I do say so myself." He knelt at her feet, turned up the hem and pinned it. "Okay, it's up to you now."

The sewing machine hummed and chattered. Danica sat on the floor in the closet and stitched. Sumiko used the toilet as a chair. Cipriana and Mercedes were on the bunk frantically sewing. Somewhere around three a.m. they were finished. Tracy stood and pressed his fists against the small of his back. Mercedes wondered if she looked as exhausted as her companions.

"Have your batBEMs bring me your dress uniform

skirts, and I'll get pants made for them too. Now that I've got your measurements and patterns there's no reason for you to come here again. Let our servants handle it."

"Is it worth going to sleep for two hours?" Cipriana asked.

"I've seen you stay up all night at a ball and go out riding in the morning," Mercedes pointed out.

"Yes, but that was doing something fun. This wasn't fun." She turned to Tracy. "Not that I don't appreciate the help."

"Of course if we'd failed to turn up in proper attire this morning we all might have gotten to go home," Sumiko said.

"Or just gotten some grotesque punishment," Mercedes countered.

"Gentle ladies, you had best go," Donnel urged.

Danica, Cipriana and Sumiko slipped through the door. Mercedes hung back, and laid a hand on Tracy's. "Thank you. I won't forget this."

He turned his hand so he could grip her fingers. The hollow jittery feeling invaded her belly again. "You're welcome."

"Are you going to go to sleep?"

"I have to finish my math homework."

"I have to start it," Mercedes said.

"I wish I could do it for you, but that would really be a violation of the code of ethics."

"As if we haven't broken a thousand rules tonight," Mercedes said with a smile.

Tracy gave an answering smile. "Goodnight… well, good morning. See you in class, milady."

• • •

As Tracy walked down the hall toward Crispin's class he saw Captain Zeng loitering in the hall. He swallowed a smile and gave the coat of his proper undress uniform a tug. It hadn't taken much work to tailor it. The FFH assholes looked surprised, but Wilson gave him a furious glare. Tracy hurried forward, caught the other scholarship student by the arm, and pulled him aside.

"I've got one for you. Dress blues too. Come to my room after dinner," Tracy said quietly.

"How?"

A rising hubbub of conversation filled the hall. Words like *outrageous, shocking, indecent* could be picked out of the confused basso hum.

"Not here. Not now," Tracy snapped.

He turned to see the four women approaching in their uniforms. Last night he hadn't been able to fully appreciate how good slacks looked on a woman. Even among the lower classes most women wore skirts or culottes. The only time he'd seen pants on women were Isanjo females. Even the Hajin had adopted the dress of their conquerors. Mercedes, tallest of the four, carried it off the best. Her chin was up, shoulders back, and she strode confidently down the hall. The small blonde tugged at the edge of her coat trying futilely to make it longer.

Tracy quickly shifted his gaze to Zeng expecting to see blazing anger there too. Instead a very small smile touched the administrator's lips. He caught Tracy looking. Tracy ducked his head and looked away.

"Find that uniform in a trashcan, did you, Cadet?"

Zeng's voice was soft and low.

Tracy tried to analyze the tone. It didn't sound threatening. It sounded more like... a suggestion.

"Yes, sir. That's exactly what happened."

"Excellent. Will there be any more... ah... trashcan recoveries?"

"One, sir."

"Good to know. Keep it to one."

"Yes, sir."

Zeng drifted away. Tracy watched the thin officer until he disappeared around a corner. *Maybe not everyone at The High Ground is an adversary*, he thought.

"Are you planning on joining us, Cadet Belmanor?" Crispin asked as he walked past.

"Uh... yes. Sir."

11

PRETTY, PETTY THINGS

Saturday. He had survived the first week. Tracy checked the clock. 5:23. No drills, no classes. Homework, but it was manageable. Zeng had said they could explore the rest of the *cosmódromo*.

Feeling indulgent he settled back on the mattress and keyed his ScoopRing. He called up a map of the space station and studied the layout. There was a hyperloop train that connected the module containing The High Ground to the central ring. From there a tram made a circuit of the ring which was comprised of docking bays for the great star cruisers, luxury hotels, restaurants, shops, small parks, nightclubs, and joy houses.

Inside the spokes that connected the great wheel to the central hub there were warehouses to store goods delivered to freighter docks on the hub (apparently it wouldn't do to have luxury liners cheek by jowl with a grubby freighter). Also in the spokes were cheap housing, cafés and joy houses for the crews of the freighters and the stevedores who managed the machines that unloaded those ships.

The massive central hub also contained command and control for the station. From there the crew monitored the wobble and yaw of the station, and fired the exterior jets that maintained the station's trim and kept the spin that provided one gee of gravity to the residents. The engineers also maintained the vast array of solar panels that provided power to the inhabitants.

Tracy switched to check the Reals in his bank account. He was surprised to see it had increased from sixty-three to one hundred and sixty-three. His dad had deposited money in the account. Tracy knew how much that one hundred Reals represented. With Tracy gone Alexander had probably hired a new employee to pick up the slack, and that person would have to be paid. Even if the new employee was an alien and could be paid less than a human it still represented a significant added cost.

His eyes slid to the closet where the impeccably tailored dress uniform hung in silent rebuke. He still hadn't called his dad to thank him. Partly because he had been so busy with classes and homework—and tailoring jobs. Now both members of the Belmanor family "made" for the royal family, Tracy thought with faint amusement. Not that he dared impart that particular bit of information to his father over an open and insecure line. From Zeng's remarks it was clear the administrators of The High Ground knew exactly what had happened, but were choosing to wink at the transgression. Better not to undermine that plausible deniability.

But schoolwork was just an excuse and he knew it. He hadn't called because he didn't know how to heal the wound that his harsh and hateful words had inflicted. How could he ever make amends for that? Was a simple "I'm sorry" going to be enough? And there was still resentment that had kept him from making the call. Tracy had realized that he'd been manipulated by Alexander and that still stung.

Irritated by his tangled and contradictory emotions, Tracy muttered a curse, threw back the covers and headed into the shower. He'd finish his homework and then head out to explore the *cosmódromo*.

• • •

Bored. Bored, bored, bored, bored, Mercedes thought as she watched Danica and Cipriana dithering between jeweled hairpins. The pins were topped with glitterflies, a bird-like species native to Ouranos. Similar to hummingbirds on old Earth, glitterflies had iridescent bodies, but faceted insect-like eyes in stunning colors of blue, purple, red, copper and gold.

The two girls were debating the relative merits of the jewels that formed the eyes on the pins.

"I bet you get those back to the academy, and have Zeng tell you to either put them in a drawer or he'll confiscate them," Mercedes groused.

In addition to all the regular rules and regulations of The High Ground there had been a special list just for the women that stated only stud earrings could be worn. No rings apart from ScoopRings, no bracelets, no pins, no dangling earrings. Apparently Cipriana thought she'd found a loophole with the hairpins.

Flipping the thick heavy braid over her shoulder Mercedes waved it at the pair. "You keep trying to game the rules," Mercedes went on, "and they just might decide to make us cut our hair."

Danica turned. She was wide-eyed with alarm. "They *wouldn't*."

"They could," was Sumiko's grim assessment.

Danica clutched at her honey-gold hair as if fearful it might escape. She spun back to Cipriana. "Let's not risk it."

"You're such a little chicken. I rather fancy having someone gently tease these out and then run his hands through my hair," Cipriana replied.

"You have anyone in mind?" Sumiko asked dryly.

"I have several candidates."

Mercedes frowned. "You get caught *y copular* and you'll be out of here."

"It would almost be worth it." Cipriana reacted to Mercedes' expression. "Oh, relax, Mer, as if I can't stop a boy at second base. For right now I'll settle for some snuggling and kissing. I promise I won't abandon you."

"You better not. So, are you buying those stupid pins or not?"

"You should maybe think about when we start *Infierno* training. Those things could come loose and be a danger in zero gee," Sumiko said.

"You are such a spoilsport," Cipriana snapped. Sumiko opened her mouth to respond.

The realization hit Mercedes that she was heartily sick of her three ladies. There was such a thing as too much togetherness. At least in the palace she had had privacy at night, and gardens to roam without an entourage. She slipped out of the shop while they squabbled and the sales clerk began to show them how to lock the pins into their hair in a way that would resist zero gee.

There was a park that formed a ribbon of green between the stores, hotels and restaurants. A small river bubbled over artistically placed rocks. Overhead fat-bellied cloudbots floated along depositing faux rain showers onto the grass, trees and bushes.

Across the pedestrian mall she saw Tracy dressed in jeans, a white shirt and his regulation issue boots standing in a shop that displayed hauntingly beautiful tapestries spun by the Sidone spiders. A handkerchief-sized tapestry rested in his hands. He held it with the same reverence a priest would show the Host. Mercedes slipped up behind him in time to hear him say, "It's amazing, but I can't afford that. Thank you for letting me see it."

Tracy handed the tiny tapestry back to the proprietor, who looked annoyed, but then noticed Mercedes. A broad smile stretched his mouth.

"Your Highness. An honor."

Tracy glanced back, and those dark grey eyes lit with pleasure. He smiled.

"What are you doing?" Mercedes asked.

"Exploring."

"Would you like to go exploring together?" The words were out before she thought better of it.

His eyes flicked about searching for her companions. "I'm not… is it… permitted… can we…?"

"I'll send for Tako. She should be chaperone enough." Mercedes keyed her ScoopRing. While she murmured to her Hajin batBEM she heard the shop owner say, "Did I tell you it was two hundred Reals?

My mistake." The man's eyes flicked between Tracy and Mercedes. "I misread. It's only one hundred, and for a friend of the Infanta I could offer a discount…"

Tracy stiffened. "I don't accept favors."

Mercedes grabbed him by the sleeve and yanked him away from the counter. "You really are an arrogant, stiff-necked prig," she said in an undertone. "This is how the world works."

"Well it shouldn't!"

"But it does. If you ever want to get ahead you have to learn to build and trade on your connections. You've scored a connection many could only dream of having, so use it."

"I won't. I'd hate it if you thought I would use you—"

Mercedes smiled at him. "I don't, and I can tell when people are just being friendly because they want something from me. Besides you weren't even all that friendly in the beginning. In fact you were rather rude."

"I didn't know who you were."

"Sometimes I wish you still didn't."

Tracy glanced again at the counter and the delicate square of silk magic resting there. "I've never owned anything like that. But buying something when it's not useful…"

"Will it give you enjoyment?"

"Yes."

"Will you treasure it?"

"My entire life."

"Those seem like useful things," Mercedes said softly.

"All right, I'll… I'll do it." There was a tremor in

his voice. Excitement? Fear? Mercedes wasn't sure.

They walked back to the counter. The proprietor looked hopeful. "What was that discount?" Mercedes asked. The man began to answer, and she quickly said before the amount emerged, "Also I fancy that piece. It would brighten a wall in my quarters." She pointed to an elaborate geometric piece one foot by two feet. Their eyes met. The man gave an almost imperceptible nod. Tako's hooves clicked on the polished floor as she slipped into the shop.

"I can sell the piece to the young lord for thirty-five Reals."

Mercedes shot a sideways glance at Tracy. His expression was bemused, probably because of the title that had been bestowed on him.

"My batBEM will take my piece. Please package it for her now." She pressed her ScoopRing against the reader, and was grateful Tracy didn't see the amount that had been deducted from her account. If he had he would know that the shop owner had practically given him the tiny tapestry.

Her hanging was wrapped and tied with a ribbon. Tako accepted the package. Tracy's purchase had been folded into a small gilt box. He placed it reverently in the satchel that he had slung over his shoulder.

They left the store with Tako trailing after them. Mercedes glanced at the jewelry store. Her three ladies were still engrossed in the trays of shining baubles. "So, where shall we go?"

"Someplace where we can look at the stars," Tracy said.

"I thought you'd want to go to the river walk."

He shrugged. "I've seen trees."

"You've seen stars too," Mercedes teased.

"Not like this. Not without atmosphere and humidity in the way. And that's our future."

"You had to remind me, didn't you?"

. . .

It turned out there were three observation lounges on the *cosmódromo*'s ring. The map Donnel had downloaded to his pad and ring proved invaluable, and Tracy and Mercedes found themselves in the smallest lounge and the one farthest from the commercial quarter. On the way the Infanta had Tako pause to buy them a picnic lunch consisting of cheese, a small loaf of French bread, and a bunch of grapes. Tracy splurged on a bottle of sparkling wine for them to share.

Now they were settled on a deep curved bench on the outer shell of the ring. There were no missile emplacements or satellites in view, and so far they hadn't seen a single ship or shuttle pass by. They also didn't have all that many stars because at this point in the station's rotation they were looking at the twining brilliant gasses of the nebula. Tendrils of red, blue and gold light seemed to reach for the stars whose light was wan and faint at the edges of the vortex.

"Here's to us—we made it through the first week," Tracy said, raising his paper cup in a toast.

"Doesn't feel like much of a victory when there are so many more weeks to go." Mercedes sighed. "And I'm afraid it's just going to get worse."

"But you've won every time," Tracy said.

"Really? It doesn't feel that way."

Tracy set aside his hunk of bread and ticked points off on his fingers. "You took down that guy who hurt your friend, and earned Deal's respect. You got the uniforms changed and then you met their impossible deadline—"

"Only because of you."

"True, I helped, but you had the idea to come to me. And I came out of it okay. Now Mark and I don't look like charity cases any more."

"It seems so stupid to treat you like this. The fleet needs you. Really smart men who want to be here."

"You might recall that isn't exactly true in my case," Tracy said and he frowned down into his drink.

"What happened that changed your mind?"

"Parent manipulation happened. My dad totally played me." He hesitated then added, "And he hit me. He'd never hit me before."

"Why?"

"I was rude to Cullen."

Mercedes looked shocked. "That seems excessive."

He couldn't stop the grin. "I also stabbed Cullen with a pin." He didn't tell her why he had done that. Less because of what Boho had said and more because of what it revealed about him.

"Oh, so *that's* why he hates you so much." Mercedes had a great laugh. Throaty and deep, like water gurgling over stones in a stream.

She sobered and asked, "Have you talked to your dad?"

Tracy shook his head. "I said some really terrible things to him when I left. I don't know how to take those back. I mean, I *can't* take them back."

"He made your dress uniform, didn't he?" she asked.

"Yeah."

"Then it sounds like he understands and forgives you."

"Which actually makes me feel worse. But you were saying that O-Trell needs us—" She giggled. "What?"

"O-Trell. How quickly we pick up this nonsensical military lingo."

Tracy grinned though his embarrassment lingered. "Your point? Anyway, *Orden de la Estrella*," he said pointedly, "needs us how?"

"Seriously? Have you looked at Yves Petek? The fact that he is going to be an officer is just scary. Not that he's not nice, but he has no more business being here than Danica, or... or me for that matter."

"Don't sell yourself short. And what happened to 'I'm going to make it'?"

"My father says twenty percent of being in charge is looking like you believe you're in charge. I was just following his advice."

Tracy gripped her hand. "You're going to make it." Tako, who had been sitting patiently on her haunches and staring at them unblinking, suddenly shifted. Tracy pulled his hand away. "And O-Trell isn't stupid. That's why they have the *prueba* at the end of first year. You don't pass you don't go on."

Mercedes looked sick and she set aside her handful of grapes. She stood up and gazed out the viewport. The light from the nebula formed a rainbow halo around her. "Then what's the point of dragging everybody up here? Why does every boy in the FFH have to do this except the ones going to the church?"

"Why do all of us *intitulado* have to do RCFC in high school?" Tracy countered. "It was all that bullshit that made me decide I didn't want to be a soldier."

Mercedes turned back to face him. "But here you are."

"Yeah. Well, at least I'll be an officer."

Mercedes crossed to him and took his hands in hers. "You'll be a good one." Dark rose suffused her cheeks. A warm spot blossomed in Tracy's chest and there was a distressing reaction in his groin. He looked away quickly.

His eyes met Tako's as she stared unblinkingly at them. That dark gaze and her very presence reminded Tracy of the gulf that loomed between himself and Mercedes and could not be bridged. He gently pulled his hands free, grabbed his cup and tossed off the rest of his wine.

"We should probably get back before someone notices that we've been together," he said shortly, suddenly remembering Cullen's warning. He started stuffing the leftover cheese, bread and fruit into the bag.

Mercedes held out her hand and pulled him to his feet. "There is one more thing..." she said.

"Okay."

"May I give you some advice? I don't know the military, but I grew up with these people." She looked down and fiddled with the sleeve of her dress. Her eyes met his. "You're proud. It's apparent to everyone, but you need to... well, hide it better."

"Excuse me?"

"My class is used to people like you being more... ingratiating. When you're not they notice you and not in a good way. I know you want to better yourself." The warmth Tracy had felt toward her turned to hurt that made breathing hard.

Better yourself. Better yourself. The words kept pounding through his head.

Mercedes went on. "Well the best way for you to accomplish that is to find a way to be useful to some of our classmates."

"Like I did with you," Tracy said harshly.

"Yes, but pick some who aren't too well born so they won't be insulted by your overtures and cultivate them."

"Well, forgive me for my mistake in *cultivating* you. Clearly I was out of line to pick someone so well born," Tracy snapped.

Mercedes' eyes widened and an expression of dismay crossed her face. "I... I've said something wrong, haven't I? I didn't mean to." Tracy spun on his heel and walked away. "What did I say?" she called after him.

He didn't look back. A churning cold rage closed his throat and made it ache. He returned to the busier areas of the *cosmódromo*. A trash incinerator panel beckoned. Tracy strode over to it and pulled the box containing the Sidone tapestry out of his pocket. He meant to throw it down the chute, but he wanted one last look before he trashed it. The colors and the intricate beauty caught him. It would be criminal to destroy such art. No, he would keep it, but as a reminder of who he was, that they couldn't be trusted, and that he was on his own.

"What did I do?" Mercedes almost wailed the question.

"I couldn't say, Cadet Princess," Tako blandly replied.

"I was only trying to help," Mercedes muttered. Tako remained silent. Mercedes gazed into the Hajin's large liquid and totally expressionless brown eyes. "I wasn't wrong. He *is* a stiff-necked idiot." Silence from the batBEM. "Oh, you're useless."

"Do you wish something from me, Cadet Princess?"

"Talk to me!"

"That would be inappropriate, Cadet Princess."

"Why?"

The long lashes that were the same butterscotch color as the Hajin's mane briefly screened her eyes. They were abruptly lifted and the alien's gaze was cold. "I know my place."

The lashes veiled her eyes again, and when she lifted them the icy look was gone. Had she imagined it? Hoped she had imagined it, but the message had been received.

"Oh. I see," Mercedes said. "But I can't apologize to him. You see, I also know my place."

12

GAMES

The first quarter had ground to an end. Three months of drills, classes, homework, slights and the first pale shoots of something that might, if one were generous, call budding friendships. Hugo of all people, the quiet and studious Ernesto Chapman-Owiti, who despite being a *marqués* didn't treat Tracy like shit, and even one of Boho's cadre, Davin Pulkkinen, though that might have been more due to the fact Tracy was tutoring him in math, and less about actual friendship.

Tracy probably could have counted Mercedes among that handful if he hadn't been such a stiff-necked ass. He hadn't spoken to Mercedes aside from polite commonplaces since their disastrous picnic. In the beginning he had snubbed her, then when his anger began to cool he had made a tentative overture only to have her snub him in return. Which made him mad all over again. Intellectually he knew they were both being idiots, but he had no idea how to now bridge the rift.

And maybe he shouldn't even try, he thought as he looked down from the choir loft to where she and her ladies sat in the front left pew. Boho, Arturo and his brother Mihalis sat with them. They were certainly the three highest born male cadets at the academy so it was appropriate for them to be with the Infanta. Just as it was completely inappropriate for a tailor's son to be with her. Still he wished he could apologize so that his last memory of an improbable association wouldn't be tinged with a residue of anger. At least he had the Sidone tapestry suspended in a Lucite cube as a tangible reminder.

The end of term had also brought a five-day pass, and a lifting of the stricture against travel to the planet. That left Tracy with a dilemma—did he go home and visit his dad or not? If he didn't his dad would think that Tracy hadn't forgiven him. If he did Tracy would *have* to forgive him.

It was a dilemma he was going to have to resolve pretty damn quickly because there was going to be a *fútbol* match on Tuesday and then leave would begin, and since Tracy was a substitute he couldn't avoid the decision by just staying on the station. Even though the chance of his actually playing was small he was going to have to be there.

It had been made very clear that every new cadet would try out for the team though the ladies had been exempted. Tracy lacked the stamina of many of the players, but he was quick and agile. He had hoped to dodge this drain on his time, but unfortunately he had made the team and even more unfortunate only as a substitute. So now he had to attend practice even though he had almost zero chance of ever playing.

Of course Boho Cullen had been selected along

with Jasper Talion, Hugo Devris, Sanjay Favreau and Mark Wilson as first-string players. Tracy tried not to care that the other scholarship student was now laughing and socializing with his well-born teammates while Tracy sat on the bench. Still it rankled.

Especially since Tracy had yet another demand on his time that left him studying far into the night, and giving up most of his weekends to school work. It had happened the very first Sunday during the opening hymn. Tracy had started to sing and noticed a few turning heads, including Mercedes. He was pleased she had noticed him, but pleasure warred with pride, and he'd pointedly looked away. When he'd snuck another glance in her direction she was once again gazing at the altar, and he could only see the back of her head. He had mumbled his way through the responses, kneeling and standing more from muscle memory than any attention to the Mass. Instead he had thought back on their final conversation torn between anger and regret.

During the second hymn he'd become aware of a very tall young man with skin the color of honey, sleek brown hair, stilt-like legs and a kettle belly pushing out the folds of his choir robe moving down the aisle between the pews. His head swung from side to side like a radar dish seeking a target. His green eyes met Tracy's and lit with delight. He smiled and nodded. Tracy had awkwardly done the same.

Right after Mass concluded he was introduced to Commander Jeffery Baldinini, the academy's music director, and invited to join the choir. Tracy had declined. A terse message from Zeng had made it clear that in the military an invitation was indistinguishable from a command. So Tracy joined the choir thus losing Tuesday nights to rehearsal as well as Saturday afternoon when Baldinini had insisted on giving him private voice lessons. Tracy didn't resent the lessons as much as the formal rehearsals because the training might be something he could use if he failed to pass the *prueba* and washed out of the academy.

The random, tumbling thoughts brought him back to the present—seated in the sweeping balcony of the choir loft while Commander Father Tanuwidjaja delivered his sermon. The chapel was a beautiful place with folded curves that made it feel like one was inside a nautilus shell. The walls were made from some translucent material and lit from within as if the grace, glory and light of God shone all around them.

Unfortunately Tanuwidjaja's rhetorical style didn't match his surroundings. He had a reedy voice, and he tended to stare down at the pulpit and read his sermon from his tap-pad. He also had a bad habit of delivering interminable homilies. Today he had already run nearly ten minutes over the allotted time. Which was just adding to Tracy's nerves. He was to sing his first solo during the elevation of the Host—for him the most moving moment in the service—and it was beginning to feel like they were never going to get to it as Tanuwidjaja droned on. And on. And on.

To hold down the flutter of nerves Tracy studied the altar. It was sculpted from the hull of a lost battle cruiser, and the metal had taken on an opalescent quality from the blast from the Cara'ot ship which had destroyed the S.L.S.S. *Paul Revere.* It seemed like an odd juxtaposition to Tracy. A fragment of a vessel of war in a place of peace. But maybe that was normal at a military academy where everyone presumed that the Lord was on your side.

Or until you got your ass blown out of space and pretty much knew He wasn't on your side.

Tracy choked on a nervous laugh and got a stern look from Baldinini followed by an encouraging smile. The choir director was seated at the keyboard of the large pipe organ. Tracy schooled his features and tried to think about anything but how nervous he was feeling. He looked back down into the congregation. From here he could see the students who were surreptitiously checking their ScoopRings or even hiding a tap-pad inside a hymnal or prayer book.

In the very back pews were the batBEMs, seeming to listen with great attention to the human priest. Tracy studied them—Isanjo, Hajin, Tiponi, and the single Cara'ot. It suddenly occurred to him that they probably had their own gods and religious practices, but here they were kneeling before their conqueror's god. He wondered why he had never thought about it before. Probably because he hadn't ever been this bored before.

So just what the hell did a Tiponi Flute think was sacred? And did the Cara'ot anthropomorphize their god or gods? Tracy had to figure they didn't since they had been altering their physical forms, even down to their genders, for thousands of years. At this point there was no longer a physical norm for the species.

It occurred to him that might be an interesting research paper for his upcoming philosophy class.

Maybe by studying the Cara'ot's religious traditions one might figure out the foundational form. Upon reflection Tracy decided it made more sense as a biology project. He'd run it past his lab partner Ernesto. Chapman-Owiti was wicked smart and would probably have some advice on how to proceed.

Surreptitiously Tracy pulled back the sleeve of his choir robe and checked the chromo set in the sleeve of his dress uniform. Tanuwidjaja was really on a roll today. The sermon was coming up on forty-five minutes. At this rate they would never get to communion... and his solo. A sharp poke in the back had Tracy looking over his shoulder to Davin Pulkkinen. Tracy studied Davin's flushed cheeks and the air of suppressed excitement, and raised his eyebrows questioningly.

Closer and longer association with Pulkkinen during choir practice had revealed the knight's son was a jokester and a clown, and when he was away from his better-born comrades he tended to actually talk to Tracy. Davin dropped one eyelid in a slow and elaborate wink, and raised his forefinger to his lips in a shushing gesture.

Tracy couldn't tell if dread or delight held sway because clearly Pulkkinen was up to something. A sharp buzzing rose from the back of the chapel. Tanuwidjaja's head jerked up from his pad and he peered about the chapel. The buzzing stopped. Tanuwidjaja resumed. Three minutes later a raucous ringing like a maddened alarm clock blared out from the right side of the chapel. There were growing mutters and laughter from the congregation. Zeng and Vice Admiral Vasquez y Markov were on their feet.

The admiral's expression was thunderous. The ringing cut off.

Tanuwidjaja's head swung from side to side. Tracy couldn't see the priest's expression, but expected it resembled a nervous rabbit contemplating an open meadow. "And so as we contemplate our burden of sin—"

From all around the chapel alarms began to blare, buzz, ring, jingle and clang. Gales of laughter wove through the cacophony. Vasquez y Markov bellowed, "DISGRACEFUL!"

Captain Father Tanuwidjaja held up a hand, and used the power of the microphone to trump the alarms, the laughter and the outrage. "All right. All right. I surrender. I promise I'll stick to the allotted time going forward. Now please. May we continue with the Mass?"

Tracy, staring open-mouthed in delight and amazement at Pulkkinen, watched as the cadet pulled aside his choir robe and slipped a hand into his pocket. The noise abruptly cut off. Tracy also noticed that Commander Baldinini was pointedly rearranging the music on the organ stand. Apparently he was also tired of Tanuwidjaja's overly long sermons. The choirmaster gave Tracy a nod.

Captain Father Tanuwidjaja left the pulpit and retired to the altar. Yves joined him, carrying the host and the chalice to the priest. Three months had peeled away the fat, but hadn't decreased the deer-in-the-headlights stare that seemed to be Yves' normal expression. Right now though he looked euphoric. *He'd probably make a great priest*, Tracy thought. Too bad he was the first son so that option was right out. For a moment Tracy considered that perhaps being born into the FFH was as limiting as his own precarious rung in the lower middle class.

The opening chords of Mozart's *Ave verum corpus* sighed from the pipes on the massive organ, pulling Tracy out of his reverie. He stood and discovered someone had replaced his knees with rubber and his belly felt hollow.

The priest raised the chalice. Light coruscated off the polished gold and glittered in the row of amethysts around the base of the goblet. Tracy's heart seemed too large for his chest and his heartbeat thudded in his ears, almost surpassing the music of the organ. There was a tingling on the back of his neck and on his shoulders as if a warm hand had been laid upon him. Tracy sucked in a deep breath, the fragrance of frankincense wafting through his nose. He released the first note, sending it floating toward the vault of the ceiling.

He should have been thinking only of the service and of his savior. Instead all he saw was Mercedes. Her head lifting abruptly from her folded hands to stare up at the choir loft.

After that he forgot about God and sang to her.

• • •

"We're going *home*!" Danica caroled.

"A long soak in a hot bath," Sumiko added almost reverently.

"Jewelry and pretty dresses," Mercedes said, joining in the fun. She stood in front of a mirror attempting to cover a dark purple bruise with foundation. Clark Kunst had managed to slip a hit past her guard on Friday.

The words passed her lips and Mercedes gave a cough, and stared down at her trousers in consternation. She looked up to meet two sets of appalled eyes.

Danica, confused, looked from Mercedes to Sumiko to Cipriana and back. "What? What's wrong?" she asked.

"There's going to be press waiting when we land," Mercedes said hollowly.

Cipriana ran a hand down the front of her thigh. "And we can't put back on our approved uniforms... since we cut them up," she said.

"You must not mention that!" Mercedes said quickly. "And whatever you do don't mention Tracy. That could get him in so much trouble."

"Better him than us," Cipriana replied.

"No." Mercedes drew herself up to her full height and looked down her nose at Cipriana. "He is not to be punished for assisting the crown."

"So, he takes one for the crown, as Chief Begay would say. That's serving too."

Pushback came from an unexpected source. Danica darted over to stand in front of Cipriana. Her hands were clenched at her sides. "No. He's nice. He helped me with geometry and... and did you hear him this morning? It was like an angel—"

"Ho ho, Dani's got a crush," Cipriana said in a singsong voice.

"I do not!" As usual Danica had gone immediately to her first line of defense—tears.

Mercedes was furious with Danica. Why did the

girl have to be an endless watering pot? Mercedes shied away from examining all the sources of her anger. Instead she said, "He's an *intitulado*. Your father would *never* allow such a misalliance," Mercedes added, and cringed because she sounded like a strict duenna.

"She doesn't have to *marry* him," Cipriana drawled. She ran her fingers across her lips, and across her breasts. "Probably more fun if she doesn't."

"You're disgusting," Mercedes snapped. "Talking like he's a prize stud—"

"Ho ho!" Cipriana's eyes were glittering with bitter fun. "Better back off, Dani. It seems Mercedes is interested and la Infanta takes precedence... in all things." She reached into her holdall and pulled out a tiny, thin square envelope. "Need one of these?"

"That's a... that's a... that's a..." Danica stuttered like a lawnmower engine trying to catch.

"A *contraceptive*. Yes, it is."

"They're not permitted," the small blonde girl gasped.

"Not in all cases," Sumiko, ever the pedant, said. "Where another child might endanger a mother's life they can be prescribed. They're not impossible to get, you just have to find an unscrupulous doctor."

"Or have a sympathetic Isanjo maid who knows how to get them from the Cara'ot." Cipriana waggled the envelope in front of Mercedes. "These are *much* better than the human version. Trust me, I know."

"You've had... You've had..."

"Danica, really you sound like an idiot. Yes, I've had sex. A number of times. It's fun."

"But they'll know. I mean, *he'll* know... on your

wedding night," Danica said, gobbling like a terrified turkey hen.

"Three stitches," Cipriana replied, holding up three fingers. "Three little stitches and you're revirginated. The Cara'ot doctors offer that service too. I'll take advantage of that once we're done with this bullshit and I get engaged." Cipriana turned back to Mercedes. "So do you want this or not?" She waved the envelope again.

A thread of worry shot through Mercedes. Had others observed her friendship with Tracy? "No! I am the Infanta, I can't... and I'm not interested in him. He's beneath my notice—"

Cipriana circled back to her original point. "So, then we can blame him."

"No!"

"You did go off with him on that first Saturday," Sumiko pointed out.

Mercedes rounded on her. She felt like a bull surrounded by picadors. "You knew? How did you know?"

Sumiko shrugged and put another dress into her holdall. "We're not actually here to learn anything or become officers. We're here so you are chaperoned and you can get a box checked that lets you be empress."

"You really think that?" Mercedes asked. "You really think we'll never have to serve aboard a ship or fight or anything?"

"How many battles has your father personally led?" Sumiko asked.

"Oh that's true." Mercedes frowned. "Although I think there was a skirmish when they had to pacify a Hidden World, but that was before I was born. Still, Daddy was on a ship, at least for a little while."

"You'll get a desk job. That's my bet," Cipriana said as she drifted to a mirror and applied lip gloss.

Mercedes chewed at her lower lip. "Do you think that means we won't get to train in an *Infierno*?"

"You sound disappointed," Danica said.

"It looks like it might be fun."

"And part of your argument for letting us wear pants," Sumiko said. "Which sorta brings us back to our present problem. I guess the *Infierno* training works as an explanation for the change."

"Or we just put on our civilian clothes," Cipriana said. "Civilian dresses. That way the press will never know."

Sumiko brought up a holo screen on her ring. Frowned at the print. "Regulation 37b: Civilian attire when on the *cosmódromo* is only permitted on Saturdays." She looked up and added unnecessarily, "Tomorrow is Monday, and until that shuttle actually lifts off we're on the *cosmódromo*."

"So, we change on the shuttle," Cipriana snapped.

"Yeah, good luck with that. Dressing in freefall. And as I recall you were puking your guts out on the flight up," Sumiko said nastily.

"Just because you're a stolid *cow* who has no sensibility…"

"Stop it!" Mercedes yelled. "You're all making me crazy." She hung her head, steadied her breathing. "We'll change after we land but before we leave the shuttle."

"Oh, good idea," Sumiko said and Mercedes resented the fact the other girl sounded surprised.

Her batBEM sidled up next to her, and placed some toiletries into the holdall. "Cadet Princess, if I might…" Tako said softly.

"Yes, what is it?"

"Might I humbly suggest that you wear your uniform and face down the critics. You have shown yourself capable of facing down all manner of obstacles. It would mean a lot to the staff." She nodded her long head in the direction of the other batBEMs.

"Why would it matter to you?"

"If you ladies succeed then more women will follow and perhaps, in time, we would be allowed to serve."

Now the alien had Mercedes' full attention. "What are you saying? That aliens should serve in the *Orden de la Estrella*?" The Hajin inclined her head in affirmation. Amusement warred with anger. "What an absurd idea. *Orden de la Estrella* exists because we can't trust you," Mercedes said.

Tako veiled her eyes with her long lashes, and backed away. "So sorry to have offended, Cadet Princess."

13

THIS IS LOVE?

The soccer team had a shuttle just for their use because before their actual leave began The High Ground was going to play the University of Caladonia. The planetside school had delivered a drubbing to The High Ground in the team's home stadium and the academy team was eager to avenge the insult by beating Caladonia on their home turf in Hissilek.

Which meant Tracy wasn't riding down the gravity-well with staff or other bits and sundries heading back to Ouranus, or unable to go at all if he couldn't have hitched a ride. The cost of a shuttle fare to the planet was well beyond his means. He might be just a substitute and resent the time, but it did mean he got to go home.

They were all strapped in while their coach, Commander Phillip McWhinnie (behind his back they all called him Whinnie or Whiny when they were really annoyed with him), floated in the front of the shuttle.

"Okay. We have to not suck tomorrow. The Conde de Vargas is going to be watching, and his prestige is on the line. I also know he and President Tummelty have a significant wager going so more than just Rohan Aubrey's pride is riding on the outcome. *So don't fuck it up and cost our patron money."*

"Also rather awkward to go to his house for a ball afterward if we've lost," Boho drawled.

The heavy paper gave a crackle as Tracy touched his coat pocket and the invitation that nestled inside. No mere ScoopVite for the conde. The invitation had been waiting on Tracy's desk. His name flowed across the front of the champagne-colored envelope in cursive script—Cadet The Honorable Thracius Ransom Belmanor. Inside, the embossed invitation elaborated on the time and place of the Salutation Ball. Dancing, champagne supper, attire formal/dress uniform. There was no refusing. Tracy wondered if he could manufacture an injury between now and tomorrow night? He turned his attention back to the coach to avoid thinking about the ball.

"So our biggest problem is their striker, Montoya. He's incredibly fast and fit so I expect you two," McWhinnie pinned Jasper Talion and Hugo with a look, "to stay on him. Boho can't do it all."

"I did what I could. At least I held them to four goals instead of seven." It was said in tones of faux humbleness, but the smirk the tall cadet gave the rest of them had Tracy gritting his teeth.

McWhinnie scrubbed at his face. "The game tomorrow is critical. If we lose again we won't make the varsity championships. That has never happened. And it's by God not going to happen while I'm coach. Got it?"

"Yes, sir," they said in obedient chorus.

"Now get a good night's rest tonight. Don't go out drinking and whoring. Technically your leave doesn't start until *after* the game."

"So we can get drunk at the ball?" Pulkkinen called merrily.

"If you're that stupid, sure," McWhinnie shot back.

"Then I guess whoring at the ball is right out too," Boho drawled and there were more shouts of laughter.

Twenty minutes later the blunt nose of the shuttle and its broad stubby wings began to nuzzle the outer fringes of the atmosphere. Their re-entry speed formed a cushion of air in front of them but the atmospheric gasses still ignited, treating Tracy to a spectacular if alarming light show as fire licked along the sides and wings of the shuttle.

They broke through the final cloud cover. Their speed had been reduced so that the flames were gone, but a corona of heat pulsed on the edges of the wings. The pilot banked and took them in toward the military side of the Cristóbal Colón Spaceport. The engines gave a final burst, pressing Tracy back in his couch, and then they landed with the delicacy of a swan dropping onto the water.

Tracy hung back as the others headed for the doors. The babble of conversation faded. He unhooked his webbing and walked slowly off the shuttle. Enlisted *fusileros* had unloaded the cadets' holdalls. Tracy was surprised to see Talion loitering while his batBEM picked up his case. Donnel stood nearby holding Tracy's small bag.

Talion approached Tracy. "Hey."

"Hey."

"Have you got a place to stay?"

Tracy hesitated, trying to decide how to answer that. Could he go to the tailor shop? Probably. Did he want to? That was less clear. Talion interpreted his silence as a negative.

"Look, my family keeps a house here on Ouranos. It's not that large and it's not in the best neighborhood, meaning it's not up on the Palacio Colina, but you're welcome to stay."

If you ever want to get ahead you have to learn to build and trade on your connections. A rich alto voice rang through his memory. The refusal that hovered at the tip of his tongue was swallowed, and he gave an awkward nod. "Thank you, I'll take you up on that."

• • •

The smells of aftershave and tobacco. It was warm and comforting and familiar. Mercedes paused in the door of her father's study and soaked it in. The water chuckled and bubbled in the gold-etched vase of the hookah as the Emperor pulled in a last lungful of smoke. Mercedes chuckled too.

"What's funny, Mer?" her father asked.

"Nothing. I'm just happy to be home."

He opened his arms and she ran to him. The linen of his shirt was rough against her cheek. She sighed with contentment as his arms closed tightly around her. "I... I missed you," she whispered against his chest.

"I missed you too, darling," and he kissed the top

of her head the way he had when she had been a child.

She pulled back from his embrace and the light from the lamp on his cluttered desk fell on her face. Fernán's brows twitched together in a sharp frown when he saw the bruise blooming on her cheek.

"What the devil is this?"

"Martial arts training."

"They allow a man to strike you?" It was less a question and more a statement of outrage.

"Daddy if I... *when* I graduate I'll be assigned to a ship and people might shoot at me. Truthfully being hit is a lot less scary."

"I suppose that's true."

Mercedes perched on the corner of his desk. "I'm learning this style called capoeira. It combines dance and acrobatics. And I'm really good at it."

"I bet you are. You were always the best dancer at your recitals."

She leaned forward and slapped him on the shoulder. "Liar."

"No, no. Biased perhaps. Aren't most fathers?" he asked with a smile. Resting his elbows on his knees he leaned forward. "So, how is it going?"

"Like you're not getting regular updates from Markov and Zeng," Mercedes said.

"Yes, of course I am, but I want to hear from you."

Mercedes slid off the desk and paced the shadowed confines of the office. The blinds had been drawn against the late afternoon sun. Fall had arrived so the room was quiet without the ever-present hum of air conditioning. Instead a large ceiling fan made of sek wood from Cuandru beat a slow cadence. The breeze from the blades ruffled her hair. It felt good to have it out of its braid and hanging loose and heavy down her back. While she assembled her thoughts Mercedes studied the paintings and hangings that adorned every wall.

"Well, I'm only getting Cs."

"As long as you're not failing. I don't need you to be at the top of your class. I wasn't either. I did, however, do very well at the *prueba*."

"Oh God, the *prueba*. What is it? No one will tell us anything," she cried.

"That's because it changes every year. I can tell you this much. It will evaluate how you all respond under pressure."

"Like that's any different," she muttered.

"Oh, it will be different," her father said. A smile quirked his lips. He drew a hand across his mouth. "I was disappointed to see you wearing a dress on the news. Why weren't you in your uniform?"

Mercedes licked her suddenly dry lips. "Well... um... I don't exactly have it... the old one... the first one... I mean... any more..." She looked up. Her father's gaze was dark and implacable. "What they gave us was completely impractical. It was a costume not a uniform—" She broke off and gave him an accusing look. "Wait a minute. If you've been getting reports from Zeng and Markov then you know all this. So why ask me?" He said nothing. "Oh. You wanted me to realize I was being a coward. If I can't handle the reaction to this..."

Her father braced his hands on the desk and pushed to his feet. "So what are you going to do about it?" He dropped a kiss on the top of her head as he walked past. "It's nice to have you home even for a few days."

Mercedes stared at the now empty doorway. She thought about calling the other girls and ordering them to change, but realized that would be another act of cowardice. None of them mattered. They, like the first uniforms, were mere set dressing. What mattered was her.

• • •

The house had seven bedrooms, five bathrooms, a formal dining room, a breakfast/morning room, a ladies' salon, a library, and a game room with a pool table. The expanse of green baize invited a game. After an aged butler with a grey mane and eyebrows had led him and Donnel to a bedroom, Tracy had headed back downstairs in search of his host, leaving Donnel to unpack. That so far fruitless search had led him ultimately to this room.

"We'll have a game after dinner." Jasper Talion's voice came from the doorway.

Tracy spun to face him. "Sorry, I didn't mean to snoop. I…"

Talion waved away the apology. "Feel free. I thought we'd just eat dinner in the breakfast room. Keep old Nicca from having to polish all the flatware and haul out Mum's rather hideous epergne." Tracy wondered what the hell an *ee*-pern might be as he nodded in agreement. "Anything you particularly hate, Tracy?" Talion asked as he led them out of the game room.

"No. Pretty much eat everything." Tracy decided to test the parameters of this new, odd relationship that might actually prove to be a friendship, so he added, "Jasper."

There was no objection, instead Talion just said, "Probably a good plan for a soldier."

"Is that what we are? Really?" Tracy asked.

Talion glanced back over his shoulder and gave a crooked grin. "Some of us will be. Once we jettison the deadwood."

"I take it I don't fall into that category," Tracy said, falling into step with his host.

"Oh, Christ no. You wouldn't be here if I thought that. I'm going to need people like you," he added.

Tracy's footsteps stuttered for an instant. *You're proud... but you need to... well, hide it better.* He struggled between wanting to respond and just giving a rueful head shake. He settled for the shake. "There, Mercedes, I'm taking your advice," he muttered under his breath.

"What?" Jasper asked.

"Nothing." Tracy took a deep breath, forced a smile and caught up with his host.

Jasper's hope to eat in the small breakfast room was dashed when the greying Hajin butler led them into the formal dining room. Eyeing the length of the table Tracy was glad the butler didn't seat him at the opposite end from his host. He would have needed a megaphone to hold a conversation.

Despite what Talion described as a skeleton staff they sat down to a very good dinner. Cold beet salad, spicy chicken, rice pilaf and a chilled raspberry soufflé for dessert, followed by a cheese platter and port. They discussed courses and professors, which of the recruit commanders they liked, but by the time coffee laced with liqueur was served the conversation was flagging. They had nothing in common beyond the academy.

Tracy nervously spun his cup and eyed the enormous silver affair sporting rearing horses and crossed swords and rifles that incongruously held a large bouquet of chrysanthemums. The clearing of his throat seemed loud in the room.

"So… is that thing a… an… epergne?"

"Yes. Horrible, isn't it?"

"I can't comment without either criticizing your mother's taste, or disagreeing with my host," Tracy said with a smile.

"Good point. I suppose it can't be easy for you."

Tracy shrugged. "It's okay. It certainly is a first-class education."

"Mmm." The conversation lagged again.

Jasper seemed to realize it might be his turn to lob the conversation ball. "I'm really looking forward to my brother Chris arriving. Let the hazing begin." He grinned. Tracy couldn't think of a response to that.

"So how many siblings do you have?"

"Eight. Five boys, three girls." Jasper asked. "So, are there more of you at home who we can expect to win a place at the academy?"

"I'm… I'm an only child," Tracy admitted.

The tall, elaborately carved chair gave a creak as Talion threw himself against the back. "No shit? I've never met an only before. Did something happen to your dad that he couldn't—"

"No." It emerged more sharply than Tracy had intended. "He just didn't remarry."

"Oh, a love match."

Memory flashed into his mind. His father's face twisted with grief, tears streaming down his face, his skin blotched red trying to get his shoulder beneath the casket that held his wife's remains. Tracy set aside his fork. "We don't arrange marriages in my class," he said quietly.

"I suppose you wouldn't."

The silence returned. Tracy tried another topic, hopefully one less fraught. "So... Nephilim."

Talion's grey brows twitched together. "What about it?" He sounded annoyed.

"Just that I don't know much about it," Tracy hastened to say.

Talion visibly relaxed and took a sip of his coffee. "It's a shit hole—but unless you live there you don't get to say that," Jasper warned.

"Got it."

"Cold. Rocky. We have to farm under domes. Bad radiation from the sun. It causes mutations." Jasper fingered his hair.

"So why—"

"Settle it?" Jasper interrupted. "Mineral resources. Primarily lithium. It's not all that common, and we have a shit load of it."

Tracy considered how much of the complex technology that powered the League relied upon lithium and nodded. "Ah, I see."

"So you'd think the League would value us more, wouldn't you?" Talion asked.

"I take it they don't."

"We're not exactly a hot vacation spot for the

FFH who live on the central worlds." Talion jerked a shoulder in a sharp shrug. "They think we're hillbillies. If you're finished…"

Tracy scrambled to his feet. "Yes. Let's."

Jasper grabbed a bottle of port and they carried their glasses back to the game room. Tracy measured cues while his host refilled their glasses. Silence reigned once more.

"So… you did make it into the Sabers," Tracy said as he applied chalk to his cue.

"Yes."

"Then Gelb was wrong."

"As he so often is," Jasper said, and his lips quirked in amusement. The billiard balls clicked loudly as he stacked them in the rack. Tracy laughed and wondered if it was too loud and too long. He felt ill at ease, out of his element and excited to be here all at the same time.

Jasper lifted away the rack, grabbed the cue ball and moved to the far end of the table. He positioned the ball, sighted down his cue and shot. There was a sharp crack and the balls scattered like startled birds. No ball entered a pocket.

"Shit," Jasper grumbled. "Your shot."

Tracy circled the table analyzing the lay of the balls, calculating trajectories. Orbital mechanics reduced to a ten by five foot dimension. He took his shot, banking the number four deep purple solid ball off the side and end bumpers and dropping it neatly in the pocket on the other long side.

Jasper leaned against the wall as Tracy took his next shot. "If you want to know how I pulled it off—it's because I'm the best swordsman in our class. Kunst thinks he is but he's not and at some point we'll settle the question."

Tracy looked up from pocketing his third ball. "Sorry to be dense, but…" He gestured at his own cheek not wanting to bluntly say *but you're scarred and Kunst isn't.*

Jasper grinned. "Smooth skin doesn't mean you're good. It usually means you're cautious or lucky or careful to pick weaker opponents." Jasper's fingers went to his scarred cheek. "My dad gave me these."

"Jesus!" Tracy looked up startled.

"No, it was good. I was getting cocky. It made me focus." Jasper laughed. "And how else would we know they loved us?"

By not hurting us? Tracy thought, remembering the slap.

His father had sacrificed his relationship with Tracy in exchange for what he believed would be a brighter future for his son. Was that love? Or manipulation? Tracy shook his head, lined up another shot and missed, his concentration blown by his confused and chaotic thoughts.

• • •

The boxes were opened and squeals of delight ensued. Mercedes glanced over to where Estella and Julieta sat on the bed now busily placing the jeweled pins in each other's hair. She hoped the gifts she had brought for the younger girls would be as well received.

Julieta hopped off the bed and rushed over to the dressing table to examine the pins in the mirror. "I'm going to wear them tomorrow night at the Conde de Vargas's ball."

Mercedes was startled by this news. "Papa's allowing you to go?"

"Uh huh. He said it wasn't fair for you and Essie to go, and for me to have to stay home."

"Hmm, he wouldn't let me go to a formal ball until I was seventeen," Mercedes grumbled.

Estella slipped off the bed and gave her a hug. "Parents are always harder on the first child. The rest of us get to be spoiled."

"True that," Mercedes said.

"I guess that means the little girls will be going at fourteen. Lucky things," Julieta said with a playful pout.

Estella, her expression suddenly sober, looked at her sibling. "Or it means he no longer cares what they do." She glanced at Mercedes. "Truthfully, Mer, I think the only one of us that matters now is you."

A hand seemed to clench down hard on her chest. She had heard truth and hated it. Mercedes couldn't bring herself to acknowledge that. Instead she heard herself hurriedly saying,

"Oh don't be silly. He loves us all." She whirled and offered her back to Estella. "Unzip me? I don't want to send for Flanon. She'll fuss and fiddle and I want it to be just us. I've missed you so much. Three months seemed like forever."

Estella obliged and Mercedes slipped the dress off her shoulders. Julieta gave a squeak and then a giggle. "Good Lord, look at your arms."

"What?"

Estella gripped her upper arm and squeezed. "Muscles."

"You look like a stevedore," Julieta giggled.

"They have us lift weights, and run three miles every day. You ought to see Sumiko. She's lost inches," Mercedes said.

"Well, I hope I don't have to go," Julieta said. "I don't want to look like a boy."

Estella caught Mercedes wince. "What?" her far too astute sister asked.

"Nothing."

"Liar."

"Let's just say you'll see tomorrow at the game," Mercedes muttered.

"You're going? But you hate soccer," Estella said.

"No, I *love* soccer, particularly when The High Ground is playing."

Estella nodded, "Oh, I get it. It's required that the cadets show support." Mercedes made a gun with her finger.

"But you're the Infanta. How can they make you go if you don't want to?" Julieta asked.

"Because I'm not the Infanta. I'm a cadet. No, scratch that, I'm a worm."

And she proceeded to tell them about Chief Deal, and his constant repetition of the phrase Big Damn Heroes, and she found herself making it funny instead of horrible. Because she suspected that if she failed her father might just try again with the next daughter. She wanted to save her sisters from that.

14

IS EVERYONE CRAZY?

As they ran onto the field there was a growing roar from the stands. It sounded less like humans and more like the growl of a particularly angry beast. Which probably wasn't wrong. There were going to be a lot more Caladonia fans than there were spectators affiliated with The High Ground.

The ground was softer than the field on the *cosmódromo,* and Tracy felt his cleats dig into the grass and soil. He tried to gauge his traction then told himself not to be an idiot. He wasn't going to be playing. He scanned the stands and was startled to see that the focus was not on the entering players. Everyone was staring at the large box at midfield.

The portly figure of Rohan Aubrey, the Conde de Vargas was settling into a seat. A taller, trimmer, older man, easily recognizable, was acknowledging the crowd with an upraised hand. The Emperor. And at his side—Mercedes, dressed in her *Orden de la Estrella* dress uniform. There were other people in the box; guards who were looking decidedly nervous at the crowd's reaction, and several older human women who were tending to a gaggle of little girls. There were also a number of Hajin, Tiponi and Isanjo servants arranging food and beverages on a table.

Mercedes turned to her father and snapped off a perfect salute. She then did the same to the Conde de Vargas. Finally she scanned the crowd in the stadium, and gave them a smile and a wave. The sound became more confused with both cheers and outraged yells blending and mixing.

"Well, nobody's going to give a tinker's fart what we do," Hugo muttered as he began to stretch out his muscles.

"Wonder what the news feeds are saying," Wilson added.

"I'll check once the game gets underway," Tracy promised as he moved to the benches on the sideline for the substitutes. McWhinnie was already pacing nervously up and down the sidelines giving last-minute instructions to his players as they stretched and prepared.

Tracy settled on the bench and set his ScoopRing to scroll the news sites. The teams took the field, the whistle blew and the game began. Glancing at the stands Tracy noticed that most of the spectators had begun to watch the field instead of the imperial box.

On his ScoopRing he saw a picture of Mercedes saluting her father on *The Globe* with the headline SHOCKING. *The Times* had a photo of just Mercedes in her trousers and coat with the dull but damning headline RETIRED ADMIRALS FEAR TOO ABRUPT CHANGE. Oddly enough it was the usually very conservative

Stellar that was the most supportive. Under the headline THE SALUTE SEEN ROUND THE LEAGUE the writer opined that if the Infanta was going to lead the fleets and armies of the League it was proper that she look like a real soldier and not like a child playing dress up. They felt encouraged by her evident professionalism.

There was a deafening roar from the stands. Tracy looked up to see the Caladonia striker trotting away from The High Ground's goal. Montoya was slapping hands with his teammates. Boho was storming up and down in front of the goal. The score stood at one–nil after only ten minutes of play.

"Well that blows," Tracy muttered to Gareth Goulet, a second-year student.

"Maybe they ought to give some of us a chance," Goulet groused. "We might surprise old Whinnie."

Having satisfied his curiosity about Mercedes and the reaction to her uniform Tracy turned his attention to the field. It was apparent that neither Jasper nor Hugo could keep pace with the Caladonia striker. He was unbelievably fast and agile. Montoya slipped through The High Ground's defenses like mercury. Just before half time Swanstrom, The High Ground's striker, managed to score a goal. They left for the locker room with the score tied.

McWhinnie berated and cajoled for ten of the fifteen minutes they had to rest, piss and hydrate. "Any questions?" he asked. Jasper raised his hand. "Yes?"

"How badly do we want this win?" the cadet from Nephilim asked.

"Are you daft or merely dense? Or not listening? This win is *vital*."

"Okay, that's all I needed to know." There was something in Jasper's voice that had Tracy staring intently at the back of that grey head.

McWhinnie checked his sleeve. "Well get to it. We're almost out of time."

"And whose fault is that," Wilson muttered as he rushed toward the urinals, unzipping as he went.

Back onto the field. Tracy settled onto the bench. Play began again. Caladonia took possession of the ball and began a lightning fast advance toward The High Ground goal. Boho hunkered down ready to leap to either side. There was a scrabble for the ball on the left. Reitten, one of The High Ground wing-backs, won back the ball and delivered a cross back to Swanstrom, but his cleats stuck and as he tried to spin he torqued his knee. When his foot pulled loose he was limping.

A time-out was called. A few moments later Reitten hobbled off the field. "Torn ACL." The whispers ran through the substitutes. Glances were exchanged. Someone was about to go onto the field. As his eyes flicked from substitute to substitute, Tracy ran the calculation. It would need to be someone fast with ball-handling skills rather than the larger, slower center-backs. There were only three possibilities and Tracy was one of them. He quickly began stretching. A few seconds later McWhinnie tapped his shoulder.

"Belmanor, you're in."

Tracy stripped off his jacket and slipped out of his sweat pants. He gave one final twist of his shoulders and ran onto the field. As he crossed center field he heard mad cheering from someone on the terrace at the end of the field. He glanced over. Among the crowd of working-class people in standing room, many holding Caladonia banners, there was a thin, stooped figure with the banner of The High Ground. Tracy's chest tightened, and there was a sudden ache in his throat. He raised his hand in a small salute to his father. Alexander yelled louder and held the banner over his head.

Play resumed. Tracy found that sprinting he was almost as fast as Montoya. He couldn't match the Caladonia striker in a long run, but Tracy could dart in every time Montoya tried a flanking maneuver. It was still a punishingly fast game. Breath rasped across Tracy's throat, and his chest seemed too small to contain his pounding heart. Sweat trickled down his forehead and stung his eyes.

There were quick hand signals flipping between the Caladonia players, and they switched from an outside strategy to trying plays up the center. Hugo and Jasper were formidable, but if Montoya's defenders could keep them off him, the striker was well positioned for another goal.

They began another run up the field toward The High Ground goal. Jasper and Hugo in their center-back positions moved to intercept. Tracy became aware of a Caladonia forward moving into a flanking position. His instinct told him that Montoya was going to try to deliver a cross to the other forward, and get past Hugo and Jasper to once again take control of the ball. Tracy moved in to guard the opposing forward. But the expected cross never came; instead there was a wild melee between Montoya, his defenders and Jasper. Three players went down, among them Jasper and Montoya. The air was torn with the sound of maddened whistles and a man screaming.

The game stuttered to a stop. The referees ran to the scene. Jasper was just climbing to his feet, supporting his left arm with his right hand. The other Caladonia player staggered up, but Montoya lay on the grass, screaming. His left leg was bent at a sickening angle.

Tracy, hands resting on his knees, panted and tried to process what had happened. While Montoya was clearly out it was clear that Jasper was also hurt and he was one of their best players. Disappointment lay like a stone in his belly. The one time he got to play and this was the outcome.

The Caladonia coach ran to his fallen player. McWhinnie was right behind him. A doctor came out next and looked first at Montoya and then at Jasper. Then came a stretcher. Caladonia's star player was carried off the field accompanied by the moans and boos of the fans. McWhinnie called his team over.

"How bad is it?" Tracy asked as he fell into step with Jasper.

"Broke my arm. It's not bad."

There were mumbles of sympathy from the nearest players. Jasper added, "So, you shouldn't have any trouble winning now that Montoya's out of the way." It was said in an undertone, but casually as if he were merely mentioning the weather, and the young baron's expression was calm and unmoved.

The realization came with sickening clarity and Tracy's steps faltered. *Dear God, he did it deliberately.* Now Jasper's question to McWhinnie in the locker room took on a dark significance.

All around him his teammates were nodding

in agreement. Starting to exchange backslaps, and muttering encouragement. Tracy was wondering what he should do. What he *could* do.

He temporized by asking, "Was it worth it?" Tracy nodded toward Jasper's arm.

Talion gave him a sharp look. He had understood the significance of Tracy's question. "Well, that's sort of up to the rest of you, isn't it? You've been given a chance. Now you have to take it."

"Because winning is that important?"

"Of course. It's everything."

A hard swat on the back of his head sent Tracy stumbling. "Get focused, *intitulado*, and let the man get to a medic," Boho said.

Tracy fell back to walk with Hugo Devris and Mark Wilson. Hugo draped an arm over his shoulders. "Hey, what's up your butt? This is all good."

"What if he did it deliberately?"

"What if he did? And even if he did he didn't get caught, so..." Hugo shrugged. "Like I said, all good." He trotted over to McWhinnie.

Tracy's good will toward the other boy curdled, but he supposed he shouldn't have been surprised. Hugo had been raised by a man whose shady dealings, outright bribery and kickbacks were well known and pointedly ignored by society at large.

"You were right there," Tracy said to Wilson. "You have to have seen everything."

"It was a little unclear." Wilson's tone was cautious.

"You saw what happened, didn't you?" Tracy accused.

Wilson thrust his face into Tracy's. His jaw was

clenched and the words emerged in a hissing whisper. "When are you going to figure out we have to go along to get along?" He ran to the gaggle of players huddled around their coach.

All those fine phrases from the code of conduct expected of O-Trell officers flashed through Tracy's mind. Just words. An illusion, a fantasy, a fabrication—like the very foundations of League society.

Tracy watched Jasper disappearing into the locker rooms in the company of a medic. A possible friend or at least ally revealed to be a ruthless son-of-a-bitch. He looked to the terrace where his dad stood proudly waving The High Ground banner. Basking in the pleasure of having a son at the academy, not caring how he had put that son there. To the imperial box where the Emperor displayed his daughter like a prize fish.

The world seemed suddenly far more complicated than it had even three months before. Principles shattered against agendas and ambitions, compromises battled conscience and inevitably won. A bleakness invaded Tracy's soul and left him exhausted. He couldn't reconcile any of it. So what to do?

Finish the match. He also had no choice but to go on.

They won the game.

• • •

Outside the tinted windows of the imperial flitter, crowds lined the streets waving and cheering. Flowers littered the walkways beneath the flight lanes. She and her father were alone except for the guard in the front seat and the driver. Her sisters and their attendants were scattered in other flitters. Mercedes glanced over at her father's profile. She decided he looked smug.

"So, was that enough visibility for you?"

He looked over at her and smiled. "It was very well done. The public got to see my heir, and they loved you."

"Now you're exaggerating. There were a lot of boos along with the cheers."

"We'll weather it. The press will come around and the public will follow."

"I was surprised to see that supportive article in the *Stellar*." Once again her father had that cat-with-a-bird expression. "Did you? You did, didn't you? You planted that."

"Let's just say that Duque Enrique is a strong supporter of the government."

"Well, if we've got that kind of help may I please wear a dress tonight? I'll look stupid dancing in trousers." She scooted around on the seat to face her father, and tucked one leg beneath her. It pained her to admit it, but there were certainly some things that were easier done in a dress. "Please, Daddy, let me be pretty tonight."

He tugged at his upper lip thoughtfully. "It's just our set at Rohan's, and I know where all of them stand."

"Not all of them are with us," Mercedes warned, thinking about Arturo and Mihalis.

"Knowing where they stand implies that yes, I do know that some oppose me and I also know who they are. I'm not leaving any of this to chance, Mer. You can be sure of that."

They fell silent for a moment. They were heading

up the hill toward the palace grounds. "Daddy, why are you letting Julieta go tonight?"

"There's someone I want her to meet."

"You can't be thinking about an alliance already? She's only fifteen."

"She'll be sixteen soon, and she won't have to marry him until he finishes school."

"Who is he?"

"Lord Sanjay Favreau."

"Oh God, no, not him!"

A frown creased his brow. "And why not?"

"He's got a temper, Daddy. He can be violent."

He shrugged. "I expect he'll behave himself if he's married to an imperial princess."

"And what if he doesn't? This is Julieta we're talking about."

"His father is the head of the largest banking concern in the League. Power needs money and money loves power. I can steer the press in the direction I want. Money needs more persuading."

"So Julieta is one of those things you're not leaving to chance? She doesn't get a chance to meet someone, fall in love—"

"No. Any more than you do," he said, and in tones that were no longer fatherly, but far more imperial. "You're going to order men into battle, Mer. Some of them are going to die. You're going to have to make the same hard choices about your sisters and half-sisters. You'll be controlling the board and you have to play to win. Sometimes you have to sacrifice a piece to achieve that victory. And most importantly you have to never forget they are just that—pieces."

"I know my duty, but I can't. I can't do that," she whispered through stiff lips. "They're my sisters."

Her father smiled. "Well, I'm not planning on pegging out anytime soon so I'll handle settling Estella and Julieta so you won't have to. And I expect you'll feel less protective toward the younger girls. Especially since you won't be around them much over the next few years." He fell silent for a moment then gave her a sideways glance. "I'm a little surprised at this reaction. You didn't object when I told you to find a consort."

"That's different. It's me and I know what's expected of me—"

"And they will too. Their training is no different than yours."

She gestured at her uniform. "With one big exception." She sat with the idea for a while. "I wouldn't let Arturo or Mihalis marry Estella or Julieta. That would be too close to the throne, but maybe one of the younger girls. Tie them to us but not too closely."

Fernán didn't say anything, just looked at her with an expression that was both amused and calculating. "Okay, not a good idea I take it." She sighed and tried to analyze it like one of the math problems in Captain Xian's class. "You think they shouldn't be allowed to marry any of my sisters."

"Correct. Why not?"

It only took a moment of consideration for her to see the answer. "We don't want to give the del Campos any more validity as rivals to your rule."

"*Our* rule. And yes, that's correct." He gave her hand a pat where it was clenched in her lap. "And, honey, you can wear a dress tonight."

15

IT'S ALL A BIT INTOXICATING

Tracy stood in the street at the front door of the shop. It was locked and a sign indicated it was closed for the day. *So he could come and watch the game. I wonder how much that cost him? At least he got to see me play and not just sit on the bench.*

It was late afternoon. The setting sun threw toffee-colored light across the buildings and warmed Tracy's shoulders. Donnel, standing three paces behind him and holding his carryall, cleared his throat.

"Have you a suggestion as to how to proceed?" the Cara'ot asked.

"Yeah, we try the back door." Tracy headed down the narrow walkway between their building and the bodega next door. To his surprise the back door was locked as well. Maybe his dad had given Bajit the day off? Had the Hajin been in the alien section at the game? Tracy hadn't even thought to look for him.

He raised his ScoopRing toward the lock. What if his dad had changed the code? Jesus, that would hurt. Then he remembered he'd deleted the code off his ring.

Even if it hadn't changed he couldn't get in.

"Sir, time is fleeting. You need to shower and dress for the ball. A ball that will start in three hours." The alien's tone was pointed.

Tracy gulped and knocked. A few minutes later the door was flung open. His father stood in the door dressed in slacks and an undershirt with his old worn scuffs on his bare bony feet. The annoyed expression faded and the pale eyes filled with tears. Answering tears sprang into Tracy's eyes. Alexander pulled him into a tight hug. His dad hesitantly pounded on his back with a fist then cleared his throat.

"Ow, you're too hard to hit now. What are they feeding you up there?" Alexander asked as he stepped back from the door.

"It's pretty good, but they work it off us just as fast," Tracy said. He followed his father into the workroom. "May I stay?"

"Don't be daft. Of course you can stay." He looked at the Cara'ot still standing in the alley. "And who and what is this?"

"My batBEM, Donnel. He's a Cara'ot."

"Do you have to pay him?"

Tracy realized with some shock that he hadn't actually thought about it. He'd just accepted the service as if it were his due. He'd never asked if the tripod alien needed money.

"I… I don't know. I mean I haven't…"

"Not to worry, sir. I assumed you knew The High Ground was covering my salary during your schooling."

"What happens after I graduate?" Tracy asked.

"After that my pay becomes your responsibility if

you wish me to join you on your first posting."

"Guess that depends on how much a first lieutenant gets paid," Tracy answered.

"And if I wish to accompany you," Donnel said softly.

Had there been a very subtle rebuke in the alien's words? Tracy wasn't certain.

"Does it… he go with you everywhere?" Alexander asked.

Tracy glanced at the alien. "I guess so. This is the first time I've been anywhere."

"To answer the question, sir. Yes, I'm here to handle mundane chores so he can concentrate on his studies and various other required activities."

"We don't really have a place for him to sleep," Alexander said.

"Not a worry, sir. Perfectly capable of placing my billet on the floor or ceiling for that matter. I won't be in the way."

Tracy's father still looked a bit confused by it all, but he said, "All right then, that's settled. I'll go next door. Get us something for dinner tonight—"

"I can't, Dad. There's a thing I have to do," Tracy replied. He handed over the invitation; it was easier than trying to explain. Alexander's pale cheeks flushed and a look of exultant pride filled his eyes.

"My boy. At an FFH ball. Your mother… I wish your mother…" He sank down on a chair at one of the sewing machines, and hid his eyes behind his hand for a brief moment.

"I'll just take your bag upstairs, sir," Donnel said with a nice display of delicacy, and he scuttled out of the workroom.

Alexander took several deep breaths, then sprang to his feet. "But enough of that! You need a shower, and give me that uniform and your dress uniform as well. We don't want you going looking like a ragbag. And where did you come by that undress uniform? Did they decide you were too good for the crappy charity one? Are you hungry? Thirsty?" Alexander threw over his shoulder as he hurried toward the stairs.

The questions came flying too fast to be answered, which was probably for the best. Tracy picked the easiest one to answer. "Thirsty. I'm too nervous to be hungry."

His father came back and gripped his shoulders. "You'll be fine. You're the equal of any of them."

"Actually I'm better than most of them," Tracy said with a proud smile. "I'm the second best student in our class."

"Second best?"

"This guy, Ernesto Chapman-Owiti, he's a fucking genius. He's beating me because he's better in biology." There was once again that expression of desperate joy. His father reached out, cupped the nape of his neck, and pulled him close.

"Okay, enough. Let's get you ready." Tracy pulled out his dress uniform. His father saw the second one and gave him a startled look.

"It's a long story that I probably shouldn't tell you. Yeah, I better not. But it meant I got the undress uniform *and* another dress uniform."

"You should wear this one tonight," Alexander said, shaking out the uniform Tracy had gotten from Mercedes. "The one I made is rather piecemeal—"

Tracy grabbed Alexander by the arm. "I'm going

to wear the uniform my father made for me."

His father's expression made Tracy look away and blink hard. Alexander grabbed a tape measure off a table and swept it around Tracy's waist. "I'll get the waistband adjusted, and get this pressed. Now go, go!"

Two hours later Tracy stood on the riser studying himself in the three mirrors. His father stood behind him smoothing the shoulders of his jacket. While he had showered, shaved and fought back panic his dad had been busy. The coat had been adjusted to accommodate the burgeoning muscles in his arms, back and chest, and the waistband on the trousers had been tightened. He pulled on his gloves and settled the billed cap on his head. On his left breast he now sported one ribbon awarded for the not terribly difficult task of successfully completing the first quarter. His boots had been polished to a mirror-bright finish, and the silver braid sparkled.

"Well, thanks to you I look the part."

"You earned your place there. You're not play acting. Now, how are you getting there?" Alexander asked as they walked to the front door of the shop.

"Tram then walk."

"No." His father dug out his credit spike. "You're taking a cab."

"Dad it's too expen—"

"Now don't argue with me."

"Yes, sir." He gripped his father's arm. "Thanks. I'll take the tram home."

"I want the butler or majordomo or the footman to hand you into a flitter. Not walk off like some peddler who's been turned away at the door."

"Dad, they all know what I am."

"Ah, but they don't know *who* you are. You're going to show them all."

• • •

Julieta was a fairy queen in a sea-foam blue mermaid-style gown sewn with hundreds of tiny glittering aquamarines. Estella wore a champagne gown that complemented her ivory complexion. Mercedes had chosen an off-the-shoulder dark carmine gown with a deep V neckline and a billowing skirt. She lifted her skirt to examine her high-heeled pumps. A spray of garnets adorned the instep and sparkled in the heels. For contrast she drew on long black mousquetaire gloves. They fit more tightly over her upper arm than they had before. She noticed one of the three buttons on her left glove had popped loose, and she thrust it out. Flanon hurried forward and buttoned it closed.

"You look beautiful, La Dama," the old Hajin maid said.

Mercedes nodded toward her sisters. "Oh, they outshine me by a mile."

"But they won't hold the throne," her maid said and Mercedes heard the pride in her age-cracked voice.

"Who are you serving with me gone?" Mercedes asked as the servant gave her skirt one final twitch.

"Her Imperial Highness has assigned me to serve Beatrisa. I tried Tanis, but…" Her voice trailed away. It seemed everyone found Tanis to be a pain.

"Is Beatrisa behaving?"

"She's a darling. Gentle as a breeze and so cheerful."

"Now you're just lying. She may be cheerful, but no one could call Bea gentle. Now don't stay up. I'm sure my sisters will want to gossip, and we can help each other undress."

Flanon bowed, but Mercedes knew the old Hajin would be up and waiting and probably have a cup of hot chocolate prepared.

Mercedes hurried forward with a rustle of skirts to join her sisters. They linked arms, and headed down the hallway. The gems on Julieta's dress chimed softly with each step. *She's exquisite*, Mercedes thought as she looked down at her smaller sister. There were more aquamarines flashing among the loops and curls of her upswept hair, and a necklace like tangled flowers held still more. *But she's a baby. How can Daddy be thinking about her marriage?* The unsettling thought had her looking away to her closest friend and confidant. Estella was classic in champagne pearls. The necklace was so long that it was looped three times around her neck, and still hung almost to her waist. Pearls and diamonds flashed in her ears. Her hair was held in place by a mother of pearl and pearl encrusted comb.

There were five faces watching from four doorways. The eldest girls, Izzara and Tanis, fourteen and twelve respectively, were looking sulky and envious. The younger ones, the seven-year-old twins, Delia and Dulcinea, already in their nightgowns, were giggling and looked excited. Eleven-year-old Beatrisa made a face at them. She was not only a tomboy, but at that age where she scorned fripperies and furbelows.

If only she had been older, Mercedes thought. *She would have loved The High Ground.* She took a firmer grip on her fan. She always became nervous and overheated at these affairs.

"Will there be ices and cookies?" Delia and Dulcie cried.

"Yes," Mercedes answered.

"Will you bring us back some?" Their little voices were like the piping of songbirds.

Estella gathered them both into a hug. "Of course we will."

Izzara and Tanis were mobbing Julieta. "I don't know why you get to go and not me," Izzara was saying. "I'm almost fifteen."

Mercedes crossed to the gawky girl with her fiery red hair. Izzara and Tanis were fairer than their sisters and both showed a smattering of freckles across their noses and cheeks. Unfortunately Tanis had rather mousey brown hair as well as freckles. She seemed a small brown wren compared with her taller sister, and resentment oozed off her like a smell.

"Liar," Mercedes said, pulling at Izzara's ponytail. "It's seven months until your birthday."

The younger girl flounced away. "I don't care. It's not fair. It's boring stuck here with the little girls."

"But you'd look like a clown in a ballgown," Tanis said in that nasty, cutting tone that the entire household had come to dread. "You're flat as a pancake, and finding a color to wear that won't clash with your orange mop would be impossible." Tanis's poisonous tongue was on full display and it went as it usually went.

Izzie gave a shriek of fury, burst into tears, stormed into her bedroom and slammed the door. A look of satisfaction flickered across Tanis's face. Mercedes sighed. It was the fights between the siblings that had dictated they have separate rooms far sooner than their older sisters. Mercedes had cried when she'd been given her own quarters. Being separated from her sisters had been horrible, and she knew Estella and Julieta had shed many bitter tears as well. With Izzie and Tanis it had probably prevented bloodshed.

Delia and Dulcinea were staring wide-eyed at Tanis. Delia gave a little hiccupping sob and rubbed at her eyes. Estella smoothed her hair, setting the beads woven into her cornrows to chiming. "Don't cry, sweetling."

Mercedes rounded on her half-sister. "Go away, Tanis, until you can behave like an emperor's daughter."

Tanis gave Mercedes a cold-eyed look and went into her room. Her door closed very quietly. In some ways it was more unsettling than Izzie's tantrum.

Beatrisa marched up and stood with her fists on her hips and a pugnacious expression. "Can I knock Tanis down? Can I? Please?"

"First, it's *may I*," Mercedes said. "And be my guest."

"Can we please *go*," Julieta cried. The crystals on her gown were chiming as she bounced in agitation.

"Just a minute! You don't want to be the first to arrive anyway," Mercedes shot back. She crossed to the twins and pulled them into a group hug. "Don't be upset that Izzie and Tanis are fighting. It's just something that happens when you're a teenager."

The twins exchanged glances. They looked both alarmed and confused. "But... but I love Delia," Dulcinea said. "I wouldn't ever make her mad or make her cry."

"That's because you're twins, and twins are

special," Mercedes said. "And we'll bring you back so many treats you'll have tummy aches," she promised. Standing she dropped kisses on the tops of their heads.

They traversed a few more hallways until they reached the top of the curving staircase. Fernán and Constanza waited in the marble foyer. Her father was wearing his star command uniform; on the left breast was a bewildering array of ribbons and medals. After three months at the academy Mercedes now recognized some of them. On the right side of his jacket he wore only the Galactic Cross, on which an ebony cross overlaid the diamonds of the Milky Way. Only the Emperor could wear this particular medal. The companions in the Order of the Galaxy wore only the galaxy.

The Emperor moved to the foot of the stairs and stared up at his eldest daughters. "You're all so beautiful. And grown up. When did that happen?"

When did that happen? Mercedes wondered. It seemed only yesterday he had introduced her to her first pony, and taught her how to throw a frisbee.

Julieta hurried down to him, lost her footing in her high heels and tumbled the final steps. The Emperor caught her. "Whoa, whoa."

Julieta gave an embarrassed giggle. "I'm sorry. I'm just so excited." Her father swung her in a circle, and set her gently aside.

Seeing Julieta in her father's arms brought back a vivid memory. Her father hugging her close as they rode a sled down a snow-covered hill on Kronos where the high mountains in the southern hemisphere offered spectacular skiing. She was four. Her mother was gone and a new woman sat at her father's side, but she felt safe encircled in her father's embrace. It was a shame insecurities and fears couldn't be so easily quelled now.

Estella had already made her elegant descent to the ground floor and was greeting her stepmother. Mercedes shook off her reverie, and descended the rest of the way. Her father drew himself to attention and gave a sharp inclination of his head, making it clear to the guards and equerries gathered all around that this was no longer just his daughter, but his equal.

Mercedes mirrored the gesture, and walked past him toward the front doors. A single push from the guards to either side sent them gliding open. They gave double foot stamps and the butts of their rifles cracked against the floor as she passed. It was all a bit intoxicating.

• • •

It turned out, unsurprisingly, that a Pony Town cab driver wasn't all that familiar with the Palacio Colina, and a self-fly flitter wasn't an option. Apparently they weren't programmed with locations on the hill. Whether from worry that a cab might be rigged with explosives or because they were cheaper and might allow riffraff to gawk at their betters, Tracy wasn't sure.

What he did know was that the invitation read eight p.m., and he was arriving at eight thirty-five. Despite his nerves and anxiety over being late he couldn't help but enjoy the sight of the stately homes as they flew past. He had thought the Talion house was impressive. It looked like a shack next to these monuments to wealth and power.

On the pinnacle of the hill the lights of the imperial

palace glittered in the darkness. Tracy wondered if Mercedes was still up there. Intricate gates, the metal twined to resemble leaves and vines, rose up on their left. The driver looked at his nav system, muttered and turned toward the gates.

A guard stepped out. Tracy pulled the invitation out of his pocket and rolled down the window. The cool night air filled with the scent of star jasmine and gardenia rolled into the cab, banishing the faint odor of pastrami and coffee from the driver's unfinished dinner.

"Your business," the guard began, then he saw Tracy's uniform, stepped back and saluted. "Sir."

Tracy still offered the invitation. It was waved off. "Go ahead, sir."

Tracy left the window down and found himself ridiculously pleased by the guard's reaction. He could get used to this. He caught a glimpse of the driver in the rearview mirror looking back at him seemingly impressed, and Tracy preened a bit more.

They joined a line of limousines approaching the grand portico. Eventually it was their turn. A Hajin footman in the elaborate livery of the Aubrey family waited while the driver lowered the flitter to a comfortable height, then opened the door for Tracy and bowed as he exited.

Tracy's driver, an older human man, leaned out his window. "Hey, this took longer than I thought. Your old man didn't give me enough money to cover that. That'll be another twenty Reals."

Embarrassment and rage sent heat washing into Tracy's face. "You told my dad you knew the area. Your problem if you lied," he said in an angry whisper.

The driver raised his voice. "What kind of officer welshes on a debt?"

A bead of sweat broke out and rolled down Tracy's cheek. The limos were backing up behind them. He heard the Hajin footman murmuring into his lapel radio. Pride had turned to embarrassment. The driver in the limo behind them climbed out. Tracy reached for his credit spike.

A human in an elegant suit emerged from the front doors and came down the steps. The Hajin footman stepped aside. The man leaned in toward the driver. "I am Stephen Grassley, majordomo to House de Vargas."

The driver's expression shifted from calculating to worried. He started to whine, "I was promised—"

"You were paid in advance. If you continue to embarrass this young man you may find your license in some danger."

"Fortune fucker," the driver spat. The window rolled up and he accelerated away so quickly that dust and gravel was thrown against Grassley's and Tracy's trouser legs.

"I'm sorry," Tracy muttered. "I should have—"

"No matter. Please step out of the way so others may be dropped off." The majordomo walked back up the stairs.

Embarrassed, Tracy mumbled, "Right. Sorry. Right away."

He hurried up the broad steps leading to the elaborate front doors, torn between gratitude at the help and the implicit criticism and condescension in the man's remarks. Every time he thought he was transcending his background something always reminded him that in the eyes of these people he never would.

16

IT ULTIMATELY COMES DOWN TO NUMBERS

Tracy stepped through into the foyer. The floor underfoot was pale blue glass. Ahead there was a rather terrifying staircase, a curving expanse of crystal stairs with only a thin silver metal railing to offset vertigo.

An Isanjo maid darted over to Tracy's elbow. "If I may take your hat, young sir."

He handed it over automatically then was seized with a sudden worry. "How do I get it back? Do I get a ticket or something?"

"I have made note of your name, Cadet Belmanor," the alien said, gesturing toward his nameplate woven into the fabric of his coat.

"Oh. Right." He headed for the stairs. As he climbed he wondered why the hell someone would have a staircase with clear treads?

Then he reached the ballroom that encompassed most of the first floor, and all such extraneous thoughts vanished. Overhead enormous chandeliers seemed to drip ice and fire from long multi-sided crystal spikes. There was a loft above a pair of doors at the far end of the enormous room where a small orchestra was playing. The floor beneath his boots was polished sek wood that seemed to flex with each step, easing any possible jarring while dancing.

A delicate clearing of the throat pulled Tracy out of his dumbfounded trance. He flushed furiously when he realized there was a receiving line and that the Conde de Vargas and the condessa, an older but very beautiful woman who stood at his side, were waiting to greet him.

"Sir!" Tracy snapped off a salute.

Rohan Aubrey held out a plump white hand. "Cadet Belmanor, isn't it?"

"Yes, sir."

"Allow me to present my wife, Analise."

The condessa had long auburn hair that fell over her shoulders like a waterfall. "Cadet. Welcome to our home."

Tracy bowed. That at least he knew how to do well. His father had drilled that skill into him. "Thank you, ma'am... milady."

The condessa gave him a kind smile, and Aubrey slapped him on the shoulder. "The buffet is all set up through those doors at the far end. If you're anything like our sons you're hungry. Young men, particularly soldiers, are always hungry. Please, go, enjoy and then find a pretty girl to dance with."

"Yes, sir. Thank you, sir."

"And a word in your ear," the conde said quietly. "The only person in civilian dress that you salute is the Emperor."

"Uh, right, thank you, sir."

Tracy bowed to the conde, and once more to the condessa, and moved toward the etched glass doors the Conde de Vargas had indicated. The entire wall to his left was a series of tall cathedral-style windows. As he passed they switched; one moment clear glass, the next they became mirrors throwing back his image, and that of the swirling crowds. No one was dancing yet, but the room was still a banquet for the senses.

Tracy wondered if he dared take a surreptitious photo for his father. He decided to wait until there were people dancing and take a video rather than a static picture. There would be less chance of getting caught, and his father would get the full effect of the amazing room.

Through the doors was another large room, where five buffet tables stood against the walls, laden with a bewildering array of food. The smell of roasted meat permeated the air. Round tables with eight chairs to each table glistened beneath white tablecloths, filling the center of the room. Servants wove through the tables carrying bottles of wine and champagne. There was the roar of conversation and the syncopation of tinkling crystal.

More servants stood at carving stations at all five buffet tables. Tracy gathered up a plate and silverware wrapped in a cloth napkin and moved down the table. There were oysters on the half shell, shrimp both fried and cold, a silver bowl piled high with caviar, salads, vegetables, roasted fowl, standing rib roast, and ham. He had no idea how to eat a raw oyster, but he was determined to try it, just like he was going to try the caviar.

Once his plate was piled high he scanned the room

for a place to sit. Hugo Devris and Mark Wilson were sitting with several members of the team including Jasper Talion, whose broken arm was in a sling. Ernesto Chapman-Owiti sat with several other acknowledged geniuses from all three classes. There were tables of the gung-ho types who were clearly going to end up commanding *fusileros*. There was a table of only the highest born—Boho Cullen, Arturo del Campo and his brother. The three ladies-in-waiting were all at that table. *Trawling for husbands no doubt,* Tracy thought. There was no sign of Mercedes.

Tracy spotted a table near the doors, which meant it caught the draft from the ballroom and was well away from the food. It was empty. Perfect. He went over and sat down. After only a few bites he decided that oysters were delicious and he went back for a plate of just those. He was starting to see the china at the bottom of both plates when a shadow fell across the table.

Tracy looked over his shoulder to see his host standing behind him. He started to jump to his feet when Rohan Aubrey laid a hand on his shoulder and pushed him back down. "Mind if I join you, Cadet?"

"Uh, no, sir, of course not."

Aubrey settled into a chair with a grunt and a sigh. "Standing for that long kills my lower back. Analise would say it would help if I lost this." He slapped his paunch and gave a chuckle. "She's right of course. But for now I'm taking a break until Fernán arrives." Tracy couldn't think of a word to say to a man who could refer to the Emperor by his first name. "So, how was the first quarter?"

"Good," Tracy offered hesitantly.

"Glad to hear it. You're racking up impressive grades."

"You… you see our grades, sir?"

"Of course. I follow all of you. You're the future and more importantly our first line of defense. And The High Ground is my particular passion. Hard to believe now, I know, but I was quite the dashing *Infierno* pilot in my youth. So, where do you think your talents lie?"

"I'm good at math. I expect I'll end up a navigator or a gunnery officer."

"I hear you're also a very good shot."

"If I can line up my shots. Though I'd rather not tote a rifle."

"A cautious man. I like that. We get enough of the balls-to-the-wall variety. Everything ultimately comes down to the numbers, doesn't it? Number of ships, number of missiles, amount of available fuel, rations, supply lines in general." The conde paused. "And men, particularly men. The numbers are rather interesting out in sector 470." Aubrey stood, pressed his fists against the small of his back and stretched. "Well, lovely visiting with you. Keep up the good work, Cadet."

The conde walked back into the ballroom just as the orchestra began to play "Hail to the Emperor".

Cadets were leaving their tables and rushing to watch the arrival of the Emperor. As for Tracy, he sat still wondering, *What the hell was that about?* He replayed the conversation. *Sector 470*. Clearly he was supposed to take a look at resources flowing to that sector, and look for… what? Maybe he'd know it if he saw it. Okay, so what if he did find something? How was he supposed to report his findings back to the Conde de Vargas? He pushed that aside as a problem for another day. Mercedes was arriving. He wanted to see that, and maybe in a crowd of seven or eight hundred people he could find a way to tell her he was sorry.

• • •

Constanza had clung to her father's arm all the way up the rather terrifying staircase. Once they were all gathered on the landing her father had removed his wife's hand from his arm, placed his hand in the small of her back, and pushed her gently aside. He gestured to Mercedes.

"Come."

It was not the cajoling tone of a father, but the command of an emperor. Mercedes moved to his side and he extended his arm. She placed a gloved hand on his sleeve and they walked toward the vaulted scissor arch into the ballroom. The majordomo called in stentorian tones over the opening chords of the imperial march:

"His Most Noble and Puissant Emperor of the Solar League, Fernán Marcus Severino Beltrán de Arango. And Her Imperial Highness, Princess Mercedes Adalina Saturnina Inez de Arango, the Infanta!"

The quick glance back over her shoulder was meant for her sisters, but Mercedes caught a glimpse of Constanza's face. It was rigid and her blue eyes glittered with unshed tears. Mercedes had made a silly face, and she now struggled to compose her features so her stepmother wouldn't think Mercedes was mocking her. Mercedes wasn't sure she had been successful and then it was too late, for she and her father were through the arch and making a stately progress down the center of the dance floor while the elite of the Fortune Five Hundred bowed and curtsied at their passing.

She murmured greetings and lightly touched the fingertips of various well-wishers but it was all done by reflex. She couldn't shake the image of Constanza's face. There had been hurt reflected there and more than hurt… fear.

Mercedes' recollections of the day her mother, Maribel, left were hazy, but there had been something in Constanza's agonized expression that touched that memory. There had been an infant crying in the background. Julieta presumably. Two-year-old Estella had been sitting on the floor in their nursery playing with blocks. Maribel had knelt in front of her, and Mercedes, age four, had stood in the circle of her mother's arms. She could remember her mother's mouth moving, but she had no memory of the words spoken.

A few hours later another woman had knelt before her and also held Mercedes in an embrace. Those words she could remember. "Hello, Mer, I'm Agatha. I'm going to be your *madre* now." In her confusion Mercedes had just nodded mutely when what she really wanted to do was kick and scream and run. Agatha hadn't turned out to be much of a mother. She paid little attention to the three eldest girls except when it came time to discipline them.

Agatha hadn't looked devastated when she had been set aside for Greta. Agatha had been furious, which suggested that perhaps Tanis's unpleasant personality was due to more than just being a teenager.

Greta had actually tried to be a mother to all of them, but this time her father had only given the new bride one chance. A daughter had been born and she was out, replaced by Inez. To her credit Inez hadn't tried to be a mother to any of them. A difficult pregnancy and having twins took a toll on her health and her happiness. Mercedes suspected she had been relieved when the Emperor's roving eye had fallen upon Constanza, just recently come to Hissilek for the season.

Mercedes glanced up at her father and hoped his eye wouldn't fall upon yet another young woman. Carisa was a nervous, high-strung child. Mercedes wasn't certain the girl could be as sanguine about the mommy musical chairs as she had been.

Her father caught her look and misinterpreted it. He gave her hand a pat and said, "Duty complete. Go, dance, have fun." He smiled fondly down at her.

Mercedes curtsied to him, and looked for Estella and Julieta. Her youngest sister was flushed, laughing in a circle of admiring young men. Sanjay was among them. Quelling the impulse to run over and snatch Julieta away, Mercedes searched for a distraction. Boho, tall, elegant and impossibly handsome, seemed to glow under the lights from one of the massive chandeliers.

The dark green eyes roamed the room. His gaze fell on her, and Boho smiled. The lights seemed suddenly dim. *Is that what people mean when they talk about charisma?* Mercedes wondered. He walked directly to her and bowed deeply.

"Mercedes, may I say that while I find you disturbingly alluring in your trousers, tonight you are exquisite."

It was an odd sensation to have to look up to a man, but Boho's extra inches made her actually feel feminine and delicate. She shook her head.

"First, eeew about the trousers, and wrong adjective, Boho. I'm far too tall to ever be considered exquisite."

"Okay, stately, elegant, sumptuous... Better?"

She chuckled. "All except sumptuous. That makes me sound like an overly rich dinner."

He dropped the lightest kiss, almost a mere breath, on the back of her gloved hand. "Frankly, you're damn regal, Mer. You're going to make one hell of an empress."

"Oh bullshi—" She clapped a hand over her mouth. "Oh dear, we're not at the academy. I better watch my language."

"Very true or you'll have the debs fainting, the matrons clucking and clutching their pearls and the dowagers scolding. May I have the first waltz?" He reached to his pocket where the edge of his dance card peeped out.

"Run and get my dance card and you may write in your name. Right now I need some supper or I'm going to perish from hunger."

"I am yours to command, Your Highness," he said with another bow, but the green eyes were dancing. She slapped him on the arm with her fan and he moved away.

She moved into the supper room, but before she could reach the buffet she had to negotiate the tables filled with friends, frenemies and actual enemies. Mercedes decided to engage the enemies first. She walked to the table where Mihalis and Arturo del Campo were seated with their brother Jose, dressed in clerical robes. Her two classmates flanked their brother and they were laughing, talking and nudging him. As for the priest, he was red faced but he looked rather pleased with himself.

They didn't notice her approach so Mercedes was able to circle around behind them and eavesdrop.

"Ho, all hail the ecclesiastical stud. Bang and they're pregnant," chortled Arturo.

Mercedes dropped a hand onto Jose's shoulder. "Congratulations, Jose. Sounds like you are earning that title of father."

Jose went from rose to scarlet, and stuttered, "Really, Mer— Your Highness, it's not appropriate for you to be part of this conversation."

Mihalis, his eyes glittering, looked up and drawled, "Ah, but she's not a lady any longer, Jose— she's a soldier so it's entirely appropriate."

Arturo, ever the courtier, slid into the conversation like an otter into water. "We're just happy that Jose can't compete with us for an actual bride. Seven of the *Celestial Novias de Cristo* have picked Jose to sire their children."

Mihalis didn't follow his younger brother's lead. Instead he turned back to Jose. "So do you have to do it clothed? That would put a damper on my pecker." Even though he was talking to Jose he kept his focus on Mercedes.

She couldn't control her blush, but she wasn't going to retreat. She groped desperately for something to say that would prove Mihalis wasn't intimidating or embarrassing her. Her mind remained stubbornly blank.

"Ah, the mystery of what's beneath a nun's habit," Arturo said lightly and tried to change the subject. "So,

Princess, what have you planned—"

"*Concha,*" Mihalis interrupted. "They're no different than any other woman."

"You are such a stellar example of manhood, Mihalis. A real poster child for the FFH," Mercedes said, outraged at his use of the vulgar term for a woman's private parts.

Her cousin stood and bowed. "Why thank you, Mercedes, and may I say, so are you. Manhood, I mean."

The words cut, allowing all her insecurities over her height, her hawk nose, and her very lush figure to rise up and shake her. She turned away and headed blindly for the buffet. A gloved hand caught her elbow. It was Boho. He held her dance card in his free hand.

"You look upset. What happened?" Concern edged his words.

"Nothing. It's... I shouldn't have worn this dress, it's..."

"What? Beautiful? Like you."

"I'm not. Not like Estella or Julieta; she's growing up to be—"

"A porcelain doll. You're a woman, Mercedes. A beautiful one."

She sniffed and Boho produced a handkerchief. "Thank you. I have one, but it's with my clutch." She dabbed at her nose and returned it. She lifted the dance card from his hand, and with the tiny mother-of-pearl pen that hung from her wrist wrote in his name for the first waltz. He did the same on her card.

"Let me carry your plate for you while you select your dinner," Boho offered.

"Thank you, that would be lovely."

By lurking on the edges of the ballroom Tracy had made a surreptitious video capturing the dancers and the music, the lights drawing flashes of fire from the jewels adorning the women's necks, hair, arms and fingers. The swirl of their skirts created a kaleidoscope of color.

Hugo twirled past with a diminutive girl dressed in an iridescent sari. His dancing wasn't as polished as the scions of the more established families, but he clearly knew how to dance. Tracy spotted Mark dancing as well, and that sense of being the lonely outsider crashed down on him. He looked away from the dancers toward the wall lined by delicate chairs. A number of them were occupied by the less attractive young women. Several of them noticed his gaze, and straightened and smiled hopefully. A solicitous matron, who prowled the line of chairs like a guard dog, bustled toward him. When he had returned to the ballroom to watch Mercedes' entrance another bossy matron had made certain he had a dance card and one of the tiny souvenir pens, but he had jammed both deep into a pocket and slipped away before she could lead him over to some unclaimed lady.

He did the same now, beating a hasty retreat out onto the balcony. He comforted himself with the thought that a girl was better off as a wallflower than suffering his awkward attempts to dance.

Outside the smell of flowers replaced the scents of perfume and aftershave and the less obvious smell of sweat. He keyed his ScoopRing and sent the video to his father. Leaning on the balustrade Tracy wondered how many more of these events he would be forced to attend. Probably not many. There would probably be some kind of hoopla for graduation, but that was almost three years away. If he could just get through tonight without embarrassing himself he could stay well away from the FFH for the remaining days of his leave.

17

AFFAIRS OF HONOR

The pressure of Clark Kunst's hand in the small of her back wasn't as steady and comforting as Boho's had been. Maybe because Mercedes was eye to eye with the marqués and that made them awkward? Clark was a wonderful dancer and his grace as he swung into an elaborate allemande was unmatched, but Boho's height and strength had made her feel as light as dandelion fluff. Clark's fingers trailed the length of her arm, and caught her hand at just the right moment to pull her back into the circle of his arm, but she realized his focus wasn't on her. He danced to show off his own abilities. She was just a prop.

Since Clark was clearly so inattentive Mercedes decided she could respond in kind. She allowed her eyes to leave his face and scan the ballroom. Tracy was nowhere to be seen, but she couldn't imagine he would have been stupid and stiff-necked enough to avoid the event.

Yves Petek was seated on one of the chairs and watching Lord Estevan de Vaca and his husband Caballero Sasha Olsen. Sasha wore the shoulder ribbon and sash that indicated he was taking the lady's part. They looked happy. Yves looked miserable.

Boho was dancing with Cipriana and they were laughing. Mercedes felt a flare of annoyance.

Mihalis was dancing with Estella *again. I wonder when Daddy's going to put a stop to that?*

She looked to her father. He was smiling that indulgent rather vague smile that she knew meant acute boredom. The man doing the talking was gesturing frantically and smiling far too broadly. *I wonder what he wants?* Someday she would be the one forced to listen to importuning conversations at what should be a social event. What techniques would she develop to stave off rudeness or outright violence?

The music ended. The dancers dutifully applauded the orchestra, and began to drift away like unmoored ships in search of their next berth. Mercedes looked at her dance card. It was a set dance and her partner was Yves. He appeared at her side.

"Yves, I really need to go to the powder room. If you wouldn't mind…" Mercedes allowed her voice to trail away.

The hangdog look immediately left the young man's face. Mercedes couldn't help it. She giggled. "Well, you don't have to look *quite* so happy about it."

"I'm… I'm sorry, Your Highness."

"Why don't you ask Devon to dance?" she suggested, looking toward the young man who had been Yves' particular friend all through childhood.

Yves shook his head. "My father would have a stroke. They," he jerked his head toward the gay couple, "are third and fifth sons. They donate their sperm, pay the annual fine and are left the hell alone. Me..." He sighed. "I know my duty. Once I wash out I'm going to marry Selestina."

"Being the heir sort of sucks, doesn't it?" Mercedes said quietly.

"Yeah."

They went in opposite directions. Mercedes considered Yves as a potential consort. He was well born from a family that seemed to be allergic to politics. Growing up in the same circles she knew they shared many interests—music, fashion, a love of animals. He was kind and gentle. He would never offer any challenge to her right to rule. In short he was... weak, she concluded. And that wouldn't do either. She mentally scrubbed him off the list.

Mercedes found the ladies', relieved herself, retouched her lipstick and powdered away the shine on her nose. Returning to the ballroom she suddenly found the colors too bright, and the air too heavy to abide. She ducked quickly out onto the balcony, hopefully before anyone spotted her return.

And found Tracy. He was leaning on the balustrade staring out across the city toward the ocean, its waves iridescent silver beneath the moons. He was a dark silhouette against the nebula's glow.

At the sound of her footsteps he jerked erect and whirled with the air of a cornered animal. Mercedes held out a calming hand. "Relax. I'm not one of the mothers come to find you a partner."

"How did you know?"

"This isn't my first ball, you know."

"Really?" he said in an elaborately incredulous

tone. She laughed. He took a quick, jerky step toward her and held out his hand. "Look, Mercedes—Highness, I wanted to say... I wanted to apologize."

"It's all right. I should apologize too. I hadn't realized just how condescending we all sound. You must get so tired of it."

"But you were right."

"And you were right to be angry."

"Good thing we're both so right all the time," he said.

She laughed and joined him at the balustrade and they looked back to the ocean. "Not to sound like one of the matrons, but why aren't you dancing?"

"I don't really know how. Why make some poor girl suffer and make a fool of myself?"

"It's easy. Dancing."

"Oh yeah, sure."

"Really. It's just walking in time to music." She held out her hands. "Here, I'll show you."

He backed off, hands up, warding her off. "Oh, no, no, no. I'm a klutz."

"As Chief Begay would say, 'Don't douse me with horseshit and tell me it's perfume.'"

Tracy primed his mouth and said, "I'm shocked, shocked, Your Highness, at your language." But the grey eyes were dancing.

"Just quoting, and the point stands. You can't fool me. I've seen you spar, and I watched you move in the game today. If you can dribble that silly ball with your feet you can avoid stepping on mine. Now come on."

"Your wish is my command."

"And don't forget it, *amigo*," she said as she

stepped into the circle of his arms.

He did have the basics. His right hand cupped her waist, but with a butterfly's touch. He kept his left hand open as if afraid to clasp hers. She firmly closed her fingers on his hand.

The music filtered faintly through the double doors. Luckily it was a waltz and not a set dance. "Just stand for a moment and listen. Now we're going to just sway back and forth in time to the beat," Mercedes instructed. They did that for a few moments. He wasn't as tall as Boho, but she still had to look up and they seemed to just fit.

"Now you take one step forward and I take one step back and then we step to the side and turn a quarter to the right."

Tracy stumbled a bit on the third step, pulled away from her and walked away. "I'm hopeless."

"No, you're nervous and too hard on yourself. You're a singer. Don't think I haven't heard you." He looked over his shoulder. She stepped to him, and pressed her palm against his chest. "Just feel it. In your body." His hand covered hers and they stood for a moment. A pulse was beating in his throat. He smelled of citrus soap, and a male musk that was very pleasant. "Now come on. At least be brave enough to try."

They started again and after a few stiff steps he began to relax. Mercedes then added the next lesson. She leaned back against his barely supporting hand, and damn near fell. She didn't make any effort to save herself, and Tracy scrambled to catch her. He pulled her back upright and ended up clutching her against his chest. Their faces were only inches apart.

"Sorry, sorry. That was my fault."

"Yes it was. You have to allow me to give weight, lean back against your supporting hand. And you have to do it too. It's the only way to have a flowing dance. You have to trust your partner, believe they will never let you fall. It's an act of faith."

His expression was serious. "Bit of a metaphor for being a soldier, isn't it? We're going to have to trust our shipmates if it comes to a fight."

"Given some of our classmates I'm not sure if that's comforting or terrifying." Mercedes had tried to make it a joke, but she found herself thinking about Mihalis and wondering just how far she could trust him.

She shook off the uncomfortable thought and said, "Let's try again."

His fingers closed around hers; his right hand was a firm, warm and constant presence on her waist. A breeze sighed through the branches of the potted bonsai trees on the terrace. The susurration of the leaves matched the rustle of her skirts across the flagstone.

"One final thing," Mercedes said softly. "It's customary to look in your partner's eyes rather than at your feet when you dance."

He raised his eyes to hers, and the breath caught in her throat. And she realized it was also a pretty good metaphor for love.

• • •

His breath went short and heat raced through his body when their eyes met. They both lost the beat and faltered to a stop.

"I knew you'd be a quick study," she said and her voice was a bit higher than normal.

"You're a good teacher," Tracy replied and he hoped the shadow from the nearby bonsai would hide his embarrassingly obvious physical reaction.

"Are we done?" Mercedes asked when he just kept standing. He thought she sounded disappointed.

"They're… they're not playing a waltz any longer," Tracy offered.

"You could… hum."

"All right." He began humming the music that had just been playing. It wasn't too discordant with the sprightly set dance that was now playing.

"Next time I'll teach you some of those," Mercedes said with a nod toward the doors.

"I think I like this best," he said, smiling down at her. The smile curdled when her eyes filled with alarm, and she pulled her hand out of his and pushed him away. "Wha—" he began and then heard Boho's voice smooth and unctuous.

"Infanta, I was sent in search of you. Poor Reitten wondered if he'd offended when his partner failed to show up so we formed a search party."

"I… I thought with his knee," Mercedes began.

Boho jumped in. "He's not up to a waltz, but perfectly capable of 'Stars End'." He held out his arm. "May I escort you?"

"Yes, yes. I lost track of…" She looked back at Tracy and her voice trailed away.

Tracy bowed, the perfect deferential bow his father had taught him. "Thank you for the instruction, Your Highness."

"Do put it to good use, Cadet Belmanor," Mercedes said formally. "I'm sure some lady will be delighted with your skill."

She and Boho vanished through the doors. For an instant the vivacious four-four time music rang in the darkness then was muted as the door closed. Tracy returned to the balustrade, and stood in a happy haze recalling Mercedes' hand in his, the warmth of her smile, and her soft breath on his face.

There was a sudden choking pressure on his throat as he was grabbed by the back of his collar and yanked around. Boho was back, and he wasn't alone. Mihalis del Campo and Clark Kunst were with him. Boho's handsome face was twisted with fury.

"How dare you! You jumped up little *intitulado*. She's the heir to the throne. Not some shop girl for you to paw and pant over. You're going to learn your place, and I'm going to enjoy delivering the lesson."

Tracy dropped into a fighting stance. He prayed his uniform wouldn't be too badly damaged in the fight. Boho surprised him by stepping back. The fury on the handsome face turned to contempt. "This is how a gentleman fights, you filthy *intitulado*!" Boho slapped Tracy hard across the face. It stung and drew tears from his left eye. "Name your seconds."

"Are you mental?" Tracy's voice spiraled up. "You're challenging me to a *duel*?"

Boho smiled, a particularly sinister expression in the moment. "Yes, I am."

"Yeah, well, fuck off. I'm not playing your aristo games." He started to push past the bigger man.

Kunst stopped him with a hand on his chest. "A

gentleman doesn't walk away from an affair of honor."

"Yeah, well you're constantly reminding me I'm not a gentleman. So I repeat. *Fuck the hell off.*"

Mihalis looked to Boho and shrugged. "Your call, man."

Boho stalked over to Tracy. He was still smiling. "If I report that you ducked a challenge to the admiral you'll be expelled. He's rather fond of dueling. He'll assume you're a coward, and he won't tolerate that."

For an instant Tracy was ready to say, *Fine, do your worst. I never wanted to go anyway.* But then he remembered the pride his father took at seeing his son in his uniform. Alexander's joy waving The High Ground banner at the soccer game. How could he face his dad if he got expelled?

"Okay, fine."

"Mihalis, Clark, will you act for me?" Boho asked.

"Of course."

"My pleasure."

"So what the hell do I have to do?" Tracy asked.

"Find two students who will stand with you. Send them to us," Kunst explained. "We'll make all the arrangements."

"Do it fast," Boho said as he walked past. He paused, and flicked Tracy's cheek with a forefinger. "I'm so looking forward to this. Don't think I've forgotten that pin."

The doors opened, the music blared then faded. Tracy was alone. He sank down on the edge of a planter and tried to think of two people who would be part of this incredibly stupid farce. After several minutes he roused himself and went into the ballroom.

A long set dance was in progress. Mercedes was being escorted by the limping Reitten up the line while Ernesto Chapman-Owiti paced quickly up the outside of the line of men. All three reached the top of the set at the same time. Chapman-Owiti took Mercedes' free hand, and both he and Reitten bowed. She curtsied, released Reitten's hand and was escorted back down the set by Chapman-Owiti. Tracy shook off his distraction and scanned the room for a friend. Or at least an ally.

Davin Pulkkinen was presenting a glass of ice water to a pretty girl in a pink dress. They were both in the choir together, maybe— Tracy rejected that thought. Davin was one of Boho's acolytes and Kunst's friend. He'd never agree.

The music ended and Tracy spotted Mark Wilson handing off his partner to the next man. He hurried over to the other scholarship student.

"Hi, I need a favor."

"Sure. What's up?" The response was offhanded. Wilson, panting and with trickles of sweat running from his sideburns, was looking after his former partner with a rather stupid grin. "That's one of Caballero Balchin's daughters. I think I might have a chance there."

"Dream on," Tracy snapped.

Wilson glared at him. "Hey, he's just a knight and she's not the eldest. Why are you such an asshole all the time?"

"Sorry," Tracy muttered. "I'm a little distracted, okay?"

"So what did you want?"

"One of these FFH dickheads has challenged me to a duel—"

"Really? What did you *do*? Who?"

"I didn't do anything, don't sound so excited, and it was that asshole Cullen."

Wilson took a step back and held up his hands. "Oh, no. I'm not getting in the middle of *that*. I'm on the team with him, and he's going to be the Duque de Argento y Pepco. His family could have held the throne if things had gone differently. I'm not making him an enemy." Wilson spun on his heel and walked away.

"Fine! Kiss their asses. It won't make any difference. They'll still despise you," Tracy called after him. There were a few shocked and disapproving glances from several older women, and a very elderly man who pinched his lips and said, "In *my* day—"

"Yeah, whatever," Tracy groused at him, and strode away. He had his head down, and he caught someone with his shoulder as he headed toward the archway leading out of the ballroom.

"Hey, what's up. You look ready to kill somebody." It was Hugo. "You're not leaving are you?"

"Yeah, I am. I've had about as much of this FFH bullshit as I can take."

"Something happened."

"You could say that." He tried to shrug out from beneath Hugo's hand.

"Tell me."

"Why?"

"Because maybe I can help. That's what friends do."

"Yeah, well, friends like me won't add to your consequence. You better go find some fourth daughter of some low-ranking knight and schmooze."

"My consequence is so low it would take a microscope to see it," Hugo said quietly.

Finally Tracy actually looked at Hugo. There was a shadow of unhappiness in the big man's eyes, and he looked vulnerable. Tracy's earlier anger against the man faded. He jerked his head toward the archway leading to the landing and they left the ballroom.

"I take it this hasn't been a great night for you, either?"

"You could say that."

"So, what happened to you?"

"You first," Hugo countered.

"I got challenged to a duel. By Cullen."

"You'll need a second."

"Yeah, so I've been told."

"I'll do it."

Tracy leaned back against the thin silver balustrade. "Why? Why would you do that? Aren't you worried you'll piss off the high and mighty Vizconde Dorado Arco?"

"First, like I told you before—I owe you. And second, these wankers wouldn't let me invite my mom and dad to this shindig."

"Huh? He's a knight."

"Yeah, but not the right kind of knight. Dad lobbied like a mother for this title, and it doesn't mean dick. The worst part was that he took this insult like a grateful Hajin, all grinning and bowing. Said he and Mom wouldn't know how to go on at something like this, and they wouldn't want to take away from my shine."

They fell silent for a moment. "Maybe your kids

will be considered sufficiently well born," Tracy offered.

"Yeah, give it a generation to get the stink of commerce off them. So, yeah. I'll stand up with you."

"I'm told I need two."

Hugo frowned, thinking, then a slow smile bloomed. "I've got a crazy-ass idea…"

"Yeah."

"What about Sumiko?"

"She's a woman," Tracy blurted.

"You noticed." Hugo gave him a punch on the shoulder. "She's also a cadet and she's cool. She's been tutoring me in math."

Tracy frowned. "I would have helped you if you'd asked."

"Hello." Hugo smacked him on the forehead. Tracy decided this habit was getting pretty damn old. "Cute girl."

"Okay, okay, I get it." Tracy sat with the idea for a moment, and began to smile. "Oh, *Dios*, it'll piss them off so bad."

"Yeah, and won't that be fun?"

"Let's do it." Tracy clasped Hugo's hand. "Assuming she agrees."

"I'll go talk to her. You headed home?"

"Yeah, like I said, I've had about all I can take of FFH hospitality."

• • •

They had returned to the palace at four a.m., and Mercedes had been too keyed up to sleep. She had had a perverse reaction to seeing Tracy leave the ball.

Disappointed that he was leaving, pleased that he didn't dance with any other girl. Later she had seen her father and Sanjay's father in close conversation, and Julieta had danced a number of times with the young cadet. Mercedes had bitten her lip and stayed silent.

Back in her quarters Flanon, ignoring her order, had helped her out of her dress, tutted over the blisters on her toes and heels, and brushed out her hair. Mercedes shrugged into a dressing gown, a frothy creation of lace and silk, and slipped down the hall to Estella's room. Estella's maid was just leaving, carrying Estella's dress and inspecting a rip in the hem.

"I was hoping you'd come by," her sister said.

They settled in the bed and Mercedes pulled the covers up to her chin. "I'll have to leave day after tomorrow, so I'm not sure I'll find the opportunity, but could you talk to Julieta and find out how she feels about Sanjay?"

Estella put an arm around her shoulders. "This sounds like more than just curiosity."

"I can say this to you. I don't like him." She told Estella about the sparring incident.

"It sounds like Danica rather asked for it," Estella offered, settling deeper into her pillows.

"Isn't that sort of blaming the victim?"

"It was a sparring class. She should have expected to get hit."

"He lost his temper, and reacted with violence."

"Because he had been told to," Estella said placidly.

"You're missing the point. A man who can get that angry over a few taunts—it means he is really thin-skinned. It could happen over anything."

"Well, you were there, and I wasn't. Maybe I'd feel differently if I had been," her sister murmured drowsily.

Mercedes looked at her in frustration then sighed, kissed the top of Estella's head and slipped out of the bed. She returned to her room, sat in the window seat, watched the dawn nibble away at the night fog billowing in the garden, and remembered the touch of men's hands on her waist.

18

GO ALONG TO GET ALONG

Tracy was embarrassed to discover he'd slept until nearly eight. He also woke with a raging erection. He flushed because the last dream he remembered had been of Mercedes. Would that qualify as sedition? Maybe Cullen was right and he did deserve a lesson in manners. A normal person wouldn't have lustful thoughts about his future ruler.

He hoped a chill shower would tame the rude beast. It didn't entirely work and he was pulling jeans on over an aching hard-on. He eyed the bed and thought about taking care of the problem, but he was afraid where his fantasies might take him.

For a moment he considered the Candy Box. His dad had taken him to the small and oddly cozy whorehouse when he'd turned sixteen. It was a standard coming-of-age ritual for League males, and Sara, the madam who owned the establishment and who Alexander occasionally visited when his own needs became too great, had picked the perfect girl for a shy and awkward teenage boy.

Lisbet was in her mid-twenties, not overtly voluptuous, but rather freshly pretty. She had put him at ease, nurtured Tracy's erection, endured his fumbling entrance and brought him to climax. She had even given him a second orgasm because the first time he had come so fast.

Thinking about that experience had the desired result. Tracy took another shower and finished dressing. As he headed down the stairs he wondered about stopping by the brothel on this, his final day of leave. But if you went during the day a lot of the girls were involved with their kids in the nursery so selection was limited. He probably shouldn't spend the money and he knew his dad would want to have dinner together.

Tracy could hear the sound of the sewing machines busily chattering and felt guilty for sleeping in so late. He paused in the tiny kitchen, smeared peanut butter and jelly on a slice of bread, and entered the workroom.

Bajit was bent over his machine. Alexander was at another, and a small Isanjo female was busy hand stitching elaborate embroidery onto the cuffs and collar of a dress shirt. His father looked up and gave him a fond smile.

"You should have woken me up," Tracy mumbled around a mouthful of sandwich.

"You needed your rest. It was past one when you got home. And thank you for the video. Bajit, Nika and I enjoyed watching it. I made that uniform the Emperor was wearing," Alexander added. Pride should have edged the words, instead they just sounded humble.

"That's why it looked so good," Tracy said as he

gave Alexander a quick hug. He moved to the Isanjo. "Hi, I'm Tracy."

"Very pleased to meet you, young lord."

"Well hardly. Hey, how's it going, Bajit?"

"Very well, sir, and may I say how happy I am to see you here."

Tracy remembered their final conversation and flushed. It probably wouldn't do to tell the alien he had been right. Instead he swallowed the last of his makeshift breakfast and turned back to his dad.

"Maybe after I graduate and start pulling a regular pay check we can buy a couple of stitch printers."

"Thanks, but no. This," he gestured around the workroom, "is what sets us apart. Our clothing is made by hand, and our clientele wants that level of care. A machine can't approximate what we do."

"Yeah, because a machine can do it better than we can. Every stitch is identical, perfect. We make mistakes."

Alexander gave him an indulgent smile. "Haven't you been around them long enough to realize they're paying for those small imperfections? Those tiny differences prove the FFH and the financial class have the money and the time to rely on the labor of others. Our clothes speak to their status."

His father's face was shining with pride, and Tracy realized that by sewing the clothes worn by the FFH it gave him a sense that he was part of that world, however tenuous the connection might be. Now his father's deference to the ruling class made more sense to Tracy, and increased the pressure on Tracy to succeed at the academy.

"I just don't want you to have to work so hard,"

Tracy said softly, but knowing this was a battle he had lost.

"Because I'm getting so old," Alexander teased. Tracy gulped and his dad fondly ruffled his hair. "It's okay, I thought Granddad was a dinosaur too when I was your age."

Tracy could barely remember the bitter old man with the arthritis-gnarled hands. He had died only a year after their ignominious return from Reichart's World, the Hidden World where they had lost everything.

Tracy settled at the third sewing machine. "Well, while I'm here let me help you get a jump on the orders."

"Oh, no, no. You're done with tailoring now."

"You'd be surprised," Tracy muttered.

"You should relax, spend time with your friends."

I don't have any. What he said was, "I'd rather spend time with you, Dad."

• • •

Mercedes hurried down the corridor, her riding boots beating a tattoo on the stone floor. She checked inside her helmet and realized that while she'd remembered her gloves she had forgotten her spurs. She turned back toward her quarters when a prick on her finger signaled a call coming in.

Her stepmother's face appeared in the holo of her ScoopRing. "Mercedes, would you mind stopping by my rooms before you go?" Constanza asked.

"I'm already late. Can it—"

"I expect they will wait. You *are* the Infanta."

The connection was broken. Mercedes tried to

decide if Constanza had sounded mad. Then she realized it had been unshed tears making Constanza's voice so harsh. She stopped by her room for her spurs then went to the other wing of the palace where her father and his current wife had their quarters.

Mercedes tapped gently on the enamel-inlaid door. The pattern was abstract but still made her think of peacocks' tails. Constanza had done a complete remodel of the consort's chambers that had begun even before she and the Emperor were married. Mercedes couldn't really blame her. It would have been awful to have returned from her honeymoon to a suite of rooms filled with tangible reminders of her predecessor.

"Come in."

The words were barely audible. Mercedes pushed open the doors and entered the sitting room. Constanza was slumped in a sleekly modern chair. Her head was resting on her hand and she wore a heavy dressing gown even though the day was quite warm. She held a damp wadded handkerchief in her free hand.

"You needed me?" Mercedes said when there was no greeting from her stepmother. She walked toward the chair.

Constanza looked up. Her face was blotchy, her nose and eyes red and swimming with tears.

"What is it? What's happened?"

"Nothing. Yet." Her tone was doleful. "He's going to set me aside."

Mercedes pulled over an ottoman and sat down in front of her stepmother. "Why do you say that? Has he given you any indication that he's going to divorce you?"

"He put me aside last night. He escorted you."

A flash of irritation shot through Mercedes' breast. She wrestled it into submission, and said mildly, "Because he was making a point. A *political* point."

"And putting me aside would also be political. I can't lose my baby, my Carisa. I can't. She's all I've got." It emerged as a wail.

"Now that's just silly. You have Papa. You have all of us."

"You all hate me."

"I don't hate you. My sisters don't hate you. It's not like we haven't been to this dance before."

"The twins—"

"Were so small when Inez left that I doubt they have many memories of her. You're the only mother they've ever known, and they all love you and Carisa. They play together, Carisa, Delia and Dulcinea. They're sisters in every way that matters."

Constanza's lips quivered. "Do you think he'd let me keep my baby?"

No, he won't because we're pawns in the game of empire, Mercedes thought, but she didn't say it aloud. "Constanza, my father loves you. Look, he divorced Inez before the twins were a year old. He's been with you almost seven years. If he was going to try again he would have done it before now."

"You really think so?"

"Yes."

And then Mercedes wondered why he hadn't. She'd never really thought about it before. The carousel of revolving wives had come to seem normal to her, but the times between divorces had gotten progressively shorter with Constanza replacing Inez almost as soon as the twins had been born.

Mercedes looked at the woman seated across from her and once again reflected that Constanza was only six years older than herself. She had been seventeen when she had married Fernán. A mother ten months later. That thought sent a stab of regret through Mercedes. Marriage and motherhood, that had been her dream, and now it seemed destined to be only one small part of the nightmare that was her life. Yes she would marry—as a way to consolidate power. And she would have children—as a way to ensure the Arango grip on the throne. But she would also have to rule and lead and possibly fight. No woman could successfully do all those things. She would fail at one or several of those duties, and since a failure of leadership would have far worse consequences it was probably going to be as wife and mother where she would fall short.

Constanza spoke, pulling Mercedes out of her brown study. "I don't know why I never asked, but why doesn't Inez come to visit the twins?" Her stepmother frowned. "You all have visits with your mothers. Why doesn't she come?"

"That's not entirely true. Agatha only came to see Izzy and Tanis once, but that's because she's a bitch, and she's never forgiven or forgotten. But Inez died. Freak boating accident shortly after she remarried."

"Do you… love your mother?" Constanza's hand shot out and gripped Mercedes.

"Yes."

Constanza caught the minute hesitation, and gave her hand a shake. "You should love her!"

The conversation was starting to annoy and

disturb Mercedes. She had a brief thought that perhaps her stepmother was drunk or drugged. She pulled her hand free and stood up.

"Look, I do love her. I just don't know her very well, okay? Maribel married Hector Breganza and they live on a reclaimed Hidden World. You act like Daddy's a monster. It's not like he kept her away from us. She's just living a long way away, and she has her own kids… I mean new kids now."

"You have siblings and you don't even know them. That's sad and wrong!"

"I'm sure I'll cross paths with them sooner or later. I'll probably end up serving with my half-brothers. Look, Constanza, I really have to go. I think you're tired and overwrought. Why don't you lie down, rest for a while. Daddy isn't going to divorce you."

Small mournful sobs like the cooing of a sick dove filled the room. Constanza's shoulders shook. Mercedes sighed and pinched the bridge of her nose.

"I'll talk to my father, okay? I'll find out."

Constanza nodded mutely, gripped Mercedes' hand again, and pressed it to her cheek. Mercedes gently pulled free and gratefully escaped.

• • •

Tracy settled back against the cushions of the luxurious self-fly flitter that Hugo Devris had sent and watched the coast pass beneath him. After his conversation about stitch printers Tracy had a better appreciation of why the FFH tended to have chauffeurs. Yes, the self-fly vehicles were more efficient, but his conversation with his dad had given Tracy a new appreciation of exactly what constituted "privilege". A driver was another way to abundantly display it.

The day was overcast and there were only a few people walking along the beach while dogs cavorted in the sand ahead of them. Judging by the flitter's direction Hugo lived on the narrow peninsula that hung like a small appendix from the body of the coast. While the big houses on that spit of land had spectacular ocean views it was a swelteringly hot location, and frequently buffeted by storms, which was why it had become where a lot of families involved in "trade" had settled. But it definitely beat being in the city proper where the heat was worse and the views non-existent.

Hugo's call had come earlier that day. Tracy had just returned from picking up shawarma for their lunch when his ring pricked his index finger indicating an incoming call.

Subtlety wasn't the other cadet's strong suit so Hugo had almost bellowed out, "Hey, I've got some news about the du—"

"Shhhh," Tracy had hissed, desperate that his father not learn about the duel. Fortunately Alexander had his head bent over his work and headphones in his ears.

Hugo's face swimming in the holo had looked contrite. "Oh right, the *thing*. Anyway, want to come to the house tonight? Come for dinner, my folks want to meet you. Afterward I'll fill you in."

When Tracy had asked for his address Hugo had laughed. "If there's one thing we've got it's flitters. I'll send one for you."

Tracy had hated telling his dad that they wouldn't

have a final dinner together, but he knew this duel took precedence and as usual his father was thrilled he had been invited to the home of one of his well-born classmates.

So now Tracy found himself being delivered to the front steps of a big, pink stone house on the waterfront. There was a Hajin butler in livery so ostentatious and overblown that it wouldn't have been out of place in an operetta. Tracy didn't recognize it and realized that Malcomb Devris had probably had it designed once he got his knighthood.

The entryway was lined with mirrors set in gold filigree frames. The butler led Tracy through a set of double doors and into a cluttered salon. There was an enormous spider silk rug on the floor; on a large credenza a pair of leopard figurines snarled at one another. One was blue and studded with sapphires, the other white and studded with diamonds. An enormous fireplace at the far end of the room had been lit, but the air conditioning was going full blast to offset the heat of the flames. The pink marble mantel was heavily carved with clusters of grapes, vines and acorns. On the mantelpiece were white china figurines in eighteenth-century dress, their eyes tiny jewel chips in green and blue.

Caballero Malcomb Devris was sprawled in an overstuffed armchair, upholstered in pink and gold, his prodigious belly resting on his thighs. He was dressed in the trousers from a formal suit, a white silk shirt, and a crimson smoking jacket. Tracy assumed this was to convey this was just a casual family dinner.

And there was a lot of family. Hugo stood behind

a long sofa that held a plump, pleasant-faced older woman with the same wide-set round eyes as Hugo's. Clearly Hugo's mother. There were four girls on the sofa with her, ranging in age from the early teens to late twenties. The women were all dressed as if they were going to court.

Sprawled on the floor in front of the fireplace and playing a game on a shared tap-pad were three young boys who hadn't yet entered the gawky teen years.

Sumiko, dressed in an exquisite pale yellow kimono, was seated on an ottoman near Malcomb. The Flitter King heaved himself to his feet, and crossed to Tracy, hand extended.

"Welcome, welcome, Tracy. You don't mind if I call you Tracy? Glad you could join us for potluck. Just a little family dinner. Hugo tells us you're destined for great things."

"Hugo is too kind," Tracy murmured as his hand was enfolded in Malcomb's large paw.

"Let me introduce you. My wife, Pearl. *Lady* Pearl now. My daughters, Opal, Ruby, Topaz and Citrine. You can see a trend here, right? I figured a jewel would only birth more jewels." He beamed at his wife, she beamed back, and Tracy realized it was absolutely sincere. "My boys, Stefan, Rafe and Brandon. Of course you know Lady Sumiko Tsukuda."

Sumiko stood and walked over to Tracy with her usual flatfooted, determined gait. Placing a hand on his shoulder she stood on tiptoes and gave him a kiss on the cheek. That took him aback, but he hoped he covered his surprise.

"Good to see you. You played very well on

Tuesday. I don't think we could have scored without your passing skills," she said.

"Thanks. I was surprised to get to play."

Hugo spoke up. "I think you ought to play more. I told old Whinnie that."

"Well, thanks."

Malcomb waved him into a chair. "So, how are you spending your leave? Getting into trouble?"

Tracy shot a glance at Hugo who looked like he'd been stuffed, and at Sumiko who turned a snorted chuckle into a cough. "Uh, no, I've been helping my dad."

"Good for you! Hugo's been helping me down at the dealership. That's what our kind of people do. The FFH, they play with numbers and war; they need an infusion of good old middle-class blood now and then."

Pearl gave a small throat clearing and glanced at Sumiko. Malcomb rolled an eye toward the girl and added hastily, "Not that we aren't grateful. They keep the monsters at bay, and we're damn happy to be one of their number now."

"I completely understand, Caballero Malcomb, my father's a caballero as well."

"But you're one of the Infanta's ladies-in-waiting," Topaz blurted.

"School chum," Sumiko said. "All of the others are much higher born."

Lady Pearl looked at her husband. "I told you we needed to transfer the kids into private school."

"You're right, as always, my love. But back to the point. As soon as Hugo is done with this... his schooling." Tracy had the strong sense the man had been about to say "nonsense". "He'll be joining me.

We're about to open new dealerships on Nueva Terra and on Reichart's World. Nice place and the economy there is starting to really take off."

"We lived there briefly. My grandfather applied for a transfer license of a textile mill and showroom." Tracy hadn't meant to say anything, but hearing the name of the planet when he'd just been thinking about it pulled out the words.

"Didn't get it? I hear those lotteries can be rigged," Malcomb said.

"No, we got it. All the rigging seems to be at the other end. My dad doesn't talk about it much, but it seems there was this baron who had had his eye on the same business. Suddenly there were fees and permits that they weren't aware of. When we couldn't pay"— Tracy shrugged—"my family ended up with a lot of debts and unpaid taxes. My dad finally got them all paid off a couple of years ago."

"Huh, and my class wonders why we're resented," Sumiko said in her laconic way.

Thankfully the Hajin butler arrived to announce dinner.

Dinner was loud, long, gluttony-inducing and surprisingly fun. None of the Devris children were shy. Tracy found himself receiving several speculative looks from the two middle girls. After dinner there was a loud Trivial Pursuit game, and then the parents went upstairs to put the youngest members of the family to bed.

Hugo hustled Tracy and Sumiko into a room that held cabinets filled with Malcomb's die-cast model car collection.

"So, it's all been arranged," Hugo said quietly.

"We got it postponed until the second Saturday after we're back at school. At seven a.m."

"I'd rather have gotten this over with," Tracy objected.

"You get cut on the station you get medical care at the school's expense. You get hurt down here—you pay. Or rather your dad does," Sumiko said bluntly.

"Oh. Good point." Tracy swallowed hard. "So it's going to be swords?"

"Sabers," Sumiko corrected.

"Whatever you call them it's still nuts. Why can't we use a gun? I might have a chance then."

"Because there are strict rules about dueling. You can't blast away at somebody with a gun," Hugo said. "Too much chance somebody will get killed."

"But it's okay if I get skewered?"

"If Boho kills you he'll be expelled. He won't risk that," Sumiko answered.

"If he kills me isn't it murder?"

Sumiko looked at him like he was an idiot. "Not if it's an affair of honor. But it is frowned on. Shows a lack of control."

"Well, that's certainly comforting."

"Have you ever used a saber?" she asked.

"No. I've never even *held* a sword… saber. It's the twenty-fifth century for Christ's sake."

Hugo and Sumiko exchanged glances. "Can we get him some instruction?" Hugo asked.

"Maybe." She frowned and tugged at her upper lip. "Talion is very good."

Tracy's first impulse was to utter a loud, profane and very firm rejection of the idea, but he wrestled the words back behind his teeth and tried to stop thinking like a commoner. How would one of his better-born classmates react? They'd accept instruction even from the psychopath. And truthfully he was going to end up likely serving with the man so he'd better learn to go along to get along. He hated himself, but he also knew the large meal he'd just consumed wasn't sitting all that well because he was scared.

Tracy knew he was going to lose, but he didn't want to be utterly humiliated. He'd accept the help. He thought again about Mercedes and her previously unwelcome advice. He wasn't sure if he was being wise. Or selling out.

19

EFFICIENT WAYS TO KILL

Mercedes raced through the door into the biology lab, and stumbled to a stop. There was a cadaver lying on every table. She had known that dissection was going to start in the second quarter and she'd been dreading it. She was squeamish. She knew it and knew her limits. She had been steeling herself to face an oyster, even a frog. She knew if she had to face anything bigger that looked the least bit pet-like she'd remember her beloved Pekinese Ty Sun and be a big sobby, slobbery mess.

But the cadaver that lay on her table wasn't a pig or even a dog. It was an Isanjo. On a neighboring table was a Hajin, its lower legs cocked at impossible angles, the mouth at the end of its muzzle lolling open. On another table a Sidone was on its back, its ten legs tight against its bulbous body. Apparently when the spider-like creatures died their limbs spasmed into grotesque coils.

Her breakfast rose up, damming her throat with burning bile. A trashcan was thrust into her hands, and her long braid pulled out of the way. Mercedes made use of it. Now the smell of vomit joined the scent of formaldehyde. Unfortunately the stink set off a chain reaction among other squeamish students. Yves was doubled over barfing, as were Cipriana and Danica. Even Arturo was losing his breakfast.

Tracy took the trashcan out of her hands. Of course it had been he who had spotted her distress, she thought. He carried it over to the long, deep sink and washed out the vomit, but he never met her eyes and he didn't return to her side.

Before she had time to wonder about it Commander Michael Westfield strode into the room, paused and glanced from vomit splatter to retching student, his head nodding and lips moving soundlessly.

"Five upchucks. Not too bad. One year we had eleven. That was our high-water mark. Made for a very unpleasant session let me tell you. I still rather think it was something they ate at breakfast—normally our young gentlemen aren't so squeamish." Mercedes thought he glanced toward the women and her face went hot with embarrassment. Westfield keyed his ScoopRing. "Please send staff to clean the biology lab."

A few moments later janitors arrived and quickly mopped up the vomit. Mercedes noticed that the aliens kept their eyes averted from their dead brethren on the tables.

"Okay, you're all going to work on your individual cadavers, but at certain points I'll have you rotate around the room so you can take a look at all the bodies."

As the professor walked past he keyed the readers on each table to bring up holos of the text and instructions on how to dissect each of the alien bodies. Ernesto's hand shot into the air. "Yes, Cadet Chapman-Owiti?"

"There's no Tiponi Flute."

"Quite right. Because their physiology is so unique and their vital organs and brain so evenly distributed throughout their bodies the only efficient way to kill them is by incinerating them."

"Wouldn't that apply to any of these," Tracy said with a gesture toward the tables. His tone was flat and cold.

"Very true, Cadet."

"Then why are we doing this?" Boho asked. "Why not stand off in orbit and light them all on fire?" Danica gave a small moan.

"Because there might be things we want to preserve on that planet or on an enemy ship. And more importantly because war isn't just wholesale slaughter. War is the application of controlled violence. If you make people think you're just murderous thugs they'll be less likely to surrender. Desperation will make them fight all the harder and as a result we'd take a shit load more casualties on our side. So, since occasionally we navy boys might have to engage in personal combat we want you to know how to kill these things. And since these are aliens, injuries that would kill us humans outright might not kill them, or at least kill them quickly enough to keep *you* alive. So let's get started."

Mercedes balked and indicated the holo of Isanjo anatomy. "It's right there. Why do we need to actually cut open a body?"

"Sooner or later, Cadet Princess, you are going to have to get your hands dirty," was the comfortless non-answer from Westfield.

Ernesto strolled over to her. "Allow me to help you, Highness."

Mercedes found herself studying the way his gold stud earring gleamed against his ebony-dark skin. She knew his family were well enough connected to be given rulership over a pacified Hidden World that was on the bare edge of habitable and lacking in resources, which made it clear they were not in the first ranks. Still he was clearly brilliant. At the end of the first quarter he was the top student in their class. She mentally added him to her list of potential consorts then wondered if that was mere gratitude?

He led her over to the table, saying softly, "The key is don't look at its face. Just focus on the viscera. It's just meat now."

He placed his hands under the printer, spreading his long, graceful fingers wide. Sterile gloves were applied to his hands. Mercedes followed suit, feeling the cold, wet touch of the latex before it dried to a flexible consistency. Ernesto positioned himself so she couldn't see the slack features of the Isanjo. He picked up a scalpel and cut through the fur and skin, then pulled it aside. The muscles in the abdomen were pink and gleaming. Mercedes swayed and clutched the edge of the table.

Chapman-Owiti placed the scalpel in her hands, and showed her how to part the muscle tissue. The bones of the ribcage appeared. The room seemed suddenly very hot and her head was reeling. "I'm going to faint," she whispered.

Ernesto turned her away from the table, went to a dispenser and got her a cup of water. It helped though her stomach tried to rebel. "Let me show you something interesting." He forced her to face the table again. "Note the lungs. You can see them through the ribcage, but look, here's the interesting thing." He slipped a hand beneath the intestines and pulled them gently aside. "There at the base of the spine."

Mercedes was shaking, but forced herself to look. There was another small set of pink/grey objects on either side of the spine.

"What do you think those are?" Ernesto asked. She shook her head, unable to think beyond her horror and disgust. "Look at the lungs again."

She obeyed and finally it penetrated. "They look the same. Like little lungs."

"Yes, they have two sets. They oxygenate their blood much more efficiently than we do. They're faster and more agile than we are, and they have five appendages that they can use."

"Hands, feet and tail," Mercedes said, mostly to prove that she wasn't completely brain-locked.

"Exactly, and because of that we're going to see differences in the brain structure as well."

Do we have to? was her plaintive thought, but what Mercedes found herself saying was, "That means they could have up to four guns—"

"And a laser blade held by their tail."

"How ever did we beat them?" she asked.

Boho, walking past, leaned in, winked and said, "We're much meaner."

Westfield came by, and he and Ernesto began a rather opaque conversation about dendrites. The professor then called for them to move to a different table and inspect the next butchered horror.

Ernesto actually took her arm and guided her over to the Hajin, its belly now laid open, and the top of its skull removed. Mercedes suddenly saw Flanon or Tako's features on the long face of the creature and turned away.

"The thing about Hajin is they have a complex nervous system. You've heard about how a headless chicken can still keep running?" Ernesto said. "Well Hajin are like that too. Their bodies have been known to stay upright and move even with the brain destroyed."

"Surely they can't fight like that?"

"No, but they can slam into you and maybe knock you down. The males are big, bigger than humans, and mass a lot more weight."

"But our soldiers are in armor so just getting knocked down—"

"Quite right that the knockdown isn't all that serious, but while you're down another enemy soldier might be able to shoot you."

Mercedes studied the man's sharply planed face, noted the genuine excitement and enjoyment as he discussed these finer points of alien physiology.

"You really love this," she said.

"I do. I want to focus on xeno biology. Of course I can only do so much because of the genetic laws, but what I'd give to study with the Cara'ot…" He forestalled the objection he saw rising to her lips. "Of course I know that can never happen and I accept it, but it just seems a shame. They know so much about genetic engineering and nano tech." He shook his head. "I wonder if it wouldn't be smarter to delve into their secrets. By blinkering ourselves we might be unable to see a Cara'ot threat heading our way."

They moved on to the Sidone corpse. Ernesto grinned at her. "So, you seem to be doing better with this."

"It's a giant bug. It's harder to be emotional," Mercedes replied. "And I've been served by Hajin and Isanjo my entire life." She wasn't exactly sure what she meant with the final sentence. That they seemed more real to her? That she would find it hard to kill one? Which raised a new question.

"I wonder where they get the bodies—"

Westfield's voice came from behind her. "Morgues and executed prisoners. No, Cadet Princess, we didn't go out and just randomly kill some aliens."

"We formally declare war for that," Arturo quipped. He seemed to have recovered his equilibrium, and was busily slicing into the Sidone.

Was it only her discomfort with this entire exercise that had her thinking he seemed gleeful?

"There hasn't been a real war for over two hundred years," Mercedes said. "I intend to keep it that way."

"And we hope you succeed in that goal, Cadet Princess," Westfield said.

"War is terrible for the economy," Arturo said. "So I second."

"It's also not terribly healthy for children and other living things," Westfield added dryly.

There was something in his delivery that made Mercedes think it might be a quote. One she decided she wanted to find and maybe pin on her wall.

• • •

Tracy found that his O-Trell ID did not give him access to ship's logs or the actual locations of those ships when they weren't docked. It also didn't give him access to the command centers for *Estrella Avanzada* Epsilon on the edge of sector 470. But it did give him access to manifests, requisition orders and maintenance logs for the star base, which was what he really wanted and needed based on his cryptic conversation with Rohan Aubrey, the Conde de Vargas.

He was glad to have this new task because it kept him from thinking about how he had failed Mercedes in biology. Sure he'd brought her the trashcan, but it was Ernesto who had been of real help to her. Why hadn't he offered to help? Had he taken Cullen's contempt to heart? Had the duque's son's threats truly cowed him, and made him scared to talk with Mercedes even in a school setting?

Thinking about Cullen made Tracy think about the duel, and the hollow feeling hit his gut again. A hard shake of the head did little to dislodge the fear and the regret.

Concentrate, he ordered his troubled and rebellious mind. He once again bent to his task.

The Epsilon outpost was the League's most distant base—out on the Scutum-Centaurus arm. The *Avanzada* was almost the width of the galaxy away from Ouranos, which orbited a sun in the Perseus arm. After an hour and a half an interesting pattern emerged. Ships that were listed in repair manifests would suddenly never be mentioned again. On requisition orders parts were designated for repairs on specific ships. Those orders also stopped when the ships stopped being listed in the garage.

Five ships, small, fast, lightly armed *explorador* ships carrying a complement of two hundred and twenty-five men, had vanished from the records. They were the *Mercury*, the *Ave Rapaz*, the *Challenger*, the *Restive* and the *Desafiante*. The first stopped being mentioned three years before. The most recent, the *Ave Rapaz*, vanished from the records back in May.

Curious now, Tracy looked to see if the scout ships had been repaired in any garage at the other twenty-three *Avanzadas*. They hadn't. He tried shipyards in orbit around various League worlds. Nothing. He even tried the third-rate facilities in orbit around Earth, that sad overheated and storm-racked planet where only a few End of Timers and hopeless romantics still chose to live. No mention of the ships. A dull ache settled in Tracy's temples.

So the physical ships had seemingly vanished. What about the humans who crewed them? Pay manifests proved to be impossible to access. Tracy leaned back in his chair and rubbed his chin, his hand rasping on stubble, and contemplated how to get the information. An idea occurred to him and he leaned back over his tap-pad. The League might not allow a junior (almost) officer to access actual coordinates of the myriad ships in the fleet, but security wasn't all that tight in other areas.

He checked sales receipts at the various bars, restaurants, shops and brothels on Epsilon when a ship docked and calculated the resulting increase in revenue correlated to the number of crew that would have been assigned to that ship, and that information also gave him the rotation schedule of the ships returning for resupply. He could trace the drop in revenue when any of the five ships stopped returning. Which meant their crew hadn't been reassigned to the outpost.

The data seemed to indicate that five ships and their crews had simply vanished. If that had happened why had there been no press? Usually if a League ship was lost it was front-page news. Tracy leaned back in his chair and rubbed the top of his head as if trying to push out the headache that gripped him. Maybe he had just missed the coverage. Prior to his graduation Tracy had paid little to no attention to fleet news. Tension quivered along his nerves as he bent over his tap-pad and searched the news sites. He hadn't missed anything because there was nothing. Over a thousand men had disappeared and there had been no outcry from anyone. Apparently not even their families.

Just how far would the conde wish him to go? Cowardice and curiosity warred for primacy. Curiosity won. He had managed to access names on credit spike accounts at various bars on Epsilon. He picked the name of a low level enlisted *estrella hombre*, and located his planetside address on Kronos. Discovered he was married with six kids. He created an email address that looked like it might come from the bank, and sent a query to Señora Patricia Denning regarding her husband's pay. It would take a while for the message to bounce through the Foldstream and reach her, and some time for her answer to return.

Tracy set aside the puzzle of the five missing *exploradors*, and turned to his homework assignments. The door chime sounded. It was Hugo and Sumiko.

"Come on," the man said, "Jasper says he's got

time for you now and the Sabers studio is empty."

"Let me change," Tracy said. He grabbed his gym clothes, and went into the bathroom. "I hope he's bringing swords," Tracy grumbled as he rejoined them.

"I think you can take that as a given," Sumiko said. "He strikes me as a man who has a lot of swords in his collection." Hugo made a snorting sound. Tracy tried really hard to control his features and bet that he looked like a stuffed dummy. "What?" She thought for a moment, then rolled her eyes. "Oh God, you just made something dirty out of that, didn't you? Of course you did. Boys!" She spun on her heel and marched out the door.

20

THE STRONGEST PART OF THE BLADE

The Sabers fencing society had a gym just for their own use. Apparently the Black Feathers had one as well. The High Ground took its dueling seriously, Tracy thought as he looked at Jasper standing cool and elegant in his fencing gear, a mask under one arm, saber hanging negligently from his good hand. His broken arm was in a sling, a slash of black against his padded jacket. He wore tight white breeches, white socks, and soft white shoes.

"Get a jacket and mask from the rack."

Tracy did as he was told. "Do I get to wear this padded thing when I fight Cullen?" he asked as he pressed the velcro on the jacket closed.

"Of course not. Shirt sleeves," was Talion's impatient reply. "And you won't wear the mask either."

Seeing the world through the mesh of the mask was disorienting. Tracy tried to focus as Talion held out a sword. "This is a saber. Be careful, the edge is sharp," he warned as Tracy reached for the weapon.

"All the better to cut you with," Tracy muttered.

"Exactly," was the comfortless reply. "We don't use

épées for affairs of honor. They're a stabbing weapon and there's too great a chance of death. The saber is a slashing weapon."

"How else do you get a sexy scar," Sumiko said in her acerbic way. Talion gave her a sharp look. Hugo chuckled and stared at her fondly.

Well that's interesting, Tracy thought, then jumped a bit when Talion hit him on the shoulder with the flat of the blade.

"Pay attention."

"Sorry. I just can't believe…"

"Well, it is happening so deal with it," Talion said.

Tracy inspected the sword—*saber*, he corrected himself. It was far simpler than he'd expected given what he knew of the FFH. He had expected an embossed and jewel-laden hilt. Instead the guard was a simple round bowl of metal covered with crimson enamel, shielding an austere metal handle. Talion took hold of his saber, and demonstrated the proper grip. Tracy followed suit and realized the enamel bell protected his hand quite well. He peered down the length of the blade, and bounced the thing experimentally in his hand. He guessed it weighed around five hundred grams and was perhaps one hundred and five centimeters long. He had a feeling the weight wouldn't feel all that negligible after a few minutes of trying to wave the damn thing around.

"The only really usable portion of the blade in terms of inflicting damage is the first thirty-three centimeters—from the point to about a third of the way down the blade. You can parry closer to the hilt—it's the strongest part of the blade, and best suited to take the stress from a blow. The main thing you have to remember is don't get your feet tangled. You do that, and it's over. I don't have time to teach you how to actually fence. I'm going to do my best to teach you how to defend yourself. It will work for a while, and might make Boho decide to just take the cut and get this thing over with. He won't want to look like a fool by taking too long to draw first blood."

"What happens if *I* draw first blood?" Tracy asked.

"Then you win, but that won't happen," Talion said bluntly. "You're limited to the torso, the arms and the head. Legs are off limits so don't go flailing away and accidentally hit him there. If you were to do that you'd get a beat down."

"Because cutting me with an archaic weapon isn't punishment enough," Tracy muttered.

"Okay, the first thing that will happen is the seconds will inspect the blades to make sure no one is cheating by bringing in a longer or heavier weapon. Then the salute." Talion demonstrated. He had been holding the saber at an angle pointed at the floor. He snapped it up to a vertical position, the blade in front of his face, and swept it down again. "After that you will return to the resting position until the handkerchief is dropped and Mihalis as the highest born will give the command to begin. He'll say *allez*."

Sumiko giggled. It wasn't something anyone expected and they all looked at her. "Sorry, I just think it's hysterical that you boys have established all this elaborate ritual to wrap around a basic desire to just whale on each other."

Talion looked offended. Hugo and Tracy exchanged

a meaningful glance, and Hugo patted Sumiko on the shoulder. "You're probably right, but that doesn't change the fact Tracy is about to get a whuppin'—"

"So we ought to get back to it," the baron said sharply.

"Doesn't Boho have to ask if Tracy will apologize?" Hugo asked. "I've been reading up on this," he explained in answer to Sumiko and Talion's surprised glances.

Tracy didn't care and wasn't impressed at Hugo's diligence. He burst out, "Fuck no I won't apologize. He hit *me*."

Talion ignored his outburst and looked at his seconds. "He won't in this case, because it's Boho's contention that Belmanor insulted a lady, and no apology is ever acceptable for that."

"Good, because I'm not going to apologize," Tracy said again. He almost added, *She asked me to dance*, but bit back the words deciding that such information getting out wouldn't be good for Mercedes.

"All right then. Keep your weight evenly balanced on both feet and watch my eyes and the end of my blade. We'll go slow to start."

Talion's blade wove back and forth. Tracy managed to catch about half of the hits, and he felt the shudder down the blade and into his arm. As he anticipated, about five minutes in the saber became a dragging weight, and his muscles began to cramp. He also knew that Talion was moving very slowly.

They took a brief break then started again, and this time the pace of the blows increased and Talion advanced on him with quick sliding steps. Tracy tried to hold in place, but was knocked to the ground. Talion reached down and pulled Tracy back to his feet.

"When I advance you have to retreat. Keep me at sword's length. That's when you have to be careful and not trip yourself."

"Isn't there like lunging and stuff?" Tracy asked, and he demonstrated, imitating what he had seen in movies and SimGames.

"Try it," Talion said as he took up the en garde position again.

Tracy awkwardly swung the blade trying to imitate Talion's smooth movements. He then tried lunging toward Talion's chest. Talion jumped back while at the same time sweeping Tracy's blade aside. It knocked Tracy off balance and he stumbled forward when he failed to meet the expected resistance. At the same time Talion made a quick reversal, lunged and slashed Tracy across the chest. He heard and felt the grate of the blade on the mesh that covered his padded jacket. Tracy staggered back and regained his balance. He had a pretty clear and sickening idea just what that cut would have done if he hadn't been wearing protective gear.

"And that's why you're not going to try and be aggressive and take the fight to him. You're going to retreat and retreat and retreat and defend yourself for as long as you can. It would be bad if he cuts you in the first seconds of the fight. If he does don't tell anyone I coached you."

"Yeah, it'd be a shame if I damaged *your* reputation," Tracy muttered ironically.

"Oh, you couldn't do that. They know I'm the best, but some of the Saber members might make jokes and then I'd have to school them. It could cause bad feelings in the society. Let's go again. We have four more nights to practice. Let's not waste them."

"We have soccer practice and I have choir on Tuesday."

"We'll work after."

"Homework," Sumiko reminded.

Talion shrugged. "This is more important."

"Boys," Sumiko said explosively and left the room.

• • •

Hot water pounded onto his head, and drew hisses of pain when it struck the bruises that stippled his chest, back, side and arms, making Tracy look like a pinto Hajin. Talion hadn't been gentle. Even with the protective mesh Talion had mostly just used the flat of his blade to drive home the lesson. Occasionally he would use the edge, and the searing scrape of metal on metal put Tracy's teeth on edge. He couldn't help but contemplate how that blade was going to feel against his flesh.

Snapping off the water he tottered out of the shower and wrapped a towel around his waist. Tracy had thought the training he did each morning had him in top condition, but fencing used a whole different set of leg muscles and his thighs were aching. He gave an experimental rotation of his right shoulder. Yep, that hurt too from the weight of the saber.

He opened the door of the bathroom and gave a yell when he found himself eye to eye with Donnel. "Jesus, don't sneak up on me like that!"

"Pardon, sir." The alien was holding a bottle in one hand and a jar in another.

"What are you doing here?"

"I thought you might require treatment after your training session."

"I'm not even going to ask how you knew." Tracy sighed and sat down on the edge of his bed. "What's in the jars?"

"Tiger balm, and a particular lotion that we Cara'ot find soothing. I'm pretty decent at massage too."

"No, that's creepy." Tracy went to stand, and felt his back catch. Even the brief time sitting had allowed his muscles to stiffen. He dropped back down onto the mattress with a groan.

"Have it your way. Should make physical training tomorrow morning just a lot of fun."

"Okay, damn you," Tracy said before the alien reached the door.

Tracy managed to roll face down on the bed and Donnel went to work on his back and legs. The alien wasn't kidding; those four hands worked at cramped muscles, and the lotion was soothing to his dark purple bruises. After a few minutes Tracy said quietly, "I'm going to get cut on Saturday."

"Yes, sir."

"It's going to hurt."

"Yes, sir."

"I'm scared," he said softly.

"And that's okay too, sir."

Thirty minutes later Donnel stepped back. Tracy sat up and ran a hand through his hair. "Thanks, that helped."

"My pleasure, sir."

"I gotta get started on my homework. Bring me a coffee. I think it's going to be a long night."

"Very good, sir."

Donnel whisked himself out the door. Tracy dropped his towel and changed into sweat pants and a T-shirt. The tiger balm was warm on his skin and his muscles felt like soft gel. He sat down at his desk, opened his tap-pad and found an email from Señora Denning. She reported that the automatic deposit of her husband's pay vouchers were coming through just fine.

The cracking tension gripped Tracy's body, undoing all the good Donnel's massage had done, and a pounding started in his temples. There were only two explanations—either *Orden de la Estrella* had sent the five ships on long secret missions. Or the five ships and all aboard them had been lost and the League didn't want the broader public or even their families to know.

And apparently the conde suspected that he was also being kept in the dark. Now Tracy just had to figure out how the tailor's son was going to contact the man whom some had called the Emperor's right hand and let him know.

21

WINGS & PRAYERS

The armor wasn't custom fitted and Mercedes found her breasts being squashed painfully against her chest. They were all exchanging glances, but Sumiko, the most endowed of all of them, described it succinctly: "Like having a never-ending mammogram."

The armor was carbon polymer with dura-steel edging. Servomotors at the joints made it relatively easy to move, but Mercedes wouldn't have wanted to try and dance in it. They clanked out of the changing room, helmets beneath their arms, and into the ready room where the rest of their class was assembling. This was their first meeting with the *Infierno* instructor. Apparently the man was so good that the academy sent him out to give refresher courses to the fleet during the first quarter.

The man turned at the ladies' entrance, and Danica and Cipriana actually gasped. The pilot looked to be in his mid-thirties with velvet brown eyes, black hair and a spade beard and mustache.

Cipriana leaned in to Mercedes. "He looks like he

should be riding an Arabian stallion across the Sahara on old Earth," she whispered.

"I am Captain Baron Tarek El-Ghazzawy. Now if you'll follow me into the shuttle bay we'll get started."

The two bulky shuttles had been moved. Instead the cavernous space held seven *Infierno* fighters. In a corner was another multi-crew fighter, the Talon. It looked far more like a craft of war—needle-nosed, sleek swept-back wings. Parked it looked like it was going a thousand miles an hour. In contrast the *Infiernos* were small saucers about twenty feet across with the cockpit dead center. The domes were open on all of them.

El-Ghazzawy led them to the nearest fighter. Some of the boys looked longingly back at the Talon. El-Ghazzawy didn't miss it. "Yes, it looks cooler and it had its uses to deliver strike teams, but we can use shuttles to deliver troops and cover them with this darling." He rested a hand on the curving side of an *Infierno* with the same pride and affection a man would show his favorite dog or horse. "The Talon can't match the punch of one of these. We still have a few Talons operational, but they are being phased out and sold as surplus.

"Note the weapon ports that line the rim of the *Infierno*. It carries a combination of missiles and slug weapons."

Off to her left Mercedes heard several of the men having a whispered conversation.

"I took out seventeen Cara'ot fighters in one go," Davin said.

"Still not enough for the Ace achievement," Kunst replied, his tone scornful. "You need twenty for that. I got it."

El-Ghazzawy must have had very good hearing in

addition to being telepathic because he turned toward the clump of boys, smiled and said, "Hanging out in your living room in a SimBubble is way different than when you're pulling gees, trying to read all your screens, and sometimes just using your eyes… you get mentally overloaded. And add to that that somebody is actually trying to shoot your ass out of space and you can't just reload the game if you die. But out of curiosity—how many of you have played *Star Fighter*?"

All the men raised their hands, even Yves. Mercedes was a bit disappointed to see Tracy among them, but then thought, *Well boys will be boys.* Sumiko started to raise her hand, then pulled it down. El-Ghazzawy caught the movement.

"Cadet Lady, is that an I-sort-of-played gesture?"

"I snuck in and used my brother's SimDeck. I wasn't supposed to, and I only did it once so I'm not sure that counts."

"Probably not," Sanjay said with a laugh. "You probably barely figured out the controls."

"True that," Sumiko said.

"Well, this will be an interesting experiment then," El-Ghazzawy said. "Will familiarity with the game be a help? I think this is shaping up to be an interesting experiment and possibly a battle of the sexes."

"No contest," came a voice from back in the crowd. Mercedes wasn't sure who'd said it.

"Don't be so certain." It was Ernesto. "Studies by the US Air Force back on old Earth indicated that women can pull more gee forces than men and have quicker reflexes."

"Then it sounds like we should have been using

them before now," Yves said.

"Up until now they've had a different role," was El-Ghazzawy's noncommittal reply. Mercedes couldn't get a read from his bland delivery how he really felt about it. "Okay, sort out into seven groups, and let's look at some actual cockpits."

"And what then?" Boho asked.

"On to the simulators." El-Ghazzawy reacted to the men's disappointed expression. "No, you don't get to hop in a twenty-two-million-Real fighter without some practice, and no, your gaming experience doesn't count."

Mercedes was startled when Sumiko didn't stick with them. She went off to a group that included Hugo, Davin and Arturo. Tracy walked over to where she, Cipriana and Danica stood. A few moments later Ernesto, Mark and Yves joined them. There was a moment where Mercedes felt like she had drawn the dregs, and how could that be because she was the Infanta? She should have the best people around her. She studied the faces around her, forced a smile and thought, *Well maybe I do*. She certainly had three of the smartest people in the class.

They moved to an *Infierno*. Its surface was polished mirror bright and it threw back their reflections oddly proportioned in the curved vehicle. The boys clambered up the arched side without any hesitation and headed toward the dome. Mercedes and her ladies exchanged glances. Mercedes shrugged and followed them up. There were two large metal loops set near the edges of the stationary central section of the *Infierno*.

"What are these for?" she asked, pointing at a loop.

"Cranes hook on there and lift the craft for reloading

armaments. The missiles and slugs are in the belly of the craft and fed into the outer belt," Tracy said.

Mercedes stared down into the tiny cockpit. The walls beneath the clear dome were matte black and she saw the tiny pinpoints for holo projection. Directly in the center was a gimbaled acceleration couch. It looked more like an entertainment center than a craft of war.

"There's no way to steer it," Danica said.

"You do it with shifts in the body; the cockpit couch can sense them and it's very sensitive. You don't need large movements," came El-Ghazzawy's voice from behind them.

Ernesto spoke up. "And eye movement as well. Right?"

El-Ghazzawy nodded, leaned down into the cockpit and lifted up a cable. "You jack into your helmet so it also becomes a sensing device." He took a helmet from Cipriana and demonstrated. She widened her eyes at him, her eyelashes fluttering like a frantic butterfly. He pretended not to notice. Or maybe he really didn't notice.

Cipriana pushed. "Is it that way in the game?" she asked.

El-Ghazzawy didn't answer. Mark did. "No, you have a controller for the game as well as your SimHelmet." Cipriana glared and Mark looked confused. Mercedes hid a smile.

El-Ghazzawy lectured them about the weaponry, how the rotation of the outer rim allowed each gun to have a cool-down period before it was brought to bear again, the maglevs that kept the spinning outer rim attached to the stationary inner structure of the craft.

How each *Infierno* carried seven hundred of the small, highly explosive missiles that had their own small rocket engines that ignited after they were thrown free of the fighter. They were very powerful, but best at close range. There were also several ports that just threw chunks of depleted uranium and iron. Those were only propelled by the speed of the *Infierno* and the spin of its outer belt.

"So they're a pray and spray sort of weapon," Tracy said.

"Exactly," El-Ghazzawy said with a smile.

"It's a little alarming to me how much of our success in battle seems to depend on that," was Tracy's dry response.

"Oh, on the big capital ships there's a lot more tactics involved. It's when the fight gets up close and personal that reflexes… and prayer come into play."

"Getting in close could be tough with such a reflective craft," Ernesto said.

"Speed and maneuvers will be your friends."

"Why not make the fighters dark? Sneak up on them?" Yves asked.

"First there's no sneaking—"

"But SEGU has dark ops ships," Ernesto objected.

"Weelll." El-Ghazzawy drew out the word. "That's more propaganda from our brethren in the intelligence service than fact. Despite what you see on the stream or in your games we don't have cloaking devices and using non-reflective materials does nothing more than add to the cost and make defense contractors happy. Space is cold. Really, really cold, as in minus 270.45 Celsius, minus 454.81 Fahrenheit cold. Passive sensors will find you. Even if you shut down the engines you still have to keep the humans inside alive so there's heat being generated, not to mention the people. Bodies are like little flares."

"What about putting the crew in cold sleep?" Yves Petek asked.

"Takes equipment to power the cold sleep capsules," Tracy said.

El-Ghazzawy nodded. "Now I suppose you could turn off every device on the ship, turn the crew into frozen, very dead and not very tasty FroPops, but having a multi-million inert chunk of metal floating through space doesn't make a lot of sense, and you can still be spotted if our enemies paint an area with lidar, radar or particle detectors. The downside to that is that the ship using those sensing devices is also giving away their position. Bottom line—we're always very aware of each other. Your only real hope is to be overlooked among all the junk that's floating in orbit around most advanced worlds because you're sure as shit going to get noticed when you arrive."

Danica raised her hand. "Why please?"

El-Ghazzawy smiled at her. Cipriana looked pissed and Mercedes gave a mental sigh. "Because you can't come out of Fold in orbit around a planet. Which means there's time to get spotted and tracked. So you run like hell for the target world and dive in among their orbital infrastructure. Hope the clutter confuses their sensors."

"And hope they aren't willing to shoot down everything in orbit to find the needle in the space junk haystack," Tracy said.

"That too," El-Ghazzawy said.

"That still doesn't explain why these are polished mirror bright," Cipriana complained.

"There was concern that the aliens might develop an effective weaponized laser. If the bastards did we wanted to send the beams right back in their faces."

"There are lasers in the game," Yves said and Mercedes thought he sounded disappointed.

El-Ghazzawy smiled. "Because they look good in a SimBubble. We've just never gotten them to the point where they were practical. It takes too much energy to power them up to a level where they can pack a punch."

He opened a panel on the outer skin of the *Infierno* and pulled out a chunk of depleted uranium. He grunted a bit with effort, and even through his coat Mercedes could see the muscles in his arms bunch. Cipriana sighed.

He heaved the piece of metal at Tracy who caught it and also grunted with the effort of holding it. "A million years of human evolution and we're back to throwing rocks at each other," Tracy said sourly.

"Sometimes the simplest tool is the best tool," El-Ghazzawy said.

Tracy passed it on to Wilson. "Huh, yeah, that would tear the shit out of something," Wilson said.

"The other great thing about the *Infierno* is it can skip across atmosphere to produce a slingshot effect, plunge into atmosphere without a lot of braking required, and it skips on water too. We took out the Hajin navy with a more primitive version of these. Why don't you all climb down and get a feel while I check on the other groups. Then we'll go to the simulators."

Out of deference to her rank Mercedes went first. The couch swung beneath her, then folded firmly around her armored body. Tracy laid down on the top of the *Infierno* and jacked her helmet into the controls. She found that by shifting her eyes the couch swung side to side, and when she looked straight down it even spun to have her facing down. She laughed delightedly. Unlike almost everything else at The High Ground maybe this was going to be fun.

• • •

Less fun. Discovering that The High Ground posted the simulator scores for the class. Not because she had done so badly. Because Mercedes had the top score. And not by a little—by a lot. The next closest scores were Boho and Jasper. Clark Kunst had the fourth highest. Then there was a large clump of people in the mid-range including Tracy. Sumiko was in that grouping. The lowest third held Cipriana, Yves and surprisingly Arturo. Dead last was Danica with a score so low that it had Mercedes saying in a hissing whisper, "Did you just go to sleep through the exercise?"

"It made me nauseous. And it's stupid anyway. We're never going to fly in those."

"And you know this how?" Mercedes demanded as they hurried toward their quarters for a quick shower before their regular classes. Despite the temperature controls in the armor Mercedes' body was drenched with sweat. She would be peeling off the skintight one-piece jumpsuit that was worn beneath the armor.

"Because this is all a big sham. Nobody wants us

here. They're doing it because your father has the power to force us down their throats, but even if they let us graduate they'll put us in groundside offices or at worst on some safe ship where the press can pretend you're a war leader. The rest of us will just quietly retire after our enlistment is over and pray it's not too late for us to find husbands, have a normal life."

The door to their shared quarters slid shut. "First, how do you know there won't be another war?" Rage made Mercedes yell. She realized some of her anger was fueled, perversely, by her extraordinarily high score. She was filled with anxiety that she would pay for it somehow and was taking it out on Danica. The knowledge didn't help her calm down and she raged on.

"As Captain Lord Xian says, 'Space is big.' We're pushing into new sectors. We may come up against new alien races and have to deal with them. Why wouldn't you want to help?"

"I can help by producing cannon fodder for these assholes," Danica shouted back. "And while they might take my sons I damn well don't want them taking my daughters too."

"Wars can come to you," Sumiko said. "Wouldn't you like to know how to protect those daughters—"

Danica burst into tears. Mercedes' anger evaporated and she hugged the small girl. "Dani, I'm sorry. What's wrong?"

"I'm so homesick," she cried. "Being home only made it worse. Having to come back up here. And I only got to see Ryan *once* and I'm sure his parents are going to find him a bride before I graduate, and… and… and…" Wracking sobs left her unable to speak.

Cipriana and Sumiko joined in the group hug. Mercedes wished she could offer soothing platitudes, but she knew Danica was probably right. Lord Ryan Casters was in his early thirties, his military service long over and past time to be married and starting a family. Mercedes wondered what a man of his age would find appealing in an eighteen-year-old girl, but maybe he was one of those men who like to baby women, or a less charitable explanation was that he wanted someone young and malleable.

Mercedes led Danica over to her bed, and pulled her down to sit next to her. "I understand this is a sacrifice and a hardship, but please, please don't abandon me. I need you. And I'm sure Ryan will wait for you," Mercedes lied. "What a coup to have married one of the first woman graduates from The High Ground. No other debutante can make *that* claim."

"I hadn't thought of that," Cipriana said. "We might have men lining up."

Danica brightened a bit. "You really need me, Mer? I'm such a bad student and not very good at all the soldier stuff."

"Yes. I need you. We all do. We're a team." The platitudes fell from her lips. Dross spun into words, but it seemed to do the trick. Danica wiped her eyes, and stood.

"We better hurry," Danica said. "Or we'll be late for class."

Sumiko sidled up to Mercedes and under cover of the pounding water in the showers said quietly, "So how did you rack up that score?"

Mercedes closed her eyes and recalled the

exhilaration, the sense of wild abandon she'd felt in that simulator. "I'm not sure. I thought of it as a living thing, a partner with me. Like my horses, where I can think and they do."

"Minute muscle movement generated by your thoughts," Sumiko mused. "That makes sense. I was trying to analyze which muscles to use. Thanks for the tip. I'll bet the boys are really pissed though."

• • •

At lunch Tracy gobbled curry and rice, and listened to the rants, complaints and conspiracy theories fly around the neighboring tables. There were even a few grumbles from his table, which he had mentally dubbed the Low-Born Scum Table.

"Had to have been rigged."

"It's clear she's just being carried."

"Skews the scores."

"Probably promised El-Ghazzawy a better title."

"Makes the rest of us look like fools."

Tracy pushed away his bowl, stood and walked past the table that had uttered the last remark. "No, you're all doing that just fine on your own," he said. He pitched his voice loud enough to be heard by most of the other tables. "And accusations like that could be considered disloyal at best. Treasonous at worst."

Sanjay, who had been most adamant in his complaints, jumped to his feet. "Are you questioning my honor, *intitulado*?"

"No, your—"

Hugo snagged Tracy under the arm. "You heard

him, he said no," Hugo called back over his shoulder to Sanjay as he dragged Tracy away. "You looking to fight another duel, *hombre*?" Hugo whispered. "Jesus, you're like a fucking mongoose, squaring up against anything and everything no matter how big."

"She beat us, Hugo. Beat all of us." The big man remained silent, and screwed up his mouth as if tasting and rejecting words. "Oh, not you too? Look!" Tracy spun Hugo around and pointed at the high table. "Look at them." The professors were gathered around Zeng, heads close, talking while frowns furrowed their brows. "They're fucking flabbergasted. They have no idea what to do with this."

"Then let them worry about it. You keep your head down and your mouth shut. Unless you want to end up with as many scars as Jasper," Hugo warned.

• • •

"So how did you do it?" Arturo demanded of Mercedes. "Let me in on the secret. My old man is always going on and on about how awesome he was as an *Infierno* jock. If he sees this score… well, I've got to get it up."

Mercedes kept her head down over her bowl and tried to blot them all out. She started eating faster, desperate to get away.

"Come on, Mercedes, we're cousins." Arturo was wheedling now.

"I didn't do anything… other than feel it. It just seemed obvious."

Arturo's usually pleasant expression twisted, and he didn't seem so handsome any longer. "Fine, have it your way, *coño*! Mihalis was right. You are out to destroy us."

It was a horrible and vile word—*coño, chatte, Fotze... cunt*. Shocked at the vulgarity Mercedes choked on a mouthful of curry and had it dribbling over her chin. Boho's six-foot-four body uncoiled, and his arm shot out across the table knocking over one of the floral arrangements. Water went cascading across the wood. Chairs scraped and people yelled as they escaped the flood. Boho's hand closed around Arturo's throat, and he thrust his face into Arturo's.

"She didn't do anything. Don't you think if there was a way to game this thing I would have found it?"

Did you try? Mercedes thought.

"It can't be done."

You did try.

"She beat us," Boho continued. Arturo's face was turning red and small choking sounds emerged from between his writhing lips. "You may be my friend, but you are also a fucking idiot being led around by the nose by your brother. He's going to end up in trouble. I thought you were too smart to follow him there."

All of this was delivered in an intense whisper. Mercedes could only be grateful that Mihalis wasn't presiding at their table. The third-years were on a brief rotation out with the fleet. The junior prefect was a second-year student who laid a hand on Boho's forearm.

"Let up, before they," he jerked his head toward the high table behind him, "have to intervene."

Boho released Arturo. Arturo fell back in his chair, massaging his throat. Boho's fingers had left purple marks on his skin.

"You bastard," Arturo whispered hoarsely.

"You want satisfaction? I've got room on my dance card," Boho said.

"I'm not going to fight you. I'm not that stupid."

"Then don't be stupid about this," Boho said more gently.

He stood and offered his arm to Mercedes. "May I escort you to class, Highness?"

"Please." She hesitated then added, "Thank you for defending me."

"It was my duty. As well as my pleasure." As they reached the doors he added, "But I'm going to beat you next time." His green eyes were twinkling.

"You can try," she replied sweetly.

Boho threw back his head and laughed, then laid a hand over hers where it rested on his arm, and gave it a squeeze. There was a flutter in her chest as if butterflies had been released in her lungs. Mercedes allowed his hand to stay there as they made their way to class.

22

COJONES

By the Friday session Tracy had felt like Jasper Talion was up to full dueling speed and that he was holding his own pretty well. Granted it was just defense, but he had felt good.

Now that he was in the actual duel Tracy knew that the student from Nephilim had been going easy on him. Worse, he knew that he didn't have a chance. Cullen's blade wove a dance of steel and terror before his uncomprehending eyes. Tracy was gasping and his heart seemed to be hammering somewhere in his throat. He longed to glance at the clock inset in the wall, but fought down the urge. He had to keep watching that blade, Cullen's cold green eyes, and the superior smile. Tracy longed to cut it away and hated that he couldn't.

The seconds stood with their backs against opposite walls watching. At the far end of the studio one of the school medics waited, bag at his feet. Occasionally Hugo would let out a groan as a flurry of blows sent Tracy stumbling back. In the gallery set above the fencing studio were other watchers.

Tracy heard faint laughter, the rattle of cellophane as someone opened a bag of crisps.

Then the world narrowed to just the breath searing his throat, his aching thighs and bicep, the clang of steel on steel, the resulting vibration as the blow shivered through the muscles in his arm. He wanted to scream at Cullen to *just make an end to it*. He saw Cullen frowning with concentration as his gaze flicked across Tracy's face, clearly picking the target. The blade lanced out. Despite the decision he'd made to just take his medicine and allow the blow to connect, that animal urge for self-preservation kicked in.

Tracy found himself leaping backwards and with an awkward sweep dropped his blade on top of Cullen's, disrupting his aim. Tracy's feet tangled and he staggered forward directly onto the point of the saber. Cullen turned it at the last moment so it slid along his ribs, a ribbon of agony. Tracy cried out in pain. Warm blood coursed down his side.

I'm ruining my undress trousers! What if I can't get out the stain? came the inane yet frantic thought. Because of course this absurd ritual had to be done while dressed in their uniforms sans only their jackets.

"That's first blood!" Sumiko shouted though her voice was high and shaking.

"She's right, Boho," Mihalis called. "Honor's been served."

"Hardly. A scar on his side? Where no one can see it?" Boho shook his head. He was circling Tracy, a stalking predator. "Not good enough. I want him to look in the mirror and remember his manners and his place. And never forget that I'm the one that schooled him."

"Then you have no honor," Sumiko yelled.

"I'm afraid I have to disagree," Cullen continued in that condescending, conversational tone. Tracy was getting dizzy trying to keep turning as Cullen circled him. Occasionally the other man's blade lashed out and beat against his weakening grasp. "I'm just overflowing with honor. I'm the personification of honor. Otherwise I'd never have agreed to cross blades with this *perro*. I would have sent servants to beat him. He should thank me for stooping to engage him."

The blade flickered in the corner of Tracy's eye. He had an instant to realize that the cut was going to cross his face and cut across his eye, potentially blinding him and putting an end to his military career. In that split second Tracy realized that he wanted to stay, wanted to graduate for a variety of complicated reasons. He dodged sideways, and yanked his head away. The blow which should have fallen in the center of his forehead and cut the length of his face instead caught him on the left temple and sliced through his left eyebrow. He screamed. His side had hurt. It was nothing compared to this. The saber fell from his hand, and he clasped it against the wound, felt blood pulsing between his fingers. He collapsed to his knees.

"Oh God, going to be sick now!" he faintly heard Sumiko saying, and then the clatter of running feet. Through eyes swimming with tears of pain, relief and humiliation, Tracy saw Cullen's face twist in frustration. The bigger man leaned down and in a vicious tone said, "You will stay away from the Infanta. You will never approach her again. Do you understand?" Tracy didn't reply. Cullen grabbed him by the back of the neck and gave him a hard shake. "Do you understand?" he repeated. Tracy again remained silent.

Cullen drew back his hand. Kunst was suddenly there, holding back his arm. "No, you can't. Don't dishonor yourself over this *intitulado*. You've made your point. He won't forget."

Cullen straightened. The nonchalant mask was back in place. Kunst offered Cullen a handkerchief, and after he mopped the sweat off his face Cullen casually wiped Tracy's blood off the saber blade. He then spun gracefully on his heel and sauntered away.

"So... lunch?" he asked his seconds.

The medic ran over to Tracy and knelt at his side. He removed a jar of dark brown cream from his bag, pulled Tracy's hand away from his face, and rubbed a dollop of cream into the cut. It felt like sand and burned like the blazes. Tracy yelped. The medic slapped a bandage on the face wound. He then ripped open Tracy's shirt and applied a bandage to the four-inch slice on his side. The cream was not applied to that cut.

"No medicine?" Tracy hissed between gritted teeth.

"No, we're going to sew that one up. And the cream I put on your face is to encourage keloids to form." The man sounded appallingly cheerful.

From his biology class Tracy knew that was another way to say heavy scarring. "I don't want the scar!"

"Not an option. It's an affair of honor, you know."

"I'm going to deck the next person who says that," Tracy mumbled while his face throbbed in time to his heartbeat. "That includes you."

• • •

Monday morning at drills Mercedes noticed the bandage on Tracy's face. He was also moving very stiffly, and when he took a hit in hand-to-hand he let out a gasping groan. Narrowing her eyes Mercedes watched closely as a number of her classmates aimed hits to the scholarship student's right side. The last hit from Sanjay elicited a cry of pain from Tracy.

She scanned the entire class and noted that Boho seemed to be strutting, preening and in general looked very pleased with himself. If she knew more about the game and its rules and if it wouldn't cause a scandal she would love to play poker with Boho. The man's every emotion flickered quickly and obviously across his face. She'd probably win a lot of money. And then there was Tracy, who was so closed off. The only thing she could easily read off Tracy was anger.

Sumiko was also watching the drama playing out on the martial arts mats, and she muttered, "Boys are such vile little animals."

"Girls too. We've got the mean girl syndrome," Mercedes answered. "Present company excluded, of course."

"But of course. We're practically perfect in every way."

"Is that snark or do you mean it?" Mercedes asked.

"Damned if I know. Right now I hate humans."

"You know something. Tell!"

"I shouldn't. The boys wouldn't approve. On the other hand they've clearly been spreading the word," Sumiko added as she watched another hit land on

Tracy's side, and this time he dropped to his knees on the mat.

When Tracy climbed to his feet Mercedes saw a red stain forming a Rorschach test on his grey T-shirt. She clutched at Sumiko's arm. "Is that blood?"

"Yep."

"And is there another cut under that bandage on his face?"

"Oh, no mere cut, Mer. A badge of honor. Or a punishment—I can never keep it straight what message the boys think they're sending."

"Tracy fought a duel."

"That's a generous interpretation. He staggered about and tried to fend off—" She broke off abruptly.

Mercedes frowned, surveyed the possible candidates. It was obvious. "Boho, right?"

"Ding, ding, ding, ding, ding. Give the girl a cookie."

"Why?" Sumiko gave her a meaningful glance. "*Me?* I was the reason? Why?" The answer came almost immediately. "Oh, it was that stupid dance. I was just teaching him. There was nothing to it. How *dare* Boho defend my... act like I can't..."

"Protect your own honor?" Sumiko suggested.

"Exactly. I'm going to be emperor—"

"Empress."

"Whatever. And an officer in O-Trell. I don't need him fighting my battles for me."

"Good luck selling that attitude to our other companions," Sumiko said and looked at Cipriana and Danica.

"Do they realize that if they graduate this is going to be their life for years?" Mercedes asked in an undertone.

"Of course not. And it may not happen anyway. I expect the powers that be will move heaven and earth to make sure *you* graduate, but would be just as glad if the three of us wash out."

"What do you want?" Mercedes was honestly curious.

"Three months ago I thought this might be interesting, but I was agnostic about it. Now…" Sumiko frowned at the floor. "I think I'd like to make it."

Mercedes gave her a hug. "Then we will. You and me." She cast a darkling glance at Boho. "But first I have to set the young gentlemen straight."

"And just how are you going to do that?"

"I'm not sure yet. But I'll think of something."

• • •

"Guess I better tell the old man to add fencing lessons to Stefan, Rafe and Brandon's schedule," Hugo muttered. He was sprawled on a bench in the locker room watching as Donnel adjusted the bandage on Tracy's side.

"What about you? Aren't you going to get an instructor?" Tracy asked.

"Hey, I'm an agreeable guy. I'm hoping to avoid these kinds of problems."

"Meaning I'm not?"

Hugo laughed. "You are totally not. You're all sharp elbows and glares and frowns and snarky comments."

"Gee thanks." Tracy glanced down at Donnel. "Did you get the bloodstain out of my trousers?"

"I didn't like the result so I found a way to replace the waistband."

"And just how… No, never mind, I don't want to know."

"Probably better that way, sir."

"You about ready? We're going to be late to class," Hugo said.

"Almost. You go ahead. I have something to discuss with Donnel."

The other student left, and Donnel gave Tracy an ironic glance. "It must be something embarrassing or nefarious if you can't discuss it in front of another human. So which is it?"

"You're disrespectful."

"Sorry, sir. Apologies, sir. Allow me to slink back into my place, sir."

"Not making it better," Tracy growled. Still, there was something about the crazy-looking batBEM that appealed to him, so the rebuke was not as strong as it should have been.

"I am all attention, sir."

"I need to get a message to the Conde de Vargas. I don't want to trust it to the stream so I need to have a data spike delivered. Given your nefarious connections and behaviors I thought you might have a suggestion."

"You could take a shuttle down on Saturday."

"Yeah, like I can afford that. Unless the academy is paying that's impossible for me. And I'm supposed to just walk up to the conde's house?"

"And my presence wouldn't cause comment?"

Tracy shrugged. "Nobody notices servants."

"Normally no, but they'd sure as fuck notice *me*," Donnel snapped.

"Okay, if you don't want to do it—"

"Oh, I can get it arranged. I just thought it wouldn't do *you* any harm to rub elbows with the high and mighty."

"My elbows are pretty fucking raw from the rubbing they've been getting." Unconsciously his hand went to the bandage on his face, and Tracy winced.

"It's a good thing, sir. Makes you look like one of them. And once you graduate your new comrades won't know why you got it, and most of your classmates won't remember."

"I will, Donnel. Believe me, *I* will."

• • •

The mess hall was awash with conversation, laughter, even shouts from table to table. From the high table there was a burst of laughter from the professors. Danica leaned over and whispered to Mercedes, "It seems like everyone is more comfortable with each other now."

Mercedes took a bite of the delicate ham, broccoli and cheese quiche, and chewed slowly to avoid having to reply. Given what she'd learned that morning her response probably wasn't going to be restrained, and she didn't want to alert Boho to what she was going to do. If she had any idea what she was going to do.

Cipriana shrugged. "It has been three months. We all had to accommodate... or kill each other."

At that Mercedes turned to look toward Tracy's table. She could only see his profile and it wasn't the side sporting the bandage. She noted he had his hand clenched on the handle of his knife and he was staring down at his plate, but not eating. He abruptly pushed back his chair, stood and started walking toward her table.

• • •

"What the fuck are you doing?" Hugo hissed from behind him. "You heard what Boho—" Hugo broke off as there was a sudden flurry of movement from the highborn table. Mercedes had pushed back her chair and stood.

Tracy's and Mercedes' eyes met. He found his lips quirking into a small smile that was an answer to hers. They were walking directly toward each other. The buzz and hum of conversation stuttered and died like night-singing insects startled into silence. Tracy and Mercedes met in the middle of the mess hall. Tracy could see the professors on their raised dais. They were also silent and watching. Cullen rose to his feet.

Mercedes opened her mouth, but Tracy held up a hand to forestall her. He wanted to be the first to speak, to directly challenge Cullen's warning.

"Cadet Princess, I wondered if you might coach me in the *Infierno* simulator?" He pitched his voice deliberately loud.

"Apparently great minds think alike, Cadet Belmanor," Mercedes said in an equally ringing tone. "I was going to ask if *you* might tutor me in math."

Tracy bowed. "I would be honored, Highness."

Mercedes held out her hand. Tracy took it. Her fingers were trembling, and he longed to press them reassuringly, but he knew that would be going too far. She had used a lemon-scented shampoo after drills, and the fragrance wafted gently off her sleekly confined hair.

"Thank you, you are a loyal subject, and a good *friend*," she said and then turned and stared directly at Cullen. "Well, we should finish our lunch."

Tracy bowed again and watched her return to her table with that long confident stride that had been revealed once she was freed from skirts. His eyes traced the line of that ramrod-straight back, and the curve of her hips where the jacket flared.

The unnatural stillness that had gripped the crowd broke. Nervous chatter flared across the room, silverware rang against china. Tracy gave Cullen a bitter, triumphant smile. The look wasn't what he'd expected. Instead of promised retribution Cullen just looked confused and frustrated and faintly alarmed.

Tracy returned to his table where Hugo grabbed him by the back of the neck and gave him an affectionate shake. Even Gelb gave him an approving nod and a slap on the shoulder.

• • •

Boho had settled back into his chair. He was frowning down at his half-eaten lunch. Mercedes laid a hand on his shoulder, leaned down and whispered, "Don't you *ever* speak or act for me again. Do you understand?"

"Mercedes—"

She gripped his shoulder hard enough to make him wince. "Don't! I'm too annoyed with you right now to listen to your reasons." Realizing she'd lost her appetite she turned and walked away.

There was a clatter of boot heels as Boho caught up with her. "What do you see in him?" he demanded. Anger and puzzlement edged the words.

She stopped, bowed her head and considered that for a moment. Finally she said, "Loyalty and friendship."

He caught her by the elbow as she started to move away. "And what do you see in me?"

"I don't know, Boho. I haven't figured out your agenda yet."

"Do I have to have one?"

"Of course you do. Everyone else in the FFH does. Maybe that's what's so refreshing about Tracy."

"I'd like you to see in *me* what you see in him— loyalty and friendship." His voice was low, intense.

"Add respect to that, and we might have something to discuss," she countered.

He released her arm, stepped back and bowed. "I think you just got it."

"And Tracy. Has he got your respect?"

The mobile lips quirked into a rueful smile. "He's got major *cojones*. I'll give him that. But that's as far as I'll go."

"I'll accept that for now."

She had almost stepped through the arch into the hallway when Boho called softly, "If it's not too impertinent may I say that you seem to have developed some major *cojones* too, Mercedes."

23

POLITICS, POLITICS, POLITICS

For Hissilek it was a relatively cold day so the French doors that opened onto the garden were closed on this December afternoon. A few intrepid couples had gone outside to admire the winter-blooming flowers. The girls themselves looked like inverted blossoms in their skirts and billowing cloaks, but Mercedes had noticed that a number of the young ladies were wearing tailored jackets that were clearly inspired by her O-Trell jacket. Mercedes knew that the crown set fashion trends. She'd just never expected to do it in quite this way. The effect only extended so far—the civilian ladies' jackets fell to their knees or even their ankles. Mercedes' uniform was still considered scandalous.

Evergreen permeated the air and danced with the scent of hot apple cider. The heavy beams in the ceiling were festooned with evergreen boughs dotted with tiny star-shaped lights. Fifteen-feet-tall Christmas trees anchored the four corners of the room, and a monster of a tree, fully twenty-five feet tall with its glowing star almost brushing the ceiling, was at the far end of the room. Presents were heaped at its base. In two hours children from less affluent parts of the capital city would be escorted in to receive presents directly from the hands of the Emperor and Empress.

On one of her weekend visits home Mercedes had suggested to her father that they hold a reception for the students at The High Ground before the palace Christmas event. Afterwards the young officers could deliver extra gifts to various churches around the city for distribution to children who weren't lucky or photogenic enough to be invited to the annual imperial Christmas party. Of course the press would be alerted to these activities.

"I like it," her father had said. "You're starting to think like a politician."

"I thought I was thinking like a ruler."

"What do you think a ruler is?"

"I thought we were above politics."

"There's not an interaction in life that isn't political on some level, my dear. And well done starting to put your stamp on the officer corps. That's important."

Her gaze now went to her father. His entire attitude was self-satisfied and expansive. He held a cup of eggnog by its delicate handle and was threatening to baptize the Marqués C. de Vaca with its sticky contents. Constanza was chatting with a number of matrons including Vice Admiral Markov's stout wife, but keeping a wary eye on Carisa who was squatting in front of the Christmas tree peering at the presents. Her tiny hands were twitching, desperate to reach for the gaily wrapped boxes, her human nanny hovering nearby. The twins held hands and gazed longingly at the tree. Izzie made flirty eyes at

Boho, who looked amused, while Tanis stood with her back to a wall eyeing the shifting crowd with calculating eyes. Beatrisa had Jasper demonstrating fencing moves with a bread stick, and Julieta was arranging a sprig of holly in Sanjay's lapel. Estella was seated next to Conde Alfred Brendahl. He was an older man, recently widowed, and he and her sister had their heads bent over a holo from his ScoopRing. It looked like they were reading a book together.

Even Mercedes' ladies had paired off. Sumiko was with Hugo, Cipriana with Arturo and Danica was accepting a cup of eggnog from Mihalis. Unease at seeing two of her ladies in close association with her cousin's children became an aching knot in the pit of Mercedes' stomach. Of Duque Musa de Campo himself there was no sign. It was a calculated insult and would probably cause comment within their circle, but her father seemed unconcerned so perhaps there was no reason to be worried. Now if Arturo and Mihalis were making moves on Julieta or Estella, *then* she'd be worried.

Mercedes drifted through the room smiling, nodding, exchanging pleasantries with the nobles of the FFH who had gathered for the event. There were a number of nobles from off world, and even the youngest Rothschild representing his family. A family that stubbornly clung to holdings on the climate-devastated Earth. She wasn't sure if that showed nobility and loyalty to the human home world or a desire to be at the top of the heap even if that heap was a dung heap.

"We've had women entering recruiting stations on every world. We need to construct a response." Mercedes overheard the quiet conversation from a clump of uniformed officers and a couple of men in grey morning dress who were gathered at one of the buffets. It was Vice Admiral Markov who had spoken.

"The Emperor needs to set some sort of policy," an officer with a great deal of chest candy on his breast said in heated tones.

"He let it get out ahead of him, and now the damn lawyers are involved." It was Captain Zeng talking. "And we're being sued, alleging that equal protection demands that all the daughters of the FFH should also be required to attend The High Ground."

"And some of them are bound to make it through first year and then their graduation is inevitable." This was from another highly decorated officer.

"Fortunately most of the daughters seemed to be horrified at the idea," Markov chuckled.

"But the law doesn't always reflect popular opinion." This was from one of the men in civilian attire. He gave a regretful headshake. "We should never have used the American constitution as the basis for the League."

The civilian noticed Mercedes and his eyes narrowed. The cold calculation in that look sent a shiver through her, and Mercedes quickly reversed direction. She then mentally kicked herself all the way across the room wishing she'd had the courage to speak up. Of course talking back to her commanding officer was unwise at best and catastrophic at worst. Although she could make the argument that she was actually Markov's commanding officer. Mercedes wondered if her father had ever flirted with these confusing ideas.

She spotted Tracy in a corner by one of the Christmas

trees. He was staring down into his crystal eggnog cup with a surprised expression. She joined him. The scar on his left temple was twisted and raw and it pulled his eyebrow upward, giving an ironic cast to his face.

"This is actually *good*," he said in tones of wonder. "Dad always buys it at Christmas and it's just *nasty*. And yellow."

"This is homemade."

"Wish I could take some home. If Dad tried this he'd stop buying that stuff that looks like cat vomit."

"I'll see to it you get the recipe and a bottle to take home." Her voice was jumping.

"You're laughing at me," Tracy accused.

"A little bit. Actually it's nice. Your delight in things I just take for granted makes me appreciate them more." She looked across the room to the table where the giant crystal punch bowl sparkled atop its cut-crystal pedestal. "I should get some," Mercedes said.

He correctly interpreted her hesitation. "Yeah, it is a bit of a hike."

"And I'll get waylaid by some bore," Mercedes added.

Tracy held out his cup. "Want a sip?"

"Yes, thanks." She took a sip savoring the sweetness and smoothness followed by the bite from the bourbon and rum. They stood side by side watching the glittering crowd and their classmates all nicely coupled up.

"So, how did we end up the only people without dates?" Mercedes said, trying to make it sound humorous rather than pathetic.

"Well in my case it's because I'm a loser."

"And in my case?"

"You want a serious answer or a joke?" Tracy responded.

"Serious."

"If you hook up with anyone who has the standing and rank to be with you it sends a message and disrupts the balance in this power dance you're all doing."

"True. This whole power thing is isolating," Mercedes said as she watched Davin jump down from the podium that held the orchestra.

The Christmas carols gave way to a sprightly samba and a number of couples took advantage of the sheer size of the room to start dancing. Cipriana, Sumiko and Danica were among them.

"And now they are actually dancing," she sighed.

"And you'd like to."

"Yes."

"I may have a solution," Tracy said.

"Oh really?"

"Dance with a nobody. There are no power repercussions at all."

"Just a whole other set of problems. And I thought you didn't dance."

"Somebody started to teach me, and I decided not to insult her by not continuing."

"And who's been continuing your lessons?" Mercedes asked. There was a hot flutter in her chest when she contemplated his potential partners. She smothered it.

"Hugo's sisters."

"That could be a good match for you," she forced herself to say.

"I expect Mama Devris wants to do a good deal better than me now that they're on the first rungs of the nobility ladder."

He fell silent and the frown was back. It made Mercedes sad. He had seemed so happy for a few brief moments. "So, get on with it," she pushed.

"What?"

"Invite the girl to dance." She set the cup down on a ledge on one of the supporting pillars that marched around the edges of the enormous room.

The glow was back; he held out his hand, started to speak, then his hand dropped to his side. "We can't. You know that."

"You're not afraid of Boho."

"No, but this is the palace and you're you and I'm me, and there's a limit to how much even you can push the boundaries."

She thought about the conversation she'd overheard. The societal boundaries were already creaking and cracking and people weren't happy. She couldn't afford a misstep. She nodded. They were silent once again.

Why did the holidays always make her sad?

• • •

"…you're you and I'm me."

The words seemed to hang between them. He had made her unhappy and he wanted to kick himself. Tracy struggled to shake off his own melancholy, brought on by the fact he was lying to his dad.

At first Alexander was horrified by the scar, but then delighted when Tracy had explained it had happened during one of the practice bouts at his dueling society. Just an accident. His father had read about the tradition of dueling societies at The High Ground, and was thrilled that his son had been invited to join that elite company. So the first tiny lie had ballooned into a monstrous lie, and his dad was no doubt spreading it all over the neighborhood. Tracy just prayed that none of the neighbors would find a way to check.

Mercedes gave him a quizzical look and he forced a smile. "Hey, I never thought I'd get here. And through the front door, no less. My dad comes here. Well, not here here. He makes formal wear for *your* dad. He's been in the private suites for fittings."

"I didn't know that."

"I don't know why I'm bringing it up."

"Maybe because there are these weird connections between us," Mercedes suggested. "I haven't forgotten the beach. Actually you just keep rescuing me."

"And you've repaid the favor. Thanks to you I've gotten much better in the *Infierno*. I've almost pulled even with Kunst."

"Your hit scores are much better than his. I have to say it got a lot harder when we went live," Mercedes said. "They can try to approximate the gee forces in the simulator, but it's not the same."

"No shi— kidding. The backs of my thighs and shoulders are one big bruise."

"What about your bu—" Mercedes broke off saying *butt* as abruptly as he'd cut off the unwary *shit* he had been about to utter. He looked back over his shoulder and discovered why. Rohan Aubrey, the

Conde de Vargas, was standing behind them.

"Your Highness. Belmanor."

"Sir," they said together. But neither of them saluted. Tracy had learned that lesson.

"I'd best go circulate. And keep an eye on my sisters," Mercedes said, and with a nod to Tracy she moved away.

Tracy tried to think of something to say before the silence became any more awkward. Aubrey removed the problem by leaning in and saying softly, "I received your report, Cadet. Nice work."

"Thank you, sir." Aubrey just beamed at him. Tracy couldn't help himself; he added, "What are you going to do, sir? About the missing ships?"

"The situation is being researched. I'd appreciate it if you didn't say anything to your classmates while I continue my efforts."

"Of course, sir."

Aubrey dropped a plump hand onto his shoulder. "I have my eye on you, Belmanor."

Tracy watched the portly man waddle away. He wasn't sure whether the final words were a threat or a promise of something good. You never knew with the FFH.

• • •

There was a small Christmas tree in his study. The multi-colored lights blinked languidly, illuminating the handmade ornaments, from crocheted snowflakes to gingerbread men. All of them created by his nine daughters over the years.

I know he's disappointed that none of us were boys, but he does love us, Mercedes thought as she peeked around the door. Her father seemed to sense her scrutiny. He looked up from his tap-pad, smiled and motioned for her to come in.

"You wanted me, sir?"

He held out his hand. She laid hers in it, and he pulled her close and bestowed a kiss on her cheek. "*Sir?* Is this what comes of a military education?"

Mercedes smiled. "Well, it seems inappropriate for this junior officer to call her emperor and commander-in-chief *Daddy.*"

"And while this *daddy* would prefer it I suspect you are right." He sighed. "I suppose every parent faces the moment when their child becomes an adult." He shook off the pensive mood. "But yes, I did want you. It's time for you to get a lesson in another form of warfare that you won't learn at the academy. Pull up a chair."

She grabbed one of the large leather wingback chairs from in front of the desk and dragged it around next to his. He touched his pad and a large holo appeared in the air over the desk. There were various filters overlaying each other. The top image was of a snowy world orbiting a red-tinged sun.

"Yggdrasil," her father said.

Her brows twitched together in a frown as Mercedes tried to place the unusual name. She snapped her fingers. "Hidden World. The most recent one we've found."

"Very good. Discovered and reintegrated seven years ago. I put Quentin D'Amante in charge of the place. You remember him?"

"Duque from Kronos. I danced with one of his

sons at my *quinceañera* celebration. I don't recall much about the father. I was a bit giddy that night."

He answered her smile. "You were my fairy princess."

"I think your memory is a bit hazy. I was so awkward and pimply at fifteen, and all that puppy fat." She shuddered. "Julieta was far more fairylike at hers."

"I think you are all beautiful."

"Are you going to feel that way after you get through six more?" Mercedes teased.

"At least I can combine the twins."

"Poor twins. They never get to be individually special."

He gave her a thoughtful look. "Very true, my dear. I hadn't thought about it in quite that way."

"But you were saying about D'Amante…"

"He's ambitious. We had a rather pointed conversation about his son and you while the two of you were dancing. Point being that I tend to keep an eye on men like that, and SEGU has discovered some interesting associations." He swept a hand across the holo and a new page appeared.

The letterhead was an elaborate rendering of *Seguridad Imperial*. Mercedes glanced over at her father's profile, starting to show a bit of five o'clock shadow on his dark cheeks. "Not exactly discreet for a spy agency," she said.

He turned to look at her full on and there was a quizzical expression in his dark eyes. "You continue to surprise me, Mer."

She studied the report. "He's aligning himself with Cousin Musa."

"Subtly. There's not enough here to confront him, but enough for me to be alarmed."

"So what are you going to do?"

"That's what I brought you here to see."

Another sweep of the hand and a series of financial records slipped into place. It was a bewildering array of information from tax receipts, to city and planetary budgets, and bond measures. Seeing her look of bewilderment her father walked her through the pages of figures explaining that there had been a disruption to the economy when the League moved in and new owners took over the major businesses on the planet.

"The primary export from Yggdrasil is gadolinium. It's a rare earth element that helps shield our ship crews from neutrons. D'Amante has been skimming." Her father reacted to her look of shock. "Perfectly natural for a planetary governor. Those are always plum assignments—particularly on Hidden Worlds. But I want to send a message."

"How?"

Fernán swept aside the financials, and brought to the fore another document that showed massive amounts of gadolinium in warehouses on Nueva Terra, Belán and Ouranos. He raised one eyebrow inquiringly. Mercedes chewed on her lower lip; she utilized the holo to bring up the current price of the element. It was shockingly high. She then said hesitantly, "Someone's been stockpiling gadolinium. Making it scarce. Which drove up the price?" She couched it as a hesitant half-question, unsure of her answer.

Her father nodded approvingly. "Exactly."

"Who's buying all the gadolinium?"

"Me."

"Didn't that cost a lot of money?"

"I control the Imperial Reserve. Money is not an issue. We just put more into circulation."

Mercedes shook her head, coping with the idea of magic money that could just be miraculously created. Her father seemed to sense the direction of her thoughts.

"It isn't something you do too often or too casually. Because of this quantitative easing it has increased inflation across the League."

"I'm sorry to be stupid, but what exactly does that mean?" Mercedes asked.

"Goods cost more, and money costs more." He chuckled at her confused expression. "Meaning that interest rates go up so it's more expensive to borrow money."

"Oh, okay. But I'm sorry, I sort of derailed you. Go on."

"My actions created a shortage of the commodity and the price has skyrocketed. D'Amante fell for it and has been skimming even larger amounts of gadolinium, and people are starting to notice. Realizing that he could be charged with corruption he switched from skimming and started buying up gadolinium with his own money. He assumed he would make a killing when he did sell, repaying himself and socking away enough money to fight any charges that might be brought. That's what I was waiting for."

The Emperor's forefinger hovered over the command key on his tap-pad. "So with one touch I'm going to flood the market with my gadolinium, driving the price into the toilet. Most of my supply will sell at the higher price, but by the time D'Amante can react he will be selling at a loss which will affect his fortune, but also the economy of Yggdrasil. At which point I'll send in the *Departamento de Justicia* to investigate, D'Amante's skimming will be revealed and he'll be ruined."

"You said you were sending a message, but if you ruin D'Amante it's more than a message isn't it?"

"Ah." Her father tapped the side of his nose with his forefinger. "The message isn't for D'Amante. It's for any other member of the FFH who might think to ally with Musa. D'Amante is the object lesson."

"He or his advisors will see the sudden glut on the market. What's to stop him from selling almost as quickly as you?" Mercedes asked.

"That's where SEGU will once again be useful." He cast his eyes upward in a parody of piety. "I'm afraid there will be an interruption in the Foldstream services to Yggdrasil for about ten minutes."

A stranger was grinning at her. Her father continued, "I had considered hedging the currency as Yggdrasil is making the transition from their local currency, the Krone, to the Real, but adding to the misery of the local people was too risky. We've already taken their children, and given their major businesses to League citizens—we can't destroy the economy as well."

She had known he was powerful. It wasn't until this moment she realized just how powerful. The ruler of the Solar League could affect the lives of countless millions in order to punish one man. And someday she would hold this power. She shivered.

Her father leaned back in his chair, and indicated the sell command. "Please, my dear."

"You want me…?" He nodded.

Mercedes struggled to swallow. She reached out and sent the sell order. On the League Exchange, numbers began flashing. Within three minutes the crown had made a fortune and the price of gadolinium was plummeting. She struggled to untangle her roiling emotions. Excitement, a sense of power, joy at her father's evident pride, and a bit of guilt, for she'd just helped destroy the patrimony of a boy with whom she had shared a pleasant dance back when she had been a carefree girl and not the heir to a throne.

Her father stood and stretched. She heard a vertebra or two in his back pop. He smiled down at her and held out his hand.

"And that, my dear, is how you wage war without firing a shot."

24

KNOWING WHO YOUR FRIENDS ARE

"I thought you were in trouble with your ship," Tracy asked as Donnel skittered ahead of him. The alien's three feet created an odd syncopation on the sidewalk. Here at the edge of the spaceport the air was redolent with competing smells—alien and exotic spices, ships' sewer tanks being pumped into honey wagons, the harsh throat-catching scent of rocket fuel.

"I'm in trouble with my captain, and my captain doesn't leave the ship. Cara was modified for low gravity and can't tolerate being on the surface, and aside from that, business is business. Cara'ot are happy to deal with me if I'm bringing a customer."

Alarm seized Tracy. "I thought you said I'd get a discount."

"And you will, sir," Donnel soothed.

A new worry swam into his head. "Donnel, do you think I need to buy presents for my classmates— well, some of my classmates. I mean the ones I like."

"That's a relatively short list, sir."

Tracy bridled. "Meaning what? That I don't have

any friends? Gee, thanks."

"Well, who are we talking about?"

"Hugo. Ernesto. Sumiko." Tracy hesitated then added, "Mercedes."

"And what are you going to give to the heir to the Solar League that she doesn't already have and can't buy if she does want it?"

"I don't know, okay?" He sounded defensive and angry. "Maybe your awesome Cara'ot traders will have something stellar."

"If it's stellar you won't be able to afford it."

"Christ, you're just full of shitty little croakers today. What is your fucking problem?"

Donnel sighed. "I guess I'm homesick. I hadn't really thought about it until you mentioned needing Christmas gifts and I suggested I take you to a Cara'ot shop and then I found out the *Equity* was docked and I could do you one better and take you to the warehouse, but then I thought about my friends and family, and I realized it's going to be another two and a half years before we get assigned to a ship—assuming you want me, of course— and suddenly I wanted to swim in eternity again." The long meandering sentence left Donnel breathless, or perhaps it was the emotion he'd betrayed.

"I didn't know you were so unhappy," Tracy said.

"Most of the time I'm not. It's just the fucking holidays. It reminds a person of what they don't have."

"It's not your holiday," Tracy pointed out.

"Don't all conquered people ape the practices and traditions of their conquerors?"

Tracy again had that flare of discomfort over the Cara'ot's blunt statement, but then the alien laughed and added, "And it does make for some truly surreal experiences. One year we stopped to trade on Xinoxex and got invited to a shop owner's home for dinner. The revered progenitor was in his time of torpor, standing in a pool of water and meditating or whatever the hell a Tiponi does in torpor. Anyway, the shoots had decked out the old stalk's fronds with tinsel, lights and ornaments and were tooting out Christmas carols."

It was an irresistible image and Tracy laughed too. He also returned to his dilemma. "So what kind of things does your ship clan have for sale?"

"Mostly luxury goods—unique foodstuffs, jewels, recreational drugs, art, exotic pets. It makes no sense to schlep ore or lumber, apart from sek wood, between systems—"

"Why sek wood?"

"Damn trees won't grow any place but Cuandru. Even *we* couldn't make it happen. Anyway, most settled systems have an asteroid belt and can mine whatever they need. We cater to people's fantasies and passions." Donnel hesitated then added, "We also carry medical teams and medicines."

"Legal ones?" Tracy asked.

"Mostly," Donnel said cautiously. He shook his big round head. "We really don't understand you humans. We have the finest physicians in all the known worlds, but you won't use us, and you've even made it illegal for us to care for the other species."

"Because you don't heal, you corrupt and mutilate," Tracy said, parroting what he'd been taught in school. "You force changes on creatures at a cellular level."

"Not true. We never force changes on any creature,

and we mostly do it to ourselves. It's a waste of energy and resources to change a planet to suit a people. It's much easier to change the people to suit the planet."

"And that's exactly what scares the crap out of us. It's not natural."

"It's our brains that figured out genetics. How is that not natural?"

"God—" Tracy began and broke off. The churches had been trying for centuries to resolve the theology once aliens had been discovered. God made man in his image. So who made the Hajin and the Isanjo, the Sidones and the Flutes?

"The two most valuable commodities in the universe are the creative genius—art, music, philosophy—of sentient beings… and DNA. That's what we trade in. We'd love to have some of what makes you humans so… so…"

"So what?"

"Aggressive? Opinionated? Determined? It's hard to pinpoint. We'd love to know what makes you tick. On the most basic level. In your helix."

"And we can't trust that you won't change us. Subtly and over time, and then we wouldn't be us any longer."

"You know from your physics class that this universe might be nothing more than a holographic projection."

"Meaning?"

"How do we know anything is real? Much less us."

Tracy stared, puzzled at the alien. "You don't sound like the guy who presses my trousers and sets out my shaving gear. You sound really… different."

Donnel gave a shake of his entire bulbous body like a dog emerging from water and laughed. "Sorry, going back among my people has made me rhapsodic or pedantic. Take your pick."

Scary, thought Tracy, but he didn't say it aloud.

Donnel turned down a narrow street lined with boxy buildings with large roll-up garage doors, and small doors of various sizes and shapes to either side. They went halfway down the block, and Donnel knocked on a small triangular door. It was opened by a creature that looked like a cross between a centipede and a ferret.

"What the hell world was he modified to fit?" Tracy blurted. The creature gave a silvery laugh. "Okay, not a he," Tracy added. He felt awkward and rude and completely out of his element.

"Among our people you would say, 'What world was Cara modified to fit?'" the creature said in the same bell-like tones.

Tracy gave Donnel a questioning look. "We change gender as well as form on a pretty regular basis and sometimes we're even hermaphrodites," the batBEM said. "So we have a gender neutral pronoun—Cara."

"Cara explained it perfectly," the creature said, looking up at Tracy. Its body was only a few inches above the floor of the warehouse so it had raised the front half of its articulated torso. That's when Tracy realized that what he'd taken for multiple legs were actually arms with tiny hands. He shuddered.

"So what have you got for us?" Donnel asked.

"Come. We've set out an array of products for your human, appropriate to his financial status."

"Broke?" Tracy snapped.

"We will work with you. You are Donnel's."

Feeling like he'd been relegated to the status of "pet" Tracy followed the creature as it undulated across the floor. There were resin steel crates on all sides with pathways through the stacks. Tracy glanced down all of them. Most were empty, but in a few other equally strange-looking creatures were working. One was carefully removing glittering gems from a lined case and inspecting them with its grotesquely large and distended eyes. They weren't normal gems found on almost any planet, but rather phantasm gems that had been grown in the gizzard of a female flying lizard that could only survive on a particularly poisonous world in the Sidone system. Down another row a stork-like Cara'ot was busy framing an exquisite oil painting of a serene pool, the water showing a multiplicity of shades of blue and a profusion of red and yellow flowers on the banks of the pond.

Donnel clattered past Tracy and held a quiet conversation with their guide in a lilting language unlike any he'd ever heard.

"Is that Cara'ot?" he asked.

There was again the glockenspiel laugh. "Cara'ot are the people." The "silly" was unspoken, but Tracy knew it was there.

"The language is Caratolian," Donnel explained.

"I've never heard it before."

"Because we don't speak it outside our communities, or allow it to be learned by outsiders," the Cara'ot trader explained. "As traders it's required that we know all the known languages, but now we primarily use English and Spanish. Almost all of the races do. You humans have a singular ability to...

dominate any conversation, shall we say."

"But you used Caratolian just now," Tracy objected. "And I'm an outsider." His eyes narrowed. "You very deliberately want me to know that you're keeping something from me."

Donnel cocked all four eyes at his companion. "Told you," he said simply.

Again Tracy had that feeling that unseen currents were flowing around him, and that he was caught in the undertow.

They reached a table covered with a black velvet cloth. Arrayed on it were various graceful jars, razors, and a knife with a slim handle that glimmered like grey pearl. It rested in a silvery sheath. There were medallions that Tracy recognized as decorative zipper pulls, and a few single earring studs that looked like banded onyx in shades of red and grey.

The centiferret swarmed up a leg of the table and began to pick up items using eight of its front hands. "A depilatory that removes the necessity for shaving. Shaving cream that causes the skin to tighten so you get a closer shave if you prefer the old-fashioned method. This razor's handle—" the creature pressed it into Tracy's hand and he felt it begin to morph until it conformed to the shape of his hand "—designed to perfectly fit your grip, and the blade will adjust to the shape of the face." The Cara'ot picked up the sheathed knife. "Boot knife. Same theory as the razor. It and the sheath adjust to paper thinness for greater comfort. It expands." The creature drew out the blade and it shifted into a silver glitter.

Tracy tested the edge with the pad of his thumb at

the same time Donnel shouted, "Don't!"

Tracy gave a shout of pain as the blade sliced into his skin. He sucked at the welling blood. "Shit, that's sharp!"

"Yes, we use a similar material in our scalpels. But even sharper."

"What's the material?" Tracy asked.

"Ah, that's proprietary information," the centiferret said. Tracy thought it was smiling, but it was hard to tell given the shape of its mouth.

Donnel picked up one of the jars. Cool opalescent colors shifted in the light. "This cream is very effective at treating arthritis. I noticed your father's hands, and thought this might ease him."

Tracy took the jar. Opened the lid. The smell was sharp, medicinal, but also pleasant. "It works?"

"Guaranteed."

"Okay. I'll take these zipper pulls." He picked up two shaped like an abstract rune. "The cream, this earring, the razor, and the boot knife."

"Very good, sir." The creature wore a ScoopRing on one of the middle legs. It curled into a ball, brought up a holo, figures flickered past, and a final amount settled and floated in front of Tracy. He eyed it, thought about his bank account, swallowed and nodded. It could have been a lot worse.

His purchases were individually wrapped and placed in a clamshell-shaped carryall of gold with a silver ribbon for a handle.

"Pleasure doing business with you," the Cara'ot trader said.

"And you."

Tracy and Donnel left the warehouse.

"I figure the earring is for Ernesto, what about the rest?"

"The two matching zipper pulls are for Hugo and Sumiko. I bought the razor for Jasper. Should help negotiate the scars."

"The depilatory cream would have helped more."

"Yeah, but he'd never use that. Wouldn't show how tough he is."

"I didn't think you liked him. Why buy him something?"

"I don't think he knows just how little I like him." He looked down at the alien trundling along at his side. "And God knows I have enough enemies."

"True. And the knife?" Donnel pressed when Tracy remained silent.

"For Mercedes. I figured that's not too personal."

"And it might help keep her enemies at least a few more inches away," the alien said dryly.

. . .

"Well, Merry fucking Christmas."

"Cipriana!"

Mercedes hadn't meant to sound so old-maidish, but for the most part she and her ladies had managed to avoid using the more coarse language that was heard at the academy. They were back in their quarters at The High Ground two days before Christmas.

"Well, I guess this is what the military means when they ask for *volunteers*," Sumiko said drolly, trying to lighten the mood. She then sighed and added, "I did so want to spend Christmas with Hugo and his family. It was going to be so warm and—"

"And crass," Cipriana snapped.

"Cipriana!" Mercedes said again.

"Now you've done it," Danica said to Cipriana. "You've taken her from shocked to angry."

Cipriana rounded on the small girl who sat cross-legged on her bunk. "You're taking this pretty damn placidly."

Danica shrugged. "What else can we do? Mercedes decided that she would show how dedicated she could be, and we had no choice but to come along."

Guilt seized her. "Look, I didn't want to do this, but when the message came in my father and I talked it over, and…"

"And he thought it would be a good PR stunt," Cipriana said.

If only I were a better liar, Mercedes thought. Then she could claim this was all her idea, but she knew she would never be able to pull it off. *I need to work on that. I'm beginning to think lying is part of ruling.*

Honestly she had no desire to be sitting in the nearly empty academy for the next week and a half while others got to attend balls and parties, tour the display of lights, go caroling, and hear midnight Mass at the cathedral. Mercedes had wanted to watch the twins and Carisa tear into their gifts, and watch the delight on the face of one of the younger girls when they found the coin baked into the plum pudding at Christmas dinner.

She had known when the message had arrived on her ScoopRing and five minutes later when she'd been summoned to her dad's office what was about to come.

"It's a good move for you. It will show your dedication to defend the League."

"Against what? Oh, wait, my ladies, because they are going to kill me."

But he was He Who Must Be Obeyed (and she had to accept it was a good public relations move) so Mercedes and her attendants had returned to the *cosmódromo* earlier that day.

Their batBEMS had brought up their gifts—boxes of them—and they were arrayed under a Christmas tree in the observation lounge.

"So anybody a Christmas Eve present opener?" Sumiko asked hopefully and received a chorus of emphatic noes.

"Is there anyone of the male persuasion to share our dismal holiday?" Cipriana griped.

"I think that scholarship student from Nueva Terra stayed," Sumiko offered. "He couldn't afford to go home, and nobody from Hissilek invited him."

"Big whoop." Cipriana threw herself down on her bunk and hugged her pillow.

Silence settled and Mercedes began to unpack and hang up her clothes. Tako slipped through the door and whispered to her, "Several young gentlemen have invited the ladies to join them for eggnog, cookies and carols in the observation lounge."

"Which gentlemen?" Mercedes asked.

"Who cares!" Cipriana countered and bolted for the door.

25

YOU HAVE MY PERMISSION

The observation lounge was lit only by the fire of the stars beyond the wide windows and the twinkling lights on the Christmas tree. The tree filled the room with the sharp scent of pine. There were six men ranged on the sofas—Tracy, Boho, Davin, Hugo, Ernesto and Mark. Mercedes checked in the doorway, amazed to see them. It didn't escape her notice that Tracy and Boho were on different sofas and separated by the width of the room.

"What are you all doing here?" Mercedes asked.

"Our duty to the League," Boho said gaily as he jumped up and ran over to her. He kissed her hand. "And the lady who will lead it."

Hugo was at Sumiko's side, his arm around her waist. "When we heard we knew we couldn't leave you to face the holidays alone so we all volunteered. Besides, we're no fools." He gave a grunt as Sumiko dug an elbow into his side.

Cipriana ran a critical eye over Ernesto's long, lean form, smiled and did that panther walk thing she did. She laid a hand on his arm, smiled up at him and purred, "Maybe you can tutor me in... biology."

The scholarly Ernesto looked poleaxed. Mercedes turned away to hide her giggle, and found herself looking directly at Tracy. He and the other scholarship student, Mark, were holding back, showing proper deference to their well-born classmates. Tracy's eyes met hers and there was an intensity to the stare, an urgent communication.

Holding out her hand she moved to them using what she thought of as her regal glide. In turn the scholarship students bowed over her outstretched hand.

"Thank you for your willingness to share our exile. We'll find some way to make it jolly," she said.

"Highness," they murmured.

"Mr. Belmanor, might I have a moment of your time. I have a trig question."

He bowed. Wilson stood like a clod, then it finally penetrated that she wanted him to step away. He gave a hurried bow and went off to join Hugo and Boho.

"He's not very bright, is he?" she whispered to Tracy.

"Oh, he's smart. Just not as well trained in how to behave around the Fortune Five Hundred." The mobile brows twitched together in a sharp frown.

"Say it," Mercedes ordered.

"He thinks rubbing elbows with all of you will literally rub off, and he'll be accepted. I—" He broke off abruptly.

"Know better," Mercedes finished quietly.

"I'll remain prudently silent." He reached into the pocket of his coat and pulled out a small package. It was elegantly wrapped in silver paper with a blue ribbon. "This is for you. Merry Christmas."

A quick glance around to make certain they were unobserved and she slid the present into her pocket. "Oh, Tracy. Thank you. I didn't get you anything."

She felt stupid and cruel. She had thought about putting him on the Christmas list that she presented to the majordomo, but she was afraid it might cause comment. She assumed that her father as well as SEGU inspected the people on her list, and it would draw unwanted attention to Tracy if she included a scholarship student. It wasn't as if she could do her own shopping. She didn't even suggest a gift for most of the people. That was handled in the protocol office.

"Don't worry. You taught me how to dance."

"And it earned you a scar." She wanted to touch the ridged mark at his temple, but controlled the impulse.

"Hey, it makes me look dashing." He gave a shrug that meant to indicate it didn't matter, but she knew better. She sensed the mark would torment him for the rest of his life.

"How are you two…" She cast a look at Boho, as always the center of a laughing group of people.

"He pretends I'm appropriately chastised."

She laughed. "I think you will never bend that stiff neck."

He gave her a rueful smile. "Yeah, I guess I don't do that go-along-to-get-along thing very well, do I?"

"*No*, really? I'd never noticed." She touched the package in her pocket and said softly, "Thank you. I'll open it later."

• • •

Back in his quarters Tracy was kicked back on his bunk, getting a jump on the reading for Crispin's history class. He hated the class, but also found it easy unlike many of the others. His dad had been cool with his volunteering to return to the *cosmódromo* over the holiday. It gave him such a thrill to think of Tracy rubbing shoulders with FFH, and with the Infanta, no less.

His ScoopRing pricked his finger twice indicating an incoming text. He brought up the message. It floated in the air before his eyes.

I couldn't wait to open. Had to be private. Explanations difficult. Luv it, but what???

Boot knife, he typed back.

Who am I fighting?

Never know.

Tracy thought about what Donnel had said and added: *U might need it someday. U don't have guards.*

Surrounded by soldiers.

And your hens.

Snarky. Want to thx you in person. Can we meet?

Cameras.

Didn't Donnel fix that once?

Point. Will check. Hang tight.

He pinged his batBEM. A few minutes later Donnel arrived. There was a napkin hanging down the front of his shirt.

"You were eating. Sorry," Tracy said.

The alien shrugged and pulled the napkin out of his collar. "Snacking. What's up?"

"I need you to do that thing with the cameras again. Mercedes wants to meet."

"You two are going to be the death of me." He

heaved a sigh. "Okay. Give us a little time and we'll tell you where."

"Hope it's not a mop closet or something," Tracy said.

"Beggars shouldn't be choosers."

"She's the Infanta."

"Which is exactly why you shouldn't be doing this, but whatever."

The alien clattered back through the door and it slid shut behind him.

• • •

"Are you sure you wouldn't rather go alone?"

Mercedes stopped and looked at her batBEM. Tako was gazing at the floor, hands folded, a picture of deference completely at odds with the brashness of the question.

"And why would I do that? I'm merely thanking a subject for a thoughtful gift." It sounded hollow even to her.

The Hajin's eyes rose to meet hers. "Then why not thank him in a more public venue? And why did you lie to your ladies?"

That was a question Mercedes couldn't answer. Why had she told the others she was going to the library and declined any of their company?

"I won't betray you, my lady."

Mercedes gave a sharp laugh. "You servants know all our business anyway."

"Very true, my lady."

"I wonder why we never remember that?"

The Hajin remained silent, recognizing a rhetorical question. After a few more moments of dithering Mercedes gave a quick nod. "All right. Wait for me in the library. Good thing the academy is old-fashioned enough to still hang onto dead tree books even after they've been scanned. You can pretend I'm wandering in the stacks if anyone should inquire."

"Fortunately that's not likely to happen." The alien hesitated, then reached into a skirt pocket and pulled out a thin envelope. Mercedes recognized it at once. It was the same thing Cipriana had waved in front of her. Contraception. "Would you like this, my lady?"

"No, I can't." The batBEM turned away. "Wait. Okay, I'll take it. I'm not going to use it, but don't say anything, okay?" She thrust the envelope deep into her trouser pocket.

"Of course not, my lady."

The batBEM clattered off and Mercedes continued on to the upper observation lounge, fingering the envelope. This lounge was far smaller and less well appointed than the big lounge. More like a crystal soap bubble on the outer skin of the *cosmódromo*. For anyone afflicted by vertigo it was an uncomfortable space.

Tracy was seated on the low bench that ran the circumference of the space. One hand and his forehead were resting against the clear material of the curving walls. The light from the nebula threw his profile into strong relief. He looked around and smiled, once again transforming that rather plain face.

A surge of heat raced through Mercedes' body. She firmly took her hand out of her pocket and away from temptation. He stood and started to bow.

Mercedes threw out a hand, restraining him.

"Don't. No protocol right now. Just a friend thanking another friend for a Christmas gift."

He nodded. "All right."

Mercedes sat down on the bench next to him and pulled up her trouser leg revealing her boot. "You can't even see it, can you?"

He peered down. "No."

She reached into the top of the boot and pulled out the blade. Exposed to the warmth of her palm it quickly thickened and lengthened.

Tracy leaned back. "Whoa! I didn't know it would do that. That is awesome."

Applying her left toe to the heel of her right boot Mercedes kicked it off to display the sheath strapped to her calf. "Now watch what happens when the point touches the sheath."

The instant the blade kissed the sheath the knife again thinned and shortened. She slid it home.

"That is so cool. I wish I'd bought one for myself," he said with a regretful headshake.

"Maybe Santa will bring you one," Mercedes said, and winced because she sounded arch.

"I don't think Santa's sleigh is rated for vacuum."

They fell silent. Mercedes was terribly aware of him. It was cold in the small observation bubble and he was a point of warmth. A mélange of smells wafted from his skin. Lemon from the academy soap, a dusky, spicy scent that was aftershave, a wisp of mint—he had obviously used mouthwash before meeting her. There was a tiny nick from a razor on his right jawline just below the ear. He was staring down at his hands that were tightly clasped in his lap. His breaths, quick and shallow, seemed loud in the silence.

A shivering tension gripped her; danced along nerve endings, set her heart racing. Warmth settled into her lower belly and there was a sudden disconcerting wetness in her crotch. She studied his lips, faintly pink, a little narrow. Wondered how it would feel to press her lips against them. She licked her lips, cleared her throat, waited. Nothing happened. He didn't look at her. Didn't make a move.

Insecurity seized her. How could it not when she compared herself to the diminutive beauty of Julieta or the elegance of Estella? She was scarecrow tall with a big nose and she had a bubble butt. She was suddenly back at her *quinceañera*. None of the boys had tried to kiss her then either. It seemed nobody wanted to kiss her.

The silence was becoming uncomfortable. Soon the moment would be lost. How could a girl reach eighteen and never have been kissed by a man apart from her father? What was wrong with her? Even an *intitulado* didn't want her…

I'm the Infanta. It wouldn't be proper with the Infanta. Voices swirled through her head. Not her. Her position. That was what made her untouchable. It was also why she had power.

"I'm the Infanta," she whispered softly.

"Beg pardon?" Tracy looked up.

Mercedes made the decision. "You have my permission to kiss me," she said. The words were so formal. Would they break the moment or free them from this quivering anxiety?

The grey eyes filled with excitement and longing.

He reached out and slid a hand around her shoulders, drew her toward him. His other hand snaked up into her hair which she had worn loose and long this day. He tilted his head, and pressed his lips lightly, oh so lightly against hers.

Breaths fluttered and mingled. Heat shot into her groin. She shivered. He started to pull away. She threw her arms around his neck and held him close. His mouth sought hers again. There was more authority to the kiss this time. She sighed, softening her lips. His tongue brushed gently across her upper lip. She gasped, moaned and opened her mouth. Her tongue found his, tasting, teasing, exploring.

Eyes closed, Mercedes floated in a wash of sensations. She was tremendously aware of the heightened sensitivity in her nipples as they brushed against the material of her bra. How warm his hands felt against her back. The taste of him, both sweet and astringent.

The envelope in her pocket seemed to suddenly have weight and heft. What if she…? Could she…? Dare she…? He was kissing her neck, his lips exploring the contours of her ears. Between kisses he whispered her name. She moaned and pulled him closer. He made a sound that was part groan, part muffled oath, and tore away from her.

Three strides had him on the opposite side of the room. His chest was heaving with panting breaths and his fists were clenched at his sides.

"What? Did I do something… something wrong?" Even to her own ears she sounded plaintive.

"No. I did."

"I said you could."

"I know, but things needed to stop before it got... well, very hard for me to stop."

"It does rather sweep you away, doesn't it?" she said lightly.

"Yeah. Especially for men. We're pigs. I might not be in the FFH but I want you to always think I'm a gentleman."

"There's never been any doubt." The madness was ebbing, the fever in her blood fading. Cold reality returned. "I should get back. My ladies know I'd never spend *too* long in the library." They shared a forced laugh. "Thank you again for my gift. For both of them." He shook his head, puzzled. "The kiss. My first. You'd be surprised the things you *don't* get when you're a princess. Good night, Tracy."

"Good night, Highness."

"Use my name. Just this once."

"Good night... Mercedes."

26

LOCKDOWN

The incongruity apparently hadn't struck The High Ground command so Mercedes and her ladies found themselves facing a giggling group of ten-year-old girls from one of the middle-class girls' schools in a gelato store. Christmas was past and they were in that grey emotional hangover period that always seemed to follow the holiday. The field trip had been requested by the school and Mercedes was surprised when The High Ground had agreed. Since it was girls, Mercedes and her ladies had been given the task of telling the children how great a career in *Orden de la Estrella* would be. *Because nothing says a military career like recruiting kids with tasty frozen treats*, Mercedes thought. Given the stiff features of the teacher the good sister hadn't missed the dissonance.

Judging by the dolphin-squeak giggles and the bursts of excited conversations the little girls seemed far more interested in trading bites of their various sloppy choices than hearing about life in the corps. They had all made their curtsey to Mercedes, holding up the skirts of their school uniforms with a precision that spoke of long hours of practice. After that they had been sent to the counter and all semblance of order had disappeared.

Mercedes didn't really care. Looking at the flushed faces like radiant poppies, many with a smear of chocolate sauce around their lips, Mercedes thought of her little sisters, and hated the thought of what bullets would do to those faces and small fragile bodies.

The nun watched her charges with a critical eye and after a suitable amount of sugar had been ingested she clapped her hands. "All right now. It's time to finish up and Her Highness the Infanta and her attendants are going to tell you all about going to school up here and how much they like it."

"So that's what we're supposed to do," Cipriana muttered past lips locked stiffly in a grimace-like smile as Mercedes stepped past her.

Summoning her own smile Mercedes asked, "So how did you all like the shuttle ride?"

"It was stellar!"

"It was scary."

"It made my stomach feel ooky."

"I threw up." There were several voices that offered variations on that statement.

"I'll tell you a little secret," Mercedes said. "I threw up too the first and even the second time, but you get used to it."

"I liked floating. It was like flying. I loved it," a little girl with red cornrow braids offered.

"It is, but here on the station you can walk around and it's that way on the big ships too. Do any of you know why?" Mercedes asked.

"Gravity," another child piped up.

"Well, yes, but why is there gravity on the *cosmódromo*?" There were puzzled looks. "I'm going to let Lady Sumiko explain that to you."

Sumiko started talking about spin. Mercedes decided to treat herself to a frozen lemon gelato. The young man at the counter never lifted his eyes to meet hers and he seemed completely tongue-tied. She thanked him for her cup because as her father had taught her it cost royalty nothing to be courteous.

Mercedes tossed on a lot of sprinkles and chopped almonds and hid her smile behind her spoon as she listened to the pedantic Sumiko trying to give a simple and stripped down explanation of artificial gravity.

There was a massive jolt. The cup flew out of her hand. For a wild instant Mercedes watched the scoop of gelato and the cup part company in slow motion. *Shit! The gravity's gone!* Her time spent in shuttles and the *Infierno* had Mercedes grabbing for a handhold. Mercedes noted that Sumiko and Cipriana were doing the same. Dani had already secured herself to a freefall ring. *We can be taught*, she thought. The children, the nun and the server were not prepared. They started floating, arms and legs windmilling. Fortunately the tables and chairs in the ice cream store were bolted down. The League might trust their technology, but only so far.

The gravity returned, slamming them all to the floor. There were terrified screams and wails of pain. There was another massive jolt, which tipped them all hard to the left though this time the gravity held.

The already frightened and injured children went tumbling. Glasses and bowls cascaded off the shelves, filling the air with the shattering sound of breaking glass and sending shards flying in all directions. One sliver sliced open Mercedes' chin.

The *cosmódromo* stabilized and Danica and Cipriana immediately rushed to the children. Unfortunately their teacher was also down and unconscious. Blood flowed from her temple and her right arm was bent at an unnatural angle.

"What the hell is happening?" Mercedes hissed to Sumiko as she snatched up a napkin and mopped at the blood coursing down her chin.

"No idea. Can't be a normal failure. It's too violent. It's like an entire row of stabilizing rockets fired at once and that—"

Whatever else she was going to say cut off when a helmeted and suited figure burst through the door of the café. He (she thought it was a he because of the size) carried a large shotgun, and he fired several shots. The expanding pellets blasted the shelves into pieces and left pock marks on the wall. One shot took the server in the chest and he went down, his white shirt stained red. The roar of the shotgun left Mercedes' ears ringing.

Various instructors had said that time slowed down in a crisis situation. Mercedes had thought it was nonsense. Now she was experiencing it. She saw the open mouths of her ladies, hands reaching as if to push away the shotgun or the pellets. Muscle memory took command.

Time returned to normal as she found herself with her fingers pressed against the cold tile floor and halfway through a capoeira cartwheel. The move carried her across the gap, separating her from the gunman. She had an inverted view of the suited figure as her leading leg slammed against the front of his helmet.

He staggered and his next shot went into the ceiling. Acoustic tile rained down on them. Mercedes landed on her feet, then immediately dropped onto her arm and swept the legs out from under her off-balance assailant with her leg.

She could see the ridged edges on the knuckles of the suit gloves. She dared not give him time to recover. A single blow driven by his greater mass and superior upper body strength and delivered by one of those ceramic knuckle guards might render her unconscious.

Her hand went into her boot; she yanked out the knife and flung herself onto the fallen attacker. He managed one punch that grazed the side of her jaw. *Left hand… beneath the ribcage, angle up… catch the aorta…* Chief Deal's staccato delivery echoed through her head as she threw her full weight into the thrust. It penetrated the belly plate of the suit with the ease of a spade into soft earth. The blade was flaring along the edges, pulling a sympathetic fire from the CeraSteel armor. The man made a wheezing sound and went limp. Mercedes jumped back. She left the knife in place. The figure on the floor convulsed slightly and went still.

"You… you killed him!" Danica wavered. Her voice seemed muffled by layers of cotton.

"Damn good thing she did." Cipriana's voice was shrill. She stalked over to the body and pulled the knife free. Blood coated the blade. "Handy little thing,"

Cipriana said, her voice jumping with tension as she handed it back to Mercedes.

She wasn't sure what she was feeling. Numb, shocked and cold all at the same time. *I just killed somebody!* She tried to apply emotion and meaning to the words and couldn't. It was too much to absorb. *So don't. Act!* She grabbed a napkin, and with a shudder wiped away the blood. She then sheathed the knife and grabbed up the shotgun.

"Take his pistol," she ordered her ladies.

"Why?" Danica demanded. "What are we doing?"

"We've got to find out what's happening," Mercedes answered.

"People are shooting!" Danica shrieked and Mercedes realized the muffled sounds she had been hearing were gunfire. "We need to stay here. Hide!"

Mercedes tried her ScoopRing and got a message that all services were temporarily offline. "Damn it!" She looked at the white-faced nun, the sobbing children. "Okay, you guys get everybody into the storeroom. Guard the door. I'll try to reach *cosmódromo* security or get back to The High Ground."

"You are not going out there alone," Sumiko said firmly. "And in fact you ought to stay here and let the rest of us go."

"I'm not leaving!" Dani again, sounding more petulant than scared.

"Fine! Stay then!" Mercedes snapped.

"You better have me or Sumiko stay with her. I'm not sure she could figure out which end of the gun shoots right now," Cipriana said with a jerk of her head toward Danica.

"Good point."

"Which one of us do you want?" Sumiko asked.

One of you please, please volunteer, Mercedes thought. *Don't make me pick. What if I pick wrong? What if I get you killed? If I pick you will you hate me? Who should have my back?*

Time ticked past. Precious seconds flowing away. "Sumi, come with me," Mercedes finally said.

"Right." Sumiko moved to the body and pulled a pistol off the dead man's utility belt and a strip holding half a dozen tiny grenades. "Should we take the grenades too?"

"What kind are they?"

Sumiko peered at them. "They look like flash bangs."

Mercedes felt a desperate urge to giggle. Five months ago they would have been talking about the latest makeup colors, jewelry, the latest trend in shoes. They wouldn't have known a flash bang from an ion engine.

"Take them," Mercedes ordered. She grabbed a couple and shoved them into her coat pocket.

They headed for the door while Cipriana got the children moving. She then grabbed the unconscious sister under the arms and dragged her into the storeroom. Mercedes glanced back to find Dani staring at her and Sumiko.

"I'll be all right," Mercedes reassured. Dani's lashes lowered, veiling her eyes, and she followed Cipriana into the storeroom.

"That knife is really interesting," Sumiko said, reverting to professor mode as they walked out the front door. Mercedes knew it was nothing more than a coping mechanism. "It's like it read the material it had to cut and changed on an atomic level. Did your dad give it to you?"

"No. Tracy."

• • •

The violent list of the *cosmódromo* sent Tracy tumbling to the floor. "The Pope's holy pecker!" he yelped as he started to float as the gravity vanished. It returned without warning and he hit the floor hard. "Who's driving this crate?" he yelled to the room as he rubbed at the elbow he'd cracked against the floor.

He'd been sitting at his desk playing a game on his computer. He should have been studying, but there was a certain lethargy associated with the period after Christmas. Now it was just waiting until vacation was officially over and the school and the *cosmódromo* returned to normal.

A loud screech and buzz made him jump. The PA sprang to life. "This is an emergency notice. The High Ground is in lockdown. All students and personnel are to shelter in place. You will be informed when *cosmódromo* security gives the all-clear. Make no attempt to leave the academy, and we would prefer you remain in quarters."

It sounded like Zeng's voice which surprised Tracy. He thought the second-in-command would have been on the surface with his family, leaving some low-level aide or out-of-favor professor to man the fort.

Then the awful, sick-making memory hit. *Mercedes and the girls aren't in the academy.* They were doing public outreach to a group of school kids in the central ring. He keyed his ring trying to reach Mercedes and discovered the Scoop network was down.

The lockdown of the academy implied that the threat was in the ring. Areas that were patrolled at peak times by *cosmódromo* security, but no one was likely to be on high alert. It was the dog days after Christmas. Most travelers had already reached their destinations and were tucked in with their families. They might even have only a skeleton staff.

The shopping frenzy was over, and the restocking wouldn't start until next week, which meant the flood of goods through the warehouses had also probably slowed to a trickle. There was a very good chance that the burly stevedores in the spokes and hub had taken off as well. Which left four women and a class of little girls virtually unprotected.

While inside the walls of The High Ground were guns, combat armor and men trained to use them. So they were being ordered to shelter in place like kids at an elementary school? It didn't make any damn sense.

"Fuck this," Tracy said, and he quickly pulled on his uniform. If he did run across any *cosmódromo* security he didn't want to get shot in the confusion. Also his uniform might provide him with a bit of authority.

He waved open the door to his room and took a cautious glance in both directions down the hall. It was clear. He headed left toward Hugo's room, and they nearly collided at the corner.

"Sumiko."

"Mercedes."

It was all they had to say.

"Should we get anybody else?" Hugo asked.

"Yeah, *all* of them," Tracy said.

"Oh, good point."

"Split up. We'll cover more ground faster."

"What if you find Boho first?"

"I expect even that asshole can put aside his problems with me when we've got a damn crisis."

"I wasn't thinking about him."

"Oh, gee thanks! Go."

Tracy whirled and ran back down the corridor. He heard Hugo's footfalls receding into the distance. *Am I really that much of a dick?* Tracy wondered.

He reached Mark Wilson's room first. Prayed he would be in. The other scholarship student opened the door. His expression held both fear and excitement.

"What's going on? You have any idea? What are you doing? Shouldn't you be in your room?"

"Mer—the Infanta and her ladies are out in the ring."

"So?"

"*So?*" Tracy tried to process the attitude. "We need to help."

"Our duty is to obey the order we've been given."

Tracy waved a hand in front of Mark's face. "Hello. Infanta. *That's* our duty."

"I'm not disobeying a direct order."

The almost pious tone infuriated Tracy. "You're a fucking coward!"

Mark's hands coiled into fists and he stepped up to bump chests with Tracy. "And you're a fucking troublemaker. Boho and Clark and Sanjay warned me. Warned me to stay away from you. Not get your stink all over me. They say I have a real chance to get ahead. I'm not getting cashiered for disobeying orders. So you can just go sit on a stick and spin."

Mark stepped back and the door swept closed in Tracy's face.

His teeth gritted in frustration Tracy ran to Ernesto's room, and found him already leaving.

"I take it we're doing something stupid?" Ernesto asked.

"Well *some* of us are," Tracy replied.

They moved on to Davin's room and rang the chime. He opened the door, looked puzzled for an instant, and then delighted. "Oh good, for once I'm not the ringleader. Let me dress. Don't want to play the hero in my jockey shorts."

"Mostly we don't want to look at you in your underpants," Ernesto said.

"Hurry. Somebody's going to notice we're wandering around. We've got to be out of here before the administrators can respond," Tracy said.

"How *are* we getting out of here?" Ernesto asked.

"One problem at a time."

By the time Davin was dressed Tracy had received a call from Hugo telling him he had Boho. They rendezvoused at an intersection of several corridors.

"Do we know what's happening?" Davin asked.

"Has to be some kind of attack on the *cosmódromo*," Tracy said.

"We don't know that," Cullen said with an infuriatingly superior tone. "It could have been a technical problem that caused the *cosmódromo* to lose stability."

Tracy gave him a disgusted look. "There are six

different kinds of safeguards against an accidental firing of the stabilizing rockets. This had to be deliberate."

"So what do we do?" Ernesto asked.

"Get out there and find the girls!" Hugo said.

"And get them back to The High Ground," Tracy said. "We need weapons," he added.

"Aren't you making a lot of assumptions?" Cullen asked.

"I'd rather assume the worst and be happy to be wrong," Tracy shot back.

"Tracy's right," Hugo said. "Let's get to the armory."

The armory proved to be a bust. The weapons were locked away. Ernesto spent ten minutes trying to override the lock without success. Each second seemed to be ticking past with the weight of a drumbeat.

"Forget this! We need to go."

"If I can't override this lock, I'm betting I can't override the doors from the academy into the *cosmódromo*."

"The batBEMs. Maybe they can help," Tracy said.

"Why would you think that?" Cullen demanded.

"You'd be surprised at what they can do… and what they know," Tracy snapped. He called Donnel and outlined the problem.

"I'm sorry to disappoint." The alien's image wavered in the holo. "That's beyond our skill."

"Shit."

"I can buy you a little more time before administration notices you're not in your rooms."

"Great, do that. We'll find another way into the ring."

"Maybe we should just accept we can't do anything," Davin said.

"No. We'll find a way," Tracy raged as he led them away from the armory.

"What way?" Cullen demanded.

The symbol for the shuttle bay loomed up on the wall to Tracy's right. He didn't answer. Instead he broke into a run and entered the shuttle bay. There was a single *Infierno* parked inside.

"We take that," Tracy said, pointing at the fighter craft.

"Maybe you can't count, Belmanor," Cullen drawled. "But there are five of us. The *Infierno* is a single-occupant craft."

"There's battle armor in the lockers," Tracy spat. "And if whoever is piloting takes it easy we can tether ourselves to the crane hooks and ride on the outside."

There was a flicker of something deep in Cullen's green eyes.

Hugo slapped Tracy on the shoulder. "You're a genius."

Ernesto grinned at him. "I don't know if I'd go that far, but he can certainly think on his feet."

"Let's *do* it," Davin said, his voice throbbing with excitement.

They grabbed battle armor from the lockers and stripped down to their underwear. Cullen hesitated with his hand on his belt buckle. "You need somebody to run surveillance. Access the *cosmódromo* cameras, let you know what you might encounter."

"You can do that?" Davin asked as he locked on the greaves.

"How do you think I got past all those duennas," Cullen smirked. Davin and Hugo gave shouts of laughter that owed more to nerves than the actual humor of the remark. "I'll get to the computer center and run the hack from there."

It made sense what Cullen was saying, but something niggled at Tracy as he sealed the breastplate.

"Ernesto is top of our class—including in computer science. Wouldn't that make him the better choice?" Tracy argued.

Cullen didn't respond. Was he ignoring Tracy or marshaling an argument against him? Ernesto stepped in to fill the silence. "Look, I'm happy to go. Make Cipriana think I'm a hell of a fellow."

Eyes narrowed, Tracy studied Cullen. "Which rather does surprise me that you're not hoping to score some coup with the Infanta."

"Sometimes you have to take the less glamorous role. I'm willing to do that," Cullen said smoothly.

"Look, we can't waste any more time arguing about this," Hugo interrupted.

"Good point," Cullen said. He looked at Tracy. "So if you're done delaying us…?" Tracy gritted his teeth wondering how he had suddenly become the goat at the banquet.

"Next to Boho you're the best pilot we've got," Davin said to Tracy. "Since Boho's hanging here you'll need to fly the *Infierno*."

"Okay, I'd suggest Hugo tether on one hook and you and Ernesto on the other. I'll take it slow, and make it as short a hop as possible." Tracy lowered his helmet, sealing it shut.

Donnel came clattering into the bay, his three legs beating an odd tattoo on the floor. "We've spoofed the cameras, but they're going to spot the ruse soon enough. I do hope you boys are going to take the blame," the alien added.

Boho and Davin started to bristle. Tracy spoke hurriedly. "Yeah, we'll keep the batBEMs out of it." He contemplated the alien, who had been modified to work on ships. "Look, why don't you come along?"

"Sorry, sir, but I must decline. First, I don't have a suit. And second it's better that humans do the killing of other humans. You get grumpy when we do it."

"Whatever!" Tracy snapped. He turned his back on the Cara'ot. "You all ready?"

Hugo snapped his tether onto the hook. "We are now."

"Just don't play crack the whip," Davin added.

27

SOMEWHERE IN THE DARKNESS

Looking at dead bodies in biology class had served one purpose. Mercedes didn't puke when she came across the body of a *cosmódromo* security guard. The man was crumpled on the bank of the river that ran through the large park in the center of the ring. His chest looked like it had been chewed, and blood stained the grass on which he lay. In death he seemed somehow shrunken and diminished.

Sumiko gave a hiccupping little sob. Mercedes gritted her teeth, fighting back the urge to also burst into tears.

"Get his gun," she said to Sumiko.

The other girl wiped her nose on her sleeve, nodded and plucked the pistol out of its holster.

"Glad I asked for you," Mercedes said. Grief and fear had lodged a stone in her throat. The words crawled painfully past. "Dani would have been useless and I'm not sure Cipriana would be as analytical."

"Yeah, that's me. No sensibility, Little Miss Common Sense," Sumiko said. Mercedes couldn't tell if she was trying to make a joke or not. "So, where are we going?"

"The High Ground. They'll know what's happening and help us."

"Okay." Sumiko tilted her head back to look at the ring overhead. "If the bad guys have optics they could spot us."

"I really, really wish Chief Begay had had us do more than just target practice," Mercedes muttered. "I guess it'll be like hide-and-seek with my little sisters."

They tried to use planters, bushes and trees as cover, but Mercedes wasn't sure they were all that successful.

"I wonder if we ought to get out of these uniforms, look more like regular ladies," Sumiko said as they passed a clothing store at the edge of the park.

"Regular ladies... with guns. And I don't want to take the time," Mercedes replied. "Let's just get to a hyperloop station, and get back."

"I wonder where the regular people got to," Sumiko said.

"Hiding would be my guess."

Sumiko darted out of the park and to the door of a hotel. She tried the door. "Locked."

"By the people inside?" Mercedes asked.

Sumiko ran to a shop and tried its door. It was also locked. "I'm thinking these attackers have put every building in lockdown."

"But not ours. Not the door into that ice cream shop," Mercedes said.

"Which means..." Sumiko's voice trailed away.

"They were after us."

"You."

They stared at each other. "We've *got* to get to the academy." Mercedes took off running.

Never had the curving ring seemed so large. Mercedes noted her breathing, and for the first time was grateful for those agonizing morning runs. An armored figure lunged from an opening between buildings. Mercedes dropped and slid on her hip across the sidewalk avoiding his swinging fist. She felt the burn on her skin, but it was muted by unadulterated panic. She brought the shotgun to bear and fired into his crotch. The pellets rattled off his armored suit like dried peas.

Sumiko was frantically firing the pistol. It was having even less effect than the pellets, but the kinetic force was at least staggering the suited figure. Mercedes rolled away and pulled a grenade from her pocket. She was behind the man now, and could see the clips on the belt harness that held a variety of tools and weapons. There was an empty hook.

Leaping to her feet she pulled the pin from the grenade, clutched at his utility belt, and clipped the grenade onto it. The man whirled and backhanded her. The blow lifted her off her feet and she slammed into a bench, knocking the air from her lungs and bruising her shoulder. Her mouth worked as she tried to suck in air like a fish on shore. He stalked toward her, lifted a metal-encased foot, preparing to stomp her face. She threw up her arms in a futile effort to hold him off.

The flash bang detonated in the small of his back. It wasn't technically an explosive device, but that close to his body it managed to dent his armor, and balanced as he was on only one leg the concussive force sent him sprawling. Mercedes wriggled from beneath his legs, jumped to her feet, grabbed Sumiko's hand and she ran, pulling the other girl after her.

"Shouldn't we have… well… killed him?" Sumiko panted.

"How? We don't have the right guns to get through his suit."

"You have that knife."

"I can't. Not again. I did it because I didn't have time to think. And please don't remind me."

They reached a tram stop that would carry them to the hyperloop station. There was a tram frozen partway down the maglev track. "They shut down transport services too," Sumiko said in her laconic way.

Mercedes led them back into the green belt. She knew their infrared signatures would look like flares on a suit's radar, but there was no help for it. A burst of cool water pattered on her cheek and wet the top of her head. She looked up to where a cloudbot floated past misting the vegetation. Four feet in diameter, the underside of the cloudbot was a curving bowl that held the water. Sprinklers dotted the rounded surface. The top however was flat with a port where the water could be refilled and fitted with a small motor.

She pointed. "We ride one of those. They make a circuit of the park. We get off when it reaches the junction for The High Ground module. It's going to be cozy, but we should both fit."

"And just how do we get on it?"

"We jump." Mercedes scanned the trees and the nearby buildings. It looked like the bot was going to float past a rather impressive oak.

"Oh dear God," Sumiko breathed, following Mercedes' gaze.

"Didn't you ever climb trees as a kid?" Mercedes demanded as she ran to the oak.

The lowest branch was still out of reach. Mercedes cocked up her leg. Sumiko rode so she knew what was expected. She cupped her hands. Mercedes rested her knee in Sumiko's hands, and the other girl gave her a boost. She caught the lowest branch, swung and got her leg over the branch. She then lay along its length, stretched out her arm, and grabbed Sumiko's hand.

It wasn't pretty and it wrenched her sore shoulder, but Sumiko joined her on the branch. Mercedes, one eye on the approaching cloudbot, scrambled into the higher branches. She shimmied out on a branch that thrust out toward the bot's path.

"It's three feet. If we miss…"

"We get hurt and then we get dead. Or we don't miss and we have a chance."

Reaching up she grasped a thin branch and a spray of leaves. Carefully she stood up. The branch flexed a bit. Sumiko gasped and clung to it like a baby sloth. The cloudbot floated closer, gently hissing as it deposited water on the park below.

Heart hammering, Mercedes tried to control the shaking in her knees. She watched the distance, gulped in a deep breath, and jumped. She almost plunged off the other side of the platform, but managed to stop herself, arms windmilling on the far edge. The bot slowed and dipped with her added weight.

Mercedes turned back. Sumiko was upright and

swaying. Mercedes held out a hand. "Come on! Jump! I'll catch you."

Sumiko's lips moved, she crossed herself and jumped. Mercedes caught her and they sank down, arms wrapped around each other. They were laughing wildly. Mercedes stifled her giggles and looked around. There was a small control box on the top of the bot.

"Do you think we can make this thing go faster?"

• • •

The padding in his helmet was damp. Tracy feared it would soon be unable to absorb his sweat and it would begin dripping into his eyes with no way to wipe it away. He had to hope the hyper-absorbent material would keep doing its job and recycle his sweat into drinkable water. The thought reminded him he was frightfully thirsty. He took a sip from the nipple inside his helmet.

He was terribly aware of the three bodies clipped to the *Infierno*. No sudden moves, no sudden acceleration, slow and steady. Which meant the *Infierno* was moving at a glacial pace.

The radio crackled to life. Cullen's voice loud in his ears. "Whoever they are they're in the central hub—"

Tracy couldn't control it; he snapped, "Yes, we knew that when they fired the trimming rockets."

"If you'd let me finish!"

"Go ahead, Boho." Davin's voice.

"They've shut down public transport on the station, and put the doors in lockdown. They've also hacked the station cameras, but I've been able to slip in with them and they haven't noticed me yet. There are a lot of dead bodies—mostly *cosmódromo* security, but I've found three unknowns in battle armor. Knowing that I've been scanning for their heat signatures. If unarmored bodies are like flares then these guys are like fucking novas. So far I've got a count of twenty hostiles."

A new thought became number one on the list of Tracy's worries. "You are on tight beam, Cullen, *right*?"

The hesitation made the lie obvious. "Uh… of course."

"Shit," Tracy muttered. Thanks to Boho's carelessness the hostiles might have picked up their conversation.

"Have you found the girls?" Hugo, his voice anxious and tight.

"I found Sumi and Mercedes. No sign of Dani or Cipri yet."

Tracy bit down hard. He had to let Hugo ask, and the big man didn't disappoint. "Where are they?"

Boho's voice quivered on a laugh. "Riding a cloudbot over the park."

"Headed where?" Davin asked.

"Probably toward the junction with The High Ground module, but with the lockdown they won't be able to get in."

Sensors picked up a flash of energy among the jumble of satellites and platforms that orbited Ouranos. Tracy hesitated, his hand hanging in the air over lidar control. "Reach out and touch someone," Tracy muttered to himself. "But what if they reach back?" He decided against making the scan.

"They'd have to let her in. She's the Infanta," Ernesto was saying.

"So do we turn back?" Davin asked.

"Our duty is to the crown, nothing more," Cullen added.

Irritation with Cullen pulled Tracy away from the sensors. "And I'm thinking leaving women and children in danger isn't exactly doing our duty." Tracy had tried for a sarcastic drawl, but was afraid he'd come across like a sanctimonious prig.

"May I quote Chief Begay," Cullen said. "We're not paid to be heroes. We're paid to be effective."

"Of course Chief Deal would say we are supposed to be big damn heroes," Ernesto offered.

"Tracy's right," Hugo said.

"Fine! I'm just saying—" Cullen began.

"Is there a docking bay near the Infanta's position?" Tracy interrupted.

"Yeah, I've got the *cosmódromo* schematics up now. I'll send you the coordinates."

The diagram sprang to life in the air in front of Tracy. "Got it. Thanks."

He altered his trajectory with a slight burn of the engine. A blaring alarm screamed through the cockpit, sending his stomach jumping into the back of his throat. Eyes flicking wildly Tracy read the screens flashing to life before him. Incoming slugs, three of them heading right for them. Somewhere in the clutter and the darkness an enemy ship lurked. With a sweep of his hand Tracy flipped the *Infierno* so the slugs would hit armor and not the soft bodies riding on the upper surface.

The fighter shook with the impact. There were yells of fear from his passengers. "Hang on," Tracy yelled, and he sent the *Infierno* spinning toward the docking bay coordinates.

On a screen he saw a second round of slugs rip through the space the fighter had occupied only a second before. The bay doors appeared before him. On the curving surface of the ring just above the doors was one of the giant cables. Tracy sent the opening code. Nothing happened.

"They've got the bay doors locked down too," he yelled.

"I'm trying to override." Cullen's voice was tight with tension.

"Let me try it manually," Ernesto said. Before Tracy could respond a human form shot past the clear dome of the cockpit, the jets on the battle armor flaring.

Ernesto ripped open a cover on the exterior of the ring. Tracy alternated watching Ernesto and watching the screen that showed another round of slugs heading their way.

"Hurry!"

"I'm trying."

"Try harder!" Frantic breathing was the only reply. Tracy was doing mad calculations. Slug versus missile? Missile—the slug was too much of a blunt instrument. Detonation on impact with the bay doors or just before? Before. He couldn't risk puncturing the ring and causing the sections to seal. He was out of time. "Hugo! Davin! Bail out. Ernesto, get away from the doors! Boost hard! Now!"

"Why? What are you…?"

"Missile coming!" Tracy targeted a few meters shy of the doors. He was very aware of the three small figures on his screens. They were boosting away. His missile detonated as programmed and white fire blazed and bubbled across the bay doors. He washed the area with a sensor sweep. The computer thought the molecular integrity of the metal had been degraded. Tracy prayed it was right. He accelerated toward the doors. The metal did seem deformed, slumping slightly. The leading edge of the *Infierno* crashed into the doors.

It wasn't sound but sensation. Tracy watched with horror as the leading edge of the *Infierno* deformed, crumpled, coming ever closer to the fragile bubble that held his even more fragile body. He closed his eyes and prepared to be crushed. Then realized he didn't have the luxury. He had to bring the craft to a stop before it plowed into the inner wall of the *cosmódromo*.

Hands outthrust as if he could hold back the momentum, he keyed the forward rockets. The *Infierno* hit the far wall, but it was a kiss rather than a blow. He lowered the battered craft to the floor of the bay, popped the dome, yanked the jack from his battle armor and ran for the airlock mechanism.

"You are fucking *crazy*, man!" Davin shouted as the three men entered the ruined docking bay. "I *love* it."

"Quick. We need to get into the station," Tracy ordered. "They will have alerted their forces inside. Sent them to intercept us."

"What's to stop them just lighting up this bay?" Hugo asked.

"Their men inside," Ernesto replied. "They may be in armor, but eventually they'll need oxygen, and in space you don't willingly poke a hole in the thing that keeps the air inside."

"Unless you're Tracy," Hugo chuckled.

"I took the risk it wouldn't penetrate the inner hull," Tracy said defensively. "Now come on."

They ran to the inner airlock controls. This time Ernesto was able to manually override. They piled into the airlock and waited for it to stabilize.

"We need to stay in the armor, but click back the face plates, preserve our oxygen," Tracy said.

"And hope nobody shoots us in the face," Hugo grunted.

"How did they spot us?" Davin asked.

Before Tracy could speak Ernesto slid in smoothly and said, "Probably read our signature. With four bodies plus the engine on the fighter we looked like a flare."

The dark eyes shifted to Tracy and they held a warning. Tracy bowed his head, accepting the reality.

"Cullen, have you got a location on the Infanta?" Tracy radioed.

"Yes. Syncing it to your suits. Good luck. Get her to The High Ground."

"That's the plan."

• • •

Since they were prone on the top of the cloudbot Mercedes hoped they wouldn't be noticed. And that the battle-suited figures wouldn't notice that this particular bot was flying rather lower than its companions. So far it had worked and Mercedes filed away that bit of information in case she ever again found herself in a combat situation—people didn't think to look up. Or at least not nearly often enough.

Their attempt to increase the speed of the bot had proved futile so it had been an agonizingly slow journey, but they were finally approaching the junction with The High Ground. The park ended there, and didn't resume until the far side of the station facilities module.

"This is our stop," Mercedes said.

"If we jump one or both of us will likely get hurt," Sumiko pointed out.

"Then we need to force the thing down. We might not have been able to reprogram it, but I bet we can break it." Mercedes wondered if her cocky smile looked as forced as it felt.

Sumiko crawled to the control box and opened the panel. She began randomly pushing buttons and pulling wires. The bot shook, and dropped its entire load of water in a great deluge, but it didn't sink closer to the ground. Muttering a curse, Sumiko pulled out her pistol and shot the controls. The bot headed down rather faster than was comfortable.

"Oh shit! Jump and roll like Deal taught us!" Mercedes yelled as the ground came up to meet them. Clinging to each other, they climbed to their feet on the platform. Mercedes frantically tried to judge the distance, gave up and just let instinct take over. She jumped, took the shock in her knees and went into a forward roll. It jarred into her knees and now her other shoulder was bruised, but otherwise she was undamaged. Her uniform hadn't fared so well. Her coat sleeve was torn and grass stains smeared her white shirt.

She looked around. Sumiko was climbing to her feet, brushing flower petals out of her hair. "Fine," she said in answer to Mercedes' inquiring look. "Let's go. Somebody might have heard that gunshot."

They ran for the transfer station that would carry them down the massive cylinder to the doors of The High Ground and safety. Out of the corner of her eye Mercedes saw four suited figures running toward them. She swung the shotgun to bear then realized that all four figures were frantically waving, and they weren't carrying guns. At the last instant she recognized Tracy and she yanked up the barrel of the shotgun, sending the pellets into the air over the men's heads.

They dove to either side and Tracy yelled, "Mercedes… Highness! It's us. Don't shoot."

Sumiko ran to Hugo. He opened his arms and enfolded her. Mercedes so desperately wanted to do the same, but fought the impulse. She did run to Tracy, but stopped a few feet short and gave him her best regal nod. He bowed, which looked ludicrous in the battle armor.

A cacophony of overlapping conversations began. "Why are you?" "How did you?" "No guns?" "What's going on?" "Who are they?"

"Shut up!" Mercedes yelled and amazingly everyone did. "None of this matters. We've got to get Cipriana and Dani and the kids then get to safety."

"No." It was Tracy, of course. Who else would have the nerve to contradict her so bluntly. "We've got to get you to The High Ground. Once you're safe we'll go back for the others."

Mercedes opened her mouth to object, but Sumiko said in her matter-of-fact way, "He's right and you know it."

"Well then let's split up. Not all of you have to escort me," Mercedes objected.

"Yes we do," Tracy said. "We can ring you and keep you shielded. So give us the guns."

"Yeah, it's a well-known fact that gentlemen make awesome bullet magnets," Davin joked.

They were right and she did know it so Mercedes finally gave a reluctant nod. "This just doesn't seem real," she sighed.

"Probably feels pretty real to that man you killed," Sumiko said bluntly.

The men looked at her with varying degrees of awe. They formed themselves into a rough knot and headed down the cylinder toward the academy.

With a gesture Mercedes pulled Tracy to her side. "Walk with me, Mr. Belmanor." The formation shifted and he was next to her, his shoulder almost brushing against hers.

"I want to thank you." He cast her a sideways glance. "For the knife," Mercedes elaborated. "It's what stopped that man. It cut right through his armor."

"I... I had no idea it could do that." He fell silent. The only sound was their boots ringing on the walkway. "How are you doing?" he added softly.

"Holding it together. Barely." She drew in a ragged breath.

"You've been amazing. To get this far." His voice trembled with suppressed emotion. Mercedes suddenly wanted to feel his arms around her again. She fought back the impulse to cry.

The radio in Tracy's helmet went live. Because of the open faceplate she could hear Boho's voice deep and worried. "Mercedes, are you all right?"

"Yes."

"Where are you?"

"About halfway down the strut."

"I've been trying to raise the Academy staff, but no one is responding."

"This is a mess! What is going on?" Mercedes raged.

"I have no idea. Just get here as quickly as you can. Where you'll be safe."

A voice boomed out over the station's emergency broadcast system. "Infanta." They all froze. Mercedes had only seen this level of quivering focus from terrified horses. "I have men waiting at the Hilton. You'll go there now."

"Yeah. No," she said, assuming that the man could hear her.

"I thought that might be your reaction. So I'm going to give you a bit of an incentive." The *cosmódromo* gave a lurch, and they tumbled onto the tram tracks. Tracy threw his arms around her, and twisted so his body cushioned her fall, and then they were floating. Mercedes clutched him tighter, and he reciprocated.

"Those were the boosters firing. I'm sending this station directly for Ouranos. We'll drop it on your daddy's head if you don't comply."

Coiling fear filled her belly. "You're crazy! Who are you? Why are you doing this?" Mercedes cried.

"You stole our world. Think it's only fair if we wreck yours. Or you can avoid that by turning yourself over to us. Better hurry, Princess. In a few hours we'll be caught in the planet's gravity-well and won't be able to pull out."

There was a click as the PA clicked off then a burst of agitated voices as everyone began to talk at once.

"They're mad!" Sumiko cried, showing far more emotion than usual. She was hanging onto Hugo's ankle.

"Who are they?" Davin sounded plaintive.

"Based on what they're saying they're probably dead-enders from some Hidden World," Ernesto said.

"You're not going!" Boho's voice came in her ear while his holo floated in the air in their midst.

Tracy cut through it all. "It's a false threat." His voice was low and grim.

"What do you mean?" Sumiko asked.

"The orbital weapons platforms will tear this station to shreds long before we enter the atmosphere."

"They're not going to fire on the Infanta," Hugo argued.

"They will if it means keeping a three-hundred-and-twenty-million-kilo space station from crashing onto the capital city of the Solar League," Tracy countered.

"Maybe we should rethink this," Boho said.

"Now you *want* her to surrender?" Sumiko said. Her voice was spiraling with outrage.

"No, Boho's right." Mercedes shook her head. "I have a duty to my subjects on the planet, and there are civilians aboard who don't deserve to die." She paused, fear making her reluctant to say what had to be said. She coughed and forced the words past a sudden obstruction in her throat. "There's no choice. I have to surrender." Her voice sounded smaller than normal.

Seeing that objections were about to start rising from all sides she hurried to add, "Look they won't kill me. Probably. If they did they'd have no leverage with my father." There were reluctant nods of agreement from all around, but not from Tracy.

"There is another option," he said in that intense way he had.

They were at once eye to eye, matching challenges with a look. "So tell me," Mercedes ordered.

28

BIGGER PROBLEMS

"We've never done this." Sumiko's voice had lost its usual flat intonation and was jumping with tension.

"I know," Tracy said.

Space, too large and too empty, hung before them. Suddenly his confident statement that they could "take back the hub" sounded like insane hubris. Tracy clutched a handgrip in the airlock and noticed that his palm felt clammy inside his glove. With the station on a trajectory toward the planet and no longer spinning, the gravity was gone. He wondered how the civilians aboard, especially those kids, were coping. Badly was his guess. He and his little gang needed to get control of the station and fast. Unfortunately he was having trouble taking that first step out of the lock and onto the skin of the ring because he was gazing out at eternity. An insignificant human could get lost in the vastness of space, die, and an uncaring universe wouldn't give a damn. He tried to figure out how to twist around to allow his boot to grip for that first step. In this moment he understood the utility of Donnel's multiple arms and legs. He wished the alien was with him now.

He shook off the fear and went on. "We've got magnetized boots and jet packs. We're not going to float off into space."

"We can't use the packs until Mercedes neutralizes that ship. Otherwise they'll burn us like ants under a magnifying glass," Ernesto pointed out.

"You really are just Mr. Fucking Sunshine, aren't you?" Davin said.

Ernesto shrugged. In the bulky suit it was an exaggerated movement. "Just pointing out the reality."

"Not looking forward to walking along those spokes. That's gonna be scary," Hugo said.

"They're huge." Realizing that might have sounded argumentative rather than reassuring Tracy added, "I know they don't seem like it when we see them from a shuttle, but we'll be fine. Trust me."

"*Trust me.* Why does that always feel like famous last words," Davin muttered.

It couldn't be delayed any longer. Tracy stretched out a leg and felt his boot clamp onto the skin of the ring.

"You know you sent the heir to the Solar League off to fight an armed ship filled with terrorists," Ernesto said conversationally as he stepped out onto the skin of the *cosmódromo*.

"She's the best pilot in the class, and if things get hairy she can boot for the planet." Tracy knew he sounded defensive because he *was* defensive, but it had been the right call. Well, he hoped it had been the right call.

"She also wasn't accepting any argument about it, and she *is* the heir to the Solar League," Sumiko offered.

Her voice had returned to its usual placid range now they were actually walking up the curving side of the station.

"*Deber, Honor, Fidelidad.*" Ernesto intoned the motto of the Arangos.

"We need a motto too," Davin said as they made their way past the anchor for one of the massive cables that linked the ring to the hub. "I'd like to propose *bolas a la pared.*"

"First, I don't have balls," Sumiko said. "And second, *ovarios hasta la pared* or *útero para la pared* just doesn't have the same ring."

"Not to mention I'm getting visual of a uterus plastered on a wall and it's really gross." Davin did sound disgusted.

"Let's cut the chatter," Tracy snapped. "We may be on tight beam, but they might be sweeping for radio communications." He actually heard teeth snapping shut.

After a few minutes he wished he hadn't issued that order. The only sound was his own harsh breath inside the helmet, and a sensation as each boot pulled free and clicked back onto the skin of the *cosmódromo.* Time dragged. They seemed to be *inching* their way across the ring, heading for the nearest of the five massive spokes. Against the backdrop of stars and nebula Tracy did indeed feel like the ant that Ernesto had evoked. He was also wearing just a standard station spacesuit filched from an emergency decompression locker. He'd given his battle armor to Mercedes so she could jack into the *Infierno.* Sumiko was wearing the same type of unarmored suit.

As if summoned by his thoughts, the girl, moving like Frankenstein's monster, closed the gap with Tracy.

"I wonder if we'll see when Mercedes engages that ship," Sumiko said.

"Depends. Our view might be blocked by the station."

"I kind of hope it is… blocked I mean. I only have so much fear and worry to go around," Sumiko muttered. A thin thread of hysteria ran like a leitmotif through the words.

"Only fear? I'm at flat-out bowel-loosening terror," Tracy said, hoping he'd infused some humor into the words. Behind the distorting faceplate he saw her smile so it must have worked.

Sumiko whispered, "I don't want to die…"

"Hugo's not going to let that happen," Tracy said and realized he'd said exactly the wrong thing.

"And *I'm* not going to let Hugo die," she snapped.

"Of… of course not." Tracy cut the link.

He found himself pondering the delicate dance between the genders that was taking place. How would they resolve centuries of training that said men protected women—not the other way around? Of course Mercedes was doing that for him right now, and he wasn't having a big problem with it. So maybe it wasn't going to be a thing.

They reached the spoke. The hub hung like an exclamation point at the center of the five converging spokes and the ten cables running from the top and the bottom of the ring and attaching at the end points of the hub. Though with the wing-like solar panels the hub had the look of a hapless insect trapped in a web of steel.

"Long walk," Hugo grunted.

"Then we better get started," Tracy said.

Boho beamed the coordinates of the mystery ship to her console. "Are you okay?" he asked gently.

"Yes. No. I don't know. You?"

"Someone is trying to get through the door and into computer ops. I'm doing what I can to prevent that. With luck I'll force them to have to get cutters. Still, we better hurry."

"I can't just blaze right at them," Mercedes argued. "I'm using the *cosmódromo* for cover, trying to get around where the sun will be behind me."

"They'll still read you."

"Which is why I'm going to fire chaff the minute I begin my approach."

"Sounds like you've thought of everything, my dear," he said softly.

"I hope."

"I sent off a tight beam warning to the planet," Boho added.

"Good thought. Though I expect the satellites will have noted the station moving," Mercedes said. "Where are the others?"

"On the spoke now moving toward the hub. Do you want me to patch you through to your father?"

The suggestion brought a surge of memory—warm embraces, the rasp of stubble from his cheek at the end of the day, the smell of whisky on his breath, his basso hum as he sang her to sleep after a particularly bad nightmare. It was a fist to the gut and tears tightened her throat.

"No. I need to concentrate so I need you to go away now too."

"All right. *Te adoro*, Mercedes," he said softly.

The click had a finality that left her shaking. It affected the trim of her fighter, and she had to struggle to get it under control. The sensitivity of the coach controls had a downside when you were actually scared. She was good against simulators. Good against drones. This time she would be matching wits with actual human minds. If she succeeded they would die. If she failed she would die.

The hijackers were burning the trim rockets on the station. Mercedes used their brilliant flare to hide the boosters on her fighter. She worked with the computer to calculate the best route to place her with the sun behind her *Infierno*. She burned as long as she could then abruptly changed trajectory and cut the engines. Inertia would have to do the rest. She just hoped the station and its escort wouldn't move too fast for her to get situated for maximum effect.

Apart from her breaths the silence in the cockpit was total. "Te adoro, *Mercedes*." Boho's voice throbbing with suppressed emotion. "*Go get 'em, girl.*" Tracy's voice as he jacked her helmet into the *Infierno*, and gave her a slap on the top of her head to show she was secure. One a voice of fervency and passion. The other a voice of admiration and confidence.

She flicked a finger to bring up her weapons load. Not at full capacity with either missiles or slugs. Well it was what she had. It would have to do. She longed to know what she was up against, but didn't dare paint the enemy ship with her radar or lidar. If she did it would be like lighting a flare and screaming, *Here I am!*

Silence. She knew she was moving only because of the pressure of her body against the restraints and the acceleration couch. The distances were just too vast and objects too small for her to see any real appreciable movement. She knew from her display that she was closing the distance with the other ship, but it didn't feel real. She had to figure out when to light the engines again and start firing. She couldn't just spray and pray. She needed her limited shots to count.

The minutes dragged, the silence filled with her heartbeats and breaths. She keyed her radio on a tight beam to Tracy. "Hey," she said softly.

"Hey yourself."

"Where are you?"

"Little over halfway to the hub," he replied. "It's slow going."

"I'm a bit closer than that."

"You'll be fine. You're the best among us."

She sat with that for a moment, forced into unnatural stillness by the sensitivity of the couch. Once again the difference between the two men was evident. "How do you always know what to say?"

"I don't. Most times and with most people. I only know with you." It was said humbly, almost apologetically.

"Tracy, I want to ask—"

"Shit! Shit! Oh God, no!"

"What's wrong? Tracy? Tracy?" But the connection had been broken.

• • •

"Tracy, I want to ask—"

It was again sensation not sound that gave him a millisecond of warning. A shifting beneath his boots that told him something had changed. Sumiko's helmeted head swung around, and he saw her face behind layers of plexicrystal. He watched as her eyes widened and her mouth opened in a scream.

Tracy tried to spin around, and wrenched his back as his boots refused to release. Out of the corner of his eye he saw a snake writhing across a backdrop of stars. It took a moment before his mind resolved what he was seeing. One of the massive cables that connected the ring to the hub had broken loose and was snapping like a silent whip.

"Shit! Shit! Oh God, no!" He broke the connection to Mercedes and went on open band to his companions. "Down, down! Everybody down!"

Against the stars the cable had seemed a thread. Hugo was directly in the path of the massive braid of metal. Tracy lunged toward his friend, hand outstretched. Too late. With the speed of a falling blade the cable sliced Hugo in half at the waist. It was grotesque. From the hips down the legs remained upright, held in place by the magnetized boots. A halo of blood crystals sparkled around the body. The upper torso was floating away from the station following the trajectory of the cable that had killed him. Tracy had a glimpse of Hugo's slack face before the body spun away, blood crystals and dangling intestines like the tail of some monstrous comet. As he watched the battle armor tried to seal the massive tear in a futile attempt to save a dead man.

Bile, hot and sour, rose through his throat. Tracy

fought it down. Vomiting in the suit could doom him. *But Hugo!* His mind was screaming. His friend. Perhaps his closest friend. *I killed him. God forgive me.*

Sumiko's screams clawed at his ears, pulling him out of his panic and grief. Davin was also screaming. He had been next to Hugo. Tracy yanked his horrified gaze from Hugo's body, searching for Davin. He too had been torn loose from the spoke and was tumbling wildly in space. As Davin spun around Tracy was able to see that his right arm was missing. The screaming stopped. This time the suit did its job and sealed the tear. Shock, blood loss, and a sedative applied by the suit had knocked Davin unconscious. Which meant he couldn't fire his maneuvering jets and return to the station. Someone was going to have to go after him. Which would alert the lurking ship.

Sumiko was sobbing, a heartbreaking sound in the darkness. "Hugo, Hugo, Hugo. No. No. Please. Hugo. No."

"What's happening?" Cullen's voice ringing in his ear. Tracy ignored him.

Ernesto grabbed Tracy by the shoulders. "What do we do?" His voice was cracking with fear.

Tracy chinned on the radio. "Mercedes. Take out that ship. NOW!"

"What? Why?"

"Just *do it*!"

"How dare you address—" Cullen began.

"SHUT UP!" Tracy bellowed. There was a flare of light against the darkness. An answering flare from the mystery ship. *Please God, keep Mercedes safe. Let her save us all.*

"You piece of shit—" Cullen began again.

"Boho, SHUT UP." It was the soft-spoken Ernesto and Tracy stared at him in surprise. It also seemed to surprise Cullen into silence. "Hugo is dead and Davin's hurt."

"And we've got to get Davin," Tracy added. He stared at the rapidly receding bodies. He kicked loose from the skin of the spoke and fired his maneuvering jets. And immediately put himself into a tumble. He fought back panic and nausea and tried to analyze what he'd done wrong. He worked out the amount of force needed to produce thrust in the proper direction and thumbed the jets again. This time he shot straight to Davin's body. He braked a foot away and analyzed the wild tumbling. If he just grabbed he'd be pulled into the same giddy whirl. He worked out the direction, fired the left jet, and grabbed Davin's utility belt. Davin stabilized. Tracy cut the jet, tethered a line to Davin's suit and towed him back to the spoke. Ernesto had recovered his composure enough to catch Davin and pull him down.

"What do we do now?" Ernesto asked.

"Nothing's changed. We still need to get to the control room."

Ernesto rolled an eye toward Sumiko's hunched figure. "We should send her back to the ring with Davin."

"No. I need everybody. You and I can't do this alone."

Ernesto shook his head. "So what? You're just going to tether Davin to a clip and *leave* him out here?"

"No. We'll take him with us. At least get him in atmosphere." *And he might still be useful*, Tracy thought, but he didn't say that out loud.

Ernesto looked back at Sumiko. "I still don't think she'll be much use."

Tracy stepped to the woman and touched her on the shoulder. She looked up at him; her face was blotched and wet with tears. Snot hung on her upper lip. The moisture had begun to fog her faceplate. "Sumiko. We're going to get to the hub and kill the bastards who forced us to be out here. Okay? You want to do that?" She gave a gulping snort followed by an emphatic nod. "Good. Let's go."

Ernesto looked toward the still distant hub. "It's going to take a while."

Tracy looked to where flashes sparked against the blackness of space. "No. We don't have to walk any more. That ship has bigger problems than us right now."

29

SOMETHING TO BURY

Something had happened. Something bad. Tracy's order to her had been blasted on an open channel, which meant she heard what he was hearing. Sumiko sobbing. Boho blustering. Ernesto screaming at Boho to shut up. It sounded like good advice. She needed to focus. To concentrate. She cut the link with her friends and began scanning her instruments. Go in slow and sneaky? Or try to intimidate them with a frontal assault?

"Don't be stupid." The words emerged like an order. She decided to obey herself.

She still had a momentary advantage from the sun, but the ship had no doubt heard the order and would be scanning for her and it wouldn't take long for them to spot her. She needed them to find her, but hopefully miss the present she was going to schedule for late delivery. She programmed three missiles to delay for forty seconds before igniting and heading for their target. At the same time she fired the missiles she was going to fire the engines, give the *Infierno* full throttle and send it looping beneath the stealth ship. At that point she could paint the enemy and read its specs.

The maneuver would bring her to a position on the bow of the ship. Hopefully her sudden appearance would distract them and they wouldn't notice the three small but deadly objects waiting at their stern. She needed to capitalize on that.

She sucked in a deep breath and realized that she was oddly calm. She had one wildly inappropriate little thought go fluttering past—*Daddy's going to kill me for this!*—just before she executed her plan. Acceleration crushed her into the couch. Holos flickered all around her. Alarms blared as the mystery ship painted her. She painted back and stared at the readout. The ship was a Talon. And not just a Talon, a SEGU black ops ship. Stolen? How had the terrorists obtained an older model League assault vehicle? She remembered El-Ghazzawy telling them they were being sold as surplus. *Maybe not the League's best plan*, she thought.

She couldn't worry about that right now. If she survived she'd bring it up with her father and the Chancellor of the Exchequer. Right now it was time to drive home the distraction. Breathless because of the gee forces, Mercedes sent a message on an open channel.

"You bastards wanted me. Well, here. I. Am!" The defiant yell she'd been hoping to achieve emerged more as a breathless little squeak.

Other readouts informed her that her opponent was delivering its own deadly gifts. She allowed her eyes to lose focus so she could see the entirety of her display and not concentrate on just one image. Five missiles were streaking at her. There was no time for fear. She relaxed and let her body, glances of her eyes and flicks of her fingertips take control. Working in concert with the *Infierno*'s sensors she launched slugs on intercept paths with the incoming missiles. She felt the fighter jerk as the slugs were hurled from the rim of her craft.

Another display informed her she would intercept three of the incoming missiles. The other two would hit. Evasive maneuvers held only a thirty-two percent chance to avoid one. To avoid both was a scant thirteen percent.

Now the fear arrived copper bright in the back of her mouth. She fought the impulse to close her eyes. Was it worse to see death approaching? She wanted to simply give up, cry for her daddy, but her body was reacting, instructing her fighter to evade even though she knew it to be hopeless. *One fights for life*, she thought as her slugs tore apart three of the missiles. Then the other two simply detonated. A mist of fragments swept past the *Infierno*, a few large enough to patter against the hull.

Mercedes knew she hadn't done a damn thing. The remaining missiles had spontaneously detonated. No, nothing just spontaneously exploded, she realized. There had to have been a command from the enemy AV to self-destruct. But why? Why not blow her out of space? Only one conclusion—because of who she was. On the station they had wanted her alive and a hostage. Even out here as she tried to kill them the enemy still wanted her alive. Why? They couldn't hope to capture her now.

Forty seconds had elapsed. The rockets on her missiles ignited. It was detected by the enemy ship and in response their starboard engines fired. Her sensors picked up their chaff being released as the Talon attempted to evade.

She watched for return fire from the dark running Talon, but it didn't come. Her computers ran simulations based on the enemy ship's trajectory. It had been pacing the *cosmódromo*. Now it was moving to intercept. Mercedes had no idea if her friends were still exposed on the skin of the station. She couldn't take the chance. She fired off a barrage of depleted uranium slugs, and worked with the targeting computer to create an intricate trajectory for her remaining missiles.

She then tensely watched for returning fire, and waited for her weapons to reach the fleeing ship. Minutes ticked past. The enemy AV began frantic evasion maneuvers. In addition to her new barrage one of her original missiles had survived the cloud of chaff and was still doggedly pursuing.

In a few minutes the Talon would be too close to the *cosmódromo* for her to safely fire a third time. Her friends aside, there were civilians aboard the station. She pictured Dani and Cipriana, the injured nun and the little girls all huddled in a storeroom. She couldn't be punching holes in the habitat. Sensors informed her that one of her plugs had torn through the AV. A little halo of frozen air and other detritus tumbled into vacuum. One of the readouts indicated two bits of floating trash were organic. *I just killed two more people.* The thought flickered through her mind. It had no power. Not like the armored soldier she'd killed. This really was just like the simulator. She began calculations to decide if a final assault could safely be made when the decision was made for her. One of the missiles found its target. There was a bright blossom of fire as the oxygen in the ship burned an angry orange against the blackness. The ship went into a tumble, shedding parts of its structure as it went.

She frantically ran calculations as to the angle of impact. She hoped the missile strike would throw most of the debris onto a new trajectory and not into the station. The pieces weren't big enough to penetrate the ring, but they would kill Tracy and the others if they were still exposed.

• • •

When they reached the airlock the panel was green, signaling it was ready to open. Tracy and Ernesto exchanged glances and Tracy shifted Davin's inert body higher onto his shoulder. "Our first piece of good luck or *come into my parlor said the spider to the fly*?" Tracy asked.

Ernesto chinned his radio. "Boho, the airlock is ready to cycle—"

"Yeah, I know. I opened it for you guys." The nobleman sounded impatient.

"So why didn't you open the damn docking bay?" Tracy growled as Ernesto keyed the panel.

"Because my counterpart on the other side was monitoring like crazy and he spotted every hack I tried."

"So what's changed?" Ernesto asked as they piled into the airlock and the outer door rolled closed.

"I'm not getting pushback. It's like he's gone or distracted."

"Mercedes," Tracy said softly. "But he's not going

to miss an airlock into the hub opening." He gently shoved Davin up to the ceiling and unlimbered the shotgun. Tracy lightly touched Sumiko on the elbow. "Are you okay to do this?"

She gave a sharp nod and drew a pistol from a utility pocket on the thigh of her armor. She gripped a stun grenade in her free hand. Tracy studied the line of her mouth, the set of her jaw and the vast emptiness in her eyes. He cleared his throat. "All righty then." He waved them to either side of the inner door.

He kicked loose from the floor and sent himself drifting to rest with a foot against the ceiling of the airlock. He grabbed hold of Davin by his utility belt. The inner door cycled open with a sigh. A barrage of gunfire greeted them. Bullets whined and pinged off the interior. Sumiko tossed out two stun grenades. A thunderclap resulted. His helmet adjusted volume so Tracy wasn't deafened. He hoped their opponents were out of their helmets.

"Demagnetize," Tracy subvocalized, then he kicked hard and sent himself and Davin diving toward the floor of the airlock. As he flew past the door he shoved Davin's body into the corridor. He had a brief flash of two figures crouched in the corridor bringing their weapons to bear on Davin's form. Tracy fired. His shotgun blast took the man in a *cosmódromo* uniform in the groin and thighs. He staggered, driven backwards by the force of the bullets impacting his body. And not just from Tracy's gunfire, for Sumiko and Ernesto were blazing away as well.

As he hit the floor Tracy tucked, rolled; a touch of one foot had him flying through the airlock door.

In trying to avoid Davin's limp, floating body, Tracy misjudged his trajectory and smacked into the far wall of the corridor. The impact sent him careening off on a tangent. His helmet screens recorded bullet impacts and suit integrity reduced by forty-six percent. The emergency suit was not designed to withstand gunfire.

"You *bastard*! You fucking *bastards*! You killed him. I'm going to kill you!"

The magnetized boots had Sumiko lurching across the corridor. Her target was slow raising his gun. Panic hammered in Tracy's temples because like him Sumiko wore a normal spacesuit not battle armor. *Female voice*, Tracy thought. *He's hesitating because of that but dear God what is she doing?*

He struggled to find purchase on a wall, ceiling, floor—anything so he could go to her aid. Ernesto shot past Tracy forming a human spear in the air and slammed head first into the terrorist. Sumiko was climbing their enemy, battering at the faceplate with her pistol. Tracy joined in the pile-on, trying to grip the man's wrist and keep him from bringing his pistol to bear. It was a flailing confusion of arms, hands and legs. Whoever he was the man was far more at ease in zero gravity than the three students. He plucked Sumiko off his chest and threw her down the hall. An elaborate somersault in the air dislodged Ernesto. He then fired his suit jets directly into Tracy's face, burning and scarring his faceplate. Blinded by the fogged faceplate Tracy panicked, yelled and pushed away. There was no choice; he pushed back his helmet and saw the terrorist flying around a turn in the corridor.

"Come on! Come on! We've got to get to Control," Ernesto babbled.

Tracy brought up the schematics of the hub and they set off using handholds to help propel themselves through the corridor. The elevators were in lockdown, but they cut through the ceiling and went up the elevator shaft to the top level.

Mercedes' voice rang through their radios. "Ship is neutralized! I repeat ship is... dead." Her voice was filled with excitement, wonder and an edge of hysteria.

"*Brava*, Highness!" came Boho's voice.

At the same time Tracy said, "Nice work, Mer— Highness," he quickly amended.

"Where are you? Are you all right?" There was now worry and tension in her voice.

"We're fine. Almost to Control," Tracy soothed.

Boho joined the conversation. "Holy shit!" His voice was a hoarse whisper.

"What?" Tracy demanded.

"Oh my God!" Mercedes said.

"Good," was Sumiko's comment.

"Why?" from Ernesto.

Since Tracy wasn't wearing his helmet he had no access to the pictures they were clearly seeing.

"What's happened?" he demanded.

They rounded a final corner. The doors to Control were in front of them. "You'll see soon enough," Ernesto said as he overrode the door lock.

The doors slid open. There were five bodies in battle armor on the floor. Their helmets were back, their eyes were bleeding holes and their heads bloody pulps with the top of their craniums blown off. It was what happened to a skull when a shotgun was placed beneath a man's chin and fired.

"Why?" Ernesto repeated in a tight voice.

Tracy considered possible explanations while Sumiko said in a hard tone, "I don't care. I'm just glad they're dead."

Mercedes got to the answer first. "No exit strategy. I blew it out of space."

"So we never had to do this. Cross the struts, get Hugo ki… ki…" Sumiko couldn't say the word, and the look she gave Tracy left him feeling as if he'd been bathed in acid.

"No, it was necessary," Ernesto said quietly. "We had to get control of the *cosmódromo*."

"And now we've got to get it stopped before planetary defenses blow *us* out of space," Tracy concluded grimly.

• • •

Stopping a giant space station and returning it to its stable LeGrangian orbit proved to be harder and far more complex than they expected, but fortunately the trio had help from engineers on Ouranos, and many of the actual *cosmódromo* personnel had been detained and not killed. In fact Tracy, Ernesto and Sumiko were firmly shooed away. Once that happened Sumiko retreated to a corner, tethered herself into a seat and just sat rocking back and forth in misery while she silently cried. Tracy and Ernesto sidled up next to each other and cast helpless glances at the girl.

"Should we say something?" Ernesto asked.

"What? I have no idea what to say," Tracy muttered.

"Me neither." They stood in silence for a moment. "I should get some medics. Go get Davin."

"Yeah. Good idea." Tracy coughed. "I should go recover Hugo... his body... I guess."

"Yeah." Ernesto called for a medical team and they all went off to recover Davin who was still floating in a corridor four levels down. Tracy went along since he would need to use the same airlock to recover Hugo. Or what was left of him.

Ernesto and the medics strapped Davin onto a backboard and headed for a hospital. Tracy stood outside the airlock and tried to force himself back out onto the strut. Hugo's upper body was lost forever. Locating it would be a Herculean task and they had other more pressing issues, but shouldn't he at least bring back something for the family to bury? Of course what would be returning might be more horrifying than comforting. Tracy tried to decide what was best. Go into vacuum and cut the body loose? Tell the family Hugo had been swept away by that snapping cable rather than cut in half?

Through the radio chatter he picked up the information that Mercedes was bringing the battered *Infierno* into a docking bay in the hub. He decided on cowardice and headed there instead.

30

NOT WITHOUT COST

The bay doors were closing at a glacial pace. Mercedes lay quivering in the cockpit couch. Despite the clear dome, claustrophobia seized her and she desperately wanted out of what now felt like a coffin. The screen flared green indicating that atmosphere had been restored to the docking bay. She keyed back the dome, yanked out the helmet jack, pulled off the helmet and scrambled out of the *Infierno*. She ended up against the roof of the docking bay with the force of her exit. Her braid had come loose and tendrils of hair wove in a dance over her head.

There were a lot of people entering the docking bay. Most wore station uniforms. One wore a spacesuit and magnetized boots held him to the floor. It wasn't conscious, she just flew to him and Tracy caught her. His arms closed around her and despite the metal and composite material that separated them she felt warm and safe.

"You did it. I knew you would," he whispered.

She pressed her cheek against his and their floating hair, dark and light, entwined over their heads. He felt hot to the touch. "And so did you. You retook the hub."

A shiver went through him. "Not without cost."

"What happened?"

"Hugo is dead and Davin's badly hurt." It emerged flat and harsh.

Mercedes pulled back and pressed a hand against her mouth. "Oh *Dios*. So I guess this is what it's like," she said softly. "Really like." Their hands reached for each other. Reassurance against the inevitable darkness.

"Can you do it?" Tracy asked softly.

"I don't know." She paused and thought about Davin and his pranks and practical jokes. Would that cheerful and blithe personality be warped by this? Hugo she hadn't known all that well, but his death— "Oh God, Simi. How is she?"

"Not good. It would probably help if she had a woman to talk to."

"Have you got Cipriana and Dani yet?"

"No. Everybody's running around trying to get the station stabilized."

"Which makes us nicely... superfluous," Mercedes said. "So we can go."

That crooked grin appeared. "And here I thought we were—" Tracy began.

"Big damn heroes," they concluded in chorus, quoting Chief Deal's constant refrain.

Mercedes grew serious. "You are."

High color flared in his cheeks. "What? Me? No." Tracy was vigorously shaking his head.

"Yes. You came up with the whole plan. Just like that." Mercedes tried to snap her fingers. It didn't work in battle armor.

"Yeah, well, you took out that ship."

"And you took the hub."

"Not really." The excitement that had lit his eyes died and he looked much older than his eighteen years. "All I did was get Hugo killed and Davin hurt. Most of those *pendejos* committed suicide before we reached them."

The station personnel were hovering, literally with the lack of gravity. Mercedes magnetized her boots and reluctantly clomped over to greet them. "Highness." It was an older man with skin like old yellowed ivory who had spoken, and he gave her a courtly bow. "We have instructions to take you to the manager's quarters until the imperial yacht arrives. Your father wishes you to return planetside as soon as possible."

"Thank you, but I still have a pressing duty to perform."

"I appreciate that, Highness, but I must insist," the man said.

She glanced at the nameplate woven into his jacket. "Really, Señor Hsieh, you're going to overrule me? Really?"

Mercedes watched the internal debate. Good sense won out. It probably also didn't hurt that she was larger than the slender older man in her heavy battle armor. Hsieh nodded and stepped back. "I'll inform the palace."

"No need for you to be the bearer of that particular bit of news, señor. I'll let them know myself." The man looked pathetically grateful.

She gestured to Tracy and he clicked his way to her side.

They stepped into the hub. Mercedes shot him

a glance and they burst out laughing. "God I love it when you're so badass. I mean regal."

Suddenly shy, she looked at him from beneath her lashes. "Do you honestly think that? That I'm badass?"

"Absolutely." He paused and looked awkwardly away. "And I wouldn't worry. I think you can do anything."

There was a sudden obstruction in her throat. "Tracy, I—"

At the same time he said. "Mercedes."

And then they were in each other's arms and kissing passionately. Panting breaths, moaning cries. She realized with shock they were hers. She wanted to tear off the confining suit, crawl inside him. Her belly seemed filled with molten honey. His arms were trembling, his mouth hungrily seeking hers. He kissed her eyes, his lips played across her ears and his tongue darted into her ear. Her knees went weak. Then back to her lips. He gave a groan and whispered against her mouth:

"Mercedes… I… I love you."

Inexpressible joy swept through her. *I love you. I love you. I love you.* She wanted to kick loose from the wall of the station where their boots held them. Go spinning and diving and spiraling through the air.

"I love you too." The words were out before she had time to consider and deep inside a small voice warned this was unwise. She pushed it aside and melted back into his embrace. They kissed and time stood still. Ironically it was he who reminded her of her duty.

"We… we better get going."

"Yes, yes." She tried to smooth her hair and realized that was silly.

Mercedes checked the *cosmódromo* schematics, and

picked a spoke that would bring them into the ring at a point relatively close to the gelato store. Because they were in a hurry they demagnetized their boots and tried freefall flight while holding hands. They made it with only a few unplanned tumbles, spins, giggles and wall crashes. She wondered if it was wrong to be giddy after all that had happened, but she had won and Tracy was here, and they were young and alive and in love.

The bodies of the terrorist and the counter clerk had drifted to the same area above the buckets of gelato where they spun lazily in a macabre semi-embrace. Mercedes' mad euphoria came crashing down around her and a whimper slipped out. Tracy laid a hand on her arm.

"It's okay."

"I didn't even think about it. I just killed him. What does that make me?" she whispered.

"Alive?"

"That's flippant!"

"You're right. I'm sorry." He raised her hand to his lips though she couldn't feel the touch through the heavy gloves. "I think it says that you are very brave and that our instructors taught us very well. We react, do what we have to do, and brood about it later."

"Right. Later." Mercedes kicked over to the storeroom door and gave it a shove, expecting resistance. It swung open and she stifled her annoyance. They couldn't have found anything to block the entrance?

Boxes of cones and paper bowls floated in the air along with twenty little girls, the nun and Cipriana. There was no sign of Danica. The tiny room was also filled with floating gobbets of vomit and drops of blood. Cipriana gave a wordless cry of joy and launched herself at Mercedes only to get hit with vomit on one cheek and go into a spin as she wiped it furiously away.

"Oh gross! Oh God, gross!"

The little girls began to wail, the sad gull-like cries interspersed with calls of "I want to go home!" "I want my mommy!"

"Let's get you all out of this muck. Tracy—" Mercedes began.

"I'll get the sister to a hospital," he said. As usual he understood without her having to spell it out.

He left with the unconscious woman. Mercedes looked after him for a long moment until a touch on her elbow by Cipriana brought her back to the present.

"So, you're going to have to tell me everything," Cipriana said.

"I will once we take care of these kids," Mercedes promised. "Okay, everybody. We're going to play a game. All of you hold hands." She scanned the little faces and picked the little redheaded girl who seemed the calmest and had said she loved freefall. "And you—what's your name?"

"Nihala."

"Okay, Nihala, you're going to hold my hand, and I'm going to take us all in a long line to the park."

"I want to get *down*," a girl sobbed.

"And we will soon, but it'll be fun in the park. We'll play like birds in the trees. Okay. Everybody take hands."

Cipriana helped and eventually they had the kids in a long human chain. It was awkward and there were a few bumped heads as they made their way out of the gelato store and into the park. Mercedes was relieved to see station personnel in their grey and maroon uniforms moving through the buildings. Once they were spotted people arrived to help with the children. One thing that could be depended upon—League citizens would always spring into action and care for kids.

Once the girls were handed off Mercedes and Cipriana retreated to a park bench, grabbed hold and hung there. "So where is Dani?" Mercedes asked.

Cipriana shrugged. "I haven't got a clue. She was weirdly calm during the crisis…"

"Wow. That seems so unlike her."

"I know, right? But when the announcement came that the station was once more under League control she took off like a cat running from a hose."

Unbidden a sharp and vivid memory came to mind. Dani already tightly gripping a freefall ring on the wall of the gelato store while Mercedes and her other two ladies struggled to find handholds. Dani—awkward Dani who put the least amount of effort into any exercise and any assignment. Dani who complained daily about everything she was missing at home. *That* Dani beat them all out to find a handhold?

Unless she knew what was coming.

An emotion cold as death gripped Mercedes.

• • •

Ernesto had secured himself to a chair in the *cosmódromo*'s hospital waiting room when Tracy kicked through the door with the sister in his arms. The nun had regained consciousness during their leaping journey to the hospital, and through lips gone white with pain thanked him for his help. Hospital staff wasted no time in taking command of the situation. A male doctor had made a quick exam, then ordered the nurse assisting him to locate a female physician even if it was an alien. The trio vanished through the doors and Tracy settled into a chair next to his classmate.

"Hell of a day," he said, but nothing could dampen his mood. *Mercedes loves me. She loves me.* It was like a hum that ran through everything, made colors brighter and life sweeter.

"Yeah. You can say that again," Ernesto sighed.

Tracy found himself fascinated by the slow movement of the tap-pads and potted plants that were floating around the lobby. For a hospital it was a pleasant place with one wall of windows tinted a pale green. An entertainment screen hung on one wall and was playing a rerun of an old comedy show that had been popular a decade or so ago. The clerk at the front desk was watching the news on his ScoopRing. Tracy hadn't been in a hospital since that final visit before his mother died. It was bringing back memories of a skeletal figure, her sweet voice reduced to a thread. His father in tears and Granddad berating a nurse. The cold in the waiting room and the odors brought it all back and he shuddered.

Tracy finally stirred himself to ask, "How's Davin?"

"They took him into surgery. They need to trim off the bottom of the arm. The suit didn't seal as quickly as hoped so there's a lot of damage to the tissue from the cold and vacuum."

"They told you all that?"

"No. I saw the arm, or what was left of it, when they took him out of the suit."

"Do you think he'll come back to school?"

Ernesto shrugged. "He could with a good prosthetic. Question is—will he want to?" Ernesto shot Tracy a sideways glance. "Has Hugo's family been informed?"

Tracy shook his head. "I haven't done it."

"Did you ever deal with the body?"

"No." Tracy then added, "I should go do that." But he found himself unwilling and almost unable to move. Fatigue had hit him like a hammer between the eyes. "But first I need your advice."

"Okay."

"Should I recover the body or cut it loose?"

"Jesus! You want me to make a call like that?"

"Well, I can't. Not all on my own."

Ernesto leaned forward and closed his hands between his knees. "You know the family?"

"A bit."

"What would hurt less?"

Tracy thought about the loud, boisterous Devris clan. "Not seeing him… like that."

Ernesto rubbed a hand across his face as if trying to wipe away fatigue. "It's just meat at this point. Hugo is gone. His soul gathered to heaven."

"So let them remember him as he was?" Ernesto nodded.

Tracy unclipped from the chair. Ernesto's hand shot out and gripped his arm, holding him in place. They formed a human right angle with Tracy floating horizontal to Ernesto. They were face to face. "There's going to be an inquiry," the marqués said.

"Yeah, and this is news how?"

"They're going to want to know why the cable snapped."

It felt like a trickle of ice water had gone down Tracy's back. "I take it you have a theory?"

"More than a theory. I ran some numbers. The cable was secured just over the bay doors…" Ernesto's voice trailed away.

"The bay doors I weakened with a missile and then rammed," Tracy said slowly.

"Yes."

"So I damaged the structural integrity." He tried to keep his voice flat and emotionless but inwardly he was quaking. He had killed his friend.

Despite his efforts Ernesto seemed to sense Tracy's turmoil. "All the jinking the station was doing didn't help. It's nobody's fault. Well it's these assholes' fault—"

"But the FFH will blame the dirty *intitulado*!" Tracy broke Ernesto's hold and pushed away. Harder than he intended. He ended up halfway across the lobby without any convenient surface to use and even out of reach of the furnishings. He fired the suit jets only to have them sputter and die before his boots could connect with the metal-infused floor. The helpless spinning just added to his grief and fury.

Ernesto untethered from the chair, magnetized the boots on his armor and clumped over to Tracy. He dragged him down until Tracy's boots connected. "Not if they don't know." His voice was low and intense.

"What? What are you talking about?"

"Hugo is dead. Davin's been badly injured.

Between shock, trauma and anesthesia his memories are going to be garbled. Only you and I know you fired at and then rammed those doors—"

"The *Infierno* was crumpled—"

"And Mercedes took it out and fought a battle. Who's to say when that happened? I'm not planning on telling. Are you?"

The anger leached out of him. Tracy dashed the betraying moisture from his eyes. "I can't believe... you'd do that—"

"If it weren't for your planning and Mercedes' skills we'd all be dead now along with everyone on this *cosmódromo*."

"Boho knows. He was monitoring our communications."

"I expect Boho will follow my lead. It's hard to look like a big damn hero when you stayed behind and let a girl fight for you."

"So you saw what I saw."

Ernesto nodded. "And we're *never*, *ever* going to talk about it again." The bright smile eased the tension in his face. "And hey, if we should end up serving under him we can depend on him to keep us out of danger. Better probably than somebody who is more courageous."

31

THE BEST YOU CAN HOPE FOR

"It seemed like every other building was in lockdown, but not our store. We were the target."

"Well of course you were," Boho said. "But they clearly didn't want you dead. Probably wanted to use you as a bargaining chip with your father."

It was just the two of them in the small observation lounge. Mercedes had shed the battle armor and was once more dressed in her uniform. She longed for a shower to wash away the sweat that coated her entire body, but that would have to wait until the station could resume its spin. She had no idea how to bathe in freefall. They were floating face to face, but it was dim in the lounge and she could barely make out his features.

"It sure didn't feel that way at the time, but based on what happened with those missiles... I think you're right but for the wrong reason. But let me finish what I started to tell you—"

He didn't. He interrupted and asked, "Why were you even in the ring?"

She smothered her irritation and answered,

"Zeng had set up this field trip. I didn't want to do it. I thought it was too soon. Particularly with such little kids, but Dani was all gung-ho which is so unlike her, and that's what I wanted to discuss."

"Okay, I'm listening."

Mercedes desperately wished she could pace. Movement helped her focus and marshal her thoughts. She used Boho's shoulder to launch herself at the wall behind her. She tapped it with the toe of her boot and flew to the other wall. Another touch and back again. Boho's head followed her like a cat watching a feather as she ping-ponged back and forth.

"Dani knew the station was going to lurch. I'm sure of it. She had a grip on a handhold before it occurred."

"Dani in league with Hidden World terrorists?" Boho threw back his head and laughed, which sent him tumbling.

"Which means they weren't terrorists, Boho," Mercedes snapped. "Listen to me. There was no way for me to evade both missiles. My chaff didn't take them. They self-destructed." That had his attention. He had stopped laughing and was groping for a handhold. "And then there's the suicide of the remaining attackers. Terrorists would have wanted a big public trial, a lot of ballyhoo and publicity to air their grievances."

He was looking stricken. "Oh, shit. Pardon me."

"No, I think that pretty much sums it up."

"So, we're looking for somebody who wasn't willing to go so far as to kill the Emperor's eldest daughter, but wanted her endangered," Boho mused.

"But why and to what end?" Mercedes said. Boho was muttering, running a hand across his face. "What are you thinking?" Mercedes demanded.

"Forcing you onto the throne has damaged your father's popularity—"

"People are really that upset about me? I know the press were huffing but—"

"Oh yeah. My dad hears it all the time."

"I haven't heard anything."

"That's because you're not in our clubs."

"And that's the problem, isn't it? We *aren't* in your clubs." She had stopped kicking off and now hung aimlessly twisting in the air. "What are they saying?"

"That this social experiment endangers the League. That the troops won't follow you. That the aliens will get uppity and come for their money and their wives, and do unnatural experiments on their kids."

"That's just stupid."

"Yeah, but that's how fear works. If you'd all gotten captured there would have been holos of you tearfully asking for help. Your dad sends in the *fusileros*. Terrorists flee—"

"I get sent home. Cousin Musa is once again heir."

"But if they killed you all the sympathy would swing back to your father."

Her rage had curdled into exhaustion and sadness. "Dani," she said thickly. "How could she?"

Boho shrugged. "They must have made her a very attractive offer."

Mercedes grasped at a hopeful straw. "Or maybe they threatened her. Or her family. She might have been forced to be part of this."

Boho caught her by the hand and pulled her close. "Come on, Mer, don't be naive. We've known Dani since we were little kids. If somebody had threatened her she'd have been a watering pot."

What he'd said was true though she hated to acknowledge it. She gave a reluctant nod. "So what do we know so far? Dani was involved which means her father was too."

"Zeng. He set up the meeting so you'd be outside the walls of The High Ground. And he has to have issued the order to shelter in place."

"And of course Musa." Mercedes gripped Boho's shoulder and fought the tears. "Do you think Arturo and Mihalis and Jose knew?"

"God, I hope not." Boho once again ran a hand across his face. "There's never been a crisis of rule like this."

"Because no other emperor only had daughters," Mercedes said sadly.

"God what a spectacle. Trials, executions. You need to tell your father all of this. Get SEGU on it."

"First I'm going to find out just how much Dani knows."

She tried to pull away, but Boho didn't release her hand. "Wait. You should never have been in that fighter. It should have been me... keeping you safe."

She opened her mouth to object, but before she could speak he kissed her. It was very practiced, proving Boho's horndog reputation wasn't just brag and boast. Confusion filled her. She should pull away, but it was only her third kiss and Boho was very handsome and she was curious. She was also beginning to regret the incautious words that had been spoken. As the full measure of Dani's treachery had become clear the world of the FFH and the League came crashing back.

Her father had told her to find a consort. Would he accept Tracy? Tracy was undoubtedly brilliant and she would make it clear it had been Tracy's tactics that had saved them all, and they had two more years to make the point, but... but... but... No, that was an analysis for another day.

Boho seemed to sense her distraction. His right hand moved to a more intimate location. As his fingers stroked across her left breast a tingle leaped from her nipple to her groin. She was horrified at the reaction and felt disloyal. Her confusion deepened. Did this mean she didn't love Tracy?

"I've never made love in freefall," he whispered into her ear, pressing his advantage. "It's always been an ambition of mine."

"I can't. I don't have... protection." It wasn't true, but things were moving too fast and she was too confused.

"Don't worry. I *always* have protection."

That reminder of his tomcat ways put an end to her confusion. She put a hand in the center of his chest as the public address system crackled to life.

"Prepare for gravity spin in three minutes. Please seek a secure location, gravity spin will initiate in two minutes forty-three seconds."

Mercedes pushed herself away from Boho. "I guess you're going to have to keep waiting to try that particular experiment."

"Damn. Terrible timing. To whom do I complain?"

His grin was bright against his tan skin and Mercedes found herself smiling back despite her annoyance. She inched her way down the curving sides of the observation lounge as weight began to tug at her joints. Eventually enough gravity had returned for there to again be a sense of up and down, and once her feet could stay connected to the floor she held out her hand to Boho. He kissed it and then rubbed her hand against his cheek. The contrast of soft skin and prickly stubble was rather pleasant. He released her and Mercedes walked carefully to the door.

She glanced back. "And by the way, Tracy's decision made perfect sense. I *am* the best in the class in the *Infierno*."

"Only because they destroyed those last two missiles," he snapped and she wondered if it was from wounded vanity or the mention of Tracy's name.

"You realize you just insulted me, right?"

For an instant he looked like a dog caught stealing from the table, then he said smoothly, "I apologize. I'm just upset because you could have been killed."

"No, it's good I had to face that. For me to fulfill my father's dream I have to be a soldier… and soldiers die."

The reduced gravity allowed him to reach her side in two long steps. He lifted her hand and kissed it again. "I won't let that happen."

• • •

His breaths and the slow beep of the heart monitor in his suit were a grating wound on the profound silence of the galaxy. The stars seemed cold and remote, like an infinite number of hostile eyes gazing down on him and judging him. Tracy had prayed that the boots would have failed and what remained of Hugo's body had already been lost to the void, but that prayer was not answered.

The lower body was like some grotesque broken piece of ancient statuary silhouetted against the stars. Tracy fought nausea and forced himself to walk down the length of the strut. He kept a wary eye out for the broken cable but with the tension gone and the *cosmódromo* once more stabilized it spun at the same speed as the station, a silver sweep hand marking time on the face of the universe.

He reached the body, clamped his own boots firmly to the skin of the strut, grabbed the utility belt and yanked. The boots released and he was holding the corpse. He wanted to just thrust it violently away from him, but he wasn't sure he could generate enough momentum that it would be lost forever.

After the beating it had taken Tracy didn't trust the emergency suit so he had returned to the academy for battle armor. Now he released his boots, fired his jet pack and boosted away from the station. This far out he didn't need to worry about the body being caught in the gravity-well of Ouranos and being spotted and recovered by a missile platform or some passing ship. Still he wanted the evidence to be lost forever, so he calculated a trajectory that would ultimately carry the body into the sun. The ultimate funeral pyre.

The moment was approaching. Catechism lessons ensured that Tracy had a selection of prayers committed to memory. He had been sure to shut down all radio transmissions, and as he released Hugo's body he murmured:

"May God remember forever Hugo Devris who

has gone to his eternal rest. May he be at one with the One who is life eternal. May the beauty of his life shine forevermore, and may my life always bring honor to his memory. Amen."

He pushed the body away from him, and fired his jets to halt his momentum. He hung in space watching until he could no longer see the corpse. Then he boosted back to the *cosmódromo*.

He was confident his space walk had not been observed. Everyone was still taken up with the cleanup and aftermath of the attack. He would carry this secret to his grave.

• • •

Danica wasn't in their quarters, and it was clear the girl had left in a very big hurry. Clothes were strewn on the floor. A few outfits were missing and the jeweled hairpins were also gone. Mercedes wanted to stalk down every hall and every building on the station until she found her but knew that was stupid. She considered informing *cosmódromo* security and sending them out hunting, but the more people she involved the less discreet this became and she didn't want to do that until she'd had a chance to talk to her father.

Which left her with Cipriana rolling a desperate eye toward her and then giving a significant nod toward Sumiko, who sat on the edge of her bed with crumpled tissues like fallen camellias all around her feet. She was crying but her face was twisted with rage as well as grief.

"I'll… I'll just leave you… two," Cipriana said and she ducked out the door.

Mercedes opened her mouth to object but it was too late. She steeled herself and turned to face Sumiko. "Sumi, I'm so sorry. Umm… are you… all right?"

The face that was revealed when she looked up was wet, blotched, red and ravaged. "Of course I'm not all right! What a stupid thing to ask me! My love is gone. I'll never find anyone ever again. And I don't want to. My Hugo is dead." The final word was a cry of anguish.

Mercedes settled on the bed and put her arm around Sumiko. "I'm sorry. He was… he seemed… I mean I didn't know him all that well, but I know how much he meant to you and you wouldn't love anybody who wasn't wonderful." *I'm a babbling fool*, Mercedes thought.

"It cut him in half, Mer. I watched it happen. His intestines were trailing. The blood was like red snowflakes. He just floated away. I saw his face in the helmet spinning, spinning until I couldn't see it any longer."

No, no, no. Don't tell me this. I don't want to hear. Horror held her silent for a moment. "I didn't… know. Tracy just said he'd been killed." *Oh God, it could have been Tracy. Thank God it wasn't Tracy.* She immediately felt horrible for thinking about herself and the man who was dominating her thoughts.

"I know there's nothing I can say or do—" Mercedes began only to be interrupted.

"Yes, actually there is." The tears were gone and Sumiko looked fierce. "I want out of here. I *never* want to come back. Get me out of this."

"Sumi, I'm not sure I can—"

"Well you better or otherwise I'll tell!"

"Tell what?"

"About you and Belmanor."

"There's nothing to tell," but she knew her blush betrayed her.

"I know you were snogging him in the observation lounge. If you thought Danica's father would be upset, well, just think about how *your* father will react. Let me leave and I'll keep your secret."

"You're threatening the crown."

"No, I'm threatening him. You'll be protected like you always are, but he'll be destroyed when it comes out. And it will. The closer you get to graduation the more you'll be scrutinized."

The truth of the statement quelled the bubble of anger she had felt rising. "All right. I agree." She then added, "What will you do?"

"Try to find somebody. It won't be the same, my true love is gone, but I'll try to be good to him, whoever he might be, and at least I'll have children. That will help." She sighed. "It's the best I can hope for."

And the best I can hope for too, Mercedes thought. For she now knew what she must do to protect Tracy. Would it make it easier knowing it was also her duty?

32

THE GAME OF KINGS

Tracy was once again at the imperial palace. This time in a formal garden. Fortunately the weather was obliging for this outdoor event. A grandstand had been erected and draped with Solar League banners. There were chairs for the dignitaries on the grandstand and a very impressive throne for the Emperor. Tracy and his companions were standing behind that elaborate piece of furniture. Neither the Emperor nor Mercedes had yet arrived. Overhead a flock of camera drones bobbed and weaved, beaming pictures to ScoopRings across Ouranos and into the Foldstream so citizens from all around the League worlds could watch.

On the grass in front of the stage were more chairs for attending dignitaries and family members, and in the final row, last chair on the left, sat his father. He was too far away for Tracy to discern his expression. One thing Tracy knew for certain: his father's grey morning suit would be as beautifully tailored as any worn by the FFH. Hugo's family was also in the last row, but on the other side from Alexander. Clearly proximity to the stage was an indicator of rank.

Behind the attendees' chairs reporters churned and jockeyed for better positions and technicians were setting up lights. Deeper in the garden, tents and tables were being set up for the reception that would follow this presentation of medals. Hajin and Isanjo servants slipped in and out of the palace carrying tablecloths, utensils, glasses, and trays of food.

It had been a chaotic nine days. The imperial yacht and yachts belonging to the Cullen, Tsukuda and Pulkkinen families had arrived a few hours after the *cosmódromo* was returned to stable orbit to whisk away their children. Ernesto's family had chartered a shuttle. Danica had found some way off the station, and her family was several days' travel away from Ouranos. Which left Wilson and Tracy as the only students at the academy.

They had carefully avoided each other, which was blindingly obvious in the mess hall since they were the only students at The High Ground. The fact they picked tables well away from each other and ate alone did not go unremarked by the master chiefs and the few professors who had remained aboard. Zeng never put in an appearance and Tracy wondered what had happened to him.

He had talked with his father a few times, and had been assured by station communications personnel that he wouldn't be charged for the calls. Classes were supposed to have resumed two days before, but the start of the new semester had been postponed while repairs were made to the *cosmódromo*.

He passed the time by reading news reports about

the attack. The part played by Mercedes had been prominent and rightly so, but Cullen was the other individual who got the most press, which galled Tracy to his core. Davin had been praised for his bravery and his injury. Hugo was mentioned, but more attention was paid to his father, and there were images of Caballero Malcomb Devris, his fat face streaming with tears, fists clenched, mouth open as he bellowed his grief. Ernesto was mentioned, and finally Tracy—the afterthought. Except in the *Alibi*, the independent news outlet read by those not in the FFH. There had been a very large article about Tracy there. To be fair every time Mercedes had been quoted she credited Tracy with the plan that had liberated the station.

Then eight days after the attack a message was delivered that a shuttle would be arriving to take Tracy planetside for a medal ceremony. He had found Mark in his room and made an effusive apology about how he was going to have to leave Mark for a few days and why. The look of rage on the other scholarship student's face had given him more than a little delight. As he walked away Tracy had tossed back over his shoulder, "Too bad you didn't come, but then you're an expert on how to get ahead."

And now he was standing in his dress uniform, in the palace garden and about to be decorated by the Emperor himself with the *Distinguido Servicio Cruzar* for extreme gallantry and risk of life in combat with an armed enemy force. On a table to the right were nine polished wood boxes with the blue enamel and silver medals nestled in dark blue velvet. Two of the medals were accompanied by a small silver bar indicating meritorious service.

Those were reserved for him and Mercedes.

He glanced at his fellow recipients. Davin looked pale and his empty sleeve was pinned across the front of his jacket. A frown had settled between Sumiko's brows. She seemed to sense his gaze and met his eyes. What he saw there had Tracy recoiling; it was pure, naked hatred. He wanted to break ranks, rush to her and apologize again. Ernesto seemed distracted, head bowed, lost in his own thoughts. Cipriana stood at rigid attention and she looked proud. Cullen had his usual expression of superior confidence. Danica was milk white; even her lips seemed bloodless and there was a blank look in those blue eyes. She looked like a dumb animal facing the slaughterhouse, not somebody about to receive a medal.

Tracy wondered what *his* face would tell to the *billions*—he tried to process that number and failed—who might be watching. He wished his thoughts hadn't gone there because now his gut felt like an empty cavern filled with butterflies with razor blade wings. No wonder Lady Danica was looking poleaxed.

• • •

"What is Dani doing here?" Mercedes demanded. "After everything I told you. Didn't—"

The Isanjo valet gave a final adjustment to the sash at the Emperor's waist. He was wearing his *Orden de la Estrella* uniform with his admiral epaulets and a mass of medals and honors glittering on both sides of the jacket. Her father held up a restraining hand, and turned away from the full-length mirror. "She's here to receive her medal," he said mildly, but there was a clear warning in his dark eyes.

Mercedes flushed with embarrassment and bit her lower lip. The Emperor waved toward the door. The servant bowed his way out of the bedchamber.

"I'm sorry, I know better than to talk in front of servants, but what the hell? I mean really, didn't SEGU find anything?"

"Yes, they did, and please watch the profanity."

"Then what…" She bit back the *fuck* she wanted to utter and said, "…are you doing? She was part of a plot to kill me."

"No, she and her family were part of a plot to point out how incompetent and useless you are, and how foolish I was to think you could ever take my place. The whispers would begin that I would endanger the safety of the League rather than see any but my own blood on the throne—"

"Well, isn't that true?"

She was hurt and hoped the barb might rattle him, but he just gave her a smile and flicked a forefinger across her cheek. "But you weren't useless, and you didn't fail and have to be rescued by the troops I was preparing to send to the station. Unfortunately for our plotters they had assumed that their view of reality was the correct one rather than corroborating that view with actual facts."

Mercedes sank down on the elaborate bed. The enamel and gold headboard extended almost to the ceiling and covered half the wall. All nine sisters could comfortably have slept in the bed itself.

"What did they offer? What was so tempting that

Dani would betray me and endanger all those people?"

"A secret betrothal to Mihalis."

Grabbing a pillow Mercedes held it tight against her aching stomach. Her throat was tight and she swallowed hard several times. She couldn't decide if she was furious or just devastated. Her father strolled to his jewelry case and slid rings onto his fingers while she processed the information. Mercedes shook her head.

"Then I don't understand what you're doing. And who were the others who were involved, the fake terrorists?"

He joined her on the bed and slipped an arm around her. "It took a while for DeLange to follow the threads," her father said, referring to the head of the intelligence service. "They were disgruntled members of the FFH, outraged officers in *Orden de la Estrella*, and of course my cousin, Musa. The operatives on the station had been recruited from disgraced members of SEGU or cashiered soldiers. They had had their fingerprints removed and made it impossible for retinal scans to be used to verify their identities, but you realizing Lady Danica was part of this plot gave us a thread to pull." He smiled. It wasn't a pleasant expression. "And pull it we did."

"But nobody has been arrested."

"No, nor will they be. No one must know I was challenged by my own nobles or the military."

"So they just walk away?"

"Oh no. Captain Zeng is being promoted and assigned to a particularly dangerous post—"

"He seemed so sympathetic," Mercedes blurted.

"And thus you learn another valuable lesson, my dear. Take nothing at face value. In fact assume every pleasant face hides a lie."

I can't live like that, Mercedes thought, but her father was still talking.

"Lady Danica and her family will meet with a tragic Foldspace accident while returning home to Kronos; others will have similarly bad luck."

"You're going to just kill them without charging them or giving them a trial…?"

"Yes. I am."

"And they're just going to show up and go through this charade?"

"I've generously placed security on their youngest children back on Kronos. The parents will play their part."

A shiver went down Mercedes' back. "And Cousin Musa?" she forced out.

"Will be greeted with kisses on both cheeks as is proper with a close relative." He looked at her and his expression was serious to the point of being grim. "This is the game of kings, Mercedes. We play it to win."

He started for the door. "Wait," Mercedes called. He looked back. "That task you gave me… I've made my decision."

• • •

The *Distinguido Servicio Cruzar* had some heft to it. Mercedes was very aware of its weight against her left breast. With the ceremony concluded people were streaming toward the buffet and settling at tables beneath the billowing tents. Dani had been standing at the other end of the line of recipients and had tried to reach Mercedes. Mercedes had turned her back and left the stage. It was the direct cut with an exclamation point added. Cipriana had given her a startled glance as Mercedes hurried past.

Yes, she was furious with Danica but she also couldn't bear to face the other girl. *She's going to be dead soon. I didn't try to argue about it. I wouldn't have won. But should I have tried?* The thoughts tormented her as she hurried through the crowd.

Boho stood in a circle formed by his family. His mother's exquisite Madonna face was framed by a shimmering silk scarf. His father, the powerful Duque de Argento y Pepco had a hand on his youngest son's shoulder. The ten-year-old had a mulish expression, the father an exasperated one. The youngest Cullen stood very close to her mother and clung to the folds of her skirt. Her older sister, who was fourteen, was trying to fit into the circle of young women who orbited the family like rings around a planet. *Boho's groupies*, Mercedes thought. *They're in for a surprise*. She inclined her head to the group. The duque and Boho performed sweeping bows, the ladies curtsied. Mercedes didn't stop. She had a more pressing errand.

Accepting bows, curtseys and congratulations Mercedes glided through the crowd dispensing a smile and a nod, but continuing her search until she found Sumiko and her family. Her mother, Mikazuki, kept touching her daughter, hands fluttering from Sumiko's hair to her shoulder to her hand as if to reassure herself that Sumiko was still there. Her stepfather, Ari, looked bored. None of the sons from either marriage seemed to be present.

"May I borrow Sumiko for a minute?" Mercedes asked as she joined them.

More bows and more curtsies. "Of course," Ari said. He had one of those Voice-Of-God bass voices.

She and Sumiko headed to an arbor roofed with the glossy leaves of a winter jasmine plant. Tiny white flowers wildly threw aroma into the wind. "Well?" Sumiko demanded once they were screened from view.

"You're out. They're drafting a statement about a family emergency that will stress you're not quitting, but taking a leave of absence to deal with a family matter. By the time the public realizes you're not coming back I'll be graduating and all the focus will be on me."

"Isn't it always?"

Mercedes flushed at the bitter tone. "Look, I'm sorry, Sumi, but what happened to Hugo is not my fault. It isn't anybody's fault." Mercedes cocked her head and considered. "No, that's not right. It's those terrorists' fault." She knew she had stumbled a bit when she said *terrorists*; fortunately Sumiko was too absorbed in her own pain to notice.

The other girl slumped. "I know. But I'm just so angry all the time, and they're all dead and I can't kill them over and over again. So I blame the people I can reach. If we hadn't been on the strut—"

"We had to get control of the hub."

"But it ultimately didn't matter."

"But it might have. If I'd failed to take out that ship it would have been up to all of you to retake control," Mercedes said softly. "We can't change the past. All we can do is try for a better future. I've done what you wanted. You don't have to go back."

"And I appreciate it. Is your dad going to conscript

a bunch more girls to be your attendants?"

"No. Cipriana is staying and I convinced him she was enough of a chaperone."

That got a laugh. "Your dad obviously doesn't know Cipri all that well."

Mercedes smiled back. "Well, for God's sake don't tell him." They hugged. "I'll miss you. So much."

"We'll see each other during the holidays." They left the arbor and Sumiko returned to her family. Mercedes' gaze shifted to a table near a fountain. The rising wind meant spray was wafting into the tent, so it was being avoided by the noble guests. Tracy and his father were at that table.

Mercedes stood looking at the father and son. Tracy knelt next to his father's chair looking up into the man's lined and weary face. Perhaps it was only the water from the fountain, but Mercedes suspected the man was weeping. She spun on her heel and walked away, not wishing to intrude and trying to postpone the conversation that had to take place.

• • •

"So proud of you. So very proud." Alexander sniffed and he groped for a napkin on the table and wiped away the tears and the moisture from the fountain. "If only your mother..." He shook his head.

"Dad, I... I want to say something. I'm glad you—" Tracy broke off, trying to think how to phrase it that wouldn't make it sound sullen instead of the thank you he was trying express. "I'm glad you found a way to make me see that I should go to The High Ground."

A long bony hand was laid on his shoulder. "I knew I might lose you, but it's what you do for your child. Giving you a future was more... well, I had to do it."

"I know."

"Remember that when you have children of your own."

"Okay."

"Have you spoken to the Devrises yet?"

"No." Tracy hung his head. "I don't know what to say. They'll blame me. Like Sumiko."

"Doesn't matter. Do what's right. Go." His father nudged his shoulder.

Tracy stood, blotted the wet patch on his right knee with a napkin and nodded. "Okay, but get us some food, all right? I'm starving."

"What do you want?" Alexander asked.

"Everything. But lots of oysters if they've got them." His father gave him a quizzical look, shook his head and smiled.

It was like pushing through molasses to force his legs to move. Tracy slowly crossed to the tent where the Devris clan was huddled. Hugo's sisters and brothers were looking scared, Lady Devris was clinging to her husband's arm with a desperate look on her face. Malcomb was red-faced and he clutched the medal in his hand.

"Bastards aren't getting another of my boys! Not happening! Not *ever*!"

"Malcolm dear, hush, they'll hear you," Lady Devris pleaded, her hand patting the air as if placating an angry dog. People at nearby tables were staring, expressions haughty; some began to drift away as if grief was déclassé and death might be catching.

"Let 'em. How dare they give me this piece of shiny crap when they took my boy from me." He jerked free of his wife's grasp and stormed toward a trashcan tucked discreetly behind a flowering bush.

"Don't do it, sir," Tracy said. His tone was soft but urgent.

Malcomb whirled, a bull coming around to confront the matador. "Give me one good reason."

Tracy stepped in close and said very quietly, "Because they *will* get your boys. You know that. And if you insult them like this it'll be Stefan, Rafe and Brandon who'll pay the price." Tracy sucked in a breath. "And if you want to blame somebody, blame me. I'm the one who took us out on that strut."

The fat man gave a gasping sob, flung his arms around Tracy and wept. "He was brave, wasn't he?" he snorted.

"Yes, sir. Braver than… well, he was the first to say we had to go. He was my friend and it's going to be very hard to go on without him." Tracy's throat ached as he uttered the words and contemplated his remaining years at the academy. Yes the snubs and the insults would continue, but he had made some friends and… *Mercedes*. The name sung in his heart and his head.

Malcomb released him and stepped back. "It's not your fault, son. But this required military service. This bullshit has to stop. I'll be working for that."

Tracy nodded; he bowed to Lady Devris and the daughters, nodded to the boys, who were wide-eyed from the raw emotions being expressed. He walked away, eyes raking across the elegant gathering. None of whom knew that a poisonous splinter had wedged itself into the body of the FFH. Would they co-opt Devris, eventually quench his rage? Or would he find supporters and would fractures start to appear in the seemingly impregnable facade of the Fortune Five Hundred?

He met Mercedes partway across the lawn. "I was hoping you'd introduce me to your father," she said.

"Of course. He's likely to become a puddle," Tracy said with a smile.

"That's cute. I'll come over as soon as I've spoken to Caballero Devris."

"Uh... I wouldn't." At her inquiring look he reluctantly continued, "He's taking Hugo's death... hard. He might say something that you couldn't ignore."

"Oh, I can ignore quite a lot."

Tracy kept his hand at his side, but lifted a finger toward the branches of a nearby tree. "And there's a press camerabot pacing you. Whoever is monitoring the feed might not be so discreet," he whispered.

She sighed. "The press was bad before. It's going to be unbearable now since we're—"

"Big damn heroes," they said in chorus and shared a smile.

"And I have some really great news for all of us big damn heroes," Mercedes said. "We've been excused from the *prueba*. If we keep our grades up we will automatically return for the second year."

"Midshipman Princess Arango."

She made a face that wrinkled her nose. Tracy couldn't pull his gaze away. "That is an appalling mouthful."

"Wait until it's Admiral Empress." A shadow of something—worry, fear—swept across her face, and he realized he'd stepped in it. "I'm sorry. Of course that's decades away. Your father will reign for many more years." She looked even more upset at that. He touched her hand. "What? What have I said?"

"Come away." She led him to an arbor where they were shielded from cameras. She twisted her ScoopRing and it emitted a high-pitched electronic buzz designed to confound microphones.

She was hesitating about something. Now that they were unobserved he reached to take her hands in his. She pulled her hands away and stepped back. "What's wrong?"

She had the expression he had dubbed The Royal Mask. The lush mouth was set, the lips folded into a tight line. The dark eyes gazed into his for a moment and he saw turmoil. Then she looked away and addressed the twining leaves and flowers. Her voice was flat and emotionless.

"I wanted to tell you in person before you heard or read the news. I'm marrying Boho. The engagement will be announced in a few days."

"Boho?" he said stupidly. Then louder and with growing heat, "*Boho!* Mercedes, you can't!"

She looked at him now and her eyes were cold. "I can. I am."

"Why?" It sounded anguished, even to his own ears.

She looked at him. "My father sent me to The High Ground with two tasks. Graduate. And find a consort. I'm going to get one of those out of the way so I can focus on the more important task."

"But you love *me*."

"Yes, I do." He started to move to her, but she held up a hand. Only a gesture but it froze him in place. The boundary had been set and he knew he would never cross it again. "But Boho is the right choice. Really the only choice. Well born, handsome, charismatic. He'll graduate with ease and he's everyone's idea of a military officer. Having him as my consort will reassure and mollify any conservatives who question my abilities."

"Mercedes." She drew herself up and a flash of anger glinted in her eyes. "Highness," he amended and the word tasted of ash and gall. "He's a coward. I didn't want to tell you but—"

"Then it's a good thing I have you, isn't it? You will be a great captain, Cadet Belmanor. I expect you'll even rise to admiral and I know you'll serve me with great distinction and with the same fervency and loyalty you have shown thus far, but I do what I must."

"And what about happiness? Love? You'd trade all that for a handsome egotist who will never respect you?" Bitterness edged each word and an aching filled his chest as if hearts really could break.

"I am not an ordinary person who can seek those things. I know my duty. Goodbye, Cadet."

She was gone.

He stood empty and desolate. He unpinned the medal, gazed at it as it rested in the palm of his hand. *Quit?*

No. It had never been more than a foolish dream. She needed him and he would be there for her. Always.

• • •

The afternoon was drawing to a close. People were beginning to take their leave. Servants were clearing dirty plates and the buffet tables were nearly depleted.

Mercedes had almost made it to the garden steps and the privacy of the palace when Dani came running up. The tendons in the girl's neck were stretched, her eyes were dark with terror. She clutched Mercedes' arm. Two large men in well-tailored suits were closing on them, and the camerabots in the area suddenly sank to the ground and switched off.

"Please. Please. I didn't mean to. I didn't realize. Please. I don't want to die. Mercedes, *help me!*"

Grief, anger, embarrassment, shame. The conflicting emotions crashed through her and bile filled Mercedes' mouth. She stared down into the agonized face of her childhood friend. She was on the verge of slipping an arm around Dani and sweeping her into the palace, taking her to her quarters, guarding her somehow.

The men, sporting deceptively pleasant expressions, stepped to either side of Danica. "Your father is looking for you, my lady. If you'll come with us."

Dani gave a cry of terror and grief and sank to the ground. The SEGU agents lifted her to her feet and hustled her away. Danica threw back one final desperate look and mouthed her name. Mercedes ran, crying, to the safety of her bedroom, and found it offered no solace to the emotional agony she felt.

The game of kings.

It had cost her her soul.

Read on for the first chapter in the next installment
of the Imperials Saga

IN EVIL TIMES

Coming July 2017

1

FOR YOUR OWN GOOD

"We *wouldn't* want to make you *uncomfortable*. Put you in a *situation* where you might find yourself issuing *orders* to one of your betters."

Ensign Thracius—Tracy—Ransom Belmanor stared down at the Lieutenant Junior Grade bars. They glittered against the black velvet that lined the clear Lucite box. The box itself sat in the exact center of the desk belonging to Vice Admiral Duque Maximilian Vertrant, the Commandant of the High Ground. A small man, the massive furniture seemed to dwarf him.

When Tracy had started school three years earlier Vice Admiral Vasquez y Markov had led the Solar League's preeminent military academy. Big and burly Vasquez y Markov had dominated the room and the academy, but the admiral had been forced to retire at the end of Tracy's first year at the High Ground. The ever useful *spend more time with his family* being the stated reason. The real reason was because Vasquez y Markov had missed a plot against the emperor of the Solar League and his chosen successor, his daughter,

Mercedes, that had been going on right beneath the commandant's aristocratic nose.

Which brought Tracy back to this moment: listening to Vertrant's rather high-pitched voice complete with a prissy upper-class accent and an annoying habit of stressing random words. Vertrant never forgot his title and never let others forget it either, and he had all the characteristics of the Fortune Five Hundred that Tracy most loathed and despised. The commandant finished by saying,

"*Especially* given the *high station* held by *one* of your *classmates* in *particular* and you a *mere* scholarship student..."

Tracy and his fellow scholarship student Mark Wilson had endured countless such snubs and less than stellar assignments during their three years at the High Ground. That had certainly been the case for the shipboard trials that had occupied part of this, their final year. Tracy wished that he and Mark could have shared beers and bitches, but the other scholarship student had never forgiven Tracy for receiving the *Distinguido Servicio Cruzar* for his service to the Infanta. They had barely spoken beyond what was required for the past two years.

And now mere days before the graduation ceremony another insult. Instead of graduating as a newly minted first lieutenant like every other ensign in the senior class he was one step below his classmates. Except for one. He hoped. Tracy couldn't help it, he blurted out,

"Is this being done to Ensign Wilson as well?"

The thin brows snapped together in a sharp frown and Vertrant's nose wrinkled as if confronted by a particularly noxious odor. "*Nothing* is being *done* to you, Belmanor. I *do* this as a *favor*, for your *own good*."

"Oh, of course, sir, how could I not have realized that."

Unfortunately Vertrant wasn't stupid. He stood and leaned across the desk, his small body almost vibrating with rage. "*Only* your *stellar* academic achievement is preventing me from responding, Lieutenant *J.G.*, but be advised—*school is over*. You are an *officer* in the *Orden de la Estrella* and insubordination can and will be *punished*. *You* are dismissed."

Tracy slammed his boot heels together, snapped off a perfect salute, swept up the now tainted emblems of his new rank and left the office. He wanted to find Davin or Ernesto and vent, but everyone was busy overseeing the batBEMs who were clearing out their quarters.

The person Tracy most wanted to talk to was Mercedes, but he knew that was impossible. Their closeness during the freshman year had ended with the announcement of her engagement to Beauregard Honorius Sinclair Cullen, Vizconde Dorado Arco, Knight of the Shells, Shareholder General of the Grand Cartel and heir apparent to the 19th Duque de Argento y Pepco, known as Boho to his friends and as Asshole to Tracy. The wedding of the Infanta and her dashing fiancé was set for one week after graduation. Tracy was very glad he'd be aboard a ship and hopefully far away from Ouranos and Hissilek, the planet's capital city. He just prayed his future captain wouldn't insist the crew watch the royal wedding. Maybe he could arrange to be on duty or something.

He entered his room. Donnel his Cara'ot batBEM

was snapping shut his holdall. Tracy threw the clear box at him. The batBEM caught it with one of his four hands, the six fingers closing tightly on the box.

"Here, get these on my jacket."

The Cara'ot stared at the bars then looked up at Tracy, the four eyes blinking at him. "One last kick in the nuts before you leave the hallowed halls, I see."

"I'm sure it won't be the last," Tracy replied sourly.

Donnel's three legs propelled him quickly to the closet where the O-Trell dress uniform jacket hung waiting for the graduation ceremony. "Wish we knew where we were heading. Big capital ship gives us more space. Small frigate and we'll need to leave some things with your dad."

"We'll know by three o'clock Saturday when our postings get announced."

"It'll be good to be in space again," the alien said.

"We're in space."

"*Moving* through space. Not stuck on this stationary behemoth. New worlds. New stars."

Tracy dropped onto his bunk. "You've missed it."

"Yeah. We Cara'ot are by nature gypsies. We spend most of our lives on trading ships."

"And stealing and manipulating the DNA of other races," Tracy shot back.

"We *traded* in DNA until your people came along and put a stop to it."

"And a good thing we did too. You're a goddamn horror," Tracy said, eyeing the alien.

Two of the four eyes rolled down the length of his squat body, and Donnel gave himself a pat with all four hands. "Made to order for a specific purpose," he said in tones of satisfaction.

Tracy shuddered. "Like I said… a horror."

"You don't give a shit what we do among ourselves. It's just your own precious human DNA that's *so* sacred. Sir." It was added as an obvious and calculated afterthought.

"Our League, our rules. If the Cara'ot don't like it they can leave."

"Not really an option. You humans would go bugfuck if we tried to leave and kick the shit out of us again."

"Yeah, you're right. We know we can't trust you. Any of you."

"You know all of us aliens," three of the arms gestured widely, "got along just fine until you guys showed up."

"You startled us. We really had thought we were alone in the universe."

"Well God help us if we ever actually scare you if this is how you react when you're just startled."

"Why are we even having this idiotic conversation. Get the bars on my uniform!"

"Yes, sir. Right away, sir. Boy, somebody's in a mood." Donnel's expression softened and he dropped the mocking tone as he said gently, "You let them get to you, sir."

The sudden kindness broke Tracy's control. "I'm second in our class behind Ernesto. I've got *that*." He pointed at where the *Distinguido Servicio Cruzar* glittered on the left breast of his jacket. "But I'll never rate. Not unless the FFH gives me a title."

"I'd say that's highly likely given your… connections."

Tracy gave a violent gesture. "Don't. Don't bring

her up. I can't... I can't bear it."

"You knew it was impossible," the alien said in even gentler tones.

"I know. But knowing doesn't help."

• • •

Mercedes Adalina Saturnina Inez de Arango, the Infanta stood on a riser while three Isanjo seamstresses knelt at the hem of her dress. The claws on their clever, long-fingered hands were retracted so only the soft pads arranged the flowing material over the stiff petticoats. Occasionally one of them would look up, large eyes set in fur-covered faces. Mercedes could read nothing in those eyes. No hint of what they might be thinking. The human designer stood back, fingers at his lips, eyes narrowed, a frown between his brows, evaluating the wedding gown. Tiny diamond beads covered the dress, glittering and flashing. More jewels formed a pattern on the bodice, the symbol of the Solar League. Mercedes drew in shallow breaths because said bodice felt like it was trying to crush her ribcage. The only good thing about the bodice was the deep V of the neckline that made her neck seem longer and displayed her décolletage, one of her better attributes.

After three years spent wearing primarily an O-Trell uniform complete with trousers or battle armor Mercedes found the elaborate wedding gown to be confining and uncomfortable. She dreaded how the stiff netting of the petticoats would feel on the back of her thighs when she finally did get to sit down at the reception banquet. Tall as she was she felt like the enormous belled skirt and lace flounces made her look dumpy.

Señor Vasilyev was approaching, holding a cloud of lace in his hands. He shook it out and it chimed as the tiny crystal bells kissed each other. The twenty-foot-long train was attached to the shoulders of the gown. He stepped back and beamed. Mercedes realized that his eyes were sweeping across his creation. He didn't even see her. How absurd she looked.

"Lovely. Lovely. His Majesty wishes you to wear your grandmother's tiara. I'll complete the design of the veil after I've seen it."

Mercedes held her breath and repeated the mantra—*courtesy, respect, civility*. Qualities always to be remembered and applied, particularly when dealing with a person who was not a member of her class. But the reminder of her grandmother's tiara, delicate twisted leaves of platinum, diamonds, pearls and moonstones brought into focus how much she hated this dress. Only one week until the wedding. How could she say anything now? She should have spoken up months ago.

"*Madre de Dios*, you look like an over-decorated bonbon," came a new voice, a light soprano with sarcasm dripping off every syllable.

Lieutenant Lady Cipriana Delacroix leaned against the doorjamb, one booted foot cocked over the other, completely at ease in her O-Trell uniform. Once one of Mercedes' ladies-in-waiting, she had joined Mercedes at the military academy. Smarter than she pretended, Cipriana was also an accredited beauty with jet-black hair shot through with strands of red, dark eyes, ebony skin and perfect features. She also lacked even a vestige of tact when it came to members of the lower class.

Her blunt assessment of the dress had Vasilyev puffing and bristling. Mercedes found a reserve of diplomacy. "I'm certain that Señor Vasilyev's goal is to make me look like a fairy princess, and I appreciate his efforts despite the deficiencies of his subject."

"Well, then he's an idiot." Mercedes again cringed. "You're damn near six feet tall, Mer, and you've got a figure. There's nothing fairy-like about you. Now Dani, she could have pulled this off." Cipriana's voice trailed away into sadness.

"I don't want to die. Mercedes, help me!"

Lady Danica Everett's agonized words just before she was pulled away by agents of Seguridad Imperial. Mercedes shuddered because she hadn't, in fact, helped her one-time friend and lady-in-waiting. She hadn't even tried.

"Sorry. Bad memories. I shouldn't have brought her up," Cipri said, contrite.

Of the three ladies-in-waiting who had accompanied Mercedes to the High Ground three years before only Cipri remained. Sumiko had been allowed to leave after the traumatic events of that first year with the fig leaf that she would someday return. That wasn't going to happen because Sumi was married, had a child and was pregnant with her second.

As for the third girl, there would be no return. Lady Danica Everett had died, but not, as Cipriana believed, in a tragic Foldspace accident. Something had indeed gone wrong when her parents' ship entered the Fold but it had been no accident. The Conde de Wahle's ship had been sabotaged by SEGU agents on orders from the Emperor. It was punishment for their involvement in the plot to discredit Mercedes, and undermine the Emperor's rule. The parents had accepted the death sentence in return for their youngest children being spared, but Dani had foolishly gotten herself secretly engaged to a claimant to the throne so she suffered the same fate as her plotting father.

"It's just the two of us now," Cipriana concluded and pulled Mercedes back to the present.

Mercedes pushed away the guilt and the residual anger that she still felt toward Dani, waved away the Isanjo seamstresses and Vasilyev, and stepped off the riser. She tucked Cipriana's arm under hers.

"Yes, but we made it, and the good news is that you won't have to be my chaperone after Saturday."

"But who's going to chaperone *me*? Oh wait, I won't have one. Just me... posted to a warship with all those lovely men. And did I mention... just me?" She gave Mercedes a droll look.

"You are impossible," Mercedes said, giving the other girl a slap on the arm. "And you won't be alone for long. There are two second-year women, and a whole four females in the freshman class."

"Who knows, maybe we'll break into double digits some day," was Cipriana's reply. "Though I doubt it."

The doors closed behind the designer and his minions. Mercedes gripped Cipriana by the upper arms. "Okay, tell me truthfully. How awful is this dress?"

"Awful doesn't begin to describe it. Try ghastly. Horrendous. Maybe monstrous—"

"Okay, okay, I get it." Mercedes clutched at her hair and took a turn around the room. The petticoats crackled and rasped against her legs. "Oh God, what am I going to do?"

"Get a different dress."

"I'm getting married in one week."

"You're the Infanta. An army of seamstresses will sew night and day, and what designer wouldn't love the chance to craft your wedding gown? Frankly I'm wondering if this clown is trying to undermine the succession by putting you in this… this…" Words failed her and she just gestured helplessly at the dress.

"Get me out of it," Mercedes ordered.

Cipriana's fingers were cold on Mercedes' back as she unzipped and unhooked. The yards of material puddled around her feet and Mercedes yanked off the stiff petticoats. It seemed to form a scratchy wall, trapping her inside. She stepped over it, padded over to the bed and sat down. With the tight bodice she wasn't wearing a bra. She found herself contemplating her bare breasts and wondered what it would feel like when Boho finally touched them without any intervening material? Despite every governess and duenna's objection there wasn't a girl in the FFH who didn't read the romantic novels or "little bonbons" as they were called, and dream about dashing space pirates, or FFH nobles in disguise who fall in love with innocent and sweet *intitulado* girls.

Strange there aren't any books about FFH noble ladies who fall in love with intitulado *men who are anything but sweet but rather prickly and opinionated and who love her and save her and whom she rejected—*

Mercedes forced her thoughts away from Tracy Belmanor and back to her fiancé.

"I want to be pretty. It's my wedding day, and Boho is so handsome."

Cipriana joined her on the bed. "Mercedes, you are pretty. No, that's wrong. You're dramatic and that lasts. Pretty fades. And Boho loves you."

"Well he certainly loves the Infanta."

"Same thing." She hesitated then asked, "Mer, do you love him?"

They stared at each other for a long moment while Mercedes wondered if Cipriana had suddenly developed telepathy. She groped for a pillow, clutched it to her bare chest. "I... think so? I don't feel for him the way I felt for—" She cut off the words, as if saying his name was dangerous because it probably was. She took a breath and resumed. "We understand each other. We grew up together. We know our duty and he's what I need. What the crown needs." She gave Cipriana a quick smile. "And did I mention he's handsome."

"He'll be a good ruler."

Mercedes stiffened. "He won't be ruling. I will be."

Cipriana looked startled then embarrassed. "Right of course, I just meant... I mean, do you really want all that on you? You'll have children and look at Sumiko. She was the most ambitious of all of us, but she seems so happy with her daughter and a new baby on the way."

"Which brings up another problem. I can't get pregnant too soon." Mercedes stood, crossed to the closet, pulled out a dressing gown and shrugged into it. "I've got to do at least one rotation on a ship to satisfy the old guard. Otherwise they'll never accept me." Mercedes frowned. "I'll need to discuss that with Boho. We'll be serving on the same ship, but we'll need to be careful."

"Use birth control."

"I can't do that. I thought I was hemmed in when I was a princess. Now that I'm the Infanta it's much worse." She sighed. "I never thought I'd say this, but I miss the High Ground. I had a lot more freedom there. Anyway, if I got a pill or a patch somebody would find out, talk, and God what an uproar there would be."

"IUD?"

"And who's going to insert it? No human doctor would agree."

"So go to an alien doctor."

"You have noticed I have a lot of security around me." Mercedes shook her head. "No, Boho's just going to have to be patient and understanding."

"Not his strong suit. He's a man of strong appetites, and you've got to do the deed on your wedding night. With your luck you'll get pregnant the first time you fuck, then none of this will be an issue," Cipriana concluded.

"I know we're supposed to outbreed the aliens, but there are five known alien races we've encountered. There's no way we can overcome the deficit."

"Paranoia's a bitch," Cipriana agreed. Then in quavering old lady tones she added, "There are more of them than us and even though we beat them they're wily and they're plotting and they have secret weapons and they'll win and take our women and produce monstrous half-breeds... Like that could ever happen," Cipriana said in her normal voice, then reverted to the trembling dowager's voice. "And... and... Oh God The

Sky Is Falling!" she concluded with a shout.

Mercedes was rolling on the bed, clutching her stomach and laughing. She finally sat up, wiped her eyes and said, "I'll worry about the coming alien apocalypse later. Right now I've got to deal with *that*." She pointed at the tumbled mass of material. "There isn't time to hand sew another one."

"So get one printed."

Mercedes was appalled. "You know what all the gossiping, back-biting bitches will say."

"And what do you think they're going to say if you come down the aisle wearing *that* thing? Billions of people are going to watch the live feed of your wedding. Over the Foldstream no one will be able to tell if the dress was hand stitched or not. They'll want to see their princess and the future ruler of the Solar League marrying her handsome consort. It would be better if they're not giggling."

A wild thought intruded. "I wonder…" Mercedes began.

"What? You've got a look that I've learned to distrust."

"Tracy's father. He's a tailor. He's made suits for my father."

"Yeah, emphasis on *tailor*."

"Tracy told me his mother was also a seamstress. She might have left behind a design or something."

Cipriana jumped to her feet. "You should not be doing this. You've stayed well away from him for the past two years. Which was very wise."

"He's still up on the station and I'm sure he couldn't afford to come home before graduation. And any money they had would go toward getting his father up the High Ground for the ceremony. It'll be fine," Mercedes said. "I can at least start there. And I never did get to meet his father."

"And you shouldn't be meeting him now," Cipriana argued.

"No, this could work, and be a great public relations coup. Vasilyev is known as the designer for the FFH. If I pick a little known commoner... well, we could make something out of this."

Cipriana pursed her lips, considered. "Now that's actually a good reason for this crazy idea." She hopped off the bed. "Come on, get dressed. I'll go with you."

ACKNOWLEDGEMENTS

This book wouldn't have happened without the help and input from a lot of people. First thanks to my amazing agent, Kay McCauley, who was determined to find the right home for this story. My patient stockbroker, Brian Bower, who spent a long time talking with me about how to ruin a person's finances or a planet's economy. Thanks to Daniel Abraham and Ty Frank aka James S.A. Cory for being so helpful during the plotting session that created the arc of Imperials. To Eric Kelley and Sage Walker who let me brainstorm with them on tricky bits, and to my writers' group—Sage and Matt Reiten for their firm and fair critiques. I also want to thank my editor, Miranda Jewess, and my publisher, Titan Books, for believing in this project enough to allow me to tell the whole story. This is merely the first act in my five-act drama.

ABOUT THE AUTHOR

Melinda Snodgrass is the acclaimed author of many science fiction novels, including the *Circuit* and *Edge* series, and is the co-editor with George R.R. Martin of the *Wild Cards* series, to which she also contributes. She has had a long career in television, writing several episodes of *Star Trek: The Next Generation* while serving as the series' story editor, and has written scripts for numerous other shows, including *Odyssey 5*, *The Outer Limits*, *Reasonable Doubts* and *Seaquest DSV*. She was also a consulting producer on *The Profiler*. She lives in Santa Fe, New Mexico.

IN EVIL TIMES

THE IMPERIALS SAGA

MELINDA SNODGRASS

Thracius "Tracy" Belmanor and the Infanta Mercedes de Arango have graduated from The High Ground and have become officers in the *Orden de la Estrella*. Tracy's posting aboard a battleship leads him to further doubt the intentions of the Solar League, as he and his comrades are required to "assimilate" the settlers of a Hidden World. Meanwhile, Mercedes' own posting—and her difficult marriage to Beauregard "Boho" Cullen, made to assure her succession of the throne—divides her loyalties. In a society where most humans and all aliens are second-class citizens, the two young officers will have difficult choices to make...

AVAILABLE JULY 2017

NEW POMPEII

DANIEL GODFREY

In the near future, energy giant Novus Particles develops the technology to transport objects and people from the deep past to the present. Their biggest secret: New Pompeii. A replica of the city hidden deep in central Asia, filled with Romans pulled through time a split second before the volcano erupted.

Historian Nick Houghton doesn't know why he's been chosen to be the company's historical advisor. He's just excited to be there. Until he starts to wonder what happened to his predecessor. Until he realizes that NovusPart have more secrets than even the conspiracy theorists suspect. Until he realizes that NovusPart have underestimated their captives…

"Evokes Michael Crichton at his best."
Financial Times

"A treat for fans of well-thought out science fiction."
Impedimenta Magazine

TITANBOOKS.COM

EMPIRE OF TIME

DANIEL GODFREY

New Rome is cut off from the rest of the world in a new Cold War. They have control of the time travel technology, which keeps western governments at bay. But the public want the destruction of New Rome, a place where slavery and deadly gladiatorial combat flourish. Meanwhile Calpurnia is fending off threats to her control over her people, aided by Decimus Horatius Pullus, the man who was once Nick Houghton… Has Nick truly embraced the Roman way of life? Can the Romans harness the power of time travel or will the new world destroy them?

THE EXPLOSIVE SEQUEL TO *NEW POMPEII*

AVAILABLE JUNE 2017

ESCAPOLOGY

REN WAROM

Shock Pao is not just any Haunt—he's the best. In the virtual world the Slip there's nothing he can't steal for the right price. Outside the Slip, though, he's a Fail—no degree, no job, no affiliations to protect him from angry ex-customers. These days he takes any job offered and wastes his money on subdermal amphetamines. So when his ex comes around with a simple-enough job, breaking into a corporate databank, he accepts—it's either that, or find himself a nice bench to sleep under. But what she wants stolen turns out to be something else entirely, something that holds the entire Slip together—and Shock finds himself in the crosshairs of a battle that has been fought unseen, both in the Slip and in the gang warrens of the city.

*"Grabs cyberpunk by the throat
and drags it into deeper, stranger waters."*
Barnes & Noble

THE RACE

NINA ALLAN

A child is kidnapped with consequences that extend across worlds... A writer reaches into the past to discover the truth about a possible murder... Far away a young woman prepares for her mysterious future... In a future scarred by fracking and ecological collapse, Jenna Hoolman lives in the coastal town of Sapphire. Her world is dominated by the illegal sport of smartdog racing: greyhounds genetically modified with human DNA. When her young niece goes missing that world implodes... Christy's life is dominated by fear of her brother, a man she knows capable of monstrous acts and suspects of hiding even darker ones. Desperate to learn the truth she contacts Alex, a stranger she knows only by name, and who has his own demons to fight... And Maree, a young woman undertaking a journey that will change her world forever.

"Every now and then, a debut novel knocks you blind... The Race will, as the best fiction should, have your compass spinning." Strange Horizons

TITANBOOKS.COM